Dear Reader,

My name is Holly Denham. I wanted to write and say, first of all, a huge thank-you for buying this book. I also thought I should explain how my personal emails came to be published! It all started with the website www.hollysinbox.com. Before that, I was your ordinary, boring 9–5 receptionist, working in London, seeing my friends Jason and Aisha, having various disastrous relationships, and generally getting on with my life. After my inbox was posted on the Web, I was told that thousands of people from 120 countries (!!!) were logging on every day to read my emails—how spooky is that! To be honest, it's been amazing, and I've received loads of messages from the loveliest people, saying how much they've enjoyed reading the site. And it was this overwhelming response from fans that led to a publishing deal! Anyway, I really hope you enjoy reading this book, and that you'll visit the site *www.hollysinbox.com*.

Thank you again for all your support!!!

Lots of love,

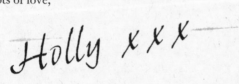

Holly xxx

Holly's
inbox

HOLLY DENHAM

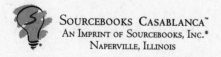

SOURCEBOOKS CASABLANCA™
AN IMPRINT OF SOURCEBOOKS, INC.®
NAPERVILLE, ILLINOIS

Published by Sourcebooks Casablanca, an imprint of Sourcebooks, Inc.
P.O. Box 4410, Naperville, Illinois 60567–4410
(630) 961–3900
FAX: (630) 961–2168
www.sourcebooks.com

Originally published in 2007 by Headline Review, an imprint of Headline Publishing Group

Library of Congress Cataloging-in-Publication Data

Denham, Holly.
 Holly's inbox / Holly Denham.
   p. cm.
 Originally published: London : Headline Review, 2007.
 1. Receptionists—Fiction. 2. Chick lit. I. Title.
 PR6104.E566H65 2009
 823'.92—dc22

                    2009008803

Printed and bound in the United States of America
VP 10 9 8 7 6 5 4 3 2

month 1

week 1
monday

Subject: To Holly—New Job

From: Mum and Dad
To: Holly

Holly,

Exciting news about the job. Are you enjoying it?

Your sister has a parcel (books or something) that needs bringing out with you, when you come to see us. Alice says it's very important and 'Ferret,' a friend of hers, is passing by Maida Vale next week to drop it off.

Love, Mum

PS Send us your flight details!

From: Holly
To: Mum and Dad

Job—I don't know yet, only been here an hour, very busy.

Ferret—what? How does anyone get to make a friend called Ferret?

Parcel—no problem, as long as it's not too heavy.

xxxx

Subject: Welcome

From: Roger Lipton
To: Holly

Dear Holly,

Glad to have you on board.

I hear everything went well with your induction on Friday and you are now familiarising yourself with our systems and policies.

It's a shame the reception area is so separated from the rest of us here, but you know where we are if you need anything.

I hope you'll be very happy here.

Roger Lipton, Director of Human Resources, H&W, High Holborn WC2 6NP

From: Holly
To: Roger Lipton

Dear Mr Lipton,

Thank you for your email. I'm sure I'll be very happy; everyone has been so welcoming.

Kindest regards,

Holly

Receptionist, H&W, High Holborn WC2 6NP

Subject: Reception experience

From: Patricia Gillot
To: Holly

Holly,

I told them to get me a receptionist I could work with, like the one I had before with lots of experience. Not having a go at you on your first day, but I feel like giving up, I really do. Where've you worked again?

Trish

Patricia Gillot, Senior Receptionist, H&W, Holborn WC2 6NP

From: Holly
To: Patricia Gillot

Hi Patricia,

In 5* Hotels—on reception.

Holly

From: Patricia Gillot
To: Holly

Great.

From: Holly
To: Patricia Gillot

It was really busy there.

From: Patricia Gillot
To: Holly

That's nice for you, darlin. Just keep grinning at people for today, and I'll do the rest. Hopefully by the end of the month you might know your arse from your elbow.

Trish

PS Stop trying to talk to me; this is a corporate bank. If you wanted to natter; you should've taken a job in a salon. Email me when you have a problem.

Subject: A good luck message

From: Alice and Matt
To: Holly

Holls,

Glad things are going so well again. It sounds wonderful there, and you've got yourself a new start. Just what you wanted.

Love,

Alice & Matt

From: Holly
To: Alice and Matt

I hate the job and everyone's awful.

From: Alice and Matt
To: Holly

Oh dear, by the way, thanks for agreeing to bring out our parcel. It's really nice of you.

xxxxxx

From: Holly
To: Alice and Matt

No problem. What's in it?

From: Alice and Matt
To: Holly

Oh, nothing, just a box of essentials.

From: Holly
To: Alice and Matt

What—books and things?

From: Alice and Matt
To: Holly

Yes, all that. I've given Ferret your number.
xxx

From: Holly
To: Alice and Matt

Oh good

tuesday

Subject: A little advice from your Mum

From: Mum and Dad
To: Holly

Holly,

Sorry to bother you again, dear. Glad to hear you bumped into Jennie from school. You were always very fond of her. Sounds like she's doing so well there.

I've given it some thought, and the only way you're going to get as far as she has done is by using any contacts you come across. My advice is: take her out for lunch as fast as possible. You never know what doors she could open for you.

What are you doing there at the moment again, PA work?

Mum xxx

From: Holly
To: Mum and Dad

Mum,

Jennie has been nice on the couple of occasions I've seen her, but I'm fine doing what I'm doing, which is RECEPTION work.

x

Holly

From: Mum and Dad
To: Holly

That's what I said, darling, it's the same thing.

Just make sure you eat properly, especially if you're going to be greeting all those people. You could pick up an infection from one of them.

Mum

Subject: A few pointers

From: Patricia Gillot
To: Holly

Stop standing up when people come to the desk!

I'm off for a fag. I'll be on the other side of the glass doors, and I'll be keeping an eye on you.

Got any problems—don't shout whatever you do. Just think you're working in a library, and you'll be halfway there.

From: Holly
To: Patricia Gillot

OK, Patricia. What time are toilet breaks?

From: Patricia Gillot
To: Holly

Any time you can't hold on, darlin—also, it's just Trish. No one calls me Patricia.

Subject: School Friend!!!

From: Jennie Pithwait
To: Holly

Hi Holly,

You went off the map for a few years. Where've you been??

So glad you're working here; sorry about the misunderstanding yesterday. I should have told you what Mr Huerst looked like; lucky he was so forgiving, even when you told him he needed an appointment.

Jennie

Jennie Pithwait, Associate, Corporate Finance, H&W, High Holborn WC2 6NP

From: Holly
To: Jennie Pithwait

Hi Jennie,

I felt like a real idiot. I even chased after him with his security pass.

Holly

From: Jennie Pithwait
To: Holly

He was fine. I said it was your first day.

What's it like sitting with Trisha?

From: Holly
To: Jennie Pithwait

Awful, rude, I can't stand her.

From: Jennie Pithwait
To: Holly

Tough old girl, probably doesn't get laid much. Great with clients, but that's about it.

Jennie

From: Holly
To: Jennie Pithwait

xxxx

Thanks Jennie.

Subject: Pretty P'Holly

From: Jason GrangerRM
To: Holly

Hiya,
How's the job going? Is it OK to email you?

Jason Granger, Reception Team Leader, LHS Hotels, London, W1V 6TT

From: Holly
To: Jason GrangerRM

Emailing is good, the job stinks, and I'm about to take a contract out on my mum.
How are you?

xx

From: Jason GrangerRM
To: Holly

I'm good.
Talking of stinky, guess what smelly celeb we've got staying here?

From: Holly
To: Jason GrangerRM

Smelly?

From: Jason GrangerRM
To: Holly

(Housekeeping told me she's got a few personal hygiene problems.)
Who cares though—she's famous!!!

From: Holly
To: Jason GrangerRM

That makes it OK then, does it?

From: Jason GrangerRM
To: Holly

Of course! You don't like her though (she's a bit of a marriage breaker)—can't tell you who it is. If you were still working here, I could, but I can't. It's a trust thing.
Enjoy your nasty bank.

From: Holly
To: Jason GrangerRM

JASON!!!

wednesday

Subject: Totty

From: Jennie Pithwait
To: Holly

Morning. Let me know if any hot guys are coming up, so I can look out for them.
Jen

From: Holly
To: Jennie Pithwait

Will do.
Holly

Subject: Ferret

From: Ferret
To: Holly

Hi Hollsie,

Ferret here. Alice gave me your email.

I've managed to get hold of more than she even wanted. Just make sure you keep it in the freezer until you go.

Chairman Mow once said 'Feel the rhythm.'

Subject: Bit slow

From: Patricia Gillot
To: Holly

Holly,

Speed it up a bit, darlin. By now you should be getting two badges printed off while calling the host to let them know their guests have arrived.

It's all got to happen at once, otherwise the place'll start looking like Piccadilly station with nowhere for people to sit.

Sorry to hassle you, but you're not picking things up fast enough.

Trish

Subject: PARCEL

From: Holly
To: Ferret

Freezer? I don't understand?

Subject: Totty

From: Jennie Pithwait
To: Holly

Thanks for the heads-up on that one. Not strictly my usual type. I do like them a little taller, without the lurch, corduroys, rotting teeth, and the smell.

Pref also for the future: can you prep them on first impressions? I like people who still have the ability to retain their spittle. The string from his shoulder wasn't working for me.

PS I'll get you back

Jen

From: Holly
To: Jennie Pithwait

Ooops, sorry (I didn't actually think he was that bad).

Also, where's good to eat around here?

xx

Holly

From: Jennie Pithwait
To: Holly

Out of here, turn left, there's a good sandwich shop on the other side, or up to the lights and turn right… nice arcade place up there.

… oh, and to answer your question earlier, there's nothing worth chasing here.

By the way, be careful about dumping on your own doorstep.

So come on then, give me some gossip. What's Holly been doing since school? I want to know everything. I heard you got yourself engaged, or married?

Jen

From: Holly
To: Jennie Pithwait

Nope, never married, love life's been much of a nonevent. What about you?

From: Jennie Pithwait
To: Holly

The odd one or two, quality guys, all prime beef.

xx

From: Holly
To: Jennie Pithwait

You lucky thing!

Holls

From: Jennie Pithwait
To: Holly

Let's meet up for lunch. I'll give you a complete tourist guide. Call you later.

From: Holly
To: Jennie Pithwait

Thanks.

Holls

Subject: Hi Jason—I'm worried—it's Holly

From: Holly
To: Jason GrangerRM

Jennie's asking questions.

Holly

From: Jason GrangerRM
To: Holly

PHOTOS Puppy-lickin

Just keep your cool and keep yourself to yourself (well, as much as you can on a main reception desk).

xxx

I'll call tonight

Subject: Team night out

From: Judy Perkins
To: Holly

Dear Holly,

Being new, I think it would be nice if we welcomed you to the team by a few of us going for a drink in the next couple of weeks.

Let me know what night would be good for you.

Regards,

Judy

Judy Perkins, Facilities Manager, H&W, High Holborn, WC2 6NP

From: Holly
To: Judy Perkins

Hi Judy,

Thanks for the invite. Any day next week would be OK.

Regards,

Holly

Subject: Shella Hamilton-Jones—PA to Jane Jenkins

From: Shella Hamilton-Jones
To: Holly

Dear Holly,

From looking at the schedule I can see you have booked meeting room 7 on Friday for Jane Jenkins. As you are aware from my previous call, this meeting is very important, and Jane's preference is always ROOM 12.

I understand you are new here, and it's difficult to begin with until you get your bearings; however, you should know Jane Jenkins has priority over other staff.

Please would you secure this room ASAP and then email me a confirmation when you have achieved this. You could also make a note that Jane Jenkins always has this room in the future.

Yours sincerely,

Shella Hamilton-Jones, PA to Jane Jenkins, MD Corporate Finance, H&W, High Holborn WC2 6NP

thursday

Subject: Ferret

From: Holly
To: Ferret

Ferret,

You haven't replied to me… You told me to put it in the freezer. Why the freezer???

Holly

Subject: To Shella—Re Your Meeting Room Request

From: Holly
To: Shella Hamilton-Jones

Dear Shella,

I can only apologise for not booking meeting room 12 for you. I will make a note of Jane Jenkins's preference for the future and move James Lawrence's meeting now.

Yours sincerely,

Holly

Subject: Important update

From: Mum and Dad
To: Holly

Holly,

I've set your granny up on a laptop, so she can email you. I think she's settling into the old people's home just fine.

Love, Mum

From: Holly
To: Mum and Dad

Oh good, but I didn't think Granny liked it out there?

Holly

From: Mum and Dad
To: Holly

Holly,

She misses the rain, but apart from that she seems very happy.

Love, Mum

Subject: Ordering duty free?

From: Holly
To: Alice and Matt

Alice,

I've left two messages on your phone. I want to know what's in that parcel—if it's drugs, you can forget it!?

Holly

From: Alice and Matt
To: Holly

Hi Holly,

Don't be so crazy, what kind of sister do you think I am? I wouldn't ask you to bring drugs out?????? GOD NO!! No, these are just your common or garden rats.

Love you.

Alice xx

From: Holly
To: Alice and Matt

What???????

Subject: Alteration to my meeting

From: James Lawrence
To: Holly

Dear Holly,

Just received your voice mail. I understand re: change in the meeting. No problem at all, and sorry I haven't stopped to introduced myself. It's been a hectic few days up here.

Regards,

James

PS You sounded shaken. Don't let people get you down. People just get stressed here sometimes.

James Lawrence, VP Corporate Finance, H&W, High Holborn WC2 6NP

From: Holly
To: James Lawrence

Dear James,

Thanks for that, it's kind of you. Have a fab day.

Holly

Subject: A question for you Jennie ...

From: Holly
To: Jennie Pithwait

Who's James Lawrence?

Hols

From: Jennie Pithwait
To: Holly

—Why ?

friday

Subject: Rats

From: Holly
To: Alice and Matt

Alice,

When I said, 'What?' that meant—what, are you crazy??? Rats?? Email me back or forget it!

Subject: Only just saw your reply

From: Alice and Matt
To: Holly

Sorry Holly,

I didn't tell you, because I didn't want you to worry about them.

They're rats, but English ones, and you won't have to touch them, they're all sealed up.

xxxx

Alice

From: Holly
To: Alice and Matt

Oh, thank God they're English rats, they'll be so much more refined????

From: Alice and Matt
To: Holly

Don't tell Mum, you know how squeamish she is with these things. We need to bring some rats into the country for the pythons to eat. Here they cost 3 euros each, it's not economical, and the quality is poor.

Alice

From: Holly
To: Alice and Matt

So these are quality rats. That is good.

NO, I'M NOT DOING IT!!!

From: Alice and Matt
To: Holly

If we don't feed them, the pythons will DIE, and Matt will be devastated. There's nothing to worry about, they're not alive…

From: Holly
To: Alice and Matt

They're not alive. Oh that's fine then—so you want me to fill my case with DEAD rats? Fab, I'll just rearrange my packing; tuck them between my swimming cozzie and my knickers?!

From: Alice and Matt
To: Holly

Please give it some thought. Remember, breeding snakes is our only source of income.

Love, Alice

xx

Subject: It's going to be a mad day—from Trish

From: Patricia Gillot
To: Holly

… so get that smile ready, girl!

Subject: Help!—Aisha needs Holly

From: Aisha
To: Holly

Hols,

Still not recovered from last weekend, think I ate something bad, feel terrrrrrrrrrrrrrible. Tell me something nice pleasssssse, Hols. I'm really depressed.

xxxxxxx

From: Holly
To: Aisha

You didn't eat anything bad, it was the bottle of vodka you drank—where was Shona?

From: Aisha
To: Holly

Mum's looking after her.

x

From: Holly
To: Aisha

Come on sweetie, get yourself together. You said you'd look for a job this week?

From: Aisha
To: Holly

I went out last night, but I wasn't feeling good when I left the house, felt really weak. Also, I'm worried about Henry. I texted him an hour ago, and he still hasn't texted back.

From: Holly
To: Aisha

He's probably just busy. When someone's at work (try and picture this)—they don't have time to check their phone every 5 mins to see if they've been texted.

From what I've heard, working in Production can take you all over the place. He could be outside. Stop worrying!

From: Aisha
To: Holly

He's not in Production.

From: Holly
To: Aisha

Yes, he is. You told me he was in TV Production.

From: Aisha
To: Holly

That's Jimmy.

From: Holly
To: Aisha

So who's Henry?

From: Aisha
To: Holly

Henry is the guy I was with on Saturday.

From: Holly
To: Aisha

So who's Jimmy?

From: Aisha
To: Holly

He's the one in Production.

From: Holly
To: Aisha

I know he's in Production. I mean, who is he to you?

From: Aisha
To: Holly

He's with me too. Look, you're not making me feel any better.

From: Holly
To: Aisha

Good, so you shouldn't. Stop feeling sorry for yourself and get a job.

From: Aisha
To: Holly

Can I come over and stay next weekend? Let's have the whole weekend in, no drinks, no partying???

xxxx

From: Holly
To: Aisha

Of course, although I might have someone called 'Ferret' popping in, not sure.

From: Aisha
To: Holly

Is he sexy?

From: Holly
To: Aisha

Good-bye.

Subject: You've got to keep an eye on people who are waiting!

From: Patricia Gillot
To: Holly

I'm sure that bloke with the yellow tie has been sitting there for 10 mins??

From: Holly
To: Patricia Gillot

He has. I've tried calling them upstairs three times but can't get through to them. Sorry, I didn't know what to do.

From: Patricia Gillot
To: Holly

Then ASK. You need to go up and look for the host, because the meeting could've started already without this one.
Come on, Holly, use your noodle.

Subject: Celebrity Pics

From: Jason
To: Holly

Remember to ask the other receptionist for the directory of senior staff. Then you can take it home over the weekend and learn what they look like (hopefully they'll have pictures). Otherwise next week, it could be the other founding partner you ask to sign in.

From: Holly
To: Jason

I hope not, he's dead.
But thanks. I'll ask her about the directory at the end of the day.

Subject: You owe me

From: Holly
To: Alice and Matt

OK, I'll do it. Presumably it's legal.

From: Alice and Matt
To: Holly

Oh, you're the best!!
xxxx
I'll remember this, thanks lots.

week 2
monday

Subject: I got a right ear bashing off them upstairs!

From: Patricia Gillot
To: Holly

Because they want two receptionists on the desk when it's busy, lunchtimes usually. I'll go through it with you once we get some peace. They're doing my head in. So, one of us needs to go before 12 p.m. slot and one after the 2 p.m. slot.

From: Holly
To: Patricia Gillot

Sorry Trish, I didn't know. I'll be careful. I can go to lunch whenever you want.

Subject: Shootings

From: Patricia Gillot
To: Holly

All these shootings, it gets worse every day. Even my youngest one says most of his classmates take weapons with them to school. It really gets to me.

From: Holly
To: Patricia Gillot

How scary!!? That's awful.

Subject: Terrible news!

From: Jason GrangerRM
To: Holly

Britney's had her hair cut off!!!!!!

From: Holly
To: Jason GrangerRM

Yes, Jason, thanks for the news alert keeping me up-to-date with current affairs.

xx

Subject: Lunch

From: Patricia Gillot
To: Holly

I have to be somewhere at 2. Should be back within an hour but if it takes longer, can you cover for me while I'm gone?

From: Holly
To: Patricia Gillot

No probs, I can cover. Where should I say you are though?

From: Patricia Gillot
To: Holly

Thanks. Just say I came back, you saw me, and you think I'm around somewhere?

From: Holly
To: Patricia Gillot

OK.

Subject: Annoying calls

From: Patricia Gillot
To: Holly

I just had an 'I'm so important' pr*ck on the line, spoke like I should know who he was, shouted the person he wanted twice (couldn't catch it either time), then had the cheek to leave me hanging while he took another call—that gets to me.

From: Holly
To: Patricia Gillot

What d'you do when that happens?

From: Patricia Gillot
To: Holly

I usually hang up on them or ask them to call back and speak to Holly.

From: Holly
To: Patricia Gillot

Thanks.

From: Patricia Gillot
To: Holly

My pleasure, darlin.

Subject: What's the name of that girl in *EastEnders*?

From: Patricia Gillot
To: Holly

You know, the one who's been in all the trouble recently.

From: Holly
To: Patricia Gillot

I don't know, which one?

From: Patricia Gillot
To: Holly

If I knew, I wouldn't be asking you, now would I? Come on girl, that one who did something with Phil Mitchell. No, I mean *The Bill*, PC something?

From: Holly
To: Patricia Gillot

D'you mean the older tarty one? Sorry, I haven't watched it for a while.

From: Holly
To: Patricia Gillot

Sorry I can't help.

From: Patricia Gillot
To: Holly

DC June... someone?

From: Holly
To: Patricia Gillot

Why d'you want to know anyway?

From: Patricia Gillot
To: Holly

Sgt June Akland!!! That was her. See that girl on the couch with the brown hair. Forget it, she's gone now. I'm off to lunch, see ya.

Subject: IMPORTANT REMINDER

From: Holly
To: Holly

SOAPS remember to watch *EastEnders* and *The Bill*, oh, and buy an alarm clock.

Subject: Sexy male porn

From: Aisha
To: Holly

I'm sending you some porn—you'll love it, pic of some guy I was with at the weekend.

From: Holly
To: Aisha

Please don't.

From: Aisha
To: Holly

I'm sending it.
xx

From: Holly
To: Aisha

Don't.

From: Aisha
To: Holly

You'll love it.
x

tuesday

Subject: Allowances abroad

From: Holly
To: GovernmentCustomsDept

Dear Sir or Madam,
Can you give me a list of what I can take or can't take when I go abroad to Spain, please.
Thanks.
Holly

From: GovernmentCustomsDept
To: Holly

REF: 9222287
Dear Holly,

If you log on to our website, there are details, including the laws governing export and import of goods to EU countries.
C&E

From: Holly
To: GovernmentCustomsDept
REF: 9222287
Dear C&E,
I can't see anywhere on your list any mention of rats, and I want to take some to Spain with me. Can you tell me where I stand with this?
Hols x

From: GovernmentCustomsDept
To: Holly
REF: 9222287
Dear Holly,
Presuming you are serious, then the exportation of live animals should be listed there.

From: Holly
To: GovernmentCustomsDept
REF: 9222287
Dear C&E,
I am serious, but I intend to take only dead rats (frozen—like popsicles, I believe), not the live variety. However, I have no intention of going to prison because of a bunch of dirty rats.
Hols

From: GovernmentCustomsDept
To: Holly
REF: 9222287
Dear Holly,

It might come as a shock to you, but I have never been asked about the exportation of dead rats. But from what I have discovered, the British Government doesn't mind how many dead rats you export, you can take the lot.

The Spanish Government, however, might be more interested in their arrival. Best to contact the British Embassy in Spain.

Subject: Help Jason Help!

From: Holly

To: Jason GrangerRM

I still feel everyone's waiting for me to mess up hugely. Trish is OK with me, but I think underneath it all, she's just waiting for me to screw up. You know what I need to do… I need to have a party and invite everyone from work.

What do you think?????

From: Jason GrangerRM

To: Holly

Do NOT have a party, bad idea. You picked it up very quickly when you were here, just have some patience.

xxxxx

PS Have you got that directory of staff yet??

From: Holly

To: Jason GrangerRM

Got the book, then got in trouble with Trish for trying to take it home (security risk). Just trying to remember faces as they pass …

Subject: IMPORTANT QUESTION

From: Charlie Denham

To: Holly

What d'you look for in a toilet?

Charlie

CLUB SUBMISSION, London

From: Holly
To: Charlie Denham

I don't look in toilets, Charlie.

From: Charlie Denham
To: Holly

What's important for you though?

From: Holly
To: Charlie Denham

That I don't have conversations about toilets with my brother.

From: Charlie Denham
To: Holly

OK, but apart from clean seats and some roll—what else is important for women?

From: Holly
To: Charlie Denham

Go away Charlie.

From: Charlie Denham
To: Holly

Have you told any of your hot receptionist mates that your brother owns a nightclub yet?

From: Holly
To: Charlie Denham

No, because you don't. You own a building site.
Holly
PS We don't all hang out together in some kind of receptionist club. There's me and one other on the desk. That's all.

From: Charlie Denham
To: Holly

Is she hot?

From: Charlie Denham
To: Holly

Are you still there?

From: Charlie Denham
To: Holly

What about the sign on the door? Lots of options …

From: Holly
To: Charlie Denham

Little girls room—sounds sweet.

From: Charlie Denham
To: Holly

I think Rubber Ron has the casting vote, and he's gone for DOMS & SUBS.

From: Holly
To: Charlie Denham

What on earth does that mean?

From: Charlie Denham
To: Holly

Who knows? I daren't ask. Some kind of kinky thing, I think, and that's trendy these days.

Subject: Totty??? Where is it?

From: Jennie Pithwait
To: Holly

Come on, what's it like down there, anything on the horizon?

From: Holly
To: Jennie Pithwait

It's manic, loads of meetings going on... what's the big event?

From: Jennie Pithwait
To: Holly

Graduate recruitment day, fresh young blood, hot young men fresh off the press, cuties in their new suities, bless.
Why don't you take some pics on your phone and email them up?

From: Holly
To: Jennie Pithwait

Not too keen. What would happen if I was caught?

From: Jennie Pithwait
To: Holly

Instant dismissal, probably escorted off the premises.

From: Holly
To: Jennie Pithwait

So my mobile stays in my bag. Some of them passing through have absolutely no social skills, they're so arrogant.

From: Jennie Pithwait
To: Holly

Arrogant and suited. Tell me more!!!!

From: Holly
To: Jennie Pithwait

Ooops, here comes another, got to go.

From: Jennie Pithwait
To: Holly

Come what, one where? Don't leave me hanging...???

From: Holly
To: Jennie Pithwait

Sorry, you should have seen him. Yeeeeeeeeees indeedi, should be heading up to the fifth floor about now. Second time I've seen him too.

From: Jennie Pithwait
To: Holly

I'm grabbing the lift now, I'm making a beeline, yabadabadooooooo.

Subject: Totty??? Where is it?

From: Jennie Pithwait
To: Holly

Where'd he go??? He must have sneaked past me, the little bugger. What have they been teaching them at Uni—Ninja Warfare???

From: Holly
To: Jennie Pithwait

If they are, then you're in trouble. You'll have to just set up your office in the lift.

From: Jennie Pithwait
To: Holly

Fine, I'll move into the lift. But get some of them to use the stairs. I'm only one woman, you know. I can't be riding it all day.

From: Holly
To: Jennie Pithwait

I'm guessing you mean the lift.

From: Jennie Pithwait
To: Holly

Nope.

Subject: Membership Approved—Fetish For Everyone!

From: Fetish For Everyone SM
To: Holly

Dear Holly,
Thank you for your enquiry. We can now confirm you are a member of Fetish for Everyone SM. You will receive our regular updates, newsletter, and event notifications.
Admin

From: Holly
To: Fetish For Everyone SM

No, no, no, I didn't want to be a member! I only wanted to know what a Sub or a Dom was, that was all I wanted to know. I DO NOT want to be a member. Please remove me from the mailing list.

From: Fetish For Everyone SM
To: Holly

You have reached our automatic reply mailbox. We cannot answer your kinky question. Do not reply to us, you naughty pervert, as you'll only receive this message again and no slap on the wrist (unfortunately).
Happy spanking!

Subject: MESSAGE To: MY BROTHER

From: Holly
To: Charlie Denham

I will kill you later for something... please remind me!

Subject: Gucci bag lady

From: Holly
To: Patricia Gillot

Is she important?

From: Patricia Gillot
To: Holly

Only a bit… that was Mr Huerst's wife. She acts like butter wouldn't melt, but—I know different.

From: Holly
To: Patricia Gillot

What???

From: Patricia Gillot
To: Holly

It's only gossip. Anyway, I'd keep out of her way.

From: Holly
To: Patricia Gillot

Like her boots though.

From: Patricia Gillot
To: Holly

And it's all real, bag too.

wednesday

Subject: Meeting room mix-up AGAIN

From: Shella Hamilton-Jones
To: Holly

Dear Holly,
Oh, dear… Would you be so kind as to have a look at the room chart and tell me what you see in room 7 at 5 p.m.?

Subject: Help Holly—Aisha Needs You!!

From: Aisha
To: Holly

Morning,

Have you got a minute? I need someone to talk to... actually, if you've got a few minutes, that would be more heading in the right direction.

Aisha xx

From: Holly
To: Aisha

No, I'm busy.

Subject: Meeting room mix-up

From: Holly
To: Shella Hamilton-Jones

Dear Shella,

Yes, I see Jane Jenkins is booked in for a meeting. Is this OK?

Kindest regards,

Holly

From: Shella Hamilton-Jones
To: Holly

Oh dear Holly,

Do you not remember our little chat? I really can't believe you didn't bother to make a note of it.

From: Holly
To: Shella Hamilton-Jones

Yes, I did make a note of it. Jane Jenkins has a preference for room 12.

From: Shella Hamilton-Jones
To: Holly

Then why, if she has a preference for room 12, is Jane Jenkins's name not in room 12?

From: Holly
To: Shella Hamilton-Jones

Because Mr Huerst also has a preference for Room 12, and I've heard he's quite important.

From: Shella Hamilton-Jones
To: Holly

Then WHY HAVEN'T YOU PUT HIS NAME IN THE BOX!!???

From: Holly
To: Shella Hamilton-Jones

Because he's still standing in front of me, giving me details of the catering facilities he wants.
Is there a need for capitals? (or are you meant to be shouting?)
Feel free to come down and shout if you'd prefer.

From: Shella Hamilton-Jones
To: Holly

Out of Office AutoReply: Meeting room mix-up
Shella Hamilton-Jones is currently out of the office. Please contact Jeremy Anderson in the case of an emergency.

Subject: Ferret Here Again

From: Ferret
To: Holly

Hiya there Hollsie,
What time d'you want to see your little friends?

From: Holly
To: Ferret

Preferably never.

Subject: URGENT URGENT Quickly Jennie—can you help me please!!!

From: Holly
To: Jennie Pithwait

I think I made a boo-boo. One of the MD's PA's, Shella, got upset with me, so I asked her to come down if she had a problem. Now she's out of the office? I hope she's not actually coming down?

From: Jennie Pithwait
To: Holly

I'm sure she is going down, but you won't want her to. Try not to mix it with her, she's a bit of a Rockweiler, or Rottweiler (not sure of spelling), but sure you get the message. She's like one of those big scary vicious dogs with the German names. Anyway, love 'made a boo-boo'—got to use it more instead of 'I f*cked up.' I'm sure my boss would appreciate the change.

Subject: HELP TRISH—it's urgent

From: Holly
To: Patricia Gillot

Trish,
Should I be worried? I think Shella is on her way down to have a go at me.

From: Patricia Gillot
To: Holly

Sh*t!
What did you do to get her attention? I suggest you hide.

Subject: Sunday beers—your place

From: Ferret
To: Holly

What about Sunday? And we can kick back and sink some bevies together (I've a few urban battle stories of my own to share).

Ferret x

Chairman Mow once said 'Free the force.'

From: Holly
To: Ferret

Sounds great.

Subject: Matthew McConaughey or a Mark Ruffalo?

From: Jennie Pithwait
To: Holly

Any hunks on the horizon?

From: Holly
To: Jennie Pithwait

Possibly Jennie. What d'you think of the swampy type?

From: Jennie Pithwait
To: Holly

What—the type that are overaffectionate and clingy?

From: Holly
To: Jennie Pithwait

No, the type that have strong political views and like to burrow.

From: Jennie Pithwait
To: Holly

Sounds good. Put me down for two.

From: Holly
To: Jennie Pithwait

By the way, I was thinking of having a dinner party on Saturday. You know, just a few friends around, nothing special. Do you fancy it? I thought it would give us a chance to catch up on old times.
Holly

From: Jennie Pithwait
To: Holly

Too right, a dinner do round at Hols in 'maida boo-boo'—couldn't turn it down.

Subject: Reception Problems

From: Shella Hamilton-Jones
To: Holly; Roger Lipton

Dear Holly Denham & Roger Lipton,

I've included you on this email too, Roger, because I feel our new receptionist isn't quite grasping how we operate here. I knew it wouldn't be an easy transition for her, making the step up into the corporate world, but there are a few things she needs to learn quickly.

Holly mentioned to me that perhaps I would be better coming down to shout at her if something went wrong, and I'd like to just point out that this is not how employees at Huerst and Wright like to operate. Every person in this building tries to pull together as a team. This is something she needs to understand. Communication is the key to success.

Maybe Holly could perhaps benefit from a training course on her communication skills and the booking of meeting rooms, just to get her up to speed. Holly has great potential but a long way to go, and I would like to offer my assistance to ensure her rapid progression.

Yours truly,
Shella

Subject: Dinner at mine

From: Holly
To: Jennie Pithwait

Dinner definitely on.
Holly

Subject: Quick break

From: Holly
To: Patricia Gillot

Hi,

I'm really sorry, Trish, but can I go for a toilet break again?
Holly

From: Patricia Gillot
To: Holly

Of course you can, sweetheart, you look white as a sheet—you OK?

From: Holly
To: Patricia Gillot

I'm fine.
Hols

From: Patricia Gillot
To: Holly

Is it about that email?

From: Holly
To: Patricia Gillot

Sorry Trish.

From: Patricia Gillot
To: Holly

You don't have to apologise, you're in a bad way, aren't ya? Stay there, I'll get someone from facilities to cover the switch while you tell your aunty Trish all about it.

x

Subject: Aisha

From: Holly
To: Aisha

Are you still on for Saturday?

From: Aisha
To: Holly

Hiya sweetie, of course! I'll bring bubbles—are you cooking?

xxxxxx

From: Holly
To: Aisha

Of course, I've been preparing it all week, so don't be eating before you come!

Holly

x

Subject: Recipe suggestions, please

From: Holly
To: Cooking Right Now

Dear Sir/Madam,

Can you recommend a recipe for a three-course dinner for 5 people?

Kindest regards,

Holly

From: Cooking Right Now
To: Holly

This week's gourmet suggestion is below:

A special roast with a regal cranberry and apple stuffing. The roast will make any dinner party into a sophisticated occasion, and your guests will feel like royalty. Original recipe yield: 6 to 8 servings.

Servings: 6

INGREDIENTS:

- 6 pounds crown pork roast
- 1⁄4 teaspoon ground black pepper
- 2 cups chopped cranberries
- 8 cups white bread cubes
- 1⁄2 cup white sugar
- 2 apples—peeled, cored
- 1⁄2 cup butter and chopped
- 2 onions, chopped
- 1⁄2 cup apple juice
- 2 cups chopped celery
- 1 egg
- 2 teaspoons salt
- 1 teaspoon poultry seasoning

DIRECTIONS:

1. Preheat oven to 375 degrees F (190 degrees C).
2. Season pork roast with salt and pepper to taste, then place on a rack in an open roasting pan, rib ends down.
3. Bake at 375 degrees F (190 degrees C) for 2 hours. Roast will be only partially cooked.
4. Meanwhile, in a medium bowl, combine cranberries and sugar and mix well; set aside. Melt butter or margarine in a large skillet over medium heat. Add onions and celery and sauté until tender, about 10 minutes. Add cranberry mixture, 2 teaspoons

salt, 1/4 teaspoon ground black pepper, bread cubes, apples, apple juice, egg, and poultry seasoning. Toss well.

5. After the two hours, remove roast from oven. Turn rib ends up and fill cavity with cranberry/apple stuffing. Insert meat thermometer between two ribs in the thickest part of the meat, making sure that end of thermometer does not touch any bone.

6. Return stuffed roast to oven and continue roasting at 375 degrees F (190 degrees C) for about 11/2 hours, or until internal temperature of meat reaches 175 degrees F (80 degrees C). (Note: If stuffing becomes too brown, cover it with aluminium foil.)

7. To Serve: Place roast on warm platter and let stand for 15 minutes for easier carving. Slice between ribs to carve and serve with stuffing.

Subject: Dinner Party Enquiry

From: Holly
To: GourmetFoodDeliveredToTheDoor

Hi,

I am having a dinner party for 5 people. Can you tell me how much it would be to deliver food to my door? (Maida Vale)

Kindest regards,

Holly

From: GourmetFoodDeliveredToTheDoor
To: Holly

Dear Holly,

We'd be delighted to help you. Our prices start at around £400 for 5 people. We can email you a full price list if you can give us more details.

Regards,

Francis

Gourmet Food, Delivered To The Door, London

Subject: Mum—can you give me some food advice please

From: Holly
To: Mum and Dad

Hi Mum,

Can you tell me what I can cook for 5 people for a dinner party on Saturday, with a budget of about £20?

Love, Holly

From: Mum and Dad
To: Holly

What about shepherd's pie?

From: Holly
To: Mum and Dad

I'm not sure shepherd's pie is the answer this time. But thanks.

Holly x

From: Mum and Dad
To: Holly

Why only £20?

From: Holly
To: Mum and Dad

Because I can't get to the bank on time.

x

Subject: Saturday night

From: Patricia Gillot
To: Holly

I've just checked with him indoors, and we'd love to come to your dinner party. What kind of thing should we be wearing?

From: Holly
To: Patricia Gillot

Anything—it's just a friendly get-together.

x

Subject: Who's James Lawrence?

From: Holly
To: Jennie Pithwait

Hey, just met that James for the first time. He's good-looking and seems really sweet.

Holly

From: Jennie Pithwait
To: Holly

Rumour has it, he's after half the girls in the company—so if your idea of sweet is a dose of crabs, then yes, I guess he's a real sweetie.

Jennie

From: Holly
To: Jennie Pithwait

That's a shame. Oh well, have a good night.

Holly

thursday

Subject: Get ready girl

From: Patricia Gillot
To: Holly

It's another big day today… keep calm, keep smiling, and we'll get through this lot together. Don't let anyone wind you up. If the

Directors or VPs get stressed and shout, don't take it personal. Keep that smile coming.

Ship 'em in and ship 'em out!

> **From:** Holly
> **To:** Patricia Gillot

Surf and Turf!

> **From:** Patricia Gillot
> **To:** Holly

What?

> **From:** Holly
> **To:** Patricia Gillot

I've no idea, I think it's from *Top Gun*, sorry. Had a bit of an Ice Man obsession when I was about 10.

Subject: Life on the campo

> **From:** Mum and Dad
> **To:** Holly

Holly,

We were sitting on the terrace the other night, sharing a quiet sherry, talking about how when we made the move to Spain, everyone thought we'd be back within a month, but we weren't. Your father was just saying something to me about how well we'd done and how beautiful the evening was, as the sun set behind the avo trees, and just then a huge tractor ploughed through the field next to us before disappearing down the hill on the other side. Then another, and another.

Apparently they built our house on a right-of-way, a country highway apparently. So we'll be having quite a bit of traffic passing by.

Mum x

Subject: Bit of info about your friend

From: Patricia Gillot
To: Holly

Shella (or Cruella, as Mags used to call her) can be a right cow, she's rubbed a load of people up the wrong way here. I take my hat off to you for standing up to her. I know at least two people she fell out with big time. But because she's a PA to an MD, she gets away with it.

From: Holly
To: Patricia Gillot

Does Jane know what she's like?

From: Patricia Gillot
To: Holly

MDs like Jane want results, and anything else is brushed under the carpet. Didn't you have any bitches like that in the hotel you worked at?

From: Holly
To: Patricia Gillot

No, they were all really nice.

From: Patricia Gillot
To: Holly

In four years you never came across anyone who was just pure evil?

From: Holly
To: Patricia Gillot

How d'you know I was there 4 years?

From: Patricia Gillot
To: Holly

Comes with the territory—you have to put up with so much cr*p sitting here, but we're the eyes and ears of the company—so yes, seen your CV, read it, think I even got a copy on me hard drive.

From: Holly
To: Patricia Gillot

Oh, great.
Re: Shella—can I tell HR what's happening?

From: Patricia Gillot
To: Holly

You could tell HR if you wanted. The other two did.

From: Holly
To: Patricia Gillot

Did it help?

From: Patricia Gillot
To: Holly

You could ask them, if they were still here.

From: Holly
To: Patricia Gillot

Oh great.

From: Patricia Gillot
To: Holly

She's a wrong un. If she were around my way, me and me sis would put our boots on and go round there.

From: Holly
To: Patricia Gillot

Why, does she live on a farm?

From: Patricia Gillot
To: Holly

What?

From: Holly
To: Patricia Gillot

I just realised my guy over there is going to be late for his meeting, the one with the blue tie.

From: Patricia Gillot
To: Holly

His meeting starts in two minutes. I'll take him up now, score us some brownie points, then I'll be off. See ya after lunch.

Subject: Are you around Jen?

From: Holly
To: Jennie Pithwait

What does Trish mean when she says—she'll be around there in her boots? She's said it a couple of times?

From: Jennie Pithwait
To: Holly

I didn't know what she meant either, until I went to an office party in Canary Wharf. I was drunk, and a few of us ended up back at hers on the Isle of Dogs. She's got these boots, we're talking steel toecapped boots, that they really do put on when they go around to sort out a neighbour.
Scary.

From: Holly
To: Patricia Gillot

Oh Sh*t.

From: Jennie Pithwait
To: Holly

Why?

From: Holly
To: Jennie Pithwait

She said she'd go round to Shella's in them. I thought it was because Shella lives on a farm (thought maybe it was muddy)... oh dear.

From: Jennie Pithwait
To: Holly

Classic. I'll be telling everyone.
Thanks!

From: Holly
To: Jennie Pithwait

No Jennie, please don't.
x

friday

Subject: Charity People in Holborn

From: Holly
To: Patricia Gillot

Are there charity people everywhere in Holborn?

From: Patricia Gillot
To: Holly

Always outside the tube. You've just got to tell them where to go.

From: Holly
To: Patricia Gillot

I find it difficult not stopping for them.

From: Patricia Gillot
To: Holly

Is that why you were late?

From: Holly
To: Patricia Gillot

I didn't think I was that late. I thought maybe a couple of minutes?

From: Patricia Gillot
To: Holly

They watch the clock around here. They expect you to be here a while before you start.

From: Holly
To: Patricia Gillot

Oh God! I'm so sorry. Has anyone said anything?

From: Patricia Gillot
To: Holly

No, not yet …

Subject: Sophisticated Dinner—Are you coming Jason??

From: Holly
To: Jason GrangerRM

You haven't let me know if you can make my sophisticated dinner do on Sat. night. Some of my new friends from work are coming. I think you'll have a ball.

From: Jason GrangerRM
To: Holly

I've already told you. VERY VERY DODGY, HUGE MISTAKE. DO NOT HAVE A PARTY.

Sorry I can't come. I've got a shift that night. Remember, I work on a reception desk, which isn't just the place to park your coffee mug (wish you were still here).

Can't believe you're partying with colleagues. Cancel it fast.

From: Holly
To: Jason GrangerRM

Why is it dodgy, why can't I?

From: Jason GrangerRM
To: Holly

RULE 1

Never get drunk with 'work people,' ESPECIALLY ex-school mates who are now 'work people.' EVER EVER EVER (except if forced, at the Christmas party, but it's still wrong).

From: Holly
To: Jason GrangerRM

OK, but I don't intend to drink, so that's not a problem, is it?

From: Jason GrangerRM
To: Holly

RULE 2

Never under any circumstances invite 'work people' into your home. It's like offering a bunch of hungry cannibals your naked body on a plate and asking them to choose from a selection of forks.

The people you think are your friends will be running around your flat, picking up evidence they can use against you. Skeletons in the closet... porn on the computer... really it's endless ...

Stop before it's too late ...

From: Holly
To: Jason GrangerRM

I don't have skeletons or porn??

From: Jason GrangerRM
To: Holly

Skeletons... oh, yes yes yes you do... and you know it ...
Porn—what about that naked strumpet you've got hanging up in the hall???!

From: Holly
To: Jason GrangerRM

That's an oil painting of my granny?

From: Jason GrangerRM
To: Holly

Really?? Saucy minx...
Anyway, you're an open book as it is.
But, your flat is a library... and you'll be judged from one glance inside your bathroom cabinet—and a sniff of that basket in your hall!

From: Holly
To: Jason GrangerRM

What's wrong with that basket in my hall?

From: Jason GrangerRM
To: Holly

It stinks, for heavens sake, do some washing. Anyway, got to go, love you hugely. BUT STOP THAT PARTY!!!

From: Holly
To: Jason GrangerRM

Wait, wait, I can hide pictures, I can keep any reference to that time hidden. Surely????
It is a bad idea, isn't it, a terrible idea, but I've already invited people, and it's nearly 5 p.m. I was feeling rotten, Jason, because of that PA and wanted some friends on my side. Heeeeeeelp help help help help help help help help help help help help help help help

help help help help help help help help help help help help help
help help help help help help help help help help help help help
help help

Help me!!!!!!!!!!

From: Jason GrangerRM
To: Holly

Calm down, cancel it if you can. Grab them before they leave for the
weekend and tell them your home's been flooded–that's what staff
usually tell me when they're hungover and don't want to come in.

If not… don't panic whatsoever, your sophisticated dinner party
will, I'm sure, be a success.

(It's probably me just being silly and worrying too much, because I
haven't slept enough.)

xx Got to go. I've got a 'room's too small' emergency on the fourth
floor.

Subject: ORDER 2190007 Ace Internet Food Delivery CARD

DECLINED

Thank you for your order. Unfortunately your payment was
unsuccessful. Please reorder using a different credit card.

Thank you for choosing AceInternetFoodDeliveries—the easier
way to do your shopping.

Subject: Saturday Night

From: Patricia Gillot
To: Holly

Les just called, and he sounds really excited about tomorrow. We're
both looking forward to it.

Thanks Holls.

Subject: Can't Cancel!!!

From: Holly
To: Jason

It's too late, I can't cancel!

Subject: Change of plan

From: Ferret
To: Holly

Hollsie,

Can't imagine you're still at work, but I tried calling you, and your phone was off.

I'm coming over a day early (not Sunday), so I'll be at yours around 7 p.m. Saturday night.

Look forward to seeing you.

Ferret x

week 3

monday

Subject: Sleeping with the enemy???

From: Jason GrangerRM
To: Holly

Oh Holly,

All I want to know is… WHICH colleague did you go to bed with? (I got your message late Sunday.) Man or woman?

From: Holly
To: Jason GrangerRM

Let me start at the beginning, because it's not fair to judge me till you've heard the state I was in!

I got my hair done in the morning—no problem there, was quite pleased with it, got some streaks put in too. I was going to make a spicy chicken dish, and I ordered the essentials off the web: milk, chicken, eggs, and lots of other stuff—of course none of it arrived, at all …

My crappy old washing machine/dryer had broken down, and apparently it'll be too expensive to repair therefore I had no clean clothes to wear, and I had a dinner to make and an hour to do it in.

Ferret came and went before anyone got there. He turned out to be quite funny actually. He brought a card for Alice and put the rodents in the freezer.

While I was waiting for guests to arrive I managed to get through a bottle of wine while deliberating on how to explain the lack of food. By the time Jennie and Trisha had come I'd solved the food problem by filling up a large glass bowl with jellybeans, which I thought at the time looked both colourful and trendy for the modern dinner party guest. I think they thought I was only kidding, and I had to dodge a few 'when's the real food coming' questions. In the end,

I heated up some frozen pizzas in the microwave... I know, you don't have to say a word.

By the time they'd finished their pizzas, I was very drunk, and I kept catching a strange smell, which was only ever there when I turned around quickly (I came to realise it was coming from the top I'd rescued from the dirty clothes basket you warned me about—which no amount of perfume could help). About this point someone then reached in the freezer for more ice and pulled out a frozen rat, which seemed to really put a dampener on the evening, and it was then that I decided people needed to hear me sing.

From: Jason GrangerRM
To: Holly

What did you sing?

From: Holly
To: Jason GrangerRM

What I always sing before I pass out—'Over the Rainbow.'
I woke up the next day in my bed.

From: Jason GrangerRM
To: Holly

Holly,

You are the only person I know who could invite people for a dinner party and not give them any bloody dinner.

Without any doubt, you are quite the most fabulously entertaining sophisticated dinner party host in history. I feel this time your high point must have been offering rat ice cubes—genius! I'm duly devastated I couldn't witness it. Damn it.

From: Holly
To: Jason GrangerRM

Spent the whole day on Sunday with raging hangover, worrying about what I did, and what people are going to think of me today.

From: Jason GrangerRM
To: Holly

I can picture the scene—curtains drawn, too scared to leave the flat or answer the phone, binging yourself on fatty foods and chocolate, Jalapeños, onion rings, chips, with side orders of *Quality Streets*, *Love Actually*, *Bridget 1 & 2* and probably a couple more with Hugh Grant in.

From: Holly
To: Jason GrangerRM

You think you know me.

I just wish I knew who put me to bed… embarrassing.

Subject: Extreme Weight Busters

From: ExtremeWeightBusters.com
To: Holly

Course chosen: Standard

Thank you for registering for a free trial as a member of WeightBusters.com.

You will now receive all our special messages of encouragement and daily dieting advice.

Remember, our methods are extreme, but we believe psychology to be the grounding in losing weight.

So come on, let's beat this together!

Your membership number is 7980

Your password is OLARGE99876

Subject: Celebrity news

From: Holly
To: Jason GrangerRM

Noticed Helen Mirren did well at the Oscars.

From: Jason GrangerRM
To: Holly

I've spent my life playing a queen, and no one's given me diddly squat.

From: Holly
To: Jason GrangerRM

Oh… poor Jason.

From: Jason GrangerRM
To: Holly

Actually that's a lie. I once got chased through Camden by a bunch of thugs who wanted to give me a 'f***ing kicking,' bless.

From: Holly
To: Jason GrangerRM

You've once again brightened up my day.

xxxx

(Not by the thought of you being chased across Camden—just because you're funny.)

xx

tuesday

Subject: Your Party

From: Jennie Pithwait
To: Holly

Nice party, thanks for the invite.

From: Holly
To: Jennie Pithwait

What time can you do lunch today?

From: Jennie Pithwait
To: Holly

Sorry, won't be able to make lunch today.

Subject: Meeting Room Request

From: James Lawrence
To: Holly

Holly,

I've scheduled a meeting with an important client today at 3pm. I'd like one of the better rooms (for a change). Word on the street is that Holly takes bribes. Is this correct?

James

James Lawrence, VP Corporate Finance, H&W, High Holborn WC2 6NP

From: Holly
To: James Lawrence

Dear James,

Bribery is essential (we run a mafia-style front of house down here).

If you don't pay us, we can make it very uncomfortable for you. No air-con, the wrong food, interruptions, and faulty AV equipment.

Holly

From: James Lawrence
To: Holly

Holly,

Please forgive my previous ignorance in this matter. I'll pay like a good boy.

Can I have the gourmet menu for our guests, also—you think you could russle up a room with a view?

James

From: Holly
To: James Lawrence

Not sure what you're expecting to see from a window in central London—the Egyptian Pyramids? Or the Hanging Gardens of Babylon?

You've got room 15. Hope this suits your requirements.

Holly

From: James Lawrence
To: Holly

Central London city smog will be fine (are we now in an episode of *Faulty Towers*?).

Room 15 is perfect, please accept my thanks. Oh, and the offer of lunch sometime?

J

From: Holly
To: James Lawrence

Thank you. Lunch some time could be nice.

Holly

Subject: Thanks Aish!

From: Holly
To: Aisha

Thanks for coming.

From: Aisha
To: Holly

I know you probably hate me and think I'm a useless friend, and I can understand it if you never want to talk to me again. But it wasn't my fault, I told you I was having problems. If it makes you feel any better, I've been crying all weekend.

From: Holly
To: Aisha

It doesn't make me feel better. I would have just liked you to have been there.

From: Aisha
To: Holly

I was a mess Sat night—through to Monday afternoon. How did it go anyway?

From: Holly
To: Aisha

It went very well. You missed a classy night.
X

Subject: Holborn Today

From: Holly
To: Alice and Matt

PHOTOS Rush-Hour
Fab weather (see photo attached). Forgot my umbrella, got a few bad looks from people for my hair looking like bush.
Pooh.

From: Alice and Matt
To: Holly

PHOTOS Rush-Hour
Rush hour in the campo—see attached.
Alice
xxx

Subject: Complaint

From: Maxi Hazier
To: Holly

Holly,

Did you hang up on someone last week, because they were rude to you?

Maxi Hazier, VP Corporate Finance, H&W, High Holborn, WC2B 6NP, London

Subject: Not funny—in trouble again

From: Holly
To: Patricia Gillot

This time for hanging up on a client. Any suggestions?

From: Patricia Gillot
To: Holly

Why did you hang up on them?

From: Holly
To: Patricia Gillot

They were gabbling and being a bit offish.

From: Patricia Gillot
To: Holly

A bit offish?? And you hung up on them? You can't do that!

From: Holly
To: Patricia Gillot

But you told me to only the other day!

From: Patricia Gillot
To: Holly

I was having a laugh!

You can't hang up on clients, there could be a shed-load of money waiting on that call. I know they're rude sometimes, but you never know what's going on their end, so you just got to grin and bear it. You messed up there babe, big time.

Trish

Subject: Got your urgent phone message!

From: Aisha
To: Holly

PHOTOS HELP-FOR-HOL
HOLLY,
I GOT YOUR URGENT PHONE MESSAGE about hanging up on a client.
See attached—this could be useful …

From: Holly
To: Aisha

That's great, thanks for that, Aish, really helpful in my current state.
PS—what is he meant to be doing anyway?

From: Aisha
To: Holly

What d'you think—I'm lying on the bed.

From: Holly
To: Aisha

What, underneath?

From: Aisha
To: Holly

Yes underneath.

From: Holly
To: Aisha

And you're taking pictures????

From: Aisha
To: Holly

I'll be honest, the view was better than the performance.
Anyway he didn't mind holding still for a couple of piccies, kept his hat on too. Yummie.

xxx

From: Holly
To: Aisha

I would send you the pictures I took on my phone today, but they're probably too wild and wet for you.

xxx

Subject: Miserable

From: Holly
To: Jason GrangerRM

Jason,
Do you have any friends who, without meaning to, remind you all the time how much of a nonevent your love life is?

x

From: Jason GrangerRM
To: Holly

Are we feeling a bit low today? Don't worry about it. Some people always have lots of partners, when the rest of us would just settle for one. There's probably one just lurking around the next corner.

From: Holly
To: Jason GrangerRM

I'd like to think of them as waiting for me patiently. (Not keen on lurkers.)

xxx

wednesday

Subject: Can you help me Trisha?

From: Holly
To: Patricia Gillot

Help, what should I do about Maxi?

I still haven't emailed her back about me slamming the phone down. What should I say?

From: Patricia Gillot
To: Holly

It's your mess. Sorry. You sort it out.

Subject: Advice needed please Mum

From: Holly
To: Mum and Dad

I'm not sure, but I think since the party, people aren't very happy with me. I imagine I probably made a fool out of myself. Trish, the other receptionist, is definitely annoyed with me. I'm just too worried to ask her why.

Oh and I think I messed up again here.

Not a great week so far, Mum.

x

From: Mum and Dad
To: Holly

Holly,

Don't worry about them not speaking to you again. Your father has spent a lifetime embarrassing me at parties, and it's all forgotten in the morning. Although the Petersons have never spoken to us since that night he swapped his clothes for their Christmas tree decorations, and I was beginning to get some strange stares in Budgens, but then it all seemed to sort itself out in the end.

Love, Mum

From: Holly
To: Mum and Dad

Mum you emigrated, I don't want to have to emigrate.

From: Mum and Dad
To: Holly

You won't have to, it'll all be fine. My advice is just keep being friendly, keep plugging away in life, keep smiling, and keep your clothes on. That's the advice I gave your father. Seems to have helped.

Let me know if they talk to you again.

Love, Mum

x

Subject: Trouble at work

From: Holly
To: Jason GrangerRM

No one's talking to me today. Saturday night could have been worse than I thought, but the problem is I can't remember what I've done to upset everyone.

From: Jason GrangerRM
To: Holly

Ask them what's wrong. I would, otherwise you'll never know. It could be just some misunderstanding from Saturday night—they mistakenly thought they were at a dinner party at Maida Vale, whereas you thought they were attending your stage debut at the Albert Hall. Misunderstandings happen.

From: Holly
To: Jason GrangerRM

I would laugh... but also I've messed up big time again; I cut someone off while they were talking, and it's hit the fan. The worst thing is—I admitted doing it on purpose, because I thought it was just some raving lunatic talking gibberish. Turns out it was a private client talking about derivatives (whatever that means)!?

Subject: Sorry to bother you Holly

From: Aisha
To: Holly

Are you there?

From: Holly
To: Aisha

Yes, but quite busy. Are you OK?

From: Aisha
To: Holly

Yes, I'm just not sure I did the right thing and want to ask your opinion.

xxxxxxxxxxxxxxxxxxxxxx

From: Holly
To: Aisha

You can't keep juggling all these men at once, and you said yourself Alex wasn't THAT hot in bed—and you certainly weren't with him for his personality!! Believe me, you did the right thing. He's gone and forgotten.

xxxx

Got to work.

Holly

From: Aisha
To: Holly

He's in the other room sleeping.

Sorry.

?

From: Holly
To: Aisha

Oh, so you're back together, then, I didn't mean he was that bad. I'm sure he's a fun, interesting guy, underneath it all.

From: Aisha
To: Holly

I was going to end it, but ended up having sex with him instead.

From: Holly
To: Aisha

Easy mistake to make, have you been to sleep yet?

From: Aisha
To: Holly

No

From: Holly
To: Aisha

Then go to sleep.

x

love you very much, and you've got nothing to worry about, you're a fun, crazy girl, and everyone loves you.

From: Aisha
To: Holly

Thanks, that's what I needed. I really should start paying you for lifting my downers.

xxxx

thursday

Subject: TEST TEST TEST

From: Elizabethontour
To: Holly

TESTING

From: Holly
To: Elizabethontour

Granny is that you?

x

Subject: Granny online

From: Holly
To: Mum and Dad

Mum, did you set Granny up as 'Elizabethontour'—if so that's really sweet, and I think she just emailed me.

From: Mum and Dad
To: Holly

Holly,

Yes I set her up on Monday.

She's so happy in Spain. She hasn't stopped smiling since she got here. We've been cleverly watering down her drink though.

Other news: it turns out our land surrounding our finca is marked by white painted stones. This is the only way the town hall has of working out which is our land and which isn't.

Fun Fun.

All our love, Mum & Dad

Subject: Jason—your opinion please

From: Holly

To: Jason GrangerRM

I feel more positive today with Trisha. I think I just need to make more of an effort.

Subject: Watching my Soaps

From: Holly

To: Patricia Gillot

Did you watch *EastEnders* Tuesday night? It was great!!

From: Patricia Gillot

To: Holly

No, I've stopped watching it.

Subject: First a mobile phone—now you're on the Internet?

From: Holly

To: Granny

Hi Granny,

I didn't realise it was you who had just emailed me. How are you? I hear you like the new country.

Love, Holls xx

From: Granny

To: Holly

Dear Holly,

They've stuffed me into a home, like I needed it! I don't like the food, I don't like the weather, I don't like the people. I would tell your mother, but my false teeth went missing in the move, and I won't speak again until I'm all dignified, so I just smile and nod. However, when I get hold of a new set, I'll tell them where they can stick their sangria. Incidentally, they've started watering down me gin. They must think I'm stupid. I am so glad you have found a new start. I'm so very proud of you Holly.

Missing you as always.

Love, Granny

xxxx

Subject: Update

From: Roger Lipton
To: Holly

Dear Holly,

Although you have been here just less than three weeks, I think it's time we had a review. Can you book a meeting room for next Wednesday around ten o'clock?

Yours sincerely,

Roger

Subject: Extreme Weight Busters

From: ExtremeWeightBusters.com
To: Holly

Standard Course

Remember the old equation: Overeating = Overweight = No Friends or Partner

Today's menu:

Breakfast—Dry Toast and Tea

Lunch—Low Fat Natural Yogurt and Fruit Salad

Dinner—Sushi & Green Leaf Salad

Night Snack—Salad

Subject: Lunch

From: Jennie Pithwait
To: Holly

You on for lunch today. I'm free around 2 p.m.?

From: Holly
To: Jennie Pithwait

I'd love to, but Trish always takes the 2 p.m. slot. She has to go somewhere each day at that time.

From: Jennie Pithwait
To: Holly

Where does Trisha NEED to go at that time???

From: Holly
To: Jennie Pithwait

Don't know.

From: Jennie Pithwait
To: Holly

Very suspicious. What d'you think she's up to???

From: Holly
To: Jennie Pithwait

I don't know, but I guess it's her private business, so I'm staying out of it.

From: Jennie Pithwait
To: Holly

Private my arse, we should ask her.

From: Holly
To: Jennie Pithwait

I think I'll leave it.

From: Jennie Pithwait
To: Holly

Well I won't. Something's going on.

friday

Subject: Moving Mum

From: Mum and Dad
To: Holly

Holly,
You think Granny is very happy out here then?
Mum

From: Holly
To: Mum and Dad

Of course she is. Just give her some time, and she'll come to love it there.

xxx

Subject: Our emails

From: Holly
To: Granny

Hi Granny,
Quickly, can you delete our emails, I don't want Mum getting upset about what you've told me.
Love, Hols
xxxx

From: Granny
To: Holly

Dear Holly,

I was just watching *The Last of the Summer Wine*. You mum has got me the series. You see I can't get British telly out here in the sticks, that's another reason I miss England. What do you mean delete our emails?

Love, Granny

xxx

From: Holly
To: Granny

If you highlight the email, then press the Delete button on the keyboard—that should do it. It's just that I told Mum we hadn't spoken to each other yet.

Holls

From: Granny
To: Holly

We haven't? This is email isn't it?

From: Holly
To: Granny

I know, but can you delete them, and from your deleted items?

From: Granny
To: Holly

If they're deleted, how can I delete them, and what am I deleting?

From: Holly
To: Granny

Don't worry, Granny, I love you very very much. I'll think of a way around this. Have a lovely day.

Love, Hols

Xxx

Subject: Extreme Weight Busters

From: ExtremeWeightBusters.com
To: Holly

Standard Course

Remember:

If the mountain won't come to Mohammed, it could be because mountains are big and heavy and don't move much.

Today's menu:

Breakfast—Nothing

Lunch—Chicken breast, on rice biscuits

Dinner—One of our special 'I'm a fatty' no-fat drinks (available online)

Night Snack—Banana

Subject: Extreme Weight Busters

From: ExtremeWeightBusters.com
To: Holly

We are sorry you have cancelled your free trial membership of ExtremeWeightBusters.com

We wish you all the success in the future with your weight problem.

Subject: Room Checking

From: Patricia Gillot
To: Holly

Rooms 6 & 8 need checking. I'll see you in 5.

From: Holly
To: Patricia Gillot

Are you upset with me—have I done anything wrong?

From: Patricia Gillot
To: Holly

Don't worry about it.

Subject: CLUB SUBMISSION

From: Charlie Denham
To: Holly

We're running out of money to build this club, so I've sacked the builders and me and Rubber Ron are going to do everything.
Charlie

From: Holly
To: Charlie Denham

You don't know how to build. You're rubbish at DIY. You can't even put up a shelf!

From: Charlie Denham
To: Holly

OK, if it was something technical like building the bar, or wiring the club, yes, that would probably be too much, but building walls—it's just bricks and cement. Unless you know any builders who could do it for free?

From: Holly
To: Charlie Denham

Sorry.

Subject: Your big mistake

From: Jason GrangerRM
To: Holly

So have you found out yet who put you to bed on Saturday?

From: Holly
To: Jason GrangerRM

Trish still isn't talking to me... Maybe she saw something shocking ...

From: Jason GrangerRM
To: Holly

It's probably just your imagination.

Subject: Mad calls!

From: Holly
To: Patricia Gillot

Trish,
You'll love this—you know when you ask someone where they're calling from, and they say something like 'Putney' instead of a company name ...

From: Patricia Gillot
To: Holly

Yes.

From: Holly
To: Patricia Gillot

Well I just got someone who stumbled—sounded confused—and said 'The bath?' Funny when that happens isn't it?

From: Patricia Gillot
To: Holly

Hysterical.

Subject: Jason—re: Trish

From: Holly
To: Jason GrangerRM

Pretty sure it's not just my imagination.

Atmosphere is stifling, and I'm now embarrassed as hell… I tried to
get her to laugh. She didn't even crack a smile.

From: Jason GrangerRM
To: Holly

No, she's fine. That's the normal reaction you get when you're
telling jokes.

From: Holly
To: Jason GrangerRM

Up yours.

Subject: Hi, my best friend

From: Holly
To: Jason GrangerRM

Need a favour …

From: Jason GrangerRM
To: Holly

Out of Office AutoReply
Unfortunately, no one is here to take your booking. If you would
like to contact the reservations team, someone may be able to secure
you a room.

From: Holly
To: Jason GrangerRM

Don't lie, I know you're there!!! It's only a small favour …

From: Jason GrangerRM
To: Holly

I have one eye open and a finger precariously close to the Delete
button.

From: Holly
To: Jason GrangerRM

Will you take my friend on... as a receptionist?

From: Jason GrangerRM
To: Holly

Out of Office AutoReply

Unfortunately, no one is here to take your booking. If you would like to contact the reservations team, someone may be able to secure you a room.

From: Holly
To: Jason GrangerRM

Stop it.

From: Jason GrangerRM
To: Holly

OK, who is he/she, what's he/she like, what is he/she to you? Why me? Why am I sitting here supervising children???

From: Holly
To: Jason GrangerRM

OK

Answers:

1: SHE's a good friend
2: Lovely
3: A good friend
4: Because you're a good friend
6: They're not children, you enjoy it, so stop being a woos (not sure how to spell it)

Also—you should feel sorry for me, I'm likely to lose my job next week—you're not ...

From: Jason GrangerRM
To: Holly

It's spelt wus, and fine, send her along for an interview on Monday.
It'll be quiet between 1 p.m.-2 p.m. so send her at 1, asking for me.
And I'm not guaranteeing anything.

x

From: Holly
To: Jason GrangerRM

You are the best! She won't let you down. And if she does, then it's
nothing to do with me.

From: Jason GrangerRM
To: Holly

What…?

From: Holly
To: Jason GrangerRM

Out of Office AutoReply

Subject: You lucky girl

From: Holly
To: Aisha

He said… yes …

From: Aisha
To: Holly

You're lying.

From: Holly
To: Aisha

BUT you have to PROMISE, you won't go out Saturday night, or
I'll kill you. I mean it.

From: Aisha
To: Holly

I promise, I promise …

From: Holly
To: Aisha

Make sure you dress appropriately. I'll call you later to go through some interview questions.

From: Aisha
To: Holly

Thanks honey, I won't be late. Don't worry, won't let you down. What d'you mean 'appropriately'—like something slutty but not too revealing?

From: Holly
To: Aisha

Black suit, white shirt, tights, makeup (not too much), stud earrings only, court shoes.

From: Aisha
To: Holly

Tights—sick. What about nails?

From: Holly
To: Aisha

Clear. NOT long, red, and slutty.

From: Aisha
To: Holly

Got it. Thanks for this, I owe ya. So Jason, is he straight?

From: Holly
To: Aisha

That is of no relevance to your interview.
Please be there …

xx

week 4
monday

Subject: A bit lost

From: Aisha
To: Holly

Hi Holly,

Still up from last night, havenx't gone to bedd, but I reckond I can still make it to the interviewx eitherway. Dont want to let you down, Where is it again?

Aisha.

Subject: What a small world

From: Mum and Dad
To: Holly

Dear Holly,

I said to your father only yesterday 'what a small world we live in,' and it turns out I was right.

A local farmer has been sneaking on to our land every night and moving those white painted rocks a yard closer to the house. If it carried on for much longer, we'd have been in a negative equity situation (Mummy joke). We've moved the rocks back where they were, and on the other side of them there is a steep drop. So no more tractors coming through our land, how pleasant. Although your father's a bit concerned I've upset nearly everyone I've met since our arrival. Maybe I should invite the local farmers around for a wine and cheese party. What do you think?

xxx Mum

From: Holly
To: Mum and Dad

Do you think I take after you Mum, or Dad?

From: Mum and Dad
To: Holly

Me darling. Really, we're two peas in a pod.
Mum.

From: Holly
To: Mum and Dad

That's wonderful news.

Subject: A bit lost

From: Aisha
To: Holly

Holly,

It's me again. OK, if you're not going to react or talk to me, then I guess I'll have to admit I'm lying. I didn't go out on Saturday. You're making me boring already.

Aisha

From: Holly
To: Aisha

You could never be called boring.

xxx

From: Aisha
To: Holly

As I was off the partying, I tried to call you on Saturday, but I couldn't get through to you.

(I thought we could have been sad staying-in types together.)

From: Holly
To: Aisha

I don't just sit there on my weekends, waiting for you to call up drunk from some guy's house. I have a life.

From: Aisha
To: Holly

Damn you! Where did you get this life from. Were you on a date????

From: Holly
To: Aisha

No.

From: Aisha
To: Holly

Oh.

From: Holly
To: Aisha

Doesn't mean I didn't have a great time.

From: Aisha
To: Holly

Really.

From: Holly
To: Aisha

Actually, yes. I met up with pregnant Pam and spent the day in Guildford by the river. Visited my school, then wondered why, and became incredibly scared I'd bump into old school friends who'd done much better than me. Ran away quickly with the secure intention of going back there once I was famous, thin, and deadly in martial arts. Then, I'd probably go there quite a lot, spend the days sitting outside the dark gates in a large, pink, open-top Rolls, growling at children.

| From: Aisha |
| To: Holly |

Sweetie, you can get arrested for that stuff (it's happened to me before).

| From: Holly |
| To: Aisha |

Well anyway, it's a shame you missed out.

| From: Aisha |
| To: Holly |

Fun with pregnant Pam, I'll give it a miss.

xxx

Just being a bitch. I had a lovely time with Shona; we acted like kids (me more than her), and we were generally very childish and played tricks on Mum all day/night.

Subject: Psychic Readings

| From: StarsFutureWizard |
| To: Holly |

Dear Holly,

This is the week when a fabulous plethora of opportunities will arise. It's important to know which is the puppy wrapped in a pink bow and which is a wolf draped in sheep's clothing.

Also, why not take advantage of our Mad March offer on psychic readings? Find out if you're destined for love this March for just $2.99 for 3 mins.

The Wizard

Subject: HOLLY DENHAM—IMPORTANT

From: James Lawrence
To: Holly

My previous lunch offer—I feel it's important, to welcome you properly... What about today?

From: Holly
To: James Lawrence

James,

Thank you for the kind offer. I'd love to, but lunches are a bit difficult—we can't take the kind of lovely long lunches you chaps do up there, sorry.

Holly

From: James Lawrence
To: Holly

That's a shame.

J

Subject: REMINDER James Lawrence ...

From: Holly
To: Holly

James—wolf or puppy?

Subject: Hotel Employment / Job

From: Jason GrangerRM
To: Holly

OK, just met with your friend, Aisha. Before I go on, don't you have a friend called Aisha you said was a bit of a screwup??

Jason

From: Holly
To: Jason GrangerRM

Oh, I know the one, no, that's not her (and I never said she was a screwup, just a bit mad). But that's Teesha.

From: Jason GrangerRM
To: Holly

OK. Eitherway, I thought she could have potential. She was bubbly, charming, charismatic, and stylish (although she had the tendency to talk a lot, about herself, without being asked).

From: Holly
To: Jason GrangerRM

Charismatic? Stylish? Why, what was she wearing?

From: Jason GrangerRM
To: Holly

Black suit, white shirt, very professional, polished, pretty.

From: Holly
To: Jason GrangerRM

That's all I wore when I was working for you, and you never told me I looked 'stylish!!' OR Charming or Charismatic. I can be charismatic.

From: Jason GrangerRM
To: Holly

I know you can be charismatic AND charming.

From: Holly
To: Jason GrangerRM

You should see me here. You never exactly oozed charm when you were upset with everyone.

From: Jason GrangerRM
To: Holly

You don't know what compliments I've given you behind your back! Stop being a big sulky child. I thought you wanted me to like your friend??

From: Holly
To: Jason GrangerRM

I did.

From: Jason GrangerRM
To: Holly

Well then?
I didn't want to interview your messed-up friend anyway.
GOOD-BYE!

Subject: A huge thank you

From: Aisha
To: Holly

Just got home. I really hope I did OK. I held back on a few questions. Nice guy, good-looking too! Let me know if you've got any news.
xxx you're the best.
Aisha

Subject: Women's problems

From: Holly
To: Jason GrangerRM

Sorry.
Bit stressed at the moment …
Sorry …
forgiiiiiiiiiiiiiiiiiiiiiive me
Pretty please???

(so… did she get the job? xxxxx??)
Holly loves you.

From: Jason GrangerRM
To: Holly

You have issues and stink.
And have no friends except me, because I know you're hormonal.
So she can start on Monday.

From: Holly
To: Jason GrangerRM

Love ya!
She'll make me proud, I promise.
But this doesn't mean she'll be like your new best friend??
… and you'll be hanging around with her, going to bars and being like all—'Aisha said this' and 'Aisha said that… '?

From: Jason GrangerRM
To: Holly

No.

From: Holly
To: Jason GrangerRM

Oh, and just one more thing. What compliments did you say about me behind my back? What did you say? Was it nice? Who did you say it to?

Subject: Hello—HELLO—Anyone there?

From: Holly
To: Jason GrangerRM

Hello, did you get my last email? Hello?

From: Jason GrangerRM
To: Holly

Hi,

Sorry, I was busy laughing at something funny Aisha said earlier, then I was planning what to wear when me and her go out clubbing together.

xxx

From: Holly
To: Jason GrangerRM

ha ha you're not funny.

tuesday

Subject: Holiday abroad

From: Holly
To: Alice and Matt

Hiya Alice,

Looking forward to seeing you, not long to go! Seem to be upsetting everyone here. Also got that meeting with HR tomorrow ...

xxxx

Subject: Trish please talk to me

From: Holly
To: Patricia Gillot

Please,

I can't sit next to you without us communicating at all. It's bad enough that we can't speak and we always have to write, but now it's just murder, and we're meant to be going for a drink with the others tonight. Pleeeeeeease tell me what I've done. Is it to do with my work?

From: Patricia Gillot
To: Holly

No.

From: Holly
To: Patricia Gillot

Is it about the party?

From: Patricia Gillot
To: Holly

Yes.

From: Holly
To: Patricia Gillot

If it was my dancing, or singing, or food, I'm really sorry, I'm not the best host. I have been feeling bad for dragging you out for that. Please forgive me. Everything just went wrong.

Holly x

From: Patricia Gillot
To: Holly

I loved the party, it was great. Les did too. We were really enjoying ourselves. We haven't been out somewhere different for a while, and it was great. We even liked your jelly beans, and your singing wasn't that bad.

From: Holly
To: Patricia Gillot

Then what was it?

From: Patricia Gillot
To: Holly

I didn't appreciate you and that Jennie laughing about me.

From: Holly
To: Patricia Gillot

I didn't laugh at you, ever??

From: Patricia Gillot
To: Holly

You did, and I didn't think you were like that.

From: Holly
To: Patricia Gillot

What did you think we said?

From: Patricia Gillot
To: Holly

You know.

From: Holly
To: Patricia Gillot

I honestly don't know what you think I was laughing about, but I can assure you, I've been very grateful for how you've trained me, put up with my mistakes, and been very patient. I know I haven't picked things up as fast as you thought I would. I wouldn't have said anything rotten about you—I promise!

From: Patricia Gillot
To: Holly

I guess I should feel lucky you noticed I was there, you were spending so much time with your old school friend—little Miss 'look at my legs, aren't they so young and smooth, it's amazing how I never even have to shave them!' cow upstairs.

From: Holly
To: Patricia Gillot

I don't know what you mean, I was very drunk very quickly. The night hadn't gone well with the food and everything, but I thought we'd all had fun… I'm really sorry.

From: Patricia Gillot
To: Holly

Also I hear you laughing about my 'island talk' as though I was from another planet. Made me feel very small, gossiping about me.

From: Holly
To: Patricia Gillot

Honestly I'm no gossip. We weren't doing anything like that at all!

Subject: Trisha's well-kept secret!!

From: Jennie Pithwait
To: Holly

I've sussed it! I know why Trisha goes out at that time… She's having an affair with one of the directors—must be!!

Subject: Trish please talk to me

From: Holly
To: Patricia Gillot

You can't have heard the whole story. Really, it was me who felt stupid. I'll tell you when these two have gone. Honest, I'd never say anything bad about you. It was just about those boots you said you put on… Really, it's me being a dumb ass… I thought they were for walking through the mud—it was about that farm comment I said (don't know if you remember).
Holly.

From: Patricia Gillot
To: Holly

You fool, I wondered what that was about. Tell me tonight. It just sounded bad, that's all. I felt hurt.

From: Holly
To: Patricia Gillot

OK. It was just a misunderstanding, Trish.

From: Patricia Gillot
To: Holly

PS also you were rambling drunkenly for a while about your nightmare life before in Canary Wharf. I know you lied about your CV, I did on mine too many years ago, but I wouldn't be telling Jennie. Also, when I put you to bed, you woke up screaming.

Subject: Office girls

From: Charlie Denham
To: Holly

This building thing is harder than we thought. The council is insisting on having both ends of the wall meeting the club ceiling at the same time, so Rubber Ron's gone out to buy a spirit level. Have you sorted me out yet with any of those tight-suited secretaries? Come on, there must be loads there. Have you told them I own a club???
Charlie

From: Holly
To: Charlie Denham

Not the best time to talk to you but: Stop being a pervert. You don't own a club, you own a building site, and neither of you have any kind of skill in this area at all. It's madness. You've got to find yourselves a handy man, please!

Subject: Job hunting?

From: Jason GrangerRM
To: Holly

When's that HR thing then?

From: Holly
To: Jason GrangerRM

Tomorrow, 10 a.m… (don't like your subject box, Jason). I think it probably will be an exit interview though.

From: Jason GrangerRM
To: Holly

I'm telling you for certain—it WON'T be an exit interview!

Subject: Reminder! Suit

From: Holly
To: Holly

Remember to wear best suit tomorrow!

Subject: Guildford—Saturday

From: Holly
To: Pregnant Pam

Hi Pam,

Great seeing you on Saturday. We've got to do it again soon.

xxxx

From: Pregnant Pam
To: Holly

It was, definitely. I'm up for doing it again later in month.

xxxx

wednesday

Subject: Psychic readings, Stars and the Future!

From: StarsFutureWizard
To: Holly

Stunts can only hurt your performance this week, so remember when ambiguity strikes at the heart of your consciousness, it's only a route to a blueprint that lurks behind mischievous gain. 'It's not the time of the moth' says the wizard, so keep one eye on Pluto, and you'll know which side your toast is burnt.

Also, why not take advantage of our Mad March offer on psychic readings? Find out if your destined for love this March for just $2.99 for 3 mins.

The Wizard

From: Holly

To: StarsFutureWizard

To the Futures Wizard,

What on earth does this mean??? Please explain???

I don't care about my lurking blueprint, or any wizard's moth, I just want to know if I'm about to lose my job??

Or whether the guy on the 5th floor really likes me or is just keen to rehouse a family of sea urchins?

Regards,

Holly

PS Your 3 mins psychic reading was 2 mins 50 secs thanking me for calling, then telling me about other offers, and 10 secs explaining how little chance I had of love unless I stayed on the line and spent more money ???? Did I? No, your wizardness, I did not.

PPS I didn't use the work phone—this was at home—(in case this is being read by anyone from IT).

Subject: Team drinking night out

From: Judy Perkins

To: Alvin Johnson; Dave Otto; Graham Kristan; Ralph Tooms; Samantha Smith; Patricia Gillot; Holly

Dear Team,

RE: Holly's Fabulous—welcoming night

A good night was had by all, glad most of you could make it. Let's do it again some time. Graham, you missed out.

Subject: Welcoming Night—xxx

From: Patricia Gillot
To: Holly

To me that read RE: Holly is Fabulous. Welcoming night. Ha ha…
I think you've turned her head, gal …
PS Delete this immediately and from your deleted items!

From: Holly
To: Patricia Gillot

She's not, is she?

From: Patricia Gillot
To: Holly

Me: Hols is so innocent. Of course she is.

From: Holly
To: Patricia Gillot

Oh great, and what are the chances—Judy was the one person here
looking over my shoulder when I got that stupid email on my half
day induction day—which shouted 'I'm a lesbian!'
I'll kill my brother!!!

From: Patricia Gillot
To: Holly

That's funny, but I thought you knew.

From: Holly
To: Patricia Gillot

No, not a clue. What should I do?

From: Patricia Gillot
To: Holly

Nothing, unless you want to …

From: Holly
To: Patricia Gillot

Not really my type.

From: Patricia Gillot
To: Holly

So am I still in with a shout then?

From: Holly
To: Patricia Gillot

OH, yes, I thought you'd never ask—let's get to it, sexy!

From: Patricia Gillot
To: Holly

Did you see I just spluttered over that woman's hand? Don't make me laugh!

From: Holly
To: Patricia Gillot

Hee hee

Subject: HR Meeting

From: Holly
To: Patricia Gillot

Seeing HR soon. Was it just because you were still angry with me that you said it was so bad that I cut that guy off?

From: Patricia Gillot
To: Holly

I was joking when I said I just cut people off. I don't really, sorry. That's the problem with email, you can't see when someone's having you on. It's like I said, that call could have been important. (important money-wise, anyway) ...
Sorry babes... xxx

Subject: HR Meeting

From: Holly
To: Patricia Gillot

Meeting Roger Lipton very soon. I can feel the minutes ticking down. I'm really scared.

From: Patricia Gillot
To: Holly

Don't you worry about them lot. I'll tell them that I told you to do it.

From: Holly
To: Patricia Gillot

No, don't be silly. It's my own fault.

From: Patricia Gillot
To: Holly

If your meeting is anything to do with Cruella, I'll kill her!

From: Holly
To: Patricia Gillot

I don't like the thought of them all having a go at me, especially if Shella's in there too. I'd die.

From: Patricia Gillot
To: Holly

It'll be all very formal with HR, everything by the book. I call them office rozzas.

From: Holly
To: Patricia Gillot

OK.

From: Patricia Gillot
To: Holly

Don't you cry now. Come on, let's take a break.

From: Holly
To: Patricia Gillot

But we can't leave the reception desk on its own.

From: Patricia Gillot
To: Holly

I'm the senior receptionist here, and I order you to leave your chair and come and give your Trish a hug! (Then go and get some fresh air and stop worrying! That's an order too)

Subject: Washing Machines & Fridges

From: HEM Machines
To: Holly

REF:9829833

Ms H Dinham,

Thank you for using H.E.M.

We hope you are happy with your purchase and return to us again in the future for your home electrical items.

Paula, Customer Service

From: Holly
To: HEM Machines

REF:9829833

No, I'm not happy with my purchase. I contacted your department twice last week. The washing machine you delivered was not functioning properly on arrival, so it has not been used. Can you remove the machine as soon as possible so I can order another.

Holly

From: HEM Machines
To: Holly

REF:9829833

Ms H Dinham

Thank you for your email. Have you contacted our 24 hour repair line, which will be able to assist you?

Paula

From: Holly
To: HEM Machines

REF:9829833

I did try to get through. I was put on hold for 10 minutes while told about your terrible experience of receiving an unusually high volume of calls. I would now like to just have the machine removed and be refunded.

Thank you.

Regards,

Holly Denham

Subject: Financial Credit Dept—Banking Trust

From: Security Banking Trust
To: Holly Denham

MAINTENANCE

Due to the updating of our online banking system, we need your account number, sort code, name, pin number, online username, passwords, and salary details.

Thanks.

From: Holly
To: Security Banking Trust

I could give you my account details, but I've a feeling—seeing as I don't bank with your company—that maybe, just maybe, this is a scam. So I tell you what, I'll keep my account details to myself, and you lot keep your nasty spamming emails to yourselves—what d'you think?

Subject: Meeting??

From: Jason GrangerRM
To: Holly

How did your meeting go?

Subject: From Trish

From: Patricia Gillot
To: Holly

Alright, spill the beans. What did they say?

Subject: Holly

From: Granny
To: Holly

There's a man looking through my window. I think he's a pervert.
Granny

Subject: Holly

From: Granny
To: Holly

No, it's your father. Sorry. Now we're going into town for a spot of lunch. How exciting. Hope it rains.

From: Holly
To: Granny

Glad you're OK.

Subject: Meeting

From: Holly
To: Patricia Gillot

There was Roger Lipton and someone else from HR, and Judy. He said he'd heard about a few 'issues,' which he viewed as teething problems. Wanted to know if I needed any support in the way of a training course, etc.—as Shella had suggested it could be useful for me... grrrr

From: Patricia Gillot
To: Holly

Cruella's doing, of course. Did you volunteer for it?

From: Holly
To: Patricia Gillot

No, but I did say how excited you were about the thought of going on one, said you'd been talking about the idea nonstop.

From: Patricia Gillot
To: Holly

I'll kill ya! Ha ha. What else did he say?

From: Holly
To: Patricia Gillot

They've booked me on to an intensive meeting-room-scheduling software course on Friday—which I'm sure Cruella will be laughing her head off about.

Also, he wanted to know if there were any issues that I may want to bring up. I said 'no,' so he told me they'd got a couple of their own that they DID want to bring up (the phone slamming down incident and the meeting room booking thing). I tried giving him my version of what happened with 'Miss De Vil' and how I HAD followed procedure, but they really didn't want to hear any of it (I think they know exactly how difficult she is, but they don't want to have to deal with her). Judy was good and backed me up. Roger kept talking about my hospitality background, and how I should be able to 'draw on these skills' to smooth over difficult situations. I got the impression after the fourth time he mentioned it, that he was meaning—just let Cruella talk to you how she wants, then grin and bear it.

From: Patricia Gillot
To: Holly

I'm sure that's just what he was saying, you just got to grin and bear the bitch. Did you tell them I'd told you to hang up on irritating people?

From: Holly
To: Patricia Gillot

Of course not!

I said I thought he was particularly rude—so I hung up on him. But I'd never do it again.

From: Patricia Gillot
To: Holly

You should have blamed me.

Oh well it's all over, and you survived—done and dusted. Just remember—it's not an easy job, keeping calm and happy while taking so much cr*p off everyone. But no one realises it.

From: Holly
To: Patricia Gillot

Thanks. I feel 10 ft tall.

xx

thursday

Subject: Re: Your Review

From: Judy Perkins
To: Holly

Holly,

Just one thing I forgot to talk about during our meeting. I've been looking at the switchboard figures and have noticed there are some calls being dropped—which are solely from the board you operate. Can you explain this?

Regards,

Judy

From: Holly
To: Judy Perkins

Hi Judy,

I don't know why that is, but I'll take extra care this week I promise.

Regards,

Holly

From: Judy Perkins
To: Holly

Holly,

If you feel some training on the switch would also help you, then just say. There are some really great courses out there, and maybe a refresher on the switch could help in that area also?

Judy

Subject: I've been lying

From: Holly
To: Jason GrangerRM

Jason,

You remember me telling you I was lying for Trish (because she's always late back from lunch)? When one of us takes our break, usually Dave from Facilities covers, but he leaves my side exactly after an hour because he thinks Trisha will be back any second. BUT she's sometimes AN HOUR LATE, and it's been too busy, and I've missed a few calls before they've rung off, but they don't even know she's not here! (I can't believe they can check my figures on the switch either, what's that about—Big Brother???)

From: Jason GrangerRM
To: Holly

You'll have to tell them soon. Is Trish going to be back late forever?

From: Holly
To: Jason GrangerRM

She's being evasive about it all. I'll give it till the end of the week and try not to drop any more calls.

From: Jason GrangerRM
To: Holly

Got to go, there's someone coming through from Mathew Parry's room.

Ta rar

From: Holly
To: Jason GrangerRM

Matthew Perry? From *Friends*? You are kidding, aren't you?

From: Jason GrangerRM
To: Holly

Mathew Parry—a balding, overweight businessman with a love of cigars and sarcasm.

From: Holly
To: Jason GrangerRM

Oh, shame. I was nearly on my way over… OK, see ya.

x

Subject: Jennie ? ?

From: Holly
To: Jennie Pithwait

What you up to Jen? Haven't heard from you for ages.

Subject: Thanks

From: Aisha
To: Holly

By the way, thanks so much for getting me this job. I won't let you down. I'm going to pick up my uniform tomorrow from the hotel. Going shopping Saturday. Fancy coming?
Aisha

From: Holly
To: Aisha

You want me to trail around shops watching you try on a succession of dresses—while you squeal about how you could wear it with this or that guy, and then not end up buying anything?

From: Aisha
To: Holly

Yes.

From: Holly
To: Aisha

Fine, count me in.

From: Aisha
To: Holly

xxxxx Also, do you know where they do alterations?

From: Holly
To: Aisha

Alterations for what?

From: Aisha
To: Holly

For the uniform. But don't worry, I think I know a place.

From: Holly
To: Aisha

I thought they had a uniform in your size.

From: Aisha
To: Holly

They do, just doesn't fit quite right.

From: Holly
To: Aisha

What d'you mean?

Subject: Re: Tomorrow

From: Patricia Gillot
To: Holly

Looking forward to your training?

From: Holly
To: Patricia Gillot

Oh—hugely.

Can you keep an eye on my emails—just in case Judy's around?

From: Patricia Gillot
To: Holly

Of course. Look out, look who's coming …

From: Holly
To: Patricia Gillot

The Prada queen herself. Let's see if she can manage a smile when she passes …

From: Patricia Gillot
To: Holly

oooo and she fails. Bitch.

From: Holly
To: Patricia Gillot

Another thing about 'Mrs Snooty, I'm the boss's wife'—it's not just us she doesn't like… have you seen how she talks to Ralph?

From: Patricia Gillot
To: Holly

Don't worry, he loves it …

From: Holly
To: Patricia Gillot

Really?? But she talks to him like dirt?

From: Patricia Gillot
To: Holly

Believe me, he don't mind.

From: Holly
To: Patricia Gillot

tell me… !!

From: Patricia Gillot
To: Holly

Sorry, got to take a client upstairs.

From: Holly
To: Patricia Gillot

grrrrrr.

Subject: Beachwear

From: Mum and Dad
To: Holly

Holly,

Make sure you pack your swimming cozzie when you come. It's too cold for me and your dad at the moment, but you might like to go for a dip. Now are you coming on your own? Otherwise, I'll need to make the other room up.

Mum

Xxx

From: Holly
To: Mum and Dad

Mum,

I can imagine it'll be too cold for me too for swimming, and in answer to your question—yes, I'm still single.

xx

Subject: Re: Uniform

From: Holly
To: Aisha

What d'you mean, it doesn't fit quite right??

Subject: Late

From: Patricia Gillot
To: Holly

Sorry I was so long. Did anyone notice I was missing?

From: Holly
To: Patricia Gillot

You're OK. Don't think so. You OK?

From: Patricia Gillot
To: Holly

I'm OK.

From: Holly
To: Patricia Gillot

I'm shooting off soon, and you still haven't told me about Mrs Huerst and our security guy.

From: Patricia Gillot
To: Holly

Who?

From: Holly
To: Patricia Gillot

RALPH!!!

From: Patricia Gillot
To: Holly

Ralph who?

From: Holly
To: Patricia Gillot

Patriccccccccccia !!!

From: Patricia Gillot
To: Holly

Oh, you mean our large, handsome protector?

From: Holly
To: Patricia Gillot

YES!

From: Patricia Gillot
To: Holly

Ooops, too late, it's time you left. Tell you tomorra!
Trish

friday

Subject: DIY Mistake

From: Charlie Denham
To: Holly

You won't believe what happened to me yesterday. I'm sitting in the office of this mess of a club and wondering whether this wasn't the biggest hole of a decision in my life to plough everyone's savings into this club, including, I might add, some good money from yourself over the years. I was up a ladder, not a particularly sturdy ladder, but worse than that it wasn't quite high enough. So I've balanced it on two sets of breeze blocks, to save buying a taller ladder, of course. I'm drilling a hole in the night club to-be (never, probably, I hope it will be), and the drill doesn't go in far enough. Soooo, while I'm drilling, Rubber Ron is busy trying to make gravestones out of planks of wood covered in cement and writing some very un-Christian messages on them I can tell you. Grandad wouldn't have approved, if he was still a vicar and alive. The drill hit something hard, and so I leaned on it to get some weight behind it. I slipped and my head hits the drill. There's this screeching sound, and I fall off the ladder, and it's all happening very fast, and I'm pulling at the drill to get it away from me, but every time I grip the drill, the trigger goes off again. I fall off the ladder, and the plug is wrenched from the wall. I land on the floor and I'm shouting and Ron's shouting and I'm really scared—am I OK?—am I OK? and he looks like he's trying not to laugh, and I look in the office mirror, and I see this …

(Photo attached)

Subject: Our security guard

From: Patricia Gillot
To: Holly

Only 'cause I know what a dull day you must have had on your course… and to brighten up your Monday morning, I'll tell you: Ralph got drunk a while back and told me he thinks Stephanie Huerst is the most beautiful woman he's ever seen, and when I said she's a rude arrogant b*tch, he told me he thought she was 'a goddess!' So I asked about the way she talks to him, like muck on her shoe, and he said he loved it!

The drunker he got, the more he admitted it was his 'thing'—that's why he always offers to carry her bags when she struts through.

I'm just dying for him to tell her how he feels. I think it would ruin her day if she knew he actually liked it!!!

xxxx

Subject: New Image

From: Charlie Denham
To: Holly

So, what d'you think? Thought I might just keep my long hair and hide the bald patch under a baseball cap??? (till it grows back) Some girls might find it sexy????

From: Holly
To: Charlie Denham

Hi,

This is not Holly, this is her friend, Trish. I'm checking her emails, because she's away for the day. Believe me, darlin, it's NOT sexy, it's a mess. You want to get yourself a wig (or better still, a razor).

Trish

month 2

Subject: Rent—direct debit

From: Holly
To: Nick

Dear Nick,

I've only just discovered that the direct debit set up to pay you has been cancelled. I've spoken to the bank, and they've admitted it's their fault. Sorry about this. Can you let me know the best way to proceed with payment?

Kindest regards,

Holly

Subject: REMINDER

From: Holly
To: Patricia Gillot

REMINDER

Find new route which avoids Homeless Harry.

Subject: Homeless Harry

From: Patricia Gillot
To: Holly

Why are you sending me a reminder to find a new route to avoid Homeless Harry? Who is Homeless Harry?

From: Holly
To: Patricia Gillot

Oh, sorry, that was meant for me.

I'm so used to emailing you, I did it without thinking. Sorry. x

Subject: New girl on reception

From: Holly
To: Jason GrangerRM

Hope all is going well with Aish. Let me know that she's OK and give her a kiss from me.

From: Jason GrangerRM
To: Holly

I would give her a kiss, if she were here.

From: Holly
To: Jason GrangerRM

Sh*t. I'll kill her. Tell me you're joking?

From: Jason GrangerRM
To: Holly

You're so easy to wind up.

From: Holly
To: Jason GrangerRM

I knew you were lying. So it's all OK?

From: Jason GrangerRM
To: Holly

It's just fine.

From: Holly
To: Jason GrangerRM

Good. And she seems to be fitting into the whole hotel look, etc.

From: Jason GrangerRM
To: Holly

Yes, she is.

From: Holly
To: Jason GrangerRM

Good, I'll relax.

From: Jason GrangerRM
To: Holly

If by hotel you meant brothel.

From: Holly
To: Jason GrangerRM

What?

From: Jason GrangerRM
To: Holly

It's OK, our hotel manager is very happy. I guess he likes the conundrum our guests go through—'Should I ask her for my room key, or a 5 minute lap dance?'

Personally, I'd just prefer a little less flesh on view. It's scaring me.

From: Holly
To: Jason GrangerRM

Oh, baby, sorry nasty female flesh is scaring you. I'll have a word with her tonight... Bad Aish!

Subject: Important meeting

From: James Lawrence
To: Holly

To Reservations:

I've got a late meeting today, very important at 7 p.m. Could you book me in?

James Lawrence

From: Holly
To: James Lawrence

Yes, that's fine. How many people?

From: James Lawrence
To: Holly

Just 2.

From: Holly
To: James Lawrence

What are their names?

From: James Lawrence
To: Holly

James Lawrence and Holly Denham—the meeting is at the Ivy Restaurant.

From: Holly
To: James Lawrence

What??!

From: James Lawrence
To: Holly

I had something witty to write if your answer was either a yes or a no. Haven't got anything to say to 'what??!'—I could just copy and paste the request again, I suppose.

From: Holly
To: James Lawrence

I was wondering why you didn't just email the reservations folder.
Yes, if you're asking me to the Ivy, then yes.
You should learn to ask a girl out on the phone, it's less ambiguous.
Although I don't want to be upsetting you now, do I? I mean, I've always wanted to go there.

From: James Lawrence
To: Holly

Cool. I'll pick you up at 7 p.m. Obviously not physically. I don't think Mr Huerst would like me giving you a piggyback out of the reception area.

From: Holly
To: James Lawrence

Is it OK to go in a suit (I don't have any other choices), but is that going to be OK for there?

From: James Lawrence
To: Holly

Suit is good. You look great, don't worry.

J

Subject: Desperately seeking Holly

From: Jennie Pithwait
To: Holly

Calling all manhunters. I need a progress report from my field agents... Any meat on the horizon?

From: Holly
To: Jennie Pithwait

Nothing down here. Anything up there on the mother ship?

From: Jennie Pithwait
To: Holly

What?

Look, I thought we were a team. I see you as my eyes and ears, my friend who's out there, on the front line, the first line of defence, or sometimes sitting on de-fence, when Judy's around. Hey, from what I've heard, you've been leading the Dyke on ...

From: Holly
To: Jennie Pithwait

I haven't been 'leading the Dyke on,' I don't know what you're talking about …

From: Jennie Pithwait
To: Holly

Sorry Holly, but I think you should have a bit more respect for your superiors. Does Judy know you call her a dyke?? Maybe, if so, you wouldn't mind me forwarding on your email to her???

From: Holly
To: Jennie Pithwait

I didn't—I simply repeated your phrase and to avoid confusion, even put it in quotation marks. So you're not getting me there!

From: Jennie Pithwait
To: Holly

OK, smarty-pants, keep your skirt on.

Got a very important private client meeting… mood-swinging Marcia, that 70-year-old ex-show girl from the 60s is back. Let me know what kind of mood you think she's in when she arrives.

Jen

From: Holly
To: Jennie Pithwait

Will do.

Subject: You'll never guess

From: Holly
To: Jason GrangerRM

You'll never guess where I'm going TONIGHT!!!!

From: Jason GrangerRM
To: Holly

I'm hoping it's the laundry—stinky.

From: Holly
To: Jason GrangerRM

Oh, OK, I won't bother you then. Just wanted to say I was going to the Ivy.

x

From: Jason GrangerRM
To: Holly

The Ivy??!! With who? Why? What time? You lucky bitch!

From: Holly
To: Jason GrangerRM

With… that James Lawrence, he asked me out!

Why… because I can't refuse a VP, it's against company rules.

What time… 7 p.m., I'm going straight from here.

And yes, I am! xxx

From: Jason GrangerRM
To: Holly

What does he look like again?

From: Holly
To: Jason GrangerRM

He looks like a cross between Clooney, Clinton, and Sinatra.

From: Jason GrangerRM
To: Holly

And hopefully a bit younger?

From: Holly
To: Jason GrangerRM

He's in his late thirties and seems genuinely interested in me. Kind eyes.

From: Jason GrangerRM
To: Holly

What are you wearing? We haven't much time and isn't this James, the one Jennie said was after half the company?

From: Holly
To: Jason GrangerRM

She did.

From: Jason GrangerRM
To: Holly

Having said that, maybe she's just jealous, because she's already had a try and got nowhere with him.

SO COME ON, Covent Garden is near, there's that nice blue number we saw. No no, you need Karen Millen. She's got the complete outfit. I'll meet you there at 6.

From: Holly
To: Jason GrangerRM

No, I'm going in my suit. Don't worry. I've told him, he said it's fine.

From: Jason GrangerRM
To: Holly

You are not going in a suit, my girl. Get your arse out of that swivel chair and go into the garden.

From: Holly
To: Jason GrangerRM

I'm not changing, he knows I'm coming straight from work.

From: Jason GrangerRM
To: Holly

You're playing it cool… like it.

From: Holly
To: Jason GrangerRM

That's not the main reason. x

From: Jason GrangerRM
To: Holly

Rubbish, you're playing it cool, and that's the end of it. Anyway, in fashion circles—'that suit!' is the new 'that dress!'

From: Holly
To: Jason GrangerRM

Thanks
xxxx

Subject: Underwear

From: Patricia Gillot
To: Holly

Just had another heavy breather. Started by saying something about a survey at the local shopping centre, asking me about what clothes I'm buying for the new season.

From: Holly
To: Patricia Gillot

Are you sure he wasn't telling the truth?

From: Patricia Gillot
To: Holly

I knew when he asked me if my knickers were soft silky satin or crispy crusty cotton.

From: Holly
To: Patricia Gillot

Nice.

Subject: Are you there?

From: Holly
To: Jason GrangerRM

It's 6:40 p.m. and I'm bored. I've got half an hour to wait. Don't say you've gone?

Subject: James ? ? ?

From: Holly
To: Jason GrangerRM

SH*T, James has stood me up!!! !!!

Subject: Bad bad bad bad bad

From: Holly
To: Jason GrangerRM

This is really really not how it was meant to go. You won't believe what I've just done.

I'm going home now. Wish you'd answered your phone.

Holly

tuesday

Subject: Homeless Harry

From: Patricia Gillot
To: Holly

Sorry darlin' I know it wasn't an email to me, but it's been bugging me, and this morning I woke up, and the question was sitting there staring at me, like my Les does sometimes when he's hungry, ha ha. So who the hell is Homeless Harry, because maybe I need to avoid him too?

From: Holly
To: Patricia Gillot

He's a guy who I sometimes give some money to on the way to work, but I'm trying to cut costs.

x

From: Patricia Gillot
To: Holly

Don't tell me that's why you're late? Because you found a new route around Homeless Harry?

From: Holly
To: Patricia Gillot

It takes me a bit out of my way, sorry.

From: Patricia Gillot
To: Holly

Can't you just ignore him?

From: Holly
To: Patricia Gillot

Can't, he knows my name now. It's difficult when he sees me coming from a distance and says 'Morning, Holly.'

From: Patricia Gillot
To: Holly

You've got a screw loose.

Trish

From: Holly
To: Patricia Gillot

I've been told.

Subject: The usual woman's problems

From: Alice and Matt
To: Holly

Hiya,

Looking forward to seeing you this weekend. Things here are as difficult as always. We're a bit down at the moment. It sounds like we need a licence to keep snakes. The council can't tell us where to get one, neither can the vets, the police, or the embassy. We've written to anyone we can think of for this licence, and no one can tell us where to get one. Just that we need one. Granny is looking forward to seeing you very much. She's settling in OK, a few complaints, she's not happy about the amount of sun at all. She does like the price of booze though.

xxx Ali

From: Holly
To: Alice and Matt

Sounds like you're having a rough time. Hope all works out.

xxxxx

Subject: Chelsea boy

From: Holly
To: Jennie Pithwait

That football boy started today. Although I guess he probably started yesterday, and I didn't notice him. Very cocky, still tanned. I think you'd love him!!

From: Jennie Pithwait
To: Holly

Think I've seen him, if you're referring to the trader. I'd 'love him,' would I? What about you?

From: Holly
To: Jennie Pithwait

Nope, don't think he's for me.

From: Jennie Pithwait
To: Holly

Hmm, so you're handing me your castoffs? No thanks!

From: Holly
To: Jennie Pithwait

What?

Subject: Tell Me

From: Jason GrangerRM
To: Holly

So tell me everything, come on… I've got my coffee and blueberry muffin, and I'm waiting????

From: Holly
To: Jason GrangerRM

It took me till about ten past seven before I realised I'd got it all wrong.

From six I'd been on my own, and most of the company had left. I kept making expeditions over to the plants, where I'd pretend to check the magazines on the glass coffee table, but I was actually checking my reflection in it.

It got to about 7:05 and knew what I'd done wrong: we should have arranged to meet somewhere else. He could have been sitting waiting for me. What was hugely annoying was that I didn't have his mobile number.

About 7:07 I began doubting myself and whether I'd got the meeting time right. Maybe it had been 6:30, and he'd come when I'd been checking myself in the toilets.

I checked through my emails again to make sure we had said 7 p.m., which we had. Then a bunch of people all came out of the lift together, and I thought he'd be with them, but he wasn't. I asked them if they were the last ones in the building, and one of them shouted back yes.

It's now about 7:15, and I'd left a couple of messages on his voice mail, and I was getting angry.

It was about this point I picked up the Tannoy.

From: Jason GrangerRM
To: Holly

You don't mean the public address system, do you? Tell me you don't.

From: Holly
To: Jason GrangerRM

Not the best decision, looking back on it, but I wasn't really thinking straight. I was half angry, half worried, my pride was battered, I thought I could be the laughingstock by the next day, and probably would want to leave, and I needed closure and to be sure then and there.

From: Jason GrangerRM
To: Holly

What did you say??

From: Holly
To: Jason GrangerRM

I just said into the mic, 'If you're still here, James, then I'm off. Some friends have dropped by for me. And if you're not here… then up yours, you selfish git!'

Turns out Mr Huerst popped into his meeting at the end—the others left, which were the ones I saw leaving—and James was cornered by Mr Huerst to talk about his bright future.

From: Jason GrangerRM
To: Holly

Sh*t.

From: Holly
To: Jason GrangerRM

He came out as I was leaving the building. He was wetting himself laughing. I died. Nice food they've got at that Ivy, though.

Think I like him a lot, yes, a lot.

Subject: Judy Perkins—Facilities

From: Judy Perkins
To: Holly

Holly,

I just noticed a couple more dropped calls on your switchboard this week.

Have you thought any more about that training course? Also, what about my idea I mentioned the other day of Trisha providing you with some training? Have a think about it all, because Trisha has never dropped a call for years, and she would be a great tutor. I am sure she would help if you asked her.

Regards,

Judy

From: Holly
To: Judy Perkins

Hi Judy,

Sorry about the dropped calls. Thanks for your suggestion, I'll ask her.

Holly

Subject: Lunches

From: Holly
To: Patricia Gillot

Hiya Trish,
When d'you think you'll finish taking these long lunches?
Holls

From: Patricia Gillot
To: Holly

It's time I told you where I've been going. I'll get Dave to cover for a moment.
xx

Subject: James

From: Aisha
To: Holly

Has Ivy balls called yet?

From: Holly
To: Aisha

No, but then if he did, I'd probably think he was too keen.

From: Aisha
To: Holly

Really?

From: Holly
To: Aisha

Not at all, just thinking positive. But still, you wouldn't call the next day.

From: Aisha
To: Holly

I would.

From: Holly
To: Aisha

Aren't you busy?

From: Aisha
To: Holly

Nope.

Subject: Our security guard

From: Holly
To: Patricia Gillot

Trish,

So, tell me more about Ralph. Give me some gossip. Makes the time go quicker.

x

From: Patricia Gillot
To: Holly

What—about him wanting to be Stephanie Huerst's bit of rough???
Loving it when she snaps her fingers at him to grab her bags? Here doggy, here doggy doggy …

From: Holly
To: Patricia Gillot

I think you're making it up.

From: Patricia Gillot
To: Holly

If that's what you think, that's fine. Having said that, if it's not true, then I guess he wouldn't be part of the boiler-room club, would he?

From: Holly
To: Patricia Gillot

What boiler-room club??? Our boiler room? What?

From: Patricia Gillot
To: Holly

Look out, he's coming over, hide your emails!

From: Holly
To: Patricia Gillot

Patricia Gillot,
You are, without a doubt, trying to wind me up!!

From: Patricia Gillot
To: Holly

I am. Doesn't mean to say it's not true though.
Have a nice evening.
Trishxx

From: Holly
To: Patricia Gillot

I'll get you tomorrow.
x

wednesday

Subject: Rent

From: Nick
To: Holly

Dear Holly,
I've only just received your email this morning, as I've been away. Sorry to hear about the mess up with the bank. Yes, we need payment as soon as possible. Your landlord isn't very accommodating with late rent, as I'm sure you remember.

We can have a cheque or preferably cash as soon as possible. Can you let me know when this will be forthcoming?

Yours sincerely,

Nick Harkson.

Greaves and Marchum

Subject: James

From: Aisha
To: Holly

So, has he called yet?

From: Holly
To: Aisha

No.

From: Aisha
To: Holly

I think of early relationships as baking a cake.

From: Holly
To: Aisha

Why?

From: Aisha
To: Holly

Because there's usually a cooling-off period, where it could end up looking good, or being a big flop.

From: Holly
To: Aisha

Isn't that a pie?

From: Aisha
To: Holly

Could be.

But don't panic. He might have forgotten or lost your number.

From: Holly
To: Aisha

That's true, only I'm on reception, so it's not hard to find me.

From: Aisha
To: Holly

Got to go.

xxxx

Subject: Time off—washing machine

From: Holly
To: Judy Perkins

Judy,

I know this is a bad time to ask, because I'm already taking Friday off for Spain.

But I wondered whether I could take Thursday as a half day, because I'm getting a washing machine removed—and you know they never give you an exact time, but they said it would be between 9–12 p.m.

Regards,

Holly

From: Judy Perkins
To: Holly

Holly,

That's fine, we will organise someone to cover you from receptionworld.com for those hours.

However, I will have to deduct a half-day's holiday from your entitlement.

Regards,

Judy

From: Holly
To: Judy Perkins

Thank you.

Holly

Subject: Nightclub

From: Holly
To: Charlie Denham

Hey, I got a missed call from you earlier. Can't talk on the switch. Is everything OK with the big night club boss?

From: Charlie Denham
To: Holly

Hi,

Got in trouble today with the health inspectors. Damn it.

From: Holly
To: Charlie Denham

Why?

From: Charlie Denham
To: Holly

Oh, some bollocks about having people in a confined space and them needing to breathe.

From: Holly
To: Charlie Denham

Please don't swear on emails.

I thought they were just upset with you about the noise?

From: Charlie Denham
To: Holly

They were. They said it was too loud outside, so we blocked up some holes I found. Turns out the holes were ventilation holes. It's hard trying to please everyone. Also, they weren't happy about the heating.

From: Holly
To: Charlie Denham

Too hot/cold?

From: Charlie Denham
To: Holly

Neither, it's got a tendency to make your eyes water. The council says it's something to do with leaking carbon monoxide or dioxide or something. It's just money money money.

From: Holly
To: Charlie Denham

Those inspectors are so cheeky, aren't they, wanting you to have alive, healthy clubbers.

Awful.

x

Subject: James

From: Holly
To: Jason GrangerRM; Aisha

He just called.

From: Jason GrangerRM
To: Holly

So… what did he say???

From: Holly
To: Jason GrangerRM; Aisha

We had a nice chat.

I told him it was lucky he'd called when he did, because I wouldn't have hung around for much longer.

From: Jason GrangerRM
To: Holly; Aisha

You're on reception, you're always hanging around.

From: Holly
To: Jason GrangerRM; Aisha

I know, damn it.

x

Also spoke to Trish about her extended lunch hours, found out where she's been going.

thursday

Subject: Trish's secret

From: Jason GrangerRM
To: Holly

Got your email about Trish. So, where's she been sneaking off to?

From: Holly
To: Jason GrangerRM

Trish's got some problems. I'll tell you in a minute.
Also looking forward to Spain. A little nervous. I'm hoping to get through the trip without too many questions.

From: Jason GrangerRM
To: Holly

Just lie lie lie lie, don't give in, don't tell the truth, and don't give them anything to go on. If you're smart and with a bit of luck, you can lie to your parents most of your life. I managed it for 20 years.
Now tell me the gossip about Trish.

From: Holly

To: Jason GrangerRM

A gang of kids badly beat up her son. They've also vandalised things, set fire to someone's house, stolen loads of cars. They've been terrorising their neighbourhood for months.

Now most of the neighbourhood are down at the trial, and it's getting quite heated. There's the families of the boys who've been doing all this versus the rest of the island, standing up against them. Trish catches up with them all there at lunchtime. If the gang get off, they'll be back to attack all those people who've been witnesses against them, including Trish's son. The trial's been going on for weeks.

It's coming to an end soon, they reckon—what a nightmare for her. I'd never have guessed. I'd be in a terrible state. She really doesn't want her work to know anything about it all, which I can understand I guess.

Holly

From: Jason GrangerRM

To: Holly

Oh bless, poor thing. You be there for her!

From: Holly

To: Jason GrangerRM

I will.

x

Subject: FAO COMPLAINTS DEPT

From: Holly

To: HEM Machines

REF:9829833

I really can't believe your company. I took a morning off work, that is a half day of my holiday entitlement, of which I don't get much entitlement at all.

I waited and then called up to check—for someone at your company to tell me nothing was booked in for this morning! Can you explain why?

From: HEM Machines
To: Holly

REF:9829833

Dear Ms Dinham,

Thank you for your email.

We are sorry to hear there was a misunderstanding with the removal date of your washing machine.

We have contacted our records department, however, we note the date agreed for removal is next Thursday. You called yesterday, and this would not have been enough notice to arrange for a removal the next day.

We apologise if you've misunderstood the arrangements. Do you still want the machine removed next Thursday?

From: Holly
To: HEM Machines

REF:9829833

No, I didn't misunderstand the arrangements at all, you definitely told me it was for today. I'll have to check first to see if I am able to make next Thursday.

Holly

Subject: Spain

From: James Lawrence
To: Holly

Dear Holly,

Have a great time in Spain but be careful about men abroad. The Spanish men will attempt to lead you up a garden path, and the English men are hooligans. My advice is to steer clear of them altogether. They're just trouble.

From: Holly
To: James Lawrence

You're a man, should I stay away from you?

From: James Lawrence
To: Holly

Definitely. I most certainly want to lead you up a garden path, for a kiss behind the privet hedge and a frolic in the summer house. That's before drinking 10 pints of lager, climbing on the roof, and singing football songs, naked.

From: Holly
To: James Lawrence

What an intriguing image.

From: James Lawrence
To: Holly

Something you can look forward to, when you're back. When are you back?

From: Holly
To: James Lawrence

Monday.

From: James Lawrence
To: Holly

See you then.
J

Subject: Lunch

From: Holly
To: Jennie Pithwait

Hiya,

We've not been to lunch for ages. D'you fancy doing something soon?

Hols

From: Jennie Pithwait
To: Holly

I was just thinking the same thing. Been busy with a huge deal I'm working on, and I think I've been a bit grouchy, so you have to forgive me. That's an order! You fancy coming to mine next weekend, I'm having a bit of a bash?

From: Holly
To: Jennie Pithwait

Sounds brill, what type of bash?

From: Jennie Pithwait
To: Holly

Cocktails and bubbles, some friends of mine, but you'll know a few people there from school days—Kristy, Georgie, and Sarah, not sure if Danny's coming. Also, possibly someone I haven't seen or spoken to for ages—Toby Williams. He's been working for Nicholson James, but he's about to move… rumour has it he's coming here.

From: Holly
To: Jennie Pithwait

You are kidding?

From: Jennie Pithwait
To: Holly

No, I guess you'd remember him more than anyone.
Have a great time in Spain, you lucky thing!

xxxx

Subject: Waste of holiday

From: Patricia Gillot
To: Holly

Hi,
Did Judy say you could have the half day back?
Trish

From: Holly
To: Patricia Gillot

No, I don't mind. I only got here for 11 anyway. Also, she had to pay the temp for a full half day. What was she like?

From: Patricia Gillot
To: Holly

From that reception specialist Front Recruitment. She was good. Better than you.

From: Holly
To: Patricia Gillot

Oh pi** off

x

From: Patricia Gillot
To: Holly

Language Timothy!! Think you've been hanging around me too long. Have a great time in Spain. Don't forget me fags.

xx

friday

Subject: Club

From: Charlie Denham
To: Holly

Roof's leaking. This place just gets better and better. Also got your message. No, I can't guess, so tell me—who's joining your company? Charlie

Subject: Interesting makeover

From: Jason GrangerRM
To: Holly

Hi,

When you're back, can you have a quiet word with your naughty friend. I've been watching and wondering what's different about the way SHE looks, compared to the other receptionists. Now this is apart from the slutty walk, the push-me-up tits, and the lip gloss, and I think I've worked it out. I could be wrong, but each day, her uniform gets a little shorter and a little tighter. I might be seeing things, and I can't imagine someone would go to the trouble of doing this stage by stage, on a daily basis. She wouldn't, would she? Can you ask her please?

Jason.

x

PS Hope you had a party-ripping time in Spain with the parents.

Subject: Ferret

From: Ferret
To: Holly

Hi,

It's all good. I heard from Alice that you're surviving there still. The problem with the big corporate machines is they don't give you room for personal freedom—as Oscar Wilde once said, 'let me out of here! I'm not a criminal' (I imagine).

By the way, I probably should have said before—you need to pack the rats in a cooler, otherwise they'll melt in your case. Especially if the flight gets delayed.

Have a good one.

Ferret

'There's no place like home' Dorothy said.

week 2
monday

Subject: Aisha's uniform

From: Holly
To: Jason GrangerRM

Hi Jason,

I'm back!!!

Just read your email about Aisha, and yes, I will have a word with her, although I think it's a bit unlikely she'd bother doing that to her uniform. Having said that, do you remember me telling you about that boyfriend of mine who kept getting my clothes taken in while I was at work… so I began to think I had a weight problem and went on a diet???

So who knows??

Holly

xx

From: Jason GrangerRM
To: Holly

Are you sure you weren't just getting fat?

From: Holly
To: Jason GrangerRM

Up yours. You're not getting to see my photos now.

From: Jason GrangerRM
To: Holly

Just having fun, missed you?

From: Holly
To: Jason GrangerRM

Well I didn't miss you.

And I hope Aisha pulls her skirt up over her head and shows you her girly bits, every day, standing on a table.

Nasty stinky reception manager. I was not getting fat. Hope you get fat now. Nasty boy. Rotten egg.

From: Jason GrangerRM
To: Holly

Oh please don't send me to Coventry.

xxxx

Come on, tell me about your holiday???

Subject: Returning staff

From: James Lawrence
To: Holly

Dear Holly Denham,

Like the tan.

J

From: Holly
To: James Lawrence

It was cloudy.

Holly

PS Like the walk. Was that a new one?

From: James Lawrence
To: Holly

Give me a break. It's not easy crossing 10 yards of marble while you're being watched by a couple of hot, snooty receptionists.

From: Holly
To: James Lawrence

You love it, show off.

Holly

Subject: Working here

From: Holly
To: Charlie Denham

Hi,

I'm back now. Hope you're still in one piece.

So OK, do you want to know who's coming to work here??

From: Charlie Denham
To: Holly

Who?

From: Holly
To: Charlie Denham

Toby.

From: Charlie Denham
To: Holly

Toby from school?

From: Holly
To: Charlie Denham

So rumour has it. I'm sure when he hears I'm working here, he'll change his mind. He's got a lot to answer for.

From: Charlie Denham
To: Holly

Too right he has. If he does, tell him I'll be coming to have a word with him, and I'm not happy.

From: Holly
To: Charlie Denham

Thanks Charlie (big brov comes to save me!)

xxx

Subject: Switchboard problems

From: Judy Perkins
To: Holly

Holly,

RE: Our discussion for Trisha to provide you with some more training on the switchboard. I thought we had agreed this would be a good idea?

I spoke to Trisha this morning and mentioned the training idea, and she looked completely blank, so you obviously haven't asked her yet. Please, can you schedule this with her ASAP. If you think you may find it difficult to ask her advice, I can organise this for you. I know she is your friend, but she is also a really experienced receptionist who is an expert in this area.

Welcome back, by the way. Hope you enjoyed your holiday.

Regards,

Judy

From: Holly
To: Judy Perkins

Dear Judy,

Sorry, I was going to ask her today. I'll speak to her now.

Thanks again.

Regards,

Holly

Subject: Switchboard—Meeting

From: Judy Perkins
To: Holly

Holly,

Having given it a bit more thought, I think we should schedule a meeting in for Wednesday. I can see meeting room 3 is free. Can you book it in some time in the morning?

Regards,

Judy

Subject: Training

From: Holly
To: Patricia Gillot

I've been asked to have some training from you on the switchboard ...

From: Patricia Gillot
To: Holly

That's rubbish. You don't need my help, you know what you're doing. Don't listen to her. She's talking a load of old twaddle.

xxx

Subject: Lunches

From: Holly
To: Patricia Gillot

Trish,

Any update on the trial?

Holly

From: Patricia Gillot
To: Holly

Not really, it's dragging on. Thanks for being there for me, babe, this stuff has been going on for too long. All this turf gang nonsense, I just want it to stop before more people get hurt.

xxx

tuesday

Subject: Holiday

From: Jason GrangerRM
To: Holly

So, are you going to tell me about Spain? Did you have fun?

Subject: Holiday

From: Aisha
To: Holly

So, did you get laid?

From: Holly
To: Aisha; Jason GrangerRM

Jason and Aisha,
No, I just had a nice, relaxing time, lots of sun, good food, and wine.
Holly x

From: Aisha
To: Holly; Jason GrangerRM

Just what you needed! Hope not too much, though. You've got to think of Ivy balls now, and I know your mum and her pies, it'd take a month to work one of them off.
Aisha

From: Holly
To: Aisha; Jason GrangerRM

Don't panic. I was very good.

Subject: Membership Renewal

From: Holly
To: Maida Vale Sports Gym

Hi,

I would like to renew my gym membership, please. My name is Holly Denham.

Thanks,

Holly Denham

Subject: From Charlie

From: Charlie Denham
To: Holly

I imagine during your stay you had the usual grilling from Mum—any awkward questions?

Charlie

From: Holly
To: Charlie Denham

It's not easy. They just can't stop saying things like 'at least my future is all sorted out.' If they only knew. I think it would kill them. I really do. I really messed up, didn't I.

From: Charlie Denham
To: Holly

So what? Could happen to anyone, and it's part of life. If you want to ever feel better about it all, just picture what a total cock up I usually make of everything.

Charlie

From: Holly
To: Charlie Denham

Thanks Charlie, love ya

x

Subject: A thank-you note

From: Alice and Matt
To: Holly

Hi Holly,

It was great seeing you again. Arabella and Joseph just love seeing their Aunt Holly from England. Thanks for bringing Matt's little presents, much appreciated.

xxxx good luck with work, call me when you can.

From: Holly
To: Alice and Matt

Great to see you too. Give the kids huge hugs and kisses from Aunt Holly.

xxxxx

Subject: Holiday to Spain

From: Holly
To: Jason GrangerRM

Jason,

Yes, I had fun in Spain—tell you later, but guess who I had an email from waiting in my inbox????

From: Jason GrangerRM
To: Holly

Simon Cowell, asking you to appear alongside him in a screen version of *Cats*, complete with rubber tights and thong?

From: Holly
To: Jason GrangerRM

No, also, not a pretty picture you paint there, Mr Granger.

From: Jason GrangerRM
To: Holly

A reply to the 1000 of emails you've sent 'The Hoff' asking him to honour his biggest fan with a signed pair of his used swimming trunks?

From: Holly
To: Jason GrangerRM

YUK!!!! ENOUGH ENOUGH!
No, it was from lovely James... How keen is that?? I think this is going surprisingly well!! What d'you think?

From: Jason GrangerRM
To: Holly

It certainly seems that way. You told anyone in the company yet, or is he still your secret lover?

From: Holly
To: Jason GrangerRM

Secret—friend.

From: Jason GrangerRM
To: Holly

For now... But the weekend beckons ...
PS where are the photos?

Subject: Maida Vale Sports Gym Membership

From: Maida Vale Sports Gym
To: Holly

Dear Holly Denham,
Thank you for your email.
Having checked our records, we have found you are already a member of Maida Vale Gyms, but you haven't signed in for six months.

It also looks as if you are three months behind with your membership fees.

Tammy at Memberships

From: Holly
To: Maida Vale Sports Gym

Tammy,

Oh, OK then. I would like to cancel my gym membership. I think I need to find a gym which is closer to home.

Kindest regards,

Holly

From: Maida Vale Sports Gym
To: Holly

We are based in Maida Vale. Have you moved recently?

Tammy

From: Holly
To: Maida Vale Sports Gym

No, I still live in Maida Vale, but it's not really close to my house.

Holly

From: Maida Vale Sports Gym
To: Holly

We are on Springfield Avenue, and we have your address as Springfield Avenue.

Tammy

From: Holly
To: Maida Vale Sports Gym

Yes, but maybe I need a gym which is close to my work instead of home, then I can go there straight from work before I get tired. Also, you don't have those little televisions that I've seen elsewhere, which are plugged into the machines.

Holly

From: Maida Vale Sports Gym
To: Holly

We do have televisions. They give you a virtual environment of sport—everything from racing to rowing, while you exercise.
Tammy

From: Holly
To: Maida Vale Sports Gym

What about the soap *Neighbours*. Do you have *Neighbours*?

From: Maida Vale Sports Gym
To: Holly

No.

From: Holly
To: Maida Vale Sports Gym

Home and Away?

From: Maida Vale Sports Gym
To: Holly

No. Nor *Jeremy Kyle*, *Trisha*, or *Judge Judy*.

From: Holly
To: Maida Vale Sports Gym

Then I think I just want to CANCEL my membership.
Thank you.
Holly

From: Maida Vale Sports Gym
To: Holly

Fine, but you have to give a month's notice, in writing. Also, you need to bring your membership fees up-to-date.
Thank you.

From: Holly
To: Maida Vale Sports Gym

Fine, and I am writing. This is my month's notice.
Holly

Subject: Photos of Spanish Holiday

From: Holly
To: Aisha; Jason GrangerRM

photos attached

From: Aisha
To: Holly; Jason GrangerRM

Is that it?

From: Holly
To: Aisha

Well, sorry, but I wasn't there long, and I was on my own.

From: Aisha
To: Holly; Jason GrangerRM

What a boring bunch of snaps. Didn't you meet any men at all???

From: Holly
To: Aisha; Jason GrangerRM

There's one more of me standing, waving outside Alice and Matt's house (see attached).

From: Jason GrangerRM
To: Holly

Where?

From: Holly
To: Aisha; Jason GrangerRM

Here's another one. I think I'm behind the bush. xx
Oh, and see attached one of a fab chameleon that Matt bred.

From: Aisha
To: Holly; Jason GrangerRM

I swear, this new guy needs to do something for your photo album,
if not your sex life.
Sh*t

From: Jason GrangerRM
To: Holly; Aisha

Don't be mean, Aisha. Nice photos, Holly.

From: Aisha
To: Holly; Jason GrangerRM

Yeah, really brightened up my day.

From: Holly
To: Aisha; Jason GrangerRM

Get lost, Aish!
Oh, and yes, Jason, she was taking her uniform in. She told me.
hee hee hee
So I'm going home now. Anyway, I've had enough abuse for the day.
x
Enjoy the snow

From: Aisha
To: Holly; Jason GrangerRM

You lying b*tch. It's not true, boss, honest!!!
PS I'll get you when I see you, Denham!!!
x

Subject: Our meeting

From: Judy Perkins
To: Holly

Holly,

This is just a reminder for you for tomorrow morning to make sure you don't forget about our meeting at 9 a.m.

Regards,

Judy

wednesday

Subject: Morning

> **From:** Patricia Gillot
> **To:** Holly

Feel like cr*p. Had a right old row last night over this case. It's really weighing me down at the moment.

How was your night?

> **From:** Holly
> **To:** Patricia Gillot

Sorry to hear about your row, must be a nightmare. Hope it all finishes soon.

xxx

> **From:** Patricia Gillot
> **To:** Holly

What you get up to—did you go out?

> **From:** Holly
> **To:** Patricia Gillot

No, stayed in, watched *American Idol*, had a strange dream about all three judges.

> **From:** Patricia Gillot
> **To:** Holly

Did you now? Nice dream, was it?

From: Holly
To: Patricia Gillot

It was, actually. Didn't want to wake up.

Bug**r, forgot about that meeting with Judy, late, going!

Subject: Jason, Please, Need you

From: Holly
To: Jason GrangerRM

Help.

Subject: Where are you?

From: Holly
To: Jason GrangerRM

Mr Reception Manager, I need advice.

Holly

From: Jason GrangerRM
To: Holly

I was just about to email. How did it go?

From: Holly
To: Jason GrangerRM

We sat there talking about general rubbish while she plied me with coffee, then when she had my guard totally down, she said she had to be straight with me—that while I was on holiday in sunny Spain… things had improved. Nice!

Basically, the temp hadn't dropped any calls at all while I was gone. Well, of course the temp didn't drop any calls!!!!!!!!!!!! She didn't drop any calls because she was never left on her own. Trish didn't go out for her long lunch hours because—quote: 'I couldn't leave Suzy to handle the switch on her own.' !! So of course Suzy didn't drop any calls, because she was never on her own… ! aaaaaaaaaaagh!

From: Jason GrangerRM
To: Holly

I'm confused—who's Suzy?

From: Holly
To: Jason GrangerRM

The temp.

From: Jason GrangerRM
To: Holly

Why don't you call her the temp then?

From: Holly
To: Jason GrangerRM

I was a temp once. We have names, you know!

From: Jason GrangerRM
To: Holly

OK, OK, calm down. So, while Judy was going on about how great this temp was, what did you do? Did you tell her??

From: Holly
To: Jason GrangerRM

OF course I didn't. I'm no grass. I couldn't have put Trish in it.

From: Jason GrangerRM
To: Holly

'I'm no grass' 'Couldn't have put Trish in it' ???
Sorry, I seem to have stepped out from behind my reception desk into a Guy Ritchie film.
Is this what sitting next to Trish does to you? Just don't start calling Judy 'Guv'na'—she won't like it.

From: Holly
To: Jason GrangerRM

Come on, I'm serious. I'm still shaking from the meeting. It was horrible. She thinks I'm useless.

But Trish has been doing this for a few weeks. They'll sack her if they find out.

From: Jason GrangerRM
To: Holly

OK, so if you tell Judy what Trish has been up to… you will be a bitch, and Trish gets sacked.

If you don't tell her, you get sacked… Have you told Trish what kind of doo-doos you're up to your neck in?

From: Holly
To: Jason GrangerRM

No, don't want to worry her. She's got enough on her plate. Come on—help me, I'm desperate. Wave your magic wand and make it all go away please. Please.

From: Jason GrangerRM
To: Holly

Holly, I'm calling you now. Don't you be blubbering on reception. Come on, hollybolly.

Subject: Holly call me

From: Jason GrangerRM
To: Holly

Call me when you get back to your desk. I just tried to call you, but you weren't there. Really worried.

xxxxx

Subject: Thank You

From: Patricia Gillot
To: Holly

I can't believe you'd do that. I can't believe you'd get into so much trouble for me.

From: Holly
To: Patricia Gillot

What?

From: Patricia Gillot
To: Holly

I just heard what you've been getting in trouble about, and it's my fault. Why didn't you tell me????

From: Holly
To: Patricia Gillot

Who told you?

From: Patricia Gillot
To: Holly

Someone who cares about you very much, they just called me 'cause they couldn't help themselves. They love you, darlin, so don't have a go at them.

From: Holly
To: Patricia Gillot

Jason called you.

From: Patricia Gillot
To: Holly

Don't have a go, he's a real sweetheart. Can't believe you, Hols, just can't believe you'd do that for me! I'm sorting it out right now. But first, I need to give you a hug.

xxxxxxxxxxxxx

Subject: Thanks

From: Holly
To: Jason GrangerRM

Hi Jason,

Couldn't really speak just now, sorry if I sounded rude. I'm glad you interfered, and you're the best friend a girl could have, and I'm really lucky.

x

sorry

Subject: What did she say?

From: Holly
To: Patricia Gillot

You spoke to Judy?

From: Patricia Gillot
To: Holly

Yes, she's gone to speak to HR.
Don't worry. I'm not.

x

From: Holly.
To: Patricia Gillot

What d'you think they'll do?

From: Patricia Gillot
To: Holly

Don't know. If it's gone upstairs, then I'm probably off.

From: Holly
To: Patricia Gillot

They wouldn't do that. You've been here for years, surely?

From: Patricia Gillot
To: Holly

It's how it works, besides which, it gives them an opportunity to get rid of me without a huge payout, get some dolly bird in to replace me.

From: Holly
To: Patricia Gillot

They wouldn't want to. They know how good you are here!!

From: Patricia Gillot
To: Holly

Really?

All this crap I dish about how much time it takes to learn it, I mean, you've picked it up quick, haven't you. Sometimes you come down to earth with a bump, don't you. I don't care, really, just a bit worried about going back out in the job market. It's scary for an old girl like me.

x

From: Holly
To: Patricia Gillot

Trish, I'm so sorry. I didn't want you to go tell them.

From: Patricia Gillot
To: Holly

I know you didn't, darlin. Anyway, got to sort this group out, look like a bunch of headless chickens (or penguins). None of them know who's in charge, squawk squawk squawk. Bet they all came from your type of school.

ha ha

xx

From: Holly
To: Patricia Gillot

My type of school??

From: Patricia Gillot
To: Holly

You know, posh f**ks.

Ha ha, I'm taking the penguins up in the elevator before you hit me. squawk squawk squawk, yah yah yah.

x

thursday

Subject: HEM MACHINES—My Washing Machine

From: Holly
To: HEM Machines

To Whom It May Concern:

After another morning of waiting for you to remove my washing machine, I am pleased to say you arrived on the right day. However, the man told me this was a 'two man job,' and he was just 'one man.' He told me to get in touch with you again to rebook the removal.

Picture a woman in a black suit sitting at a desk with her head blue from the neck upwards and that's how silly I look being this angry. Pllllllllllllleeeeeeeeeeeeeeeeeeeeeeeeeeease can you get this sorted. Can you also make sure you send two men next time, on the correct day.

Holly

From: HEM Machines
To: Holly

REF:9829833

Holly Dinham,

Thank you for your email.

Unfortunately, from our records you live in a basement flat, and that requires two people to get it up your stairs. We needed to know this before the booking to ensure the correct amount of removal staff was assigned.

We would be very happy to reorganise a date to suit you, as soon as possible.

From: Holly
To: HEM Machines

REF:9829833

If you had asked me if I lived in a basement, I would have told you 'yes, I live in a basement.' I mistakenly imagined you knew I lived in a basement, as you installed the machine last month—in my basement. I have managed to organise one more morning off for next Friday. For the sake of my job and all that is holy, please don't mess this up.

Regards,

Holly

Subject: Ruined Designer Clothes

From: Charlie Denham
To: Holly

We've had a bit of an inspiration today—you know, about the drainage problem that me and Ron have been worrying about.

Charlie

From: Holly
To: Charlie Denham

It's not good getting dripped on, ask any girl. You won't get any 'hot chicks' (as you call them) turning up to a place with drips.

From: Charlie Denham
To: Holly

Exactly.

So we paint the walls with Bitchumen, which is thick, black plastic paint they use for roofs to stop the water leaking through. Hopefully problem solved.

From: Holly
To: Charlie Denham

By the way—is there a reason you keep in touch so much? (I'm not complaining) but for years I barely know what you're up to, now I get emails from you every week?

From: Charlie Denham
To: Holly

I've always kept in touch.

From: Holly
To: Charlie Denham

Nope, no, you haven't. I don't mind. I'm not being the nagging sister. It's just nice now—wondered why?

From: Charlie Denham
To: Holly

OK, apart from that patch you went through (but I'm not good with that kind of thing), I've always called you.

From: Holly
To: Charlie Denham

Drunk, in the early hours, yes.

From: Charlie Denham
To: Holly

That's still caring?

From: Holly
To: Charlie Denham

I'm not moaning. It's just nice, that's all.
Holly

Subject: Cover

From: Holly
To: Patricia Gillot

How was our sexy security guard on the desk this morning?

From: Patricia Gillot
To: Holly

He was telling me how bored he gets when he does the afternoon shift in the security office (camera watching). Told him he should email us—we'd cheer him up.

(woof)

ha ha

From: Holly
To: Patricia Gillot

Bad Trish!!

(But I'm game)

Holly

x

Subject: Saturday Alert

From: Jennie Pithwait
To: Holly

Hey lover,

Remember what's coming up on Saturday, and you better be there, Miss Denham!

From: Holly
To: Jennie Pithwait

Hey Jen,

I've been looking forward to it, but I'm not sure now that I can make it. Has Toby confirmed he's going?

Hols

From: Jennie Pithwait
To: Holly

Don't fret, Toby's not coming. He's blown us out. But the rest will be there, and they're so looking forward to seeing you again. Please try your best to make it. By the way, are you bringing anyone? Any secret men in your life you're keeping under your covers?

From: Holly
To: Jennie Pithwait

No men yet, so I'd be coming alone.

X

From: Jennie Pithwait
To: Holly

Great, we can hunt together.

xx

Also, don't mention it to Trisha, as I haven't invited her—I would have done, but there'll be too many people she won't know, and it wouldn't have been fair.

From: Holly
To: Jennie Pithwait

Thanks so much for inviting me, I'll be there! Sounds like it'll be a fabulous night.

xx

Subject: Are you OK?

From: Holly
To: Patricia Gillot

Any decision from Judy yet?

From: Patricia Gillot
To: Holly

No. Everyone's being nice to me like nothing's happened. It's too quiet, if you know what I mean (from a film, can't remember which one).

From: Holly
To: Patricia Gillot

Probably some kind of action film.

From: Patricia Gillot
To: Holly

Yeah, right before they all get shot to pieces.

From: Holly
To: Patricia Gillot

Or someone brings them a lovely cake and sings happy birthday?

From: Patricia Gillot
To: Holly

It's not me birthday.

x

Subject: Here we go

From: Patricia Gillot
To: Holly

This is it, got to go see Judy.

Just in case, if I'm told to go straight off site, I don't want to come back here and pack my stuff. I couldn't take that, after so many years. So could you just look after it for me, and I'll catch up with you soon?

xxxxx

From: Holly
To: Patricia Gillot

Of course.

Good luck!

xxx

friday

Subject: I'm worried …

From: Holly
To: Jason GrangerRM

Trish hasn't turned up …

From: Jason GrangerRM
To: Holly

Oh sh*t, so I guess you're on your own till they replace her.

xxx

Subject: Tell Me

From: Holly
To: Patricia Gillot

What happened?

From: Patricia Gillot
To: Holly

Oh, late out the door, then got caught up on the Central line—it was very slow today.

From: Holly
To: Patricia Gillot

No, I mean about the meeting with Judy?

From: Patricia Gillot
To: Holly

Sorry, didn't want to think about it. She told me to start looking for another job while they begin recruiting for someone new. I'm stuffed, Holly, really f**king stuffed.

From: Holly
To: Patricia Gillot

Oh, Trish. Can I come give you a hug?

From: Patricia Gillot
To: Holly

Keep your stinking posh ass in that seat and those nasty public school hands off me… I'm pulling your leg, ha ha hee heee heee hee.

xxx

From: Holly
To: Patricia Gillot

Trish!!!! YIPPEEEEEEEEE. Now you're definitely getting hugged.

From: Patricia Gillot
To: Holly

Judy told me off, told me I should have just come clean with her. She's keeping it to herself, nice init (that means 'isn't it'—for you).

From: Holly
To: Patricia Gillot

That's great news, really brill.

So is this taking the mickey out of my background going to carry on forever now?

From: Patricia Gillot
To: Holly

It is, if you use words like mickey.

From: Holly
To: Patricia Gillot

P*ss off.

From: Patricia Gillot
To: Holly

Oh if your school friends could only see you now. A bit longer with your Aunty Trish, and I'll have you putting a c word in every sentence.

Subject: New shifts on Reception

From: Judy Perkins
To: Holly

Dear Holly,

I'm sure you are aware by now, but to ensure lines of communication are now open and clear, I have spoken to Trisha, and she told me about her son's case.

It is an unusual situation, and I'm sure we can come to some kind of arrangement whilst the case is on regarding shifts and cover (I just wish someone had come to me earlier). I answer to people above me, so I need to provide some answers, however brief, and this is something we need to handle sensitively.

On another note; whilst I don't doubt your good intentions in covering for Trisha and your loyalty as a colleague, I would appreciate you telling me the truth next time.

Incidentally, Trisha tells me the court case will come to a conclusion on Monday, so fingers crossed the little thugs get what they deserve.

Regards,

Judy

Subject: Gay bars/clubs?

From: Jason GrangerRM
To: Holly

Got your message, glad Trish's OK.

Fancy going for a drink tonight with me and Aish, we're off from 7 p.m.???

From: Holly
To: Jason GrangerRM

Can't, I'm seeing Ivy balls (as Aisha calls him). He called late last night.

From: Jason GrangerRM
To: Holly

Did he now? Keen! So where are you going—anywhere exciting?

From: Holly
To: Jason GrangerRM

Don't pretend that's just an innocent question, I know what you're up to.

From: Jason GrangerRM
To: Holly

Oh come on, we'll sit miles away from you. You won't even know we're there.

From: Holly
To: Jason GrangerRM

No no no, it'll be the last time I ever see him again—if you meet him. It's not happening.

From: Jason GrangerRM
To: Holly

If you're making a referral once again to 'Ben night,' that idiot wasn't worth it anyway—you said so yourself! AND it was a rubbish restaurant he took you too, AND—he would never have known I was there if you hadn't told him.

From: Holly
To: Jason GrangerRM

You walked past him with a place mat on your head.

From: Jason GrangerRM
To: Holly

SO! It was a Chinese restaurant!

From: Holly
To: Jason GrangerRM

How does that make it OK?

From: Jason GrangerRM
To: Holly

I'm not sure—thought I'd try sounding indignant (it could be a Chinese custom?). If you really don't want me around you, I understand, that's just fine and dandy, I just feel we're growing apart. We never get to see each other anymore… I miss you.

xxx

From: Holly
To: Jason GrangerRM

We saw each other last night???

From: Jason GrangerRM
To: Holly

OK, but we see each other a lot less. Is it because I'm gay—do you feel embarrassed about introducing me?

From: Holly
To: Jason GrangerRM

Oh shut up! I'll introduce you when it's right.

x

Subject: Your hot date

From: Aisha
To: Holly

Hiya, good luck with Privet boy tonight, have a good one. Don't tell Jason where you're off too, you know after last time you can't trust him. So what exciting place is he taking you to tonight?

From: Holly
To: Aisha

Firstly, stop changing his nickname, I can't keep up, and secondly, I know you're sitting next to Jason now, planning and scheming. There is no way you're meeting him either, not with those bright red talons. I've heard you've already got the manager there at your beck and call… You're not getting within 10 feet of James!!!

From: Aisha
To: Holly

Jason is actually on the Concierge desk, and I am hurt to think that you would view me with such disdain as to imagine me taking part in any kind of scheming against you at all. It truly hurt.

From: Holly
To: Aisha

Well, seeing the word 'disdain' is the kind of word you'd never use, but one which I've heard Jason use a thousand times, my guess is he's standing behind you, giggling, and adding his input right now.

From: Aisha
To: Holly

OK OK OK smarty-knickers, we just wanted to get involved in the fun of your night ahead—as friends. You've told us not to go anywhere near you tonight, so we wouldn't—besides which, if we don't know where you're going, then we could bump into you by mistake—then you'd be really annoyed with us.

xxx

From: Holly
To: Aisha

OK OK OK, we're meeting at Chez Gerard. Exciting!!!

You guys have a fantastic night, see you next week.

xxx

Subject: Entertain me

From: Ralph Tooms
To: Holly; Patricia Gillot

I'm bored.

From: Patricia Gillot
To: Holly; Ralph Tooms

Ralph,

Too late to entertain you, we're off.

You'll have to think about it over the weekend.

Now you be a good boy, Ralph, and you keep your eyes on those security cameras.

Trish

Subject: Trish!

From: Holly
To: Patricia Gillot

You're naughty!

From: Patricia Gillot
To: Holly

Init.

x

Hey, what you up to—anything fun?

From: Holly
To: Patricia Gillot

Not sure yet, got an invite for some kind of friends reunion—you know—through Jennie, but I'm nervous. I've been putting on a bit of weight recently, nothing fits, and you just know everyone will be rich, gorgeous, and skinny… Maybe I'll stay at home with some popcorn and films …

From: Patricia Gillot
To: Holly

Don't you dare, you look great! Don't you be nervous girl!

xxx

From: Holly
To: Patricia Gillot

Love ya, back in a sec, just going to get changed—seeing a friend later in town.

xxxx

saturday

Subject: Double bluff—sneaky mare!

From: Jason GrangerRM
To: Holly

I am horrified to think that you would think it necessary to lie to your best friends. As if me and Aisha hadn't anything better to do than snoop around your personal life! (We only hid giggling behind a flower pot for an hour in Chez Gerard before we realised the double bluff, so don't think you're so clever!)

xx I'll call you later, sneaky!

PS You try crouching with a place mat on your head for an hour. It's not funny, I can barely walk!

week 3
monday

Subject: Spies don't prosper

From: Holly
To: Jason GrangerRM

Re: your email from Saturday …
Hope you're not still hobbling this morning. Hee hee hee
x

From: Jason GrangerRM
To: Holly

Is there no more trust left between friends?

From: Holly
To: Jason GrangerRM

Apparently not. How was the rest of your night with Aisha??

From: Jason GrangerRM
To: Holly

Good, a very funny night. What happened with your date?

Subject: Friends reunited

From: Charlie Denham
To: Holly

So our clever idea doesn't seem to be working. The bitchumen hasn't dried, it's just tacky and sticky. The water still comes through the ceiling, but now it's dripping a black tarlike substance over people. How was your school reunion? Did you go? And did Toby the jerk turn up?
Charlie

From: Holly
To: Charlie Denham

I went because Jennie insisted Toby wasn't going to be there. She's got a really nice place, very tasteful and classy. The old lot from school were there, no one you'd really know. It wasn't easy evading questions, and I realised you were right quite early on. It was a mistake going. Of course Toby did turn up and everything—you know—that day, all of it, just came flooding back to me. Jennie said she was just as surprised to see him. And guess what—he IS working here too—at Huerst & Wright—starting next week!! I left soon after he arrived, couldn't handle it.

From: Charlie Denham
To: Holly

Of all the companies you could have picked to take a receptionist job in?? You're not having much luck these days, are you? What did he say anyway?

From: Holly
To: Charlie Denham

He looked shocked when Jennie said I was working at the same place. He actually looked quite sick and he tried to talk to me, but I left.

From: Charlie Denham
To: Holly

I bet he was shocked. With any luck he might do another disappearing act. Did you find out what HAD happened to him?

From: Holly
To: Charlie Denham

I didn't want to talk to him and left soon after he'd arrived.

From: Charlie Denham
To: Holly

Oh well, with that many people working there, you probably won't bump into him.

From: Holly
To: Charlie Denham

That's what I thought.

xx

good luck with your drips

From: Charlie Denham
To: Holly

Thanks

Charlie

Subject: Single in the City

From: Mum and Dad
To: Holly

I came across an old article in the newspaper about relationships and thought it was very interesting ...

Being single in big cities looks to be very normal, and you shouldn't worry at all.

Love, Mum

xxx

From: Holly
To: Mum and Dad

Thanks Mum,

Thank you for this, but I know it's OK to be single in London—I've never had a problem with it, so you don't have to worry.

Xxxxx

From: Mum and Dad
To: Holly

Good, just saw the article and wanted you to be happy with yourself.

xxxx

From: Holly
To: Mum and Dad

I AM.

xxx

Subject: Busy day

From: Patricia Gillot
To: Holly

Monday madness. It's going to be busy today, calls just keep coming!

From: Holly
To: Patricia Gillot

I know. Just then I had two on hold with four coming in and some woman 'umming' and 'arrrrrrring,' couldn't remember who she'd spoken to last week—but needed to speak to him again—was it a Tim, or maybe a Tom, she thought it began with a T although maybe it didn't and either way—'it was definitely a man, if that helps?' ...

??????????

From: Patricia Gillot
To: Holly

Don't know what you're moaning about, we could easily just bang out an email to everyone in the company, asking if anyone spoke to a woman last week.

From: Holly
To: Patricia Gillot

At some times like that, I just wish we could say something like 'I know this may sound like total lunacy to you, but we have taken the unusual approach of employing more than one man amongst the 400 staff we have here.'

From: Patricia Gillot
To: Holly

Or 'p*ss off, you daft tw*t'?

From: Holly
To: Patricia Gillot

Yes, that would work too.

Subject: Did she or didn't she?

From: Aisha
To: Holly

You haven't told me yet, so my guess is—you missed out on a great night of Privet-shagging on Friday by being a frump?
Aisha x

From: Holly
To: Aisha

Well that's where you're wrong, Miss Peters.

From: Aisha
To: Holly

I don't believe it.
x

From: Holly
To: Aisha

I spent a fab night with him and went home Saturday lunchtime.

xx
I just didn't want to talk about it yet.

Subject: Hope you got home OK

From: James Lawrence
To: Holly

Had a good time Friday. Hope you got home safely.

From: Holly
To: James Lawrence

Yes, fine. Had a good night too.
Holly

Subject: Friday night—an important question to get out of the way

From: James Lawrence
To: Holly

I forgot to ask you on Friday if you enjoy it downstairs.

From: Holly
To: James Lawrence

Why Mr Lawrence,
How kind of you to ask, yes it's OK. It's quite mad at times with some of the characters we get coming through the door.
Why?
Holly

Subject: Quickly, I need urgent advice!!!!

From: Holly
To: Jason GrangerRM; Aisha

HELP!!!!

I think I just misunderstood an email from James—he said the below... is this an innuendo or not???

'I forgot to ask you on Friday if you enjoy it downstairs.'

From: Aisha

To: Holly; Jason GrangerRM

Definitely. What did you say back?

From: Holly

To: Aisha; Jason GrangerRM

Oh cr*p, I said the below, thought it made me sound cheeky and a bit flirty?

Why Mr Lawrence,

How kind of you to ask, yes it's OK. It's quite mad at times with some of the characters we get coming through the door.

Why?

Holly

From: Aisha

To: Holly; Jason GrangerRM

No, that makes you look like you're being a bit thick—while trying to be sexy. God, Holly!! What have I taught you?

From: Holly

To: Aisha; Jason GrangerRM

OK, sorry if I'm not up-to-date with Aisha-talk, but stop being a smart arse and help me. Where's Jason?

From: Aisha

To: Holly; Jason GrangerRM

He's dealing with a problem, so it's just me, take it or leave it?

x

From: Holly

To: Aisha; Jason GrangerRM

I'll take it. What should I write back then?

From: Aisha
To: Holly; Jason GrangerRM

Wait, first tell me the truth. Did you do the dirty with him on Friday night?

From: Holly
To: Aisha; Jason GrangerRM

That's not important, I'll tell you later. Just tell me what to say quick!

From: Aisha
To: Holly; Jason GrangerRM

OK OK, I'm going to help.

But come clean first???

And remember, your next email could either make you look perverted or worse still—frigid!

From: Holly
To: Aisha; Jason GrangerRM

Aisha!!!!

OK, no, I didn't. I lied to you alright!

Now tell me what to say!!!

From: Aisha
To: Jason GrangerRM

OK, so go back and say:

Yes, I enjoy it downstairs—why Mr Lawrence—are you any good with your tongue?

From: Holly
To: Aisha

WHAT??????

From: Aisha
To: Holly; Jason GrangerRM

Or:

I am happy staying downstairs for as long as I'm told to?

From: Holly
To: Aisha

???

From: Aisha
To: Holly

Maybe something about you liking people to shoot through your reception?

From: Holly
To: Aisha

NO.

From: Aisha
To: Holly

By the way, I always like having men downstairs—I always provide the kind of service I would expect to receive????

From: Holly
To: Aisha

None of it is really me. I think I should just leave it.

From: Aisha
To: Holly; Jason GrangerRM

If you leave it, there's a good chance he'll think you're a dork. I would. (in a nice way xxx)

This could make or break your sex life. Miss this opportunity, and you'll be sending us pictures of lizards and mountains forever.

From: Holly
To: Aisha

What?

From: Aisha
To: Holly

From your holiday snaps.

Subject: By the way

From: Holly
To: James Lawrence

I always like having men downstairs—and I always provide the kind of service I would expect to receive …

From: James Lawrence
To: Holly

?????

Subject: No WAIT!!!

From: Jason GrangerRM
To: Holly; Aisha

Holly,

Just read your emails, don't email that to him!! It might not have been an innuendo, just call him first!!! (don't listen to Aisha)

From: Holly
To: Jason GrangerRM; Aisha

JASON!
WHERE HAVE YOU BEEN!!!
I'VE SENT IT.
WHAT SHALL I DO NOW????

From: Aisha
To: Holly; Jason GrangerRM

Holly,

I'll have to admit, I didn't think it was a 100% innuendo, there's a good chance he didn't mean anything by it. But I think it's always best to make the first move. How exciting, Holly, I'm proud of you—you dirty b*tch!!!!

love, Aisha xx

From: Holly
To: Aisha

Aisha, when I finish here tonight, I'm coming to find you. You better hide.

Subject: Customer Service

From: James Lawrence
To: Holly

After further consideration, I'll be down in five minutes. I'd like to give you some scoring on your customer service skills, I mean, you don't want to be caught out in the future by a mystery shopper.

From: Holly
To: James Lawrence

Any assistance you can give me would be most gratefully received, Mr Lawrence.

Subject: Aisha

From: Holly
To: Aisha; Jason GrangerRM

You don't know what you've started now.

Subject: Saturday Night Partying—Are you OK?

From: Jennie Pithwait
To: Holly

Hey, haven't managed to get through to you since Saturday. Are you OK? Why did you run off?

From: Holly
To: Jennie Pithwait

I had to leave, drunk too much and didn't want to embarrass you by being ill in front of your guests, so sorry about that. It was a fab night. Thank you so much for inviting me.

xxx

tuesday

Subject: Orders from New York

From: Judy Perkins
To: Patricia Gillot; Holly

Dear Trisha and Holly,

I hope there will be a speedy conclusion to this court case, but it has been a useful catalyst in raising some important questions concerning switchboard cover and our current rota, prompting me to review our standard operating hours.

For a while now there have been some concerns expressed amongst the management here in the UK and abroad, who feel that to compete successfully within the marketplace in London, we should operate a longer shift pattern on the switchboard, especially as so many of our clients are calling from overseas and in particular, America. Most of our staff have DDI, but there is always a chance we could lose an important call, meaning lost millions for the company.

Therefore, I would like to propose new hours, with the earliest shift starting at 8:30 a.m. and latest finishing around 7:30 p.m. Obviously you would have to rotate your shifts. I can organise a rota, or if you feel you can coordinate it between you, then I am happy leaving it to yourselves.

Let me know your thoughts.

Judy

Subject: Court Case

From: Holly
To: Patricia Gillot

Any news?

From: Patricia Gillot
To: Holly

We should hear the verdict today. I'm not holding out much hope they get it right.

Trish

Subject: Customer Service Training and Evaluation

From: James Lawrence
To: Holly

Holly Denham,

RE: Your customer service skills evaluation

Please accept my apologies for the cancellation of our meeting yesterday afternoon. Work commitments took over.

Kindest regards,

James Lawrence

From: Holly
To: James Lawrence

Mr Lawrence,

No need to apologise, I have no requirement for your instruction. It is you, I feel, who would benefit from some tuition in this department.

I hear Judy offers some excellent courses; you should consider taking her up on one.

Regards,

Holly

From: James Lawrence
To: Holly

Holly,

I fear it is not one of Judy's courses which can help me, but rather a more hands-on practical approach, the assistance of which I'm sure a woman of your ability could handle with ease.

James

From: Holly
To: James Lawrence

James,

I don't doubt I could. You may come down and sit with Trish and myself at any time today. I'll even find you a nice clean chair to make sure you don't ruffle that expensive suit of yours.

Holly

From: James Lawrence
To: Holly

It's from Marks.

From: Holly
To: James Lawrence

I doubt it.

From: James Lawrence
To: Holly

OK, maybe it's not.

PS You should wear more lipstick. I think we should slut it up a bit on reception—your thoughts?

From: Holly
To: James Lawrence

I'll wear more lipstick, when you change those awful bling cuff links.

From: James Lawrence
To: Holly

You love them.

From: Holly
To: James Lawrence

Get lost. Maybe I do.

From: James Lawrence
To: Holly

I knew it.

Subject: Real life chick lit love affair?????

From: Jason GrangerRM
To: Holly

Any gossip yet?

From: Holly
To: Jason GrangerRM

A bit more contact. It's becoming interesting… what about you— how was last night?

From: Jason GrangerRM
To: Holly

We had dinner, talked a lot, mainly about his work, but it was still good. Unfortunately, he's away now for another week, working up North. Poor me, all alone.

I was thinking of having a quick fling, but now Hugh's getting back with Jemima. I'm stuck.

From: Holly
To: Jason GrangerRM

I know, that really puts a spanner in the works.

From: Jason GrangerRM
To: Holly

So this James—he sounds possible?

From: Holly
To: Jason GrangerRM

Yes.

Subject: Parents on vacation abroad

From: James Lawrence
To: Holly

My folks are away this weekend. I wondered whether you fancied coming over Saturday?

Subject: Oh my God

From: Holly
To: Jason GrangerRM; Aisha

Sh*t, he lives with his parents. This is definitely not good—what's that about????

From: Jason GrangerRM
To: Holly; Aisha

Dump him, run run run for the hills, he likes his mummy, probably likes wigs too.

From: Holly
To: Jason GrangerRM; Aisha

Wigs?

From: Jason GrangerRM
To: Holly; Aisha

That guy from the *Psycho* films wore them, but either way, you must end it now, before he starts asking you to call him 'little Jamie,' and you spend your Saturday nights stuck at home, changing his nappy and spanking his botty in time to *Bob the Builder*.

From: Holly
To: Jason GrangerRM; Aisha

Just because he lives with his parents?

From: Jason GrangerRM
To: Holly; Aisha

Yes.

From: Holly
To: Jason GrangerRM; Aisha

Really?

From: Jason GrangerRM
To: Holly; Aisha

NO! OF COURSE NOT, GET A GRIP!!!

There's nothing wrong with living with your parents. I think even Sylvester Stallone lives with his mum.

From: Aisha
To: Holly; Jason GrangerRM

Hi guys,

Thought I'd add my input here. It's OK—but come on, Jason, it's not very sexy and isn't he closing on 40? She'll be sure once she's seen his bedroom, then if it's covered in posters of Mum and there's a train set somewhere, run.

Agreed?

From: Jason GrangerRM
To: Holly; Aisha

Aisha's just moody… because of last night.

From: Holly
To: Aisha; Jason GrangerRM

Oh baby, what happened?

From: Aisha
To: Holly; Jason GrangerRM

I met some guy in a club, and we ended up back at his place—you know, as you do.

From: Holly
To: Aisha; Jason GrangerRM

No.

From: Jason GrangerRM
To: Aisha; Holly

No.

From: Aisha
To: Holly; Jason GrangerRM

Well, as I do. Anyway don't get all on your high horses or I won't be telling you.

From: Holly
To: Aisha; Jason GrangerRM

OK OK OK, sorry, do tell… xxxx

From: Aisha
To: Holly; Jason GrangerRM

I'm back at his place, and I had gone out that night looking hot hot hot, you know, my hair's straightened, my green contacts are looking extra sparkly, and generally I'm smoking. So we're back at his place, and we're messing around, and I've come up, and in the moonlight I've seen his face, and he looks horrified, absolutely horrified, and I've caught my reflection, and my hair's standing on end now (gone frizzy from the club heat), my makeup has given me big black stains under my eyes, and I've got one green eye and one brown eye.

From: Jason GrangerRM
To: Holly; Aisha

A scary-mary!

From: Aisha
To: Holly; Jason GrangerRM

I was the original scary-mary. Soon after he kind of made his excuses about needing an early night, and I left. Very sad, and besides which, one of my favourite contact lenses is caught up in some guy's underwear in Putney. Shame. Big shame.

From: Holly
To: Aisha; Jason GrangerRM

There's not a lot I can say to that story. I love you, Aish, and I prefer you with brown eyes anyway.

xxx

Subject: Draft Copy—To James Re: Saturday night

From: Holly
To: Holly

I'm not sure I can see you Saturday night, I've kind of got some old plans booked. Could see you in the day??

Subject: Girls clubbing night out

From: Jennie Pithwait
To: Holly

You fancy coming out on the pull Saturday? A night out on the tiles??

From: Holly
To: Jennie Pithwait

Hi,
That sounds brilliant, I'll hopefully be able to come. When do you need to know by?
Holly

From: Jennie Pithwait
To: Holly

Now.
What could you possibly be doing that's more important than a VIP table at Chinawhite?
Jennie

From: Holly
To: Jennie Pithwait

Nothing, but I'm out with my uncle on Saturday (it's his birthday), and I might not be able to get away early enough.

From: Jennie Pithwait
To: Holly

That's fine. We won't be going there till 11 p.m.

From: Holly
To: Jennie Pithwait

Oh, OK. I guess it should be finished by then. Is everyone going?

From: Jennie Pithwait
To: Holly

Of course, no boys though. Well, not to start with. You have to come, you're support staff—and after a couple of bottles of Krug, I'll need your support!!

Jennie

Subject: Probation period

From: Roger Lipton
To: Holly

Dear Holly,

You are midway through your probation period and all seems to be going well.

If you have any questions or need advice that you feel our department can help you with, don't hesitate to get in touch.

Regards,

Roger Lipton

From: Holly
To: Roger Lipton

Dear Roger,

No questions really, apart from the obvious—how am I doing, etc.?

Kindest regards,

Holly

From: Roger Lipton
To: Holly

Dear Holly,

It is not for me to give feedback at this stage, however, keep trying hard and listening to senior members of staff. If you feel there's anything we can do to assist you in improving your skills or concentration whilst in this position, let me know.

Roger

wednesday

Subject: Girls in love

From: Granny
To: Holly

Holly,

I once had a passionate kiss with a girl at school. I can't say it was better than kissing your Granddad, but it made me feel naughty. I'm just saying that your old gran isn't as boring as some people make out. I've lived a good life, Holly, and I think you should do whatever makes you happy in life.

xxxx

From: Holly
To: Granny

Thanks Granny.

I'm very happy at the moment. Things seem to be going well, and thanks for your advice.

x love, Holly

Subject: Been dumped

From: Holly
To: Jason GrangerRM

Morning,

I told him I'd see him on Saturday in the day (but not the night), and he hasn't got back to me… ?

What d'you think?

From: Jason GrangerRM
To: Holly

It sounds like you've made a firm statement saying—'keep your hands OFF my silky drawers.'

From: Holly
To: Jason GrangerRM

I just want to play it out a little further. We do work together, I don't want to be the office tart.

From: Jason GrangerRM
To: Holly

Then don't worry.

From: Holly
To: Jason GrangerRM

Also, I might be going out with Jennie and her friends Saturday night.

From: Jason GrangerRM
To: Holly

Have you told her about James?

From: Holly
To: Jason GrangerRM

No, don't think it's a good idea. She sounds like she hates him. I think I'll get on much better with Jennie if I'm single.

From: Jason GrangerRM
To: Holly

But you're not.

From: Holly
To: Jason GrangerRM

I am kind of.

From: Jason GrangerRM
To: Holly

No you're not.

From: Holly
To: Jason GrangerRM

OK; somewhere in between. You're meant to just agree with me.
xxx

From: Jason GrangerRM
To: Holly

So why does Jennie not approve? There must be some kind of history there?

From: Holly
To: Jason GrangerRM

No, there isn't, I've asked James. He looked hurt when I said she didn't seem to like him.

From: Jason GrangerRM
To: Holly

Grass.

From: Holly
To: Jason GrangerRM

I know!

I didn't actually mean to. I asked him whether they got on and then he wouldn't leave the question alone. He said they weren't friends or anything but couldn't think why she didn't like him.

Maybe she had the hots for him?

She's very pretty. I hope she doesn't have the hots for him?? Oh, maybe he hadn't even noticed her until now. Oh, God, she has the hots for him doesn't she?? What d'you think??

From: Jason GrangerRM
To: Holly

I think you don't need me if you're asking questions and answering them yourself, so why don't we leave 'Holly's Hour' for now and have a quick catch up with 'Jason's 5 mins'?

From: Holly
To: Jason GrangerRM

Oh, sorry, I forgot it was your final night for a week with your Mr. How did it go?

From: Jason GrangerRM
To: Holly

It was good, very good—

yeeeeeeeeeeeeeeeeeeeeeeeeeeeeeeeeeeeeeeeeeeeeeeeeeeeeeeeeeeeeeeeeeees sir. Do you really want to know all the sexy, gory details?

From: Holly
To: Jason GrangerRM

Not sure… Just kidding, I'd love to hear.

From: Jason GrangerRM
To: Holly

You liar!… anyway, I won't waste them on you, I'll just tell appreciative gay ears. (Imagine I'm pouting and turning my head away and strutting off with a particularly camp swing.)

From: Holly
To: Jason GrangerRM

I did. Fabulous exit darling.

x

Subject: I've bitten off all my fingernails

From: Holly
To: Patricia Gillot

So… TELL ME? What happened?

From: Patricia Gillot
To: Holly

Thanks for covering late again yesterday. You'll be happy to know it's over, and they got what they deserved. The worst of the bunch won't be around for a few years.

They didn't get him for murder, but we know he's to blame for a load of shootings. Still, good riddance. I'm so relieved darlin, I can't tell you how happy I am, knowing I won't have to look at his nasty little evil face again.

xxx

From: Holly
To: Patricia Gillot

That's brilliant!!!

Good, so is it all back to normal, back to school, etc.?

From: Patricia Gillot
To: Holly

Yeah, my boy did the right thing, and I'm proud of him.

Just wish I could send him to that school you told me about that won all those awards.

From: Holly
To: Patricia Gillot

You could, if he converted to Judaism—I think it's just for Orthodox Jews?

From: Patricia Gillot
To: Holly

It would be worth it, I'm telling you.

From: Holly
To: Patricia Gillot

Oh, and his sex. I think it's an all girls school.

From: Patricia Gillot
To: Holly

A bit more tricky, but still.

Hey, not sure about these late shifts. What d'you think?

From: Holly
To: Patricia Gillot

I don't mind doing some lates.

Subject: Exclusive Celebrity Nightclub?

From: Holly
To: Charlie Denham

So when do I get to show off and bring you all the girls from the office? How big is my guest list going to be??

From: Charlie Denham
To: Holly

Might be some time.

We had the health and safety inspectors around again and with all this water dripping down the walls, they now have a problem with those metal light shades we bought, and they want all the wiring covered in trunking. Oh, and they want a 'real' electrician doing the wiring who has to have some kind of certificate.

Bugger.

Subject: Friends needed

From: Jason GrangerRM
To: Holly

I've got to talk to you tonight. I'm a bit worried about Aisha.

From: Holly
To: Jason GrangerRM

Worried about what? Is she OK?

From: Jason GrangerRM
To: Holly

She's fine. It's just what I think she's up to here. I'll tell you later.

From: Holly
To: Jason GrangerRM

No no, you can't leave me hanging. What's she up to, and are you sure?

From: Jason GrangerRM
To: Holly

I think so. I don't want to email you about it. I'll call you later.

From: Holly
To: Jason GrangerRM

OK.

x

thursday

Subject: Seeing things

From: Patricia Gillot
To: Holly

Don't look now, but I'm sure one of those kids that got off is sitting on the other side of the road out there.

From: Holly
To: Patricia Gillot

Are you sure?

From: Patricia Gillot
To: Holly

I think so. Don't go out there.

Subject: B*stard men

From: Holly
To: Jason GrangerRM

I ran to work today to see if he'd replied, but he still hasn't. This is crap, crap, crap. He's a sex-starved, one-track minded git, who's got no interest in me other than seeing what a receptionist wears under the desk. He's a stinking-nasty, self-centred, perverted prat.

Subject: phone message

From: Holly
To: Shella Hamilton-Jones

Shella,

Jane Jenkins's daughter just called. She said it was urgent that her mum called her back.

Kindest regards,

Holly

Subject: And another thing

From: Holly
To: Jason GrangerRM

A git who just treads on people's hearts. A nasty, hurtful, spineless philanderer.

Life stinks.

I've got those butterflies in my stomach again, and it's his fault. I hate feeling like this. He's a heart-stamping rotten egg who just treads around on hearts all day long, that's what he is.

Subject: Saturday

From: James Lawrence
To: Holly

Hi Holls, are you not speaking to me?

I just wanted to know about Saturday?

J

Subject: Oh no!

From: Holly
To: Jason GrangerRM

Oh sh*t, oh pooh, oh big big dollops, I never sent a reply back to him. I drafted it to myself… crappola.

From: Jason GrangerRM
To: Holly

So he's no longer a rotten egg?

From: Holly
To: Jason GrangerRM

No, not a rotten egg. He's lovely. xxx

Subject: Saturday

From: Holly
To: James Lawrence

I would love to come on Saturday. Brilliant! Sounds like a great idea, yes. Not sure about the night. I have probably committed to something, but it's not hugely essential.

Holls x

Subject: Phone message

From: Shella Hamilton-Jones
To: Holly

Which daughter????

Subject: Help

From: Holly
To: Patricia Gillot

Oh shit, I've madeabooboo, help… it's a De Vil thing.

From: Patricia Gillot
To: Holly

Don't try and make it sound cute. No point—it won't wash with that evil cow. What have you done sweetie?

x

From: Holly
To: Patricia Gillot

Well, I was waiting to hear back from a certain someone about a date and was really really worried and upset, etc., and I got a call from someone early this morning who said she was Jane Jenkins's daughter and could she call her back immediately. I tried Jane's line, but she's out all morning, so I left a message on her secretary's voice mail… Shella, and also emailed her. Problem is, there's more than one daughter. Don't know which one it was.

From: Patricia Gillot
To: Holly

Why didn't you ask her name??

From: Holly
To: Patricia Gillot

Because I was in a tiz, and also because I was probably so scared on hearing the name Jane Jenkins, I started shaking and didn't want to ask her too many questions, because she was bound to then complain about me, and then… I mean, surely she knows she's got other sisters, surely she knows she's not an only child… I mean, how stupid is she!!! She just said that it's Jane's daughter and could

Jane call her back. I was lucky I managed to get her last name… oh helllllllllllllllp.

From: Patricia Gillot
To: Holly

If it's urgent, I'm sure Jane Jenkins will know which daughter it's more likely to be, so don't panic. I would have thought she'd know their numbers too. But Cruella will make a big fuss of it all. There's no getting out of it, unless you change your name and move countries.

x

Subject: Phone message

From: Holly
To: Shella Hamilton-Jones

Shella,

I'm really sorry, the girl in question just said it was her daughter and went very quickly. I assumed she only had one, as otherwise, I would have thought she'd have left her name. Hugely sorry. Can she try them both?

Kindest regards,

Holly

From: Shella Hamilton-Jones
To: Holly

There are three of them, one of which she doesn't speak to. So no, it's not that easy. It's a screwup. Major league.

Subject: Urgent

From: Mum and Dad
To: Holly

Holly,

Do you like lavender potpourri?

Love, Mum

From: Holly
To: Mum and Dad

What?

From: Mum and Dad
To: Holly

Lavender potpourri, do you like them? And don't say 'what' on its own, it's not polite dear.

Mum

From: Holly
To: Mum and Dad

Sorry Mum, I'm in a bit of a pickle. Why d'you want to know about lavender potpourri?

Love, Holly

From: Mum and Dad
To: Holly

For your birthday. I know it's not yet, but it's coming, and we'll have to post something, which takes a while now with the post being so bad to England, and so your father and I were trying to think of something light which we could post. I came up with potpourri, because they are light and smell nice. What d'you think?

Mum x

From: Holly
To: Mum and Dad

I think it's a wonderful idea, Mum.
Thank you.
x

Subject: REMINDER

From: Holly
To: Holly

Lavender potpourri? Is Mum OK?

Subject: Your friend

From: Jason GrangerRM
To: Holly

Did you talk to Aisha?

From: Holly
To: Jason GrangerRM

Yes, I managed to catch her briefly before I went to bed, but honestly, Jason, if she is doing it, she hasn't admitted it to me. Maybe it's your imagination?

friday

Subject: New job for Ralph

From: Holly
To: Patricia Gillot

Hiya,
How was the morning—not too bad?

From: Patricia Gillot
To: Holly

It was OK. Ralph just about got through. He doesn't handle it too well when people give him a hard time. You can see his muscles tensing under his uniform. He just wants to get up and clobber them.

From: Holly
To: Patricia Gillot

Muscles bulging under his uniform?? Sounds like someone has a crush on someone?

From: Patricia Gillot
To: Holly

He's lovely, and you know what I think about men in uniforms. I'd have those gold buttons off before you could say Jack Robinson.

From: Holly
To: Patricia Gillot

Patricia!

From: Patricia Gillot
To: Holly

You watch the lift, and I'll have him on that coffee table while there's no one about.

From: Holly
To: Patricia Gillot

What's got into you today!!

From: Patricia Gillot
To: Holly

It's me hormones!

xxx

Subject: A first-class customer service

From: Holly
To: HEM Machines

To the manager:

Call me optimistic, but I was hoping after your past three failed attempts to remove my faulty washing machine, this time you would send me the correct amount of men, on the right day of the week, and that they might successfully extract my machine from my kitchen.

Two men arrived, on the right day, but apparently without a trolley, which my particular job 'required.'

OK, if you don't want to find your washing machine sitting outside our flat in the street, then I suggest you send the right amount of removal 'specialists' with the correct tools on the perfect day of the week. Oh, and please remind them to come in a van, because I'm guessing they'll need a van to get it home, and a map, a compass, a full tank of petrol, and maybe a flask of coffee to keep them going. Oh, and my name is Holly Denham, although undoubtedly you'll have me down as Dinham.

x Holly

Subject: Sex and the city

From: Jason GrangerRM
To: Holly

Drop me a line when you get in. I'm sure Aisha's been doing something with that guy, but I've also got a feeling she's doing it with my boss too. Can't you find her a hobby or something?

From: Holly
To: Jason GrangerRM

2 of them???? I'll have a word with her tonight, I promise. She doesn't mean any harm, I'm sure she just doesn't realise what a difficult situation it might put you in.

Holly x

Cheer up, it's Friday!

Subject: Very important

From: James Lawrence
To: Holly

Truth or dare?

From: Holly
To: James Lawrence

Sorry?

From: James Lawrence
To: Holly

I said 'truth or dare.'

From: Holly
To: James Lawrence

Hello Holly,

How are you Holly?

Or even good afternoon Holly.

One usually starts a conversation with some kind of greeting.

From: James Lawrence
To: Holly

Good afternoon, Miss Denham.

Truth or Dare?

From: Holly
To: James Lawrence

Bored are we? Finished playing football with the traders?

From: James Lawrence
To: Holly

You hear about those kind of things down there, do you? That wasn't me though. Traders: they can be so childish, one does well, and they start a World Cup. We're much more grown up in my Dept.

So, is Holly going to come out to play or not?

From: Holly
To: James Lawrence

Not saying I'm playing, but 'dare.'

From: James Lawrence
To: Holly

I dare you to walk past my desk sucking a lollipop.

From: Holly
To: James Lawrence

Pervert.

From: James Lawrence
To: Holly

So, do you accept the challenge, Miss Denham?

From: Holly
To: James Lawrence

No. Besides which, I thought we were meant to be keeping this a secret?

From: James Lawrence
To: Holly

Keeping what a secret?

Anyway, girls walk past my desk all day sucking lollipops. No one will notice.

From: Holly
To: James Lawrence

You should have a word with them, tell them to suck off.

From: James Lawrence
To: Holly

Cut the cr*p Miss Denham. Is it a yes or a no?

From: Holly
To: James Lawrence

No.

Subject: Cocktails and Champagne

From: Jennie Pithwait
To: Holly

Holly,

We've now got six of us up for Saturday night. Glad you're coming. It's going to be bubbles then cocktails then dancing (or trying to anyway), starting off in Henrys, 8 p.m.

xxx

From: Holly
To: Jennie Pithwait

Great Jen, hopefully I'll be there. Just got to go somewhere early on, then should be there for 8 p.m.

x

Subject: Your new bloke

From: Patricia Gillot
To: Holly

By the way, who's this 'certain someone'?

From: Holly
To: Patricia Gillot

What certain someone?

From: Patricia Gillot
To: Holly

The one on your email you sent yesterday. You said you were waiting to hear back about a certain someone about a date.

From: Holly
To: Patricia Gillot

Some guy I met at a party a while ago, nice guy.

From: Patricia Gillot
To: Holly

Oh, right, is it going well?

From: Holly
To: Patricia Gillot

So far so good …

From: Patricia Gillot
To: Holly

Where do they work then?

From: Holly
To: Patricia Gillot

He works in a shipping company.

From: Patricia Gillot
To: Holly

Doing what?

From: Holly
To: Patricia Gillot

Shipping stuff.

From: Patricia Gillot
To: Holly

What kind of stuff?

From: Holly
To: Patricia Gillot

Electrical goods mainly, he works in the electrical shipping department.

From: Patricia Gillot
To: Holly

What, like TVs and phones and Playstations?

From: Holly
To: Patricia Gillot

Yes.

From: Patricia Gillot
To: Holly

Where does he ship them to?

From: Holly
To: Patricia Gillot

I don't know, it sounds like there are countries which need them, and countries which sell them, and he sends them from one to the other. In ships, big ships.

From: Patricia Gillot
To: Holly

What a crock of sh*t. You're dating Mr James Lawrence, you know, the man who winks at you every time he thinks I'm busy talking to someone.

Heee hee hee

x

From: Holly
To: Patricia Gillot

How did you see that???

But this is a huge huge secret, pleeeeease don't tell anyone.??? You haven't, have you?

From: Patricia Gillot
To: Holly

Does Jennie know?

From: Holly
To: Patricia Gillot

No, and I don't want her knowing either.

xx

Subject: Thank you

From: Holly
To: James Lawrence

Very kind of you, but even a whole box isn't going to make me accept the challenge.

From: James Lawrence
To: Holly

Spoilsport.

Subject: Lollipops

From: Patricia Gillot
To: Holly

Who were they from???? James?

From: Holly
To: Patricia Gillot

He thinks he's funny.

From: Patricia Gillot
To: Holly

He is, darlin. Give us a red one before you go.

xx

Subject: Meeting

From: Shella Hamilton-Jones
To: Holly

Dear Holly,

I'm coming down in a moment, and I need to talk to you. What time do you finish today?

Shella

Subject: Horror films

From: Jason GrangerRM
To: Holly

By the way, keep your phone on when you get to the family home, just in case he does turn out to be a bit weird. Not saying he will.

xxx

sunday

Subject: Toby

From: Charlie Denham
To: Holly

Good luck on Monday. If he looks at ya, let me know, and e'll be swimming with the daisies.

xxxx

week 4
monday

Subject: Saturday night

From: Jennie Pithwait
To: Holly

Where were you then?????

Subject: Gangster film

From: Holly
To: Charlie Denham

Got your email—but did you mean pushing up the daisies, or swimming with the fishes?

From: Charlie Denham
To: Holly

Hi Holls,
Was wasted on Sunday. I think when I wrote that I was even slurring a cockney accent—the one I usually use when I'm negotiating with plumbers and sparkies (so they think I'm a bit streetwise and don't just rip me off).
Charlie

From: Holly
To: Charlie Denham

You told me they're always ripping you off.

From: Charlie Denham
To: Holly

Of course they are, because they see some middle-class knob putting on a fake cockney accent and instantly double their prices. You seen Toby this morning yet?

From: Holly
To: Charlie Denham

He came past. Don't worry, not a problem.

x

Subject: Re: Saturday night

From: Holly
To: Jennie Pithwait

Jennie,

Sorry, I was at my uncle's birthday, and they threw a surprise birthday party for him (and I didn't even know). This went on for ages, and I couldn't get away... sorry. What happened? What did I miss out on??

Holly

Subject: Banking Boy

From: Holly
To: James Lawrence

Is there a banker in the house?

From: James Lawrence
To: Holly

Great weekend, lots of fun ...

PS Is that a split I saw in that skirt of yours?

From: Holly
To: James Lawrence

No.

From: James Lawrence
To: Holly

Damn.

From: Holly
To: James Lawrence

Anything else?

From: James Lawrence
To: Holly

I'll give it some thought.

From: Holly
To: James Lawrence

I'm sure you will.

Subject: Reminder

From: Holly
To: Holly

REMINDER, SPLIT SKIRT—possible? Where to buy?

Subject: Working part time

From: Shella Hamilton-Jones
To: Holly

Dear Holly,

I'm not sure if you are there today? (I couldn't see you on the desk Friday morning, and you were not there Friday evening) but maybe when you ARE in, you could call me.

Regards,

Shella.

Subject: Uh oh!

From: Holly
To: Patricia Gillot

Got some hatemail from Shella.

From: Patricia Gillot
To: Holly

I can guess. She came down just after you'd gone on Friday and stormed off before I could explain.

Subject: Working full time

From: Holly
To: Shella Hamilton-Jones

Dear Shella,

I am here, and I'm not working part time. I had the morning off on Friday, and as Trish and I organise our shifts to cover the later times, we did so. I will be covering some lates this week.

Holly

From: Shella Hamilton-Jones
To: Holly

Holly,

It's nice to see you've quickly adapted your position to flexitime, I'm sure that's more convenient for you. I'm guessing management knows all about this?

Regards,

Shella

Subject: Bet she has a puppy-coat too

From: Holly
To: Patricia Gillot

What is wrong with her? She's absolutely got it in for me!!! Grrrrrrr

From: Patricia Gillot
To: Holly

Don't let her get to you, not today. There's too many of them coming in, and it's going to be worse any second. Here we go …

Subject: Come on Holly—update please

From: Aisha
To: Holly

So, what did you and your train spotter get up to then?

From: Holly
To: Aisha

Hi Aish,

It turns out, he is only staying with his parents while his house is being renovated. Apparently he'd already told me this when we'd gone for a meal last week (I wasn't listening).

Had a good time.

x

From: Aisha
To: Holly

You do that to me, the not listening thing.

From: Holly
To: Aisha

I do not! I always listen to you!! How's work? Have you made up with Jason yet?

From: Aisha
To: Holly

He made such a huge deal out of it all. I told him I haven't done anything with either of them, and now I won't, I promise!!

From: Holly
To: Aisha

OK, maybe he doesn't believe you (OK, before you start ranting… I'm not having a go), but he's worried about his job. He got you the job there, he interviewed you, and it'll be his head if things go wrong.

From: Aisha
To: Holly

OK OK OK, get off my back. I need love and friendship now, not hassle. He's just being a drama queen.

From: Holly
To: Aisha

OK, honey, I do love you, but be nice to him. He really tried helping you, getting you in there, so try and repay him by doing what he asks. It doesn't sound to me like he's in the wrong.

Subject: Something's fishy

From: Patricia Gillot
To: Holly

You're getting picked on by Shella, and we're run off our feet with calls coming in by the bucket load, bookings everywhere, and we've had clients queuing, and still you manage to keep grinning like a Cheshire cat. I know you're good, but you're grinning even when there's no one watching. What you been up to with James? Good weekend, was it??

From: Holly
To: Patricia Gillot

You've got such a naughty mind. That's not the reason. I'm just in a good mood. That's all.
x

From: Patricia Gillot
To: Holly

Oh, OK then, I won't mention it. Obviously nothing happened. I just wish I'd got some this weekend, that's all.
Trish.
Oi, so is this James Lawrence a big lad?

From: Holly
To: Patricia Gillot

Patricia!!!! Shame on you!!!

x

From: Patricia Gillot
To: Holly

Come on, brighten up my day, or I'll get Ralph to come sit between us. Lovely. Talking of which, I might send him a little email.

Subject: I've spoken to Aisha

From: Jason GrangerRM
To: Holly

I think we've sorted it all out. I've explained to Aisha the problems with starting a relationship with work colleagues etc., and she seemed to totally understand. I don't think she's actually done anything with either of them yet.

xx

From: Holly
To: Jason GrangerRM

I'm so pleased!!
Glad you've sorted it out between you.
xxx

Subject: Ralph—Receptionists's request ...

From: Patricia Gillot
To: Ralph Tooms; Holly

Ralph,
Holly and me are thirsty. Can you run off and get us a couple of glasses of water.
Pretty please?
Trisha & Holl

Subject: TRISHA!

From: Holly
To: Patricia Gillot

Don't involve me in your flirting! He won't do it anyway. He's got to keep himself in there, watching screens.

From: Patricia Gillot
To: Holly

I'm thirsty!!! (besides which, I'll laugh my tits off if he does).

From: Holly
To: Patricia Gillot

He's coming!!

From: Patricia Gillot
To: Holly

Who?

From: Holly
To: Patricia Gillot

Ralph!

Subject: Water boy

From: Patricia Gillot
To: Holly; Ralph Tooms

Cheers for that Ralph. Also, next time me and Holly want our water from the blue tap—it's colder, OK?

From: Ralph Tooms
To: Patricia Gillot; Holly

Cheeky!
OK, I'll do it next time. I had to get them quick. You know what Judy's like if I go off walking around in the afternoon.

You lot busy?
Ralph

From: Patricia Gillot
To: Holly; Ralph Tooms

Always.
Trish

Subject: help... xxxx in trouble again

From: Aisha
To: Holly

Hi Holly,
Can you do me a favour. Can you speak to Jason for me? I think I've upset him again, but not sure how bad it is.
xxxx

tuesday

Subject: In trouble

From: Aisha
To: Holly

Hi Holly,
Did you get my email from last night? I'm not sure, but I think I've really upset Jason. Can you find out for me?
xxx

From: Holly
To: Aisha

Why??? What have you done?

From: Aisha
To: Holly

Nothing too bad, I don't think. Has he said anything yet?

From: Holly
To: Aisha

No... not yet. Tell me??? You didn't get off with his GM did you?

From: Aisha
To: Holly

Of course not... I wouldn't do that!! He told me it was forbidden to go near colleagues etc. This was just a guest staying in the hotel.
xxxx

From: Holly
To: Aisha

A what?

From: Aisha
To: Holly

A guest—surely that's not as bad as a colleague? Don't give me a hard time, someone should give me some rules, and I'll stick to them. It's not that bad, is it?

From: Holly
To: Aisha

What were you doing with the guest?

From: Aisha
To: Holly

Not a lot, OK a little, but you should see him (I've got a picture, actually). He's so f**king sexy, he had the nasty East End gangster look, oh, and stinking rich too. He was just so rough about it all. Loved it!!!

xxx

From: Holly
To: Aisha

Rough about what? You didn't sleep with him, did you?

From: Aisha
To: Holly

No, just sex, he grabbed me and pulled me into one of the spare suites, it was great!!! Mmmmm

From: Holly
To: Aisha

You haven't told Jason all of this, have you?

From: Aisha
To: Holly

No, but he knows, because we got caught.

xxx

Got to go now, he's coming.

x

Subject: Urgent meeting

From: James Lawrence
To: Holly

Dear Holly Denham,
It is absolutely essential that you come up to my floor.
Right now!
James Lawrence

From: Holly
To: James Lawrence

Why?

From: James Lawrence
To: Holly

Why? Do I need a reason?

Stop being lippy I'm a VP for Chr*st's sake—get that beautiful backside into the lift and come to my desk—that's an order!

James

From: Holly
To: James Lawrence

What exactly, Mr Lawrence VP, do you want with me?

From: James Lawrence
To: Holly

You'll find out when you get here, won't you?

From: Holly
To: James Lawrence

It's very busy down here, I need the reason.

From: James Lawrence
To: Holly

Seriously, I need to discuss that client meeting I've scheduled next week, just want everything to go according to plan. Can you bring a pad with you? Also, it's casual up here today, so you can loosen a few buttons on that suit of yours.

James

Subject: My Morning

From: Pregnant Pam
To: Holly

Holly,

Do you know what it's like to throw up in your mouth and leak pee at the same time? On the Tube? In front of people? That's what happened to me this morning. Don't ever ever ever get pregnant. How are you anyway?

Pam

From: Holly
To: Pregnant Pam

I'm fine, sorry to hear about the pee thing. Must be very difficult. Do we know what sex the baby is yet?

From: Pregnant Pam
To: Holly

No, they tell me it's far too early.

From: Holly
To: Pregnant Pam

You'll find out soon enough. I can't wait, it's so exciting!

xxxx

Subject: Urgent meeting?

From: James Lawrence
To: Holly

Sorry to be pushy, but I've got to get this finalised before I call one of the clients back.

J

Subject: Meeting?

From: Holly
To: Patricia Gillot

Trish, I've got to go upstairs in a minute, someone's moaning about a room check. You OK for a second?

From: Patricia Gillot
To: Holly

No problem babe.

Subject: Your meeting

From: Holly
To: James Lawrence

Dear Mr Lawrence,

Next time you make me traipse all the way up there for no reason,
I'll invoice you for wasted company time & assets.

Holly

From: James Lawrence
To: Holly

It wasn't wasted, it was essential to correct the finer details and to
see you take my advice re: the buttons.

From: Holly
To: James Lawrence

Hate to break your fantasy, but the lifts are hot with no air-con,
that's all.

From: James Lawrence
To: Holly

Liar.

Subject: And …

From: James Lawrence
To: Holly

You're a flirt.

From: Holly
To: James Lawrence

Possibly. I think one of the buttons was undone on purpose, yes.

Holly

xx

Subject: Aisha's in love

From: Holly
To: Jason GrangerRM

Jason,

You never told me you had a problem last night there, is everything OK?

Holly xx

From: Jason GrangerRM
To: Holly

Are you referring to your horny delinquent friend?

From: Holly
To: Jason GrangerRM

I heard about it—this morning, but I've been waiting for your dreaded call, etc. Has she caused any trouble?

From: Jason GrangerRM
To: Holly

Not at all.

From: Holly
To: Jason GrangerRM

Really?

From: Jason GrangerRM
To: Holly

Really, yes, it's quite the norm for our front of house team to be discovered shagging in seemingly unoccupied rooms. I'm very proud of it. I positively encourage my staff to go around pumping the guests whenever their hormones get the better of them. If you can't help them, screw them—is our motto.

Fancy a sh*g?

From: Holly
To: Jason GrangerRM

Are you OK? You sound a bit manic?

From: Jason GrangerRM
To: Holly

I'm p*ssed off.

Don't worry, I'm getting over it. A bellboy found them, it made his day, but don't tell Aisha. I want her to stew in her own guilt for a while.

Subject: News re: friend of mine

From: Holly
To: Charlie Denham

You remember that friend of mine, Aisha, you said was really really hot? I've got to tell you this, because I know how much you'll appreciate it, and you've got to promise not to tell anyone, not that you know anyone I know. Email me back a promise.
Holly

From: Charlie Denham
To: Holly

I promise?? What is it?

From: Holly
To: Charlie Denham

She just got caught having sex with a guest in a hotel she works in! And she's also dating the Hotel Manager! (we think)

Subject: My friend

From: Holly
To: Patricia Gillot

I just heard my friend working in a hotel got caught in bed with one of the guests!!!

From: Patricia Gillot
To: Holly

I've got a friend who loves having sex in the back of dirty old vans, she can't get enough of it.

From: Holly
To: Patricia Gillot

That's nice.

Subject: Romantic encounter?

From: Holly
To: Alice and Matt

I know you don't know who Aisha is, and you live in another country, and it probably means nothing to you, but I've got to tell someone and can't tell anyone she knows. Aisha, a friend of mine, has just got caught having intercourse with a guest in a hotel she works in, on reception!! And she's also dating the Hotel Manager!!! It's like, I don't know, one of those books you read.

xxxx

From: Alice and Matt
To: Holly

She got caught having intercourse on reception? I don't believe it.

From: Holly
To: Alice and Matt

No, she works on reception. It was in one of the spare rooms.

From: Alice and Matt
To: Holly

OK, well it sounds like she has a troubled soul. Did I tell you I've enrolled on a course which helps give you more inner peace and mental stimulation—I think this could help her too.

x

From: Holly
To: Alice and Matt

What course?

From: Alice and Matt
To: Holly

Don't get all freaked out, but it teaches you how to be a white witch.

Subject: REMINDER

From: Holly
To: Holly

REMINDER
Check out witchcraft, is it a cult—and also—family tree for previous signs of madness.

Subject: YOU ARE KIDDING ME!!!!

From: Charlie Denham
To: Holly

Whhhhha hey!!! You're kidding!! Aisha's bad!!! That naughty sexy minx, love it!!!!

From: Holly
To: Charlie Denham

Thanks, Charlie—I can, at least, always count on your response.

x

(even if slightly predictable)

wednesday

Subject: Problems with Jason

From: Aisha
To: Holly

Any news? Jason's not talking to me.

From: Holly
To: Aisha

It could have been really bad for him. I think he's still waiting to see what happens.

From: Aisha
To: Holly

Sh*t, I'm in trouble aren't I?

From: Holly
To: Aisha

Sorry baby—I think you are.

x

From: Aisha
To: Holly

Why me? I think my job could be on the line, you know.

x

From: Holly
To: Aisha

I told you, he's upset.

x

From: Aisha
To: Holly

Sh*t. Still, do you want to see a picture of him!!!!!?

From: Holly
To: Aisha

Aisha!

Subject: Annual Results

From: Judy Perkins
To: Holly; Patricia Gillot

Dear Patricia and Holly,

Next month will be a busy time for Huerst & Wright. We have our 25 year celebratory Gala dinner to look forward to, and now we've been given the task of hosting this year's HW International Annual Results Conference at our London offices, so we will need to begin preparing for it. It is 10 years since our office held the annual results when I myself organised it, however, with our impending occupation of a further two floors, I'm sure you will agree I am at full stretch already.

We have therefore a couple of options. The first is that it would be handled by either: the events team, both of whom are fairly junior, or it could be organised by one of the senior PAs, assisted in part by my team. At this stage, I am looking at all possibilities, and your input would be greatly appreciated.

Kind Regards,

Judy

Subject: Annual Results??

From: Patricia Gillot
To: Holly

I don't like the sound of this at all.

From: Holly
To: Patricia Gillot

Why, what are annual results?

From: Patricia Gillot
To: Holly

It's a right pain, like a big conference where they go through how the company did—figure wise, lots and lots of figures, very dull, but a huge deal. I remember the last one, Judy almost had a nervous breakdown. That's probably why she's ducking from it this time.

Subject: Washing machine

From: Holly
To: Alice and Matt

You won't believe it, but I finally got my machine taken away last night—out of office hours!!
Now this is strange, and I know it's just a stupid washing machine, but standing up for myself and being firm with them made me feel a little stronger. It was good, especially when I got through to their manager and got them to make a special trip out of hours, etc.

xxxx

From: Alice and Matt
To: Holly

Holly honey,

I know you hate confrontation, but sometimes it's unavoidable. I hate it too, I think the only people in our family who are any good at it are Charlie and Mum. By the way, you're sounding so much better these days. Maybe soon you could even head over to Canary Wharf—get a little back of what's owed to you????

xxx

From: Holly
To: Alice and Matt

I'm never going to do that. It's gone and forgotten.

x

From: Alice and Matt
To: Holly

OK. By the way, have you heard from Granny recently? I'm worried. She seemed quite down at the weekend.

x

From: Holly
To: Alice and Matt

No I haven't. I'll send her an email and call her tonight.

x

Subject: Present for you

From: Holly
To: Jennie Pithwait

Oh oh… you'll like this present I'm sending you up now.

From: Jennie Pithwait
To: Holly

Ooo, you're getting my hopes up, I'm excited …

Subject: Yes please

From: Jennie Pithwait
To: Holly

LOVE IT!! What a lovely present, and so nicely wrapped in Armani. I'm sure he just took a detour past my desk… and now I can only paw tearfully at the air, as the last image of his backside disappears behind the closing steel lift doors, like a… f*ckit, Mr Huerst heading my way. Back to reality, see ya.

Subject: You know who

From: Aisha
To: Holly

See attached.

From: Holly
To: Aisha

Why is it all your pictures of men are from that angle???

From: Aisha
To: Holly

Do you really want me to answer that one?

From: Holly
To: Aisha

No.

x

From: Aisha
To: Holly

Hey. I think Paul could be a long-term thing though?

From: Holly
To: Aisha

So this is in the hotel room? You thought to take a picture but not lock the door???

From: Aisha
To: Holly

I know, don't have to tell me.

From: Holly
To: Aisha

I remember—you like that kind of thing, don't you!!!! The whole 'being seen' yuk thing—why did I recommend you to Jason? I must be mad—and you need a shrink, or I do. Are you working over Easter?

From: Aisha
To: Holly

If I've still got a job… yikes.

x

Subject: Mr Lawrence

From: Holly
To: James Lawrence

Hello.

From: James Lawrence
To: Holly

Sorry, been busy all day. You OK?

From: Holly
To: James Lawrence

Why wouldn't I be?

From: James Lawrence
To: Holly

Ooh, someone's moody.

From: Holly
To: James Lawrence

Not at all.

From: James Lawrence
To: Holly

Fancy a drink after work?

From: Holly
To: James Lawrence

Maybe. Oh sod it, yes.

From: James Lawrence
To: Holly

I'll be down later.
PS Like the lipstick, very 'welcoming.'

From: Holly
To: James Lawrence

I think you're imagining things again.

From: James Lawrence
To: Holly

I am now. I'll see you at 5:30 p.m.

From: Holly
To: James Lawrence

x

thursday

Subject: Annual Results

From: Shella Hamilton-Jones
To: Holly; Judy Perkins; Patricia Gillot

Dear Judy and her team:

Happy Easter.

Knowing what an important conference this is for Huerst & Wright, I would like to throw my name into the hat for the organisation of this event.

The last conference of this size was an absolute success. Judy, I'm sure it is essential for you to feel confident that the candidate stepping into your shoes will arrange this with the minimum of fuss and with the maximum of impact.

Having organised many events for the company in the past, I am extremely qualified in this field of expertise, and together we can produce one of the best conferences Huerst & Wright has ever seen. As the PA for the MD in Corporate Finance, Jane Jenkins, who will be spending the next couple of months in our New York office, I'll have less of a workload.

Our office has been chosen to host the Annual Results, which I relate to London's recent achievement of hosting the Olympics, and I know the directors of this wonderful company feel the same way.

The current events team have little if no experience in organising anything of this scale, and using them would be a risk, especially when you have a competent team of assistants and helpers down there, which I can utilise.

I am free during some limited times for a meeting together next week.

Subject: Bitch up there

From: Patricia Gillot
To: Holly

I'll kill her!!

From: Holly
To: Patricia Gillot

You know, she probably wrote 'little helpers' and then thought that would wind us up too much.

From: Patricia Gillot
To: Holly

She'll get to be in charge of us… Can you imagine? I think I'd kill myself. Or her.

From: Holly
To: Patricia Gillot

No! Please tell me Judy wouldn't let her, that would be like your mum turning her back as you got fed to the lions, or something similar! yuk

Subject: Reception Cover

From: Judy Perkins
To: Holly; Patricia Gillot

Dear Holly and Trisha,

We have a reception temp covering this afternoon from www.receptionworld.com, which Shella recommended. We'll get another to cover for Trisha next week.

I would like your input in this meeting for the Annual Results.

Judy

Subject: Friends

From: Mum and Dad
To: Holly

Holly,

How are you? How is your job? How is Jennie? Are you beginning to make friends again with her?

Mum

x

From: Holly
To: Mum and Dad

Mum,

It's so good getting back in touch with Jennie. She is funny still, but possibly more so.

xxx

From: Mum and Dad
To: Holly

Holly,

That's good news. Jennie was always a great influence, keep in there.

x

Subject: Night clubbing in London

From: Jennie Pithwait
To: Holly

Me and Katy are waiting for your 'yes.' Are you coming out tonight? ? ?
You are invited to attend the best clubs you've never seen before.
You lucky girl.

From: Holly
To: Jennie Pithwait

I'll be honest, I've nothing to wear.

From: Jennie Pithwait
To: Holly

Fine, we'll head back to mine, and you can borrow something.... let's make Holly the princess for once! Spill anything, and you're dead!
xxx

From: Holly
To: Jennie Pithwait

I'm in! Not sure your stuff will fit me?

From: Jennie Pithwait
To: Holly

Bring some shoes, and we'll get you into the rest. The carriage awaits, princess!

Subject: You're slapping on the makeup?

From: Patricia Gillot
To: Holly

Where you off to tonight?

From: Holly
To: Patricia Gillot

Going out with Jennie, feeling a lot less glam than I imagine the rest will be ...

From: Patricia Gillot
To: Holly

She's a tart. Don't worry, you've got class, darlin!

From: Holly
To: Patricia Gillot

I just don't want to look silly. Her lot are sooooo gorgeous.

From: Patricia Gillot
To: Holly

You don't look up to that lot, you're better than them!

Subject: New job

From: Aisha
To: Holly

Still not good with Jason. Any jobs going there? With you?

month 3

week 1

tuesday

Subject: Friday night

From: Holly
To: Jennie Pithwait

Hi Jennie,

Hope you had a good Bank Holiday weekend. Thanks for a great night out on Friday. I'll have your dress back to you by tomorrow.

xxx

Subject: Your opinion please, Mr Granger

From: Holly
To: Jason GrangerRM

You know we spent Saturday night in Oxford, well I've been mulling something over in my head, and something isn't right. Email me when you're in. I'm desperate to get your thoughts.

xxxx

Subject: Request for you

From: PRade@GJO.JE.COM
To: Holly

Dear sirs

I come to England and have £1,000,000.00 I need spend when I arrive. I not have bank account, so you let me store this in your account I pay you £100,000? I just need your bank details? Yes?

P Rade.

From: Holly
To: PRade@GJO.JE.COM

No. But the last people desperate for my bank details were
Administration@securitybankingtrust.com—I'm sure they could
set up an account for you.

Good luck with your millions.

x

Subject: Your dirty weekend

From: Jason GrangerRM
To: Holly

Morning

I guess you must have only just remembered those of us who didn't
get a holly-day, while you were having so much fun.

From: Holly
To: Jason GrangerRM

Don't be mean, I called you every day.

From: Jason GrangerRM
To: Holly

OK, but let me assure you:

1: I hate our General Manager

2: He made my Easter a nightmare

3: I feel mentally scarred, Holly

4: I honestly don't think I'll ever recover

Jason.

From: Holly
To: Jason GrangerRM

It can't have been that bad?

From: Jason GrangerRM
To: Holly

You weren't there!!

Can you even imagine, you're an angry guest, your room isn't the deluxe suite you booked, the TV doesn't work, the windows are jammed shut, the air-con is up too high, and you ask for the reception manager, and he walks out with a set of Easter Bunny ears on???
Can you imagine how hard it is to be taken seriously?????
I hate him.

From: Holly
To: Jason GrangerRM

You told me. But forget it now sweetheart, it's over.
xx

From: Jason GrangerRM
To: Holly

Also—Sunday night (as if it could get worse), a friend of mine with a body of a god, drops by and catches me in my furry head piece (I died).

I'm going to organise a contract killer for the GM—I know he only made us wear them so he could dress Aisha up as a bunny girl. Heaven help me.

So go on, then, tell me about James? (I'm all ears, huh!)

From: Holly
To: Jason GrangerRM

Although I looked terrible when I first woke up (from my night out with Jennie), I was looking OK by the time James picked me up at lunchtime. It was a beautiful day. We drove to Oxford, spent the afternoon walking around the town, looking at the old buildings, etc. It was gorgeous. We were meant to come back that night, but after eating we ended up in a pub, and James had too much to drink (so couldn't drive), therefore… we checked into a hotel there.

Now comes the strange bit. I was a bit drunk, but I'm sure I overheard him give his name to the concierge, and the concierge confirm his reservation.

From: Jason GrangerRM
To: Holly

So what's the problem?

From: Holly
To: Jason GrangerRM

But we hadn't reserved, it was a spur of the moment thing.

From: Jason GrangerRM
To: Holly

Obviously, Holly, your surprise romantic shag-fest was a pre-arranged romantic shag-fest... I like this James, he's baaaaaaaaaaaaaaaad. Tell me what he looks like naked!!

From: Holly
To: Jason GrangerRM

He did, didn't he? He presumed I would agree to it. What kind of woman does he think I am???

From: Jason GrangerRM
To: Holly

One who's up for it, I guess. Come on—does he have a hairy bum?

From: Holly
To: Jason GrangerRM

NO!

From: Jason GrangerRM
To: Holly

Got any photos?

From: Holly
To: Jason GrangerRM

No pictures, I'm not Aisha. I can't coordinate my lovemaking whilst directing photos.

From: Jason GrangerRM
To: Holly

Damn you and your lack of dexterity.
His best feature??

From: Holly
To: Jason GrangerRM

His arms.

From: Jason GrangerRM
To: Holly

Because they're everywhere at once, like a naughty-weekend-prearranging octopus?

From: Holly
To: Jason GrangerRM

No, they're just hairy, tanned with toned forearms (and that's all you're getting).

From: Jason GrangerRM
To: Holly

That's all I need! (fancy an extra to make up the numbers?)

From: Holly
To: Jason GrangerRM

No?

xx

Subject: Hello

From: Ralph Tooms
To: Holly; Patricia Gillot

Holly & Trisha,
Good afternoon, ladies. Just wanted you to know that I'm here,
ready and willing if you need refreshments.
Ralph

Subject: Night out

From: Patricia Gillot
To: Holly

He's keen. How was Friday night?

From: Holly
To: Patricia Gillot

It was fun, but a long night. We went to 4 bars and 3 clubs. I wasn't
feeling so good Saturday morning.
We should go out one night, fancy it?

From: Patricia Gillot
To: Holly

Love to, darlin. Not this week though, maybe next week.

From: Holly
To: Patricia Gillot

OK.
I'm still starving, I wish I'd have got more for lunch. Those packet
salads don't go very far once you've thrown away the croutons and
the sauce, and I'm not that keen on lettuce either.

From: Patricia Gillot
To: Holly

What do you fancy?

From: Holly
To: Patricia Gillot

A chicken mayonnaise sandwich.

Subject: Water boy

From: Patricia Gillot
To: Holly; Ralph Tooms

Water boy, us ladies need your attention.

From: Ralph Tooms
To: Holly; Patricia Gillot

May I say how gorgeous you are both looking today?
Ralph

From: Patricia Gillot
To: Holly; Ralph Tooms

You may, Ralph.

You aren't looking so bad yourself. Now, gorgeous women like us shouldn't have to lift a finger, should we?

From: Ralph Tooms
To: Holly; Patricia Gillot

You ladies want some more water, do you? It's no problem. I was about to do a building check anyway.

From: Patricia Gillot
To: Ralph Tooms; Holly

Lady Holly wants a chicken mayonnaise sandwich from over the road, so we'll expect you standing to attention in front of us in 5 mins. Is this understood?

Subject: Delivery Service

From: Holly
To: Ralph Tooms; Patricia Gillot

Ralph,

Thank you for bringing me a sandwich, but I want you to stand to attention next time in front of us, OK?

Cap in hand!

Trisha & Holly

Subject: Poor Ralph

From: Holly
To: Patricia Gillot

I can't believe I've just sent that. He hasn't replied back, Trish, he probably thinks I'm really rude.

From: Patricia Gillot
To: Holly

You evil cow, messing with his head, shame on you, Holly! Holly the bitch, who would have guessed?

From: Holly
To: Patricia Gillot

Stop it Trisha!

From: Patricia Gillot
To: Holly

Oh, listen to you now! You bossy cow! Lucky Ralph.

xxx

Subject: Ladies on reception

From: Ralph Tooms
To: Holly; Patricia Gillot

OK, Holly, I will.

Ralph

wednesday

Subject: Call me, I'm worried.

From: Holly
To: Aisha

Call me if you're in, sweetie. I got all your messages. First you were crying, then laughing, then crying again??

Tell me you're OK?

xxx

love you.

Subject: Southern Debt Management—Acct

20000389384374 Holly Rivers

From: Holly
To: Southern Debt Management Services

REF: Acct 20000389384374 Holly Rivers

To Whom It May Concern:

I received your letter today and feel your wording is a little unjust.

I understand my commitments fully, but threatening letters can only help in a negative way. I know my situation is not a novel one to your company, but it is, however, original to me, and it is something which has taken a while to come to terms with.

I am doing my best. I am getting there and am trying to keep to the financial program which I have committed to—mentioned in your letter.

Finally, I have posted you the documents requested—can you please let me know when you are likely to update my record to show my name as Holly Denham?

Yours sincerely,

Holly Denham

Subject: Aisha

From: Holly
To: Jason GrangerRM

Hi Jason,
I know you're annoyed with Aisha at the moment, but is she OK today?
xxx

From: Jason GrangerRM
To: Holly

Why?

From: Holly
To: Jason GrangerRM

Just wanted to know.
xx

Subject: Call me, please

From: Holly
To: Aisha

Just so you know, I've asked Jason if you're OK. Don't know whether you're even in, so don't want to get you in more trouble. Can you contact me please?
x

From: Aisha
To: Holly

I'm here, I'm here. Where were you when I needed you... tell me you love me.

From: Holly
To: Aisha

I love you very much. How are you feeling? Have you slept yet?

From: Aisha
To: Holly

No.
Don't tell Jason.

From: Holly
To: Aisha.

You should have called in sick, how did you get home?

From: Aisha
To: Holly

I thought I might as well go clubbing last night, seeing as I am counting the hours until I'm sacked anyway.

From: Holly
To: Aisha

I tried calling you. He doesn't want to sack you, just wants you to apologise to him (which I didn't know you hadn't yet done) and to prove you're taking your job seriously (which might be difficult).

From: Aisha
To: Holly

OH, don't tell me that, I want to stay here, I love my job, and I love Jason. I'm in the shit, aren't I?

From: Holly
To: Aisha

Baby, just keep it together, and you'll be OK. What happened last night?

From: Aisha
To: Holly

I'll tell you later. First I'm going to talk to Jason and tell him everything and tell him I love him.

From: Holly
To: Aisha

NO NO, don't do it, baby. I think you're still drunk. Call me.

Subject: Friends

From: Holly
To: Patricia Gillot

Do you have any mates that always seem to be in trouble?

From: Patricia Gillot
To: Holly

I've only got friends who always seem to be in trouble, you are an exception, darlin.

x

Subject: Your friend

From: Jason GrangerRM
To: Holly

Have you got something to tell me?

From: Holly
To: Jason GrangerRM

What?

From: Jason GrangerRM
To: Holly

An explanation for what just happened to me?

From: Holly
To: Jason GrangerRM

It depends. What just happened to you?

From: Jason GrangerRM
To: Holly

At first I thought I was being mugged: the alcohol breath, desperation behind the eyes, a strong grip on my arm. But then I thought—no Jason, muggers don't dress like they're in a booty-rap-video, and they don't spout on about their undying love for you. No, surely, this is one of your star employees?

From: Holly
To: Jason GrangerRM

She's loveable though, isn't she?

From: Jason GrangerRM
To: Holly

I'm guessing you know what happened to her last night?

From: Holly
To: Jason GrangerRM

No idea, she went out, that's about all I've got so far. I had some very strange calls on my answer phone, alternately crying or laughing, but the music was too loud to hear why she was happy, or she was sobbing so much, I couldn't understand a word.

From: Jason GrangerRM
To: Holly

I've sent her home now, and we've made up, bless her Jimmy Choos. Her night went something like this. She goes out with a friend to a club, having a great time, but then her bag gets stolen with everything in it. Her friend wants to go home, but Aisha realises she's not lost her wallet, it's in her back pocket—so now, very happy, decides to stay drinking. The next thing—her wallet does get stolen, more tears, but Aisha meets this American guy she's convinced herself she likes, very happy, and so goes back to his flat. He drops his pants and that's when she starts crying again. First she loses her bag, then her wallet, then tries to make herself feel better by having meaningless sex, but the guy has a todger the size of a wine-bottle. She said there was no way she could 'fit THAT up her' (horrible thought) and broke down crying again. The guy at this point throws her out. What a dick.

From: Holly
To: Jason GrangerRM

Oh, Aish.

Subject: Your Clients

From: Holly
To: James Lawrence

Your clients are still waiting for their meeting. Have you forgotten about them?

Tut-tut

From: James Lawrence
To: Holly

No, I couldn't give a damn about them, truth be told. Can't you send them away?

From: Holly
To: James Lawrence

Sorry James, I can't. I'm guessing these aren't what you like calling 'money' clients?

From: James Lawrence
To: Holly

No, they're what I call 'knobs.'

From: Holly
To: James Lawrence

Come on, I'd like to see you anyway. Do you have your sleeves rolled up today?

From: James Lawrence
To: Holly

You and your arms fetish. I don't have, but I could do, if you roll that skirt up a bit?

From: Holly
To: James Lawrence

It's a deal.

From: James Lawrence
To: Holly

I'll be there before the fat one scratches his chin again.

From: Holly
To: James Lawrence

How did you know he was doing that?

Subject: Rip off

From: James Lawrence
To: Holly

I feel conned.

From: Holly
To: James Lawrence

I only got one arm to look at, so you only got one inch higher. Anyway, what d'you expect me to do—sit there with it around my waist?

From: James Lawrence
To: Holly

Listen, Denham. I want a split in that skirt by next week, or I'll invite the fat boy back and tell him you love him.

From: Holly

To: James Lawrence

Being mean to people doesn't do it for me and you're not getting any split, so forget it.

thursday

Subject: Plans

From: Holly

To: James Lawrence

Are we doing anything this weekend? I haven't been asked yet, and time is ticking on, you know, popular girl, etc.?

Subject: Friday night

From: Jennie Pithwait

To: Holly

Holly,

Champagne-Friday is nearly here again, which should make you happy—if my memory serves me correctly, when we lost you last week, you were found hunched over a table dipping your finger in your glass and writing 'Holly loves Bolly' (I'm presuming this means Bollinger and not a sexual act) on its surface. The trading lot are coming out too, along with most of our team, so we'll be straight down from work. See you then.

Jennie

From: Holly

To: Jennie Pithwait

Hi Jennie,

Thanks for the invite. I'm still recovering from last week—I'm hopefully getting Trisha out too. Are you going clubbing again?

Holly

Subject: What are you up to Trisha?

From: Holly
To: Patricia Gillot

You fancy coming out Friday?

From: Patricia Gillot
To: Holly

Can't, I'm taking my dad to Bingo, always do on a Friday. He looks forward to it. Thanks for asking though.

xx

From: Holly
To: Patricia Gillot

You won't believe I'm still having problems with that parking fine that shouldn't have been given to me.

From: Patricia Gillot
To: Holly

They take diabolical f**king liberties, darlin. My Les thinks it's all a conspiracy.

Subject: Love affair, we need more description

From: Jason GrangerRM
To: Holly; Aisha

So go on then, we're dying to know. More details please, Holly.

From: Holly
To: Aisha; Jason GrangerRM

Are we all friends now? Are you both there?

From: Aisha
To: Holly; Jason GrangerRM

I was being crap, and Jason was rightly annoyed.

From: Jason GrangerRM
To: Holly; Aisha

She's going to be a good girl now. We love her though. So go on, tell us what he looks like again.

From: Holly
To: Aisha; Jason GrangerRM

OK, picture a tall George Clooney, but not quite as good-looking, eyes are different, but same age, etc.

From: Aisha
To: Holly; Jason GrangerRM

A tall George Clooney? George Clooney IS tall—so you're going out with a giant?

From: Holly
To: Aisha; Jason GrangerRM

Oh, is he? OK, Colin Firth.

From: Aisha
To: Holly; Jason GrangerRM

He looks like Colin Firth?

From: Holly
To: Jason GrangerRM; Aisha

No, not really, but you get the picture?

From: Aisha
To: Holly; Jason GrangerRM

No.

From: Jason GrangerRM
To: Holly; Aisha

Not at all ??

From: Holly

To: Aisha; Jason GrangerRM

Anyway, he hasn't called about the weekend yet. We're meant to be seeing each other one of the days, either Friday or Saturday, but nothing's been confirmed. I don't want to look like a pushy clingy type, but it's difficult.

From: Aisha

To: Jason GrangerRM; Holly

Sort it out girl. In the meantime, we want to know what he's like in bed.

From: Jason GrangerRM

To: Holly; Aisha

Yes, does he do the wild thing?

From: Holly

To: Jason GrangerRM; Aisha

? What?

From: Aisha

To: Holly; Jason GrangerRM

The funky Buddha?

From: Holly

To: Aisha; Jason GrangerRM

?

From: Aisha

To: Holly; Jason GrangerRM

DOES HE GO DOWN ON YOU !!

From: Holly

To: Aisha; Jason GrangerRM

AISHA!!!

From: Aisha
To: Holly; Jason GrangerRM

What??

From: Aisha
To: Holly; Jason GrangerRM

I said what? Aren't we playing any more??

From: Jason GrangerRM
To: Aisha; Holly

Aisha, go sit in the corner and serve those guests. You can't sit with the adults any more!

From: Aisha
To: Holly; Jason GrangerRM

But…

From: Jason GrangerRM
To: Aisha; Holly

I said go!

From: Jason GrangerRM
To: Holly; Aisha

That's better, she just doesn't know how to behave. So come on, does he give good head? You can tell me.

From: Holly
To: Jason GrangerRM; Aisha

JASON!!!!

Subject: Guest list

From: Jennie Pithwait
To: Holly

Re: Trisha—of course, although she might not like it at China's, and it's not easy for me to get many people on the guest list.

From: Holly
To: Jennie Pithwait

She can't come out Friday anyway, but she did say to me once that she knows someone who's a cousin of one of the doormen there, so she could probably help in that respect as well …

Subject: Penalty Charge Notice PO092384203

From: London Borough of Camden
To: Holly

Dear Holly Denham,

Thank you for your representations received on 19/03/2008 and your call this morning.

I am currently investigating your case, however, I require to see a copy of the parking permit you discuss in your letter.

You say you had this permit clearly displayed, and one of our parking attendants still gave you a penalty notice.

We will need to see a copy of this permit within 7 days.

Yours sincerely,

Tanya Duggan

From: Holly
To: London Borough of Camden

Dear Tanya,

I kept getting parking tickets from you, so I purposely went to the trouble of buying a yearly parking permit.

I parked on one of your designated bays, but still got a ticket. From what I heard at the time, your traffic warden had a whale of a time running up and down, giggling madly while attaching tickets to every car—permit or no permit. Maybe he was sick, or just sadistic, or perhaps just wanted to reach his Friday bonus.

These things happen. But please explain how am I meant to take a copy of my permit—I'm curious?

Regards,

Holly

From: London Borough of Camden
To: Holly

Holly,

Simply take the permit to a photocopy machine, take a clear copy, and fax us at the number on the bottom of your letter.

Yours sincerely,

Tanya Duggan

From: Holly
To: London Borough of Camden

Tanya,

Agh! There it is. You want me to remove my permit from the windscreen and take a copy, and while it's not in its little plastic holder, one of your chaps will give me a ticket. It's a conspiracy— (my friend Trisha told me).

Holly

From: London Borough of Camden
To: Holly

Holly,

Can you not drive to somewhere where there is a photocopying machine not far from your car?

Tanya Duggan

From: Holly
To: London Borough of Camden

Yes, my work. But then I'll have to pay a congestion charge fine for going into London.

Can't you check on your system that I bought it? Surely you keep records? (If not—it would be a good thing if you did; a tidy desk is a tidy mind.)

Holly

From: London Borough of Camden
To: Holly

Holly,

I understand. However, please be advised that if this information is not received within 7 days then a decision will be made using the information that is currently available to me. Thank you for your cooperation in this matter.

Yours sincerely,

Tanya Duggan

Subject: Penalty Charge Notices

From: Holly
To: Patricia Gillot

They want a copy of the permit—I can't take it out, because I'll get another fine. Do you have any advice? I even tried pretending to be a bit loopy, didn't work.

From: Patricia Gillot
To: Holly

Take a photo of it.

From: Holly
To: Patricia Gillot

Brilliant!

x

Subject: Missed you

From: James Lawrence
To: Holly

Missed you.

From: Holly
To: James Lawrence

Good. Where've you been?

From: James Lawrence
To: Holly

Busy busy busy.

From: Holly
To: James Lawrence

You want to go out Friday or Saturday?

From: James Lawrence
To: Holly

Do we have to do a day in the weekend?

Subject: James is a git!

From: Holly
To: Jason GrangerRM; Aisha

It's official, that's it!!!!!

Subject: Re: Weekend

From: Holly
To: James Lawrence

No, not at all, why? Are you going out partying with the others Friday? I was thinking of going, but I'm not sure.

From: James Lawrence
To: Holly

No, I'm not going out with this lot. I'd prefer to have my nuts covered in treacle and served to Anne Robinson for breakfast.

Subject: Forget it

From: Holly
To: Aisha; Jason GrangerRM

He's nice now.

From: Jason GrangerRM
To: Holly

Oh, good, thanks for telling us. I'll inform the media.

From: Holly
To: Jason GrangerRM

Good. Tell them Holly Denham is alive and happy and still able to attend premiers.

From: Jason GrangerRM
To: Holly

You misunderstand me—I thought you were now single, so I quickly stuck an ad under the personal section for you, asking for partners to participate in sick sex with parsnips and pickles—shall I cancel it or keep it? (spice up your life a bit)???

From: Holly
To: Jason GrangerRM

Cancel it—for the moment at least.

xx

friday

Subject: News from Spain

From: Mum and Dad
To: Holly

Dear Holly,

Well—what's been happening here?

I suppose I should start with your father and his painting. This is something which I feel could get us into hot water. He's being very silly, and it wouldn't surprise me if the Guardia Civil don't arrive at any moment and begin beating down our door to arrest him. Fraud is a serious crime over here, and I didn't move to Spain to begin feeling like I'm married to Ronnie Biggs. Maybe you could have a word with him. I will not tell you what he's up to, I'll leave that to him. Certainly not on email, anyway.

We haven't heard much from you recently. How is your job going? Have you made any new friends? How is Jennie? You don't keep us very well informed of what you're up to there, do you?

Has Jennie managed to open any doors for you in the banking side? I was thinking that maybe me and your father could have a word with her parents. I think if I set my mind to it and did a little investigation, I could come up with their address. Didn't you say they had a holiday house in Puerto Banus? Maybe me and your father could head down there and do a bit of Denham PR. What do you think?

Love, Mum

From: Holly
To: Mum and Dad

Hi Mum,

You sound very upset about everything, and I don't know why. I keep in touch with you and only called you a few days ago, so I think that's a bit unfair. I love you very much—but not much has happened recently. What's this about Dad?

Finally, please please don't do any 'Denham PR.' It's really, really not needed.

I wouldn't know what to do in banking, and I'm very happy doing reception and want to stay here.

Holly

x

From: Mum and Dad
To: Holly

Holly,

I told you I can't tell you about your father and fine, if you don't want me talking to Jennie's parents, I won't.

I'm only trying to be a helpful, caring mother, but if you don't want me sticking my nose in, I understand.

Mum

From: Holly
To: Mum and Dad

Please don't get upset. I'll call you tonight. I have actually got some news I guess you'd like to hear—I have a boyfriend, and he's really nice and works in the bank. There, some good news for you.

Love you.

xxx

From: Mum and Dad
To: Holly

Holly,

What lovely news! We're both so pleased for you. What does he do in the bank?

Love, Mum

x

From: Holly
To: Mum and Dad

Mum, he's a VP (Vice President) (it's an American thing).

x

From: Mum and Dad
To: Holly

VICE PRESIDENT OF THE BANK?????

From: Holly
To: Mum and Dad

No, Mum, there are many VPs. It's not what you think, but yes, it's a little senior.

x

From: Mum and Dad
To: Holly

I'm going to look it up on the web now. Vice President. I'm going to go and tell your father—take his mind off any more scams he might be thinking up.

xx

Subject: Tonight

From: Holly
To: Jennie Pithwait

Hi Jennie,

I can't make tonight, really really sorry, but I've got to go away unexpectedly for the weekend.

Please forgive me.

Holly

xxx

Subject: Sexy Underwear

From: Patricia Gillot
To: Holly

Hey, what's that on your screen? Doesn't look like you're booking a room to me, looks like you're shopping for sexy undies! You saucy thing!

From: Holly
To: Patricia Gillot

It's my brother—thinks it's funny to send me these links and just opened this stuff onto my screen. He's a nightmare, but I love him.

Subject: Something for the weekend

From: Orders@somethingfortheweekend
To: Holly

REF 8989832942 Holly Denham

Thank you for your order. We hope you'll be very happy with your products.
A39 MINI–SPLIT SKIRT SATIN

Subject: They are going global!!

From: Jason GrangerRM
To: Holly

That incredibly sexy couple are at last reaching the audience they deserve—America!!!

From: Holly
To: Jason GrangerRM

Who?

From: Jason GrangerRM
To: Holly

Come on, Holly, think… You should be proud of them, they're the most gloriously celebrated celebrity couple in the UK.

From: Holly
To: Jason GrangerRM

Does he sing?

From: Jason GrangerRM
To: Holly

Mmmm, could be.

From: Holly
To: Jason GrangerRM

Does she model?

From: Jason GrangerRM
To: Holly

Yes! Good. Glad to see all those copies of *OK!* & *Hello!* I leave strewn around your flat are paying off!!! He's a stud and she—well, she's so pink, I could probably convert for her …

From: Holly
To: Jason GrangerRM

Pete and Kate.

From: Jason GrangerRM
To: Holly

10 points to the girl at the back.

From: Holly
To: Jason GrangerRM

You fancy Pete Doherty??

From: Jason GrangerRM
To: Holly

Not that Pete and Kate gloriously celebrated celebrity UK couple, the other Pete and Kate gloriously celebrated celebrity UK couple— Katie Price and Peter Andre. Although you can keep the points, because I can see there's some confusion.

How's your morning, anyway?

From: Holly
To: Jason GrangerRM

Could you be any gayer?

From: Jason GrangerRM
To: Holly

Probably not. Talking of which, me and Aisha are going to GAY tonight... the girl has got to have some fun.

From: Holly
To: Jason GrangerRM

Oh, this is just for her, is it?

From: Jason GrangerRM
To: Holly

Of course, I'm a happily married man.

From: Holly
To: Jason GrangerRM

Great, so it's all 'Aisha and Jason' now is it, thanks for inviting me.

From: Jason GrangerRM
To: Holly

Oh shut it, hollysocks. I know you're spending the weekend with James.

xxx

Subject: Dad's Oil Paintings

From: Holly
To: Granny

Hi Granny,

It was lovely to talk to you the other night, and I was really sorry—once again—that you were left a little in the dark about what to do with the computer. Hope your screen is now refreshing and you get my email. Also, do you know anything about Dad and his painting?

Holly

X

From: Granny
To: Holly

Holly,

You are wonderful. I feel like such a ninny sitting there, staring at this computer for days on end, only to find out the thing needs refreshing. And then I had the lovely feeling of seeing all these nice letters/emails waiting patiently for me.

Your father and I have been up to mischief. He recently painted someone's baby as a commission, and the word went around the town, and everyone was talking about how super it was. So before he knew it he had people bringing their baby photos for him every day and he ended up with eight commissions for people's baby portraits. Now your father paints because he likes painting oil landscapes, not oil babies, but your mother was so proud of him, she wouldn't let him refuse a commission.

This is where I got involved Holly, because I told him to just paint the eyes, nose, and mouth of one baby and then run off another eight copies. Then all he needed to do for each one was just add a little hair or baby clothes to make each one individual, and no one would know.

As it happens, it all worked like a dream, and your mother would never have twigged except for me and my big mouth. I was there on Monday with your parents while someone had come to pick up their painting. They were saying how wonderful the portrait was, and how the little one had her father's eyes, and I said quietly to your dad, as I elbowed him and giggled, that they actually had Jose's eyes from No. 10.

This your mother overheard, and I think that's when she became upset. So that's the big news from Spain. It's really made my month. I've thought of some good ideas for your father and me to get up to new mischief in that bank of yours.

(I'm just pulling your skinny leg, don't worry.)

Miss you so much,

Love, Granny

xxxx

Subject: Romantic Break

From: Jason GrangerRM
To: Holly

So, where is he taking you then?

From: Holly
To: Jason GrangerRM

I don't know yet, he's not told me.

From: Jason GrangerRM
To: Holly

So what time is he picking you up?

From: Holly
To: Jason GrangerRM

Don't know—still waiting for a call, etc… ?

Subject: I just heard the news!

From: Aisha
To: Holly; Jason GrangerRM

I just heard about you being stood up, the little sh*t.

From: Holly
To: Aisha; Jason GrangerRM

THANKS JASON!

I am not being stood up, I think he's just really busy today.

From: Aisha
To: Holly; Jason GrangerRM

Yeah, busy today—I get that one too. They're all fuc*kers, really they are. Come out with us.

xxx

From: Holly
To: Aisha; Jason GrangerRM

Aisha, please sort out your stars!!—Jason, are you there??

From: Aisha

To: Holly; Jason GrangerRM

He's coming back in a moment, I can see he looks really busy. So we're going to GAY come with us??

Subject: The banker

From: Mum and Dad

To: Holly

Holly,

I've looked it up on the web in the Wikipedia and it says—"In business, vice president refers to a rank in senior or middle management. Most companies that use this title generally have large numbers of people with the title of vice president with different types of vice president (e.g. vice president for finance)." So it sounds promising, doesn't it.

Love, Mum

From: Holly

To: Mum and Dad

Yes, Mum, it sounds promising.

Subject: James

From: Aisha

To: Holly; Jason GrangerRM

Hey, maybe he's going out with your friends upstairs?? and hasn't thought to break it to you yet, the Sh*tbag?

From: Holly

To: Aisha; Jason GrangerRM

Haven't you got work to do? Why don't you help Jason out?

From: Aisha

To: Holly; Jason GrangerRM

He looks like he's handling it. Oh no, he's not. I'm not getting involved.

From: Holly
To: Aisha; Jason GrangerRM

Involved, isn't that what you're meant to be doing as a receptionist for him??

From: Aisha
To: Holly

Don't have a go at me just because you've been stood up. It happens to me all the time!

From: Holly
To: Aisha; Jason GrangerRM

I have not BEEN STOOD UP!

Subject: The banker

From: Mum and Dad
To: Holly

Middle management—I guess it depends how many VPs there are in your company. Do you know how many there are there?

From: Holly
To: Mum and Dad

No Mum.

From: Mum and Dad
To: Holly

OK, well, it's all good news. I shouldn't keep you. I'm sure you're very busy there. Your father and I are very proud of you.
Love, Mum

Subject: Strange but true

From: Pregnant Pam
To: Holly

There's more discharge in my knickers today than I have even eaten. I can't hold anything down. Have you got time to talk, sweetie?
Pam

x

From: Holly
To: Pregnant Pam

Sorry I can't Pam. I'll catch up on the mobile over the weekend, and you can tell me all about it.

xxx

Subject: The weekend

From: Holly
To: James Lawrence

Not heard from you—can you please tell me what is happening???

Subject: Spanish Life

From: Alice and Matt
To: Holly

Hi Holls,

Just got to tell you this, as I know how much you care about our snakes really.xx

We've just come back from the vets. Bobby (the snake) isn't very well. He's the biggest of all Matt's animals, 2 meters long and weighing in at 5 kilos of solid muscle, so I went along to help Matt hold him while he had his jabs. I think we'll now have to give him his antibiotic jabs ourselves, because I don't think the vet is very keen on having him back. Waiting their turn in the room outside were a lot of other people sitting with their pets (mostly English— reassuring their dogs/cats that a vet's surgery is a lovely place to be). You see it's not the head that's the problem, you can pin that down, but while you're keeping your eye on his mouth, you tend to forget about the rest of his body—which began happily trashing the place (Bobby likes to thrash it about a bit). We're all screaming at each other, a glass beaker has smashed on the floor, I stamped on Matt's foot in the havoc and ended up being jabbed with the needle. 'It's only antibiotica, no worries' said the vet, whilst blood poured from my hand. I can tell you, those pets outside were not looking so keen any more. When we came out, you've never seen a row of faces so transformed. One woman gasped when she saw Bobby, and Matt points at her Shih Tzu and says, 'you want to hang on to that, love, he's only bitesize, and he's already swallowed the vet!' (I was very embarrassed). How we're going to manage to do these injections by ourselves every day for the next week, I don't know.

How's your morning?

Subject: You're in trouble

From: Aisha
To: Holly; Jason GrangerRM

You're in trouble, young lady. I just called your work, and your friend Trisha said you weren't in yet!!!

Subject: Meeting

From: Judy Perkins
To: Holly; Patricia Gillot

Dear Holly & Trisha,

I need to organise a meeting with you. I am thinking of some possible times next week. Can you let me know if 6 p.m. Tuesday can be confirmed?

Regards,

Judy

From: Holly
To: Judy Perkins

Hi Judy,

Yes, that's confirmed.

Regards,

Holly

Subject: Meeting?

From: Holly
To: Patricia Gillot

Is this meeting about me? What's happened?

From: Patricia Gillot
To: Holly

Sorry, I was miles away. Don't panic, she thinks you were on the 5th floor doing room checks. This is about the annual results stuff.

xxxx

Tell me about your weekend?

From: Holly
To: Patricia Gillot

It was great. You bad woman you ...

From: Patricia Gillot
To: Holly

He made me promise, darlin. I was dying to tell you Friday, but I didn't—I was a good girl and kept shtum!!

From: Holly
To: Patricia Gillot

I thought he'd forgotten about it, I really did.

Subject: Dirty Stop Out

From: Jason GrangerRM
To: Holly; Aisha

I've just heard from Aisha—you're not even in yet!!! And why didn't I get any more messages??? No update since Saturday? We need answers, and we need them now!

Subject: My weekend break

From: Holly
To: Patricia Gillot

What did he tell you then on Friday?

From: Patricia Gillot
To: Holly

He just turned up in that lovely motor and told me to make sure you didn't get in a strop and walk out, silly b*gger—he's lucky, cause you looked like you had the right hump until you saw him. Wish I'd had a camera.

From: Holly
To: Patricia Gillot

Guess where we went ...

From: Patricia Gillot
To: Holly

Where?

From: Holly
To: Patricia Gillot

He bought me a dress for it.... ?

From: Patricia Gillot
To: Holly

I love this man!

From: Holly
To: Patricia Gillot

and a hat ...

From: Patricia Gillot
To: Holly

You lucky cow, he took you to the races?

From: Holly
To: Patricia Gillot

Had just the best weekend. I wanted to bet on a horse, but after looking at them trotting around the start, I must admit—it was slim pickings.

From: Patricia Gillot
To: Holly

Lucky you.

From: Holly
To: Patricia Gillot

Get it, 'Slim Pickings?'

From: Patricia Gillot
To: Holly

Yes, I got it, darlin, funny.

Subject: My morning

From: Holly
To: Aisha; Jason GrangerRM

Hi guys,

It hasn't stopped since I got here. We've been rushed off our feet, etc. I couldn't keep in touch on Sunday, because I didn't have my phone any more (I dropped it down the toilet). I think I've had about 2 hours' sleep, and it's really beginning to catch up with me.

xxxx

From: Jason GrangerRM
To: Holly; Aisha

I'm glad you didn't try and fish it out—tell me, my classy friend—who was snooting it up with royalty at the Grand National... you didn't have one arm of your dress halfway down a Aintree bog on Saturday, did you? Please say you didn't?

From: Holly
To: Jason GrangerRM; Aisha

Of course not. I used a brush.

From: Jason GrangerRM
To: Holly; Aisha

Oh Holly.

From: Holly

To: Aisha; Jason GrangerRM

And a few bits of toilet paper.

From: Jason GrangerRM

To: Holly; Aisha

I hope you didn't tell your escort of your adventures? Men have a thing about that. Women's nails should be manicured to perfection, not dripping with pooh.

From: Holly

To: Jason GrangerRM; Aisha

Of course I didn't! Anyway, where's Aisha? I need her advice.

From: Jason GrangerRM

To: Holly; Aisha

Our happy little sexpot has gone to lunch. I'll tell her when she's back that you are in need of her services.

Subject: HOLLY DENHAM'S SUBSCRIPTION To: HOT NAKED GIRLS

From: Charlie Denham

To: Holly

Got another inspection this Friday, so some praying might come in handy (if you can tell Alice). Also managed to talk some local artists from the college into lending me their sculptures, and I got a bunch of old cages for hot girls to dance in—by the way, do you know any hot girls who'd fancy spending a sweaty night in a cage—possibly wriggling????
Charlie

From: Holly

To: Charlie Denham

No, I don't—funny that, isn't it?
PS re: the subject box—?!!

Subject: Monday blues

From: James Lawrence
To: Holly

Miss you, honey pie, sugar lumps, squidgy fruit, strawberry knickers.

From: Holly
To: James Lawrence

You said we hadn't reached cutzie names stage yet?

From: James Lawrence
To: Holly

I know, sweet pea, but I'm feeling reckless. I called you just now and enjoyed a dirty conversation with a sex-mad toilet attendant in Liverpool. It was only after I'd agreed to a marathon bonking session over the back of a cistern that I realised it wasn't you, but a chap named Doug, and it was me who was going to be over the cistern. I politely declined.

How are you anyway?

From: Holly
To: James Lawrence

Good. I still can't believe I did that with my phone. I'm really annoyed. I can't take the parking permit pictures now. Damn.

From: James Lawrence
To: Holly

What interesting hobbies you have.

From: Holly
To: James Lawrence

No, it's because of a fine—long story.

From: James Lawrence
To: Holly

Is fumble bum tired?

From: Holly
To: James Lawrence

Fumble bum?

Not sure you've quite got the hang of this yet. Anyway, it's not me—it's Aisha—my friend who likes nicknames.

From: James Lawrence
To: Holly

Oh, I remember you mentioning your 'hot' friend—so, when do I get to meet her?

From: Holly
To: James Lawrence

When hell freezes over.

From: James Lawrence
To: Holly

Is that a definite no?

From: Holly
To: James Lawrence

I'm busy. Isn't there a deal somewhere that needs putting to bed or something?

From: James Lawrence
To: Holly

I was going to suggest it myself, but glad you made the first move. Come on, can't you leave early?

Subject: Just got your message

From: Aisha
To: Holly

Sorry, I've been busy here—you know how it is when you value your job and take it seriously… How is the dirty stop-out feeling??????

From: Holly
To: Aisha

Bad. I was going to ask your advice earlier—for how to get through the day when you've not slept.

From: Aisha
To: Holly

Oh, it's quite easy, I usually go talk to a guy called Trevor, but you'll probably prefer just drinking a few espressos.

tuesday

Subject: Claim

From: Holly
To: TOTALTFTIns-Claim-Dept

To whom it may concern:

I took out insurance for my mobile phone, and I now need a replacement please. I dropped my last one as I was getting off a bus, and it got flattened.

Can you let me know how I go about getting a new one?

Regards,

Holly Denham

From: TOTALTFTIns-Claim-Dept
To: Holly

REF 23400000000089888

Dear Holly Denham:

Thank you for your email.

Arranging a replacement phone for you could not be simpler. Simply send us the bits of the broken phone, and we'll arrange for your new one to be posted out to you.

Thank you.

Yours sincerely,

Frank Didman

Subject: Any Advice Welcome

From: Holly
To: Aisha; Jason GrangerRM

Hi you two,

I'm trying to arrange for my new phone to be sorted out, but they want to see the bits. What should I do?

From: Jason GrangerRM
To: Holly; Aisha

What bits? I thought you dropped it down the toilet?

From: Holly
To: Jason GrangerRM; Aisha

I thought I might not be covered for toilet mishaps, so I lied.

From: Jason GrangerRM
To: Holly; Aisha

What did your mother tell you about lying?

From: Holly
To: Jason GrangerRM; Aisha

That it's OK to lie about three things: your age, a man's performance in bed, and the recipe for her steak and kidney pie (it's a Denham secret). And I promise, this is what she told me. I'm never likely to need to lie about the pie, so I'm swapping that one for insurance claims.

??? What do you think?

From: Jason GrangerRM
To: Holly; Aisha

You're swapping a lie about a pie, for major league insurance fraud? I'm not sure a judge would think it a fair swap, even with the added smiley face …

From: Holly
To: Jason GrangerRM; Aisha

You're not serious?

From: Jason GrangerRM
To: Holly; Aisha

Of course I'm not serious. Just get an old phone and run over it— problem solved.

Subject: Urgent Meeting Request

From: James Lawrence
To: Holly

Accept…Tentative…Decline…Propose New Time.
MEETING REQUEST FOR HOLLY DENHAM AT 3 P.M.

From: Holly
To: James Lawrence

Tentative.
I remember the last meeting, to make sure it's a real meeting I need to know—
A: What the meeting is about
B: Where the meeting will be held
Yours,
Holly

From: James Lawrence
To: Holly

Holly,
To answer your questions:

A: What the meeting is about

Your lack of respect for senior members of staff and your ability to communicate professionally.

B: Where the meeting will be held

In the lift at approx 3:03 p.m.—where I will be conducting a thorough linguistic evaluation of our newest and naughtiest receptionist.

I will be sending the lift down for you at exactly 3: 02p.m.

I will expect you to be in there waiting for me when I enter at 3:03 p.m. on the 4th floor.

Any questions, email my secretary.

James Lawrence

A very important person

PS. I expect the top three buttons of your suit and shirt to be undone—slutty look essential.

Subject: Prank Calls

From: Holly
To: Jason GrangerRM; Aisha

I'll get you both back for that one! Those in glass houses …

From: Jason GrangerRM
To: Holly; Aisha

Oh hi Holly,

How's it going today. We've been really busy. What's up?

From: Holly
To: Aisha; Jason GrangerRM

Don't try that one!! I even heard Aisha laughing in the background!!

From: Aisha
To: Holly; Jason GrangerRM

HA HA HA HA

That was so funny. Did you actually say it out loud?

From: Holly
To: Aisha; Jason GrangerRM

Yes.

Don't worry, your time will come… both of you!

PS I just got an email from James asking me to meet him in the lift …

Subject: What was that about?

From: Patricia Gillot
To: Holly

What did you just say to them?

From: Holly
To: Patricia Gillot

I got a call from someone saying they had an urgent message for one of the gentlemen in reception—a Mr Vingbender—they said his first name was Ray. SO I just asked our clients if any of them was a raving bender. Great.

It turned out to be Jason and Aisha—of course.

From: Patricia Gillot
To: Holly

Luckily they didn't understand you, girl. Could have been bad. You should get them back for that.

Subject: How exciting—lift—meeting?

From: Jason GrangerRM
To: Holly; Aisha

TELL US??? So, are you going to go????

From: Aisha
To: Holly; Jason GrangerRM

Of course she is!!

> **From:** Holly
> **To:** Aisha; Jason GrangerRM
>
> No, I'm not going.

> **From:** Aisha
> **To:** Jason GrangerRM; Holly
>
> I'll go!!!

> **From:** Jason GrangerRM
> **To:** Holly; Aisha
>
> Unfortunately Aisha, I don't think Holly was asking for a stand-in.
> James = Holly's boyfriend
> Dave, Peter, Paul, Matthew, Mark, Luke, and any number of Johns
> = Aisha's boyfriends.

> **From:** Aisha
> **To:** Jason GrangerRM; Holly
>
> You're not funny, Jason. So come on Hollysocks—are you going
> to go??????

> **From:** Holly
> **To:** Aisha; Jason GrangerRM
>
> NO.
> I don't know. Sh*t.

Subject: Someone Once Said ...

> **From:** Jason GrangerRM
> **To:** Holly; Aisha
>
> Time waits for no man.
> COME ON HOLLY. Tick tock tick tock, you've got 7 minutes
> to decide.

> **From:** Aisha
> **To:** Holly; Jason GrangerRM
>
> Come on, Holly, do it do it do it do it!!!!!!!!

From: Holly
To: Aisha; Jason GrangerRM

oohhhhhhhhhhhhhh don't know.

From: Jason GrangerRM
To: Holly; Aisha

I'm sorry, I'm going to have to rush you on this one. I need your final answer, you have less than 2 minutes left!!!!

From: Holly
To: Aisha; Jason GrangerRM

No.

From: Jason GrangerRM
To: Holly; Aisha

30 seconds left. Is that your final answer?

Subject: Meeting—sorry

From: Holly
To: Patricia Gillot

Sorry Trisha, I completely forgot about a meeting upstairs. I've got to leave now, sorry.

xxx

Subject: Romance or Filth, we need to know???

From: Jason GrangerRM
To: Holly; Aisha

What's happening there? Don't leave us hanging????

From: Holly
To: Aisha; Jason GrangerRM

Out of Office AutoReply: Romance or Filth, we need to know???

Unfortunately, I am out of the office. If you require urgent assistance, please contact Patricia Gillot at PGillot@HuerstWright. com. Otherwise, I will be back soon.

Kindest regards,

Holly Denham

Subject: What meeting?

From: Patricia Gillot
To: Holly

I can't see a meeting in the diary. Where've you been, and why you looking so flushed?

From: Holly
To: Patricia Gillot

Sorry Trish, I didn't mean to be so long. I got grabbed as I was coming back by Judy, who wanted to talk about this conference thing.

From: Patricia Gillot
To: Holly

Coming back from where?

From: Holly
To: Patricia Gillot

Coming back from my meeting.

From: Patricia Gillot
To: Holly

With who?

I know where you went first, you saucy girl. You went up to see your fella again didn't you. Oh, I wish I could have an office romance. It's not fair.

From: Holly
To: Patricia Gillot

Ralph?

From: Patricia Gillot
To: Holly

I couldn't. I'd love to, but I couldn't. Maybe I could enjoy setting him up with that stroppy cow.

From: Holly
To: Patricia Gillot

Mrs Huerst? She'd eat him alive, poor Ralph.

Subject: Are you there?

From: Holly
To: Jason GrangerRM; Aisha

I did it.

My heart is still racing—but mainly because I thought I was in trouble when I got collared by Judy, but then she just wanted to talk about work. I grabbed the lift and went to the fourth floor …

From: Jason GrangerRM
To: Holly; Aisha

So????

From: Holly
To: Jason GrangerRM; Aisha

We went down to the basement …

From: Aisha
To: Jason GrangerRM; Holly

Holly !!!

Stop doing that dot dot dot thing. Tell us everything, we want to know, did you shag him in the basement???

From: Holly
To: Aisha; Jason GrangerRM

I wanted to take my time to write this, OK?

From the beginning …

I took the lift to the fourth floor. He stepped into the lift and grabbed me, and we kissed. But it was so passionate, he tugged my hair back and kissed me on the mouth. I was coming back up for another kiss, and he held my hair for a moment and smiled. It was raunchy as hell! While he held me there he looked over to the buttons and pressed for the basement… I never heard the doors open at all—I guess he must have blocked them open with his foot, but to be honest, I wasn't really thinking about it, he had his hand squeezing my bum and I could feel him (pressing against me). I won't go into more detail, we didn't do much more (OK I've got to tell you this bit, because I know Aisha will be proud of me. At one point, he was biting my breast hard, which drove me crazy.). Help! I want to start dancing around the reception area and singing. Do you think I should sing? ? ?

From: Jason GrangerRM
To: Holly; Aisha

Don't sing, for the love of all that's beautiful, DON'T SING!!
Love you.
x Jason.

wednesday

Subject: Jennie's party

From: Toby Williams
To: Holly

Holly,
Seeing as we're now working buddies, and you left so quickly when I arrived at Jennie's, I thought it would make sense to bury the hatchet, if you like, and go out for a drink this week.
Toby

Toby Williams, VP Corporate Finance, H&W, High Holborn WC2 6NP

Subject: Toby

From: Holly
To: Charlie Denham

First contact has been made… he just emailed me.

Subject: Kettle calling pot black

From: Aisha
To: Holly

So tell me Holly, how does it feel like to be such a slut???? Shagging in the basement, coming to work without any sleep, whatever's next? I guess it won't be too long before you're going at it on the front desk with Trisha pushing the passes out between your legs? Morning.

From: Holly
To: Aisha

Very funny, but not really fair—I didn't actually do anything much in the basement, and I've NEVER had a go at YOU.

From: Aisha
To: Holly

Never had a go?? What about the half hour lecture when I got caught in the hotel room!!!!! 'Aisha, you're not taking your job seriously, you're letting the side down, you're letting Jason down, Aisha, can't you control your urges?????!' I was thinking, maybe you should wear a T-shirt when you get in that state again, something like 'Holly's got the horn' so people know to steer clear of you, unless they want to be dragged into the lift for a gangbang Holly-style… oh, and he fingered my buttons, oh, and the doors were closing, oh, and… is it Holly Denham or Jackie Collins? Looks like you've changed over night. ha ha ha ha ha ha haaa ha that's the last word, I'm going good-bye horny Holly

xxxx

From: Holly
To: Aisha

Aisha Peters! You think you're so funny, I'll just wait until you fall off that high horse and then we'll see, yes indeedy.

Subject: TW*T

From: Charlie Denham
To: Holly

What did the sh*t bag say?

From: Holly
To: Charlie Denham

Something about going for a drink!!!!????

From: Charlie Denham
To: Holly

I'll kill him, tell him your brother still wants to talk to him, urgently.

From: Holly
To: Charlie Denham

Thanks, but I wouldn't want you to do anything.

xxxx

Hope your club's looking better. I think putting the art in there makes sense—the cages, I'm not so sure about.

x

Subject: No thanks

From: Holly
To: Toby Williams

I am on reception, you are in corporate finance. I am not your working buddy and—get lost.

From: Toby Williams
To: Holly

Like that is it?

From: Holly
To: Toby Williams

Yes.

Subject: HUERST & WRIGHT 25 YEAR BIRTHDAY

From: Randolph Timothy Huerst
To: Holly

Dear Holly,

As you are aware, here in London, Huerst & Wright will be proudly commemorating their European Headquarters' 25th year in business next month.

To celebrate this milestone achievement, we are holding a gala dinner at the Dorchester, and I wish to make it clear that I expect everyone to attend. It will be a fantastic night and certainly a wonderful way to mark this auspicious day in the history books. For this special occasion, partners are also welcome.

Randolph Timothy Huerst, Huerst & Wright

Subject: Dating

From: Holly
To: Patricia Gillot

I just got asked out on a date by randy old Randolph.

From: Patricia Gillot
To: Holly

Me too, at the Dorchester. To be honest, I don't fancy it. I might ask him back to the wharf instead, we could have a pint in the Gun, followed by a knees up at the Watermans (there's usually a disco around 11). He'd want a puke in the bushes about 12, and he could catch a lift home with dangerous Dan after that. Hey, you better be sitting with me, we'll have a right laugh.

From: Holly
To: Patricia Gillot

Of course I will

xx

Subject: HUERST & WRIGHT 25 YEAR BIRTHDAY

From: James Lawrence
To: Holly

Birthday b*llocks.

The only way I'm getting through that dribble is if I book us a suite. We can show our faces for the old man's speech then back upstairs for some interoffice bonding?

What say you, Denham?

PS How's the nipple?

From: Holly
To: James Lawrence

Sore. You've made twisting very difficult.

From: James Lawrence
To: Holly

Don't twist then. You're on reception, Holly, not *Strictly Come Dancing*.

From: Holly
To: James Lawrence

Anyway, I'll be going with Trisha.

From: James Lawrence
To: Holly

Fantastic news.

Subject: Baby clothes, boy or girl?

From: Holly
To: Pregnant Pam

How did it go today? Do we know yet whether it's a boy or girl?

From: Pregnant Pam
To: Holly

Hi Holly,

Sorry, I forgot you couldn't talk earlier. I went for the scan today and had a horrible journey on the way. It seems like you give up your right to privacy when you're pregnant—everyone wants a touch of your tummy and grabs it before you can say no. I was dying to find out the baby's sex today, and I was in such a tiz you won't believe what I did, Holly. Are you alright to chat or are you busy?

From: Holly
To: Pregnant Pam

Hi,

No I'm here, I'm here. Go on.

xxx

Subject: Keep forgetting to ask you

From: James Lawrence
To: Holly

Who's Toby?

Subject: Sister needs dating advice

From: Holly
To: Charlie Denham

I go to lunch on top of the world, I come back, and suddenly everything's going wrong. I need your help. Did I tell you I've been dating someone at work? Actually, I know I haven't told you, but there it is. I have, and he's a really nice guy, but he's just asked me who Toby is. What should I say (Toby only happens to work on the same floor)?

Holly

PS Don't worry if you have no advice at all, I know you are a guy, and you find touchy-feely problems difficult.

x

Subject: Some wonderful news Holly

From: Granny
To: Holly

Dear Holly,

It was so lovely to see you when you came here. I do wish you could come out to Spain more often, even if it's only for the weekend. I know you say it's expensive, but since your mother showed me how, your old gran has found she's a bit of a wiz at the computer. I've found flights for just £20 on a site, imagine that! I've also given them your email address and name so they can send you their information on a daily basis.

Love, Granny

xxxx

Subject: CHEAP FLIGHTS!!

From: BEST FLIGHTS AROUND
To: HOLLY

Holly Denham,

BEST FLIGHTS AROUND
FLY To: MALTA From: £19!!!!!
Simply log on to our site!!!!!
OPEN 7 DAYS / 24 HOURS A DAY
JUST CALL IN OR LOG ON

Subject: Deals Deals Deals

From: Savings at You-Fly-We-Pay
To: Holly

DEALS DEALS DEALS
YOU FLY WE PAY!!!!!!!
You're now registered with our NETWORK and will be receiving
our UPDATES!!!!!!
SIMPLY THE CHEAPEST FLIGHTS AROUND!!!!!!

Subject: Are you heading off?

From: CHEAP FLIGHTS FOR EVERYONE ALL THE TIME.COM
To: Holly

Then you need look no further. We have cheap flights for everyone
all the time, that's why we're called 'cheap flights for everyone all
the time,' crazy but true!!! If you book your flight today, we'll give
you a free plane/hat.
COOL !!!!
BOOK TODAY BEFORE THEY'RE GONE!!!!!!

Subject: So ...

From: Pregnant Pam
To: Holly

Holly,

I went into the toilet with the sample cup, and I was so on edge,
because I was thinking, if it's a girl then I can dress her up in lots of

pink stuff, and we can go out together, and it'll be all girls together, but I'd probably worry more, so it might be better if it was a boy, and that's when I dropped the cup down the loo!!! You know what it's like, because you told me about your phoneloo experiences and without thinking, I've dived in and pulled it out, full of what was left in the toilet bowl, and I'm thinking—it's alright, it's alright, they'll never know, it's the same thing anyway. So I've walked back with it, then realised what I'm doing, but she's caught me, so I had to explain she couldn't have this one, because it was toilet pee water. Oh God, Holly, am I cracking up??

Subject: It's your lucky day

From: Flights To The Moon And Back
To: Holly

FLIGHTS FLIGHTS FLIGHTS FLIGHTS FLIGHTS FLIGHTS AND FLIGHTS FLIGHTS FLIGHTS FLIGHTS FLIGHTS AND MORE FLIGHTS!!!!!!!!
You can have a cheap holiday for less than £50!!
You could be …
Eating Paella on the Costa del Sol from £20 (Spain)
Eating Pizza in the Sistine Chapel from £29 (Italy)
Eating burgers in Central Park from £80 (USA)
Book now!! Before they've gone!!!!

Subject: Granny—Cheap Flights

From: Holly
To: Granny

Thank you Granny, it's very kind of you to register for me, I'll be sure to check out those deals. No need to put my name anywhere else though, I'm looking now with much hope. Thank you so much.
Love you,
xxxxx Holly

Subject: TOBY

From: James Lawrence
To: Holly

Did you get my email about Toby?

Subject: Wait, before you do anything else ...

From: Flights To The Moon And Back
To: Holly

... TAKE A FLIGHT!!!!!!

You know you want to !!!!

You can have a cheap holiday for less than £50!!

You could be ...

Eating Paella on the Costa del Sol from £20 (Spain)

Eating Pizza in the Sistine Chapel from £29 (Italy)

Eating burgers in Central Park from £80 (USA)

Book now!! Before they've gone!!!!

From: Holly
To: Flights To The Moon And Back

Thanks for your flight info but:

Those flights are just one way and the return flights are £200 plus £100 tax plus VAT. So yes, if I only had £50 then I COULD be in Spain, eating paella, but without a return flight I'd be scraping it from the bottom of a beach bin and eating it from a hot flip-flop. SO PLEASE LEAVE ME ALONE

(and take me off your database)

Subject: Pregnant is Beautiful! YES IT IS

From: Holly
To: Pregnant Pam

Don't worry about thinking you're mad, you're not honestly. xxxxx Being pregnant is a tough thing, but it's also such a beautiful thing too. xxx

So tell me, are you having a boy or a girl??

From: Pregnant Pam
To: Holly

Beautiful?? Pregnancy??

You should see me, I'm a fat lump, my fingers have swelled up to the size of burgers, and my legs look like tree trunks. I sweat, I ache, and Holly, I puke. No, I've no idea what the baby is, the nurse really winds me up. From what I've seen I'm giving birth to a small snowstorm off Scotland. She keeps holding up this bit of plastic to the light and saying 'there's its little head, and there's its little body' and I've realised now she's mad. She's probably been doing this for so many years, she's lost it. I bet other couples have their scans, and they look at perfect pictures of their babies in clarity—my nurse had a machine which stopped working years ago and needs retuning, but no, she thinks she sees a baby. At least it's only one.

Love, Pam

From: Holly
To: Pregnant Pam

Sorry I haven't been around for a while. Can we meet up at the weekend? I'm sure you look lovely!

xxx

Subject: Where are you?

From: Holly
To: Charlie Denham

I've tried your mobile, and I can't get through. You're the only one who knows about Toby, so just wanted to run it past you. xxxx
Sh*t.

I really like the guy I'm seeing—and I haven't emailed him back yet. I'll just have to make something up.

x

Subject: Toby

From: Holly
To: James Lawrence

Yes I heard Toby had come here. He was just some guy from my
school, I didn't have much to do with him.

xxxx

Subject: Are you sure???

From: Patricia Gillot
To: Holly

You don't mind doing the later shift????

From: Holly
To: Patricia Gillot

No, I'm fine, I'm happy doing 11–6 from now on.

xxxx

have a lovely evening

thursday

Subject: Car problems

From: Holly
To: James Lawrence

Morning James,

Do you have your car here?

From: James Lawrence
To: Holly

No, Iain does, I'm sure he'd let you borrow it for a few minutes.
Where you going?

J

From: Holly
To: James Lawrence

Oh great, can I borrow it at lunch time? I won't be long. What car is it?

From: James Lawrence
To: Holly

I think it's a Mini.

From: Holly
To: James Lawrence

Oh, that's no good, do you know anyone else up there who could help me?

From: James Lawrence
To: Holly

What's wrong with the Mini??

From: Holly
To: James Lawrence

Not heavy enough, long story.

xx

From: James Lawrence
To: Holly

Why do women think putting a couple of x's at the bottom of their emails will stop men asking any more questions?

From: Holly
To: James Lawrence

Don't know.

xx

From: James Lawrence
To: Holly

I know a jerk with a Chelsea tractor up here, he's just a slap around the head away??
Xx

From: Holly
To: James Lawrence

OK, the reason a Mini is no good—I've got a Mini too, and I tried to run over my phone this morning but it didn't work, so I need a heavier car, long story.

From: James Lawrence
To: Holly

There are other ways to get back at your phone you know, if it's been naughty, you could simply make it communicate in Japanese, put it on silent, or even take away its battery privileges.
Are you OK Holly, is the job getting to you?
J

Subject: Flights—problem

From: Holly
To: Alice and Matt

Hi,

Granny's so lovely, but she's beginning to think I'm cheap… and doesn't understand why I haven't got the money to fly out more. When I mentioned it being expensive, she began looking for flights.

From: Alice and Matt
To: Holly

Hi sweetie,

Don't worry, I'll have a quiet word with her without having to spill the beans.
Xxx

Subject: Boredom

From: James Lawrence
To: Holly

Holly,

If it's simply a way of you girls getting through the boredom of a long lunch hour, I've heard backgammon is quite good. Obviously it doesn't match the thrill of seeing your phone take a beating, but I dare say very little does. Also, if you put the pieces away afterwards and resist the temptation of setting fire to the board, you can use it again?

J

Subject: Help is never far away

From: James Lawrence
To: Holly

I found this for you …

Thought it might help

Do you sometimes feel everyone's against you?

Do you often get strange looks from coworkers?

Do your friends ever worry about your mental health?

Does blind rage sometimes take over?

If so, then maybe you're suffering from stress and anger issues.

Join our team of anger management classes today.

You are not alone!!!

Anger&StressManagement-UK.CB

Subject: Toby

From: James Lawrence
To: Holly

This Toby fella, are you sure you don't know him better than you say???

Subject: Help

From: Holly
To: Charlie Denham

Help.

I'm up a huge tree without a paddle and you're not answering your phone. Help Charlie help.

From: Charlie Denham
To: Holly

Hi,

Just got your messages etc and email. Sorry, been up my own tree without a paddle with stuff here (whatever that means). The main thing I'd recommend is just not to lie, because guys talk, and you're bound to be caught out, but on the other hand, don't tell him everything obviously.

Charlie

From: Holly
To: Charlie Denham

Too late, I lied already. Aaaaaaaaaaaaaa
Holly

Subject: Earth to Holly …

From: Jennie Pithwait
To: Holly

Hi,

I haven't had a chance to call you back, because the last few days have been crazy. So, what have you been up to recently, where have you been, tell me everything???
Jennie

From: Holly

To: Jennie Pithwait

Nothing really exciting to tell you, we've got to go out again soon. Damn, lots of clients coming in. I'll call you later.

xxxx

Holly

Subject: Telling stories

From: Holly

To: Aisha; Jason GrangerRM

Do you ever find days when all your lying seems to catch up with you at once???

Subject: Toby

From: Holly

To: James Lawrence

It's manic down here at the moment, so can't get away, but I'll call you as soon as I can get a break. There's a bit more to explain.

x

Subject: Lying

From: Aisha

To: Holly

Yes, I once got caught with an ounce of dope up my snatch (wrapped in cellophane). I told them it was there because I just couldn't swallow any more. I know how you feel. x

From: Holly

To: Aisha

???

Subject: Aisha

From: Jason GrangerRM
To: Holly

She's a delight, isn't she? Aisha just told me matter-of-factly what she emailed you. But don't worry, Hollykins, people will forgive the odd lie. I'll call you tonight.

x

Subject: Interesting... So Toby was your childhood sweetheart???

From: James Lawrence
To: Holly

Don't bother calling me! You're obviously a lying, conniving harlot who has without any shadow of a doubt previously kissed someone of the opposite sex.

How can I possibly accept a dinner invitation to your flat tonight?

J

From: Holly
To: James Lawrence

Are we having dinner tonight??

From: James Lawrence
To: Holly

Of course, I love lying, conniving harlots. If you can talk your scary gatekeeper into nipping off for a fag, we could roll around behind that unfeasibly tidy reception desk. That's if we don't get disturbed by any of your previous flings. Just interested—are there any more lurking in the building?

From: Holly
To: James Lawrence

Not one—honest. Also, she's not scary, she's lovely, and lastly, I don't know what 'rolling around' involves.

From: James Lawrence
To: Holly

Toby said you do …

From: Holly
To: James Lawrence

Toby is nothing but a lowlife skank.

From: James Lawrence
To: Holly

Really? I must admit, he does strike me as the skanky type (if I've used the word correctly).

From: Holly
To: James Lawrence

You have, perfectly.

From: James Lawrence
To: Holly

So tonight?

From: Holly
To: James Lawrence

Meet at the usual place down the road—7:10 P.M.
Holly
x
PS Talking of desks… what is going on with your bombsite????

From: James Lawrence
To: Holly

Maid's been away, maybe you could get yourself up here with a duster?

From: Holly
To: James Lawrence

Maybe you could kiss my arse.

From: James Lawrence
To: Holly

Maybe I will.

From: Holly
To: James Lawrence

Maybe, oh, I've got work to do, see you later lover …

xxxxx

From: James Lawrence
To: Holly

Love the way you use your dots, makes your mind wander… Oh, talking of mind wandering, my desk, maids, uniforms—there is one thing that Toby has seen that I haven't, and I feel this is totally unfair …

From: Holly
To: James Lawrence

You can forget it! (It won't fit anymore, anyway.)

From: James Lawrence
To: Holly

No problem, I hear they've got replica rubber slutty school uniforms at most reputable sex shops?

Subject: Kinky

From: Holly
To: Jason GrangerRM; Aisha

You two, not heard much from you today. Hope you're having a ball, I'm muuuuuuuuch happier now.

xxxx

PS This relationship with James, it's quite intense.

From: Jason GrangerRM
To: Holly; Aisha

Holly,

You can't put KINKY in the subject box then talk about it being intense? ? ? ? Come on Holly, has James been asking you to do things you wouldn't normally do?

Jason x

From: Holly
To: Jason GrangerRM; Aisha

In the past all this stuff wouldn't be something I'd even consider, but we just have so much fun together. I'm so happy at the moment.

From: Jason GrangerRM
To: Holly

I KNOW YOU'RE HAPPY—I'm your best friend!!!! I say go for it, and if I'm thinking what I'm thinking you're meaning, then you'll probably love it.

xxx

(I've cut Aisha out of this email, as I've sent her off on an errand to another site for me anyway.)

From: Holly
To: Jason GrangerRM

? ? ? What is it you think he's asking?

From: Jason GrangerRM
To: Holly

Whether he can do what I do a lot of, which is good, really it is, but you want to make sure he uses plenty of KY. Oh, and you might want to buy some poppers.

xxx

How exciting!!

330 holly's inbox—week 2

From: Holly
To: Jason GrangerRM

NO!!!! YUK!!! That's not what I was saying!!

Subject: Jason!

From: Holly
To: Jason GrangerRM

Are you still there!!!! That wasn't what I was saying!!!!!!! Jason?????

Subject: Rain

From: Granny
To: Holly

Holly,

Hello dear, they say it might rain again here later. I was asleep when it did earlier this week, but let's wait and see, shall we. Many years ago, during our honeymoon in Scotland, I posed for your grandfather like a ballerina while it rained. I don't know if you remember, but your parents have a picture your grandfather took on their wall. I'd love to do that again.

Love, Granny x

friday

Subject: Rain

From: Holly
To: Granny

Granny,

I'd left by the time you sent your email yesterday, but of course I remember the picture. You looked beautiful, and you should go out and be a ballerina if it rains!!!

Love, Holly

Subject: Late

From: Patricia Gillot
To: Holly

Judy asked where you were. I said you'd called in—problems on the Tube.

From: Holly
To: Patricia Gillot

I'm so so sorry Trish, this new shift thing, and I forgot it was 10:00 this morning. I just couldn't get it all together in time.

xx

From: Patricia Gillot
To: Holly

Don't worry, darlin, you cover for me plenty.

x

Subject: Sorry I was late

From: Holly
To: Judy Perkins

Hi Judy,
Sorry I was late this morning, I had problems on the Underground.
Kind regards,
Holly

Subject: Marbella

From: James Lawrence
To: Holly

Just found out that Marbella trip is on next Friday—I've definitely got to go there for the weekend. I'll get you a ticket too if you fancy coming.
I thought we could pop in for lunch down the coast and surprise your family? What do you think?
J

Subject: Gala dinner

From: Jennie Pithwait
To: Holly

Are you coming to this Gala dinner next month—I'm guessing you'll be sitting with me??

Jennie

From: Holly
To: Jennie Pithwait

Of course!! We should all sit together in a big group of us, it'll be so much fun. I'm looking forward to it. What are you up to this weekend. How's work been this week?

Holly

Subject: RE: Late

From: Judy Perkins
To: Holly

Not a problem, Holly, the tubes are always a nightmare. What trouble did you have?

From: Holly
To: Judy Perkins

Judy,
It was a train caught in a tunnel, kept us there for ages. Nightmare.
Holly

From: Judy Perkins
To: Holly

Oh, dear, what line?

Subject: Trouble!

From: Holly
To: Patricia Gillot

Shit, Judy wants to know which line now?

From: Patricia Gillot
To: Holly

OK, check the Tube website, because I know that's what Judy'll be looking at. She's told me about it before.

From: Holly
To: Patricia Gillot

I can't see any line having problems, can you? There must be one line, THE ONE DAY YOU NEED THEM TO HAVE A PROBLEM FOR HEAVENS SAKE!!!!

From: Patricia Gillot
To: Holly

Nothin, darlin, not a fire, a fault, not even no one thrown themselves under one? Nothing?

From: Holly
To: Patricia Gillot

Wait—minor delays on Circle Line!!! And some minor on the Hammersmith and City Line too? Wait, check out the Metropolitan Line!!!

From: Patricia Gillot
To: Holly

Severe delays on the Met Line! Bingo!!! We have a winner! Get that email sent, darlin.

xxx

Subject: Tube nightmare

From: Holly
To: Judy Perkins

The Metro Line, absolute nightmare.
Holly

Subject: Marbella???

From: James Lawrence
To: Holly

Need to know now, I'm booking the tickets—you fancy surprising your family??
J

Subject: Kate or Britney?

From: Jason GrangerRM
To: Holly

Where do you stand on the whole Kate or Britney debate?

From: Holly
To: Jason GrangerRM

Are you bored?

From: Jason GrangerRM
To: Holly

Very much.

From: Holly
To: Jason GrangerRM

OK, what about helping me in the 'should Holly go to Spain with James' debate ?

From: Jason GrangerRM
To: Holly

Has he asked you????

From: Holly
To: Jason GrangerRM

Yes.

From: Jason GrangerRM
To: Holly

Well of course the answer is YES YES YES!!!

From: Holly
To: Jason GrangerRM

I'm not so sure.

From: Jason GrangerRM
To: Holly

He hasn't asked you to go dressed in some weird outfit, has he? Tell me he's not making you sit on a plane in 10 kilos of rubber and a hose up your bum or something? If so then you should seriously consider the sweat implications when you touch down in Malaga. Still, take an empty bucket and a couple of dry sponges and some more KY, and you'll be fine. You might lose some weight too???

From: Holly
To: Jason GrangerRM

NO!! And stop talking about bums and KY, it's not nice. You've been hanging around with Aisha too much!!!

x

From: Jason GrangerRM
To: Holly

FINE!!!!!

From: Holly
To: Jason GrangerRM

I was only kidding.

xxx

Subject: BUMS KY BUMS KY BUMS KY BUMS KY BUMS KY BUMS KY

From: Jason GrangerRM
To: Holly

BUMS KY BUMS KY BUMS KY BUMS KY BUMS KY BUMS KY BUMS KY BUMS KY BUMS KY BUMS KY BUMS KY BUMS KY BUMS KY BUMS KY

From: Holly
To: Jason GrangerRM

Have you finished?

From: Jason GrangerRM
To: Holly

BUMS KY BUMS KY BUMS KY BUMS KY BUMS KY BUMS KY BUMS KY BUMS KY BUMS KY BUMS KY BUMS KY BUMS KY BUBUMS KY BUMS BUMSKY BUMS KY

From: Holly
To: Jason GrangerRM

You're being very childish, Mr Granger. Where's Aisha?

From: Jason GrangerRM
To: Holly

Not around, so why don't you want to go to Spain then?

xxx

From: Holly
To: Jason GrangerRM

Don't know. Maybe I'm overworrying. We would have to see my family, and it's all a bit early …

Subject: I'm very cross with you Holly

From: Mum and Dad
To: Holly

Holly,
Did you suggest Granny dance in the rain today?
Mum

From: Holly
To: Mum and Dad

Yes, she told me about that time on her honeymoon when she danced like a ballerina in the rain. You know—that picture you have on your wall with her spinning around in that lovely long dress. Why, did it rain?

From: Mum and Dad
To: Holly

No, Holly, the picture in that long dress was taken years later. She was talking about that other one you have on YOUR wall in YOUR HALL, the one of her balancing on one leg on the grass by the lake, she is—as you will remember, without clothes, naked!!! I've never been so embarrassed. When we turned up for her usual lunch outing just now, we arrived to find your grandmother whirling around on the lawn, naked as a baby, with families coming to visit their relatives just standing around speechless. It scared the life out of them, I think one of the old boys is still in recovery. Can you please be careful what you encourage her to get up to?
Mum

Subject: Marbella

From: Holly
To: James Lawrence

Hi James,

I think all my family are away unfortunately next weekend, so we won't be able to do that. But I'd love to go to Marbella!!!

xxxxx

From: James Lawrence
To: Holly

Good, we'll have some fun.

From: Holly
To: James Lawrence

PS I got me in trouble this morning… for being late.

From: James Lawrence
To: Holly

Not my fault. You started it.

From: Holly
To: James Lawrence

So I did.

x

Subject: Lying to friends? ? ?

From: Jennie Pithwait
To: Holly

I'm guessing at some stage you'll stop lying to me—I mean, as a friend, this is something which is usually important to most genuine people. I'm going home now, good-bye.

Jennie

Subject: Granny

From: Holly
To: Mum and Dad

Sorry Mum.

Oh well, I'm sure there was no harm done and I'm sure it made her very happy.

xxx

Subject: I just heard

From: Alice and Matt
To: Holly

Holly,

I just talked to Mum and heard she's told you about Granny. What's so sad is they thought she was drunk, and now they've banned her from drinking for the next month. Of course, Granny never needs to be drunk to do that kind of thing, that's just how she is, lots of fun. From what we've heard, she put on quite a show, with her own version of Swan Lake in front of a stunned audience in deck chairs. Could you give her a call tonight and cheer her up though?

xxx

Alice

week 3
monday

Subject: Our trip to England

From: Mum and Dad
To: Holly

Holly,

We're still coming in the summer, and your father and I have come up with an idea. We'd like to meet up with some of our old friends, the ones we haven't seen for a while, have a bit of a reunion night. Would it be OK to have this at your house? It would be really lovely to show them how well you've done, and a few of them could stay over? What d'you think?

Love, Mum

xxx

PS How is James? We know so little about him. For instance, you haven't even told us what car he drives or where his parents live?

Subject: Forgive me forgive me forgive me forgive me

From: Holly
To: Jennie Pithwait

Have you forgiven me yet… Pretty please? I tried calling you a few times over the weekend to explain.

xxxx

Holly

Subject: My weekend

From: Holly
To: Jason GrangerRM; Aisha

Hi,

I saw James again (and pregnant Pam). Are either of you there? I'm
dying to tell someone about my weekend. How was yours?

xxxxx

From: Aisha
To: Holly

Hi,

Jason's somewhere upstairs sorting out problems, it's busy here. Can
we catch up after checkouts?

xx

Subject: Morning

From: Holly
To: Patricia Gillot

Morning, how was your weekend?

From: Patricia Gillot
To: Holly

OK, I spent Friday night in A&E with our Anthony. He'd been in a
fight at school. Turns out he's got a cracked rib.

From: Holly
To: Patricia Gillot

That's awful, is he OK?

From: Patricia Gillot
To: Holly

No, he's got a cracked rib! Then Saturday, you won't believe, I wake
up to find two hot battered fish on my front doorstep.

From: Holly
To: Patricia Gillot

Were they a present?

From: Patricia Gillot
To: Holly

Yeah darlin, of course, that's what we do down the East End—didn't you know?

From: Holly
To: Patricia Gillot

No, why?

From: Patricia Gillot
To: Holly

Yeah, of course we do. Around our way we always give each other fish and chips as a thank you, not like you posh f**ks with your chocolates. A bag of chips left on someone's doorstep, yeah thanks, mate, there's your chips, away you go. YOU MAKE ME LAUGH!!!

From: Holly
To: Patricia Gillot

Sorry sorry sorry, OK, so why the fish??

From: Patricia Gillot
To: Holly

They were from our garden, Les's goldfish. Les reckons it's like a warning, or a revenge killing or something.

From: Holly
To: Patricia Gillot

You mean—like the horse's head left in someone's bed in that film?

From: Patricia Gillot
To: Holly

Something like that, yes. Why are you laughing again?!?

From: Holly
To: Patricia Gillot

Fish?? Somewhere else it would probably be a child's prank, but in the East End it's a mafia killing—hand over the cash, or the fish gets it. hee hee hee

I'm off before you can get me! Toilet break.

xxx

Subject: Weekend??

From: Holly
To: Aisha; Jason GrangerRM

Anyone there? I STILL want to tell someone about my weekend!!!

xxxxxx

Subject: A truce ? xxxx

From: Holly
To: Patricia Gillot

OK, so apart from that, how was the rest of your weekend?

From: Patricia Gillot
To: Holly

Not good. Sunday we went to watch the London Marathon.

From: Holly
To: Patricia Gillot

Oh, so did I!! I went with James …

From: Patricia Gillot
To: Holly

I went with Les… he got p*ssed up, had a fight, off to A&E (AGAIN), came back, got angry about his fish, then he had a barny

with the neighbour and spent a night in the cells. I spent most the
night trying to argue him out of there.

How was your Sunday?

Subject: Be afraid, be very afraid

From: Holly
To: Charlie Denham

Charlie,

Hide your strange friends, bury your dope, clean behind your ears
and say your prayers, MUM'S COMING TO ENGLAND.

xxx

From: Charlie Denham
To: Holly

Hi Holly,

Yes, I'd forgotten she was coming. Also, what strange friends?

Charlie

From: Holly
To: Charlie Denham

Strange friends—yes, you have—what about Sticky Pete?

From: Charlie Denham
To: Holly

It's Rubber Ron, as you're well aware.

From: Holly
To: Charlie Denham

Also, guess what—Mum and Dad want a reunion party with their
friends… at my lovely house????… Where they'll all be spending
the night!!!!????

Sh*t.

From: Charlie Denham
To: Holly

That could be interesting. Don't panic, we'll think of something.
So—we had the inspection Friday.

From: Holly
To: Charlie Denham

Sorry, forgot to ask… how did it go?

From: Charlie Denham
To: Holly

Things didn't go too badly at first. BUT there was a sheet of metal
(we've got a metal bar top) leaning against one wall, and Ron
thought he'd get it out the way. He began sliding it along the floor
while I quietly spoke to the health and safety officers, but behind
them I saw Rubber Ron slide the sheet over a radio cable. There
was a huge bang (as the cable severed and made the sheet live), and
just for an instant, I saw him lit up and jumping through the air,
then everything went black. They asked me what it was, I said we
must have just blown a fuse. Ron moaned then in the darkness, but
managed to drag himself off before the lights came up again. It was
very close. He's OK, obviously a bit bruised, but the top news is… I
think we might have passed our health and safety inspection. Now
we've finished, Rubber Ron said it would probably be a good idea
to have done the whole safety DVDs thing.

From: Holly
To: Charlie Denham

That's what I've BEEN TELLING YOU ALL ALONG!!!

From: Charlie Denham
To: Holly

No—he thinks we should MAKE a safety video. You know—show
people how to steer clear of danger. This week, we'll show you how
Ron electrocuted himself, gassed 100 people, and put a nail through

his foot. Next week you'll see how I lost my hair, an arm, and why I can't have children. What d'you think?

Charlie

From: Holly
To: Charlie Denham

I think you're sick, but very funny. I would have thought Rubber Ron would have been insulated against this kind of thing??

From: Charlie Denham
To: Holly

ha ha

Charlie

Subject: Nice one

From: Jennie Pithwait
To: Holly

Listen Holly, I don't care who you shag, but sneaking around so much, then telling Trisha all about it and not me, makes me realise how little you view our friendship.

From: Holly
To: Jennie Pithwait

I couldn't hide it from Trish—she sits next to me, and I didn't want to tell you, because I thought you hated him so much.

From: Jennie Pithwait
To: Holly

Oh come on, you even thought I'd had a fling with him, or at the very least had a crush on him. That's what you said on my answerphone, and THAT IS why you didn't tell me!!!!

From: Holly

To: Jennie Pithwait

I didn't really know what to think, I just knew it was going really well and didn't want it to go wrong. I'm so so so sorry, you're my friend, and I'd never purposely upset you. Surely these kind of things can be forgiven between friends, pleeeeeeeeeeeeeeeeeeeeeeeeeeeeeeeeease.

Subject: Tonight

From: Patricia Gillot

To: Holly

Hate to be the bringer of bad news, but you know who we're seeing tonight.

From: Holly

To: Patricia Gillot

Oh, I'd forgotten about her.

From: Patricia Gillot

To: Holly

The dragon lady herself—lucky it's St George's Day, ha ha ha.

Subject: I'm in trouble

From: Holly

To: Patricia Gillot

Jennie's really really upset with me… Did you see that look she just gave me?

From: Patricia Gillot

To: Holly

Yeah, she had a face on her like a slapped arse.

From: Holly

To: Patricia Gillot

I shouldn't have lied to her.

From: Patricia Gillot
To: Holly

You're better off without her. Calling us 'support staff,' the cow. So, you ready for Shella Cruella?

From: Holly
To: Patricia Gillot

No, she's bound to have a go at us about something, I'm just hoping you brought those boots. TELL ME YOU BROUGHT THOSE BOOTS?

From: Patricia Gillot
To: Holly

Steel-toe-capped ones? No, left them at home with me chips.

Subject: Coming to England

From: Holly
To: Mum and Dad

Hi Mum,

I'm very excited about seeing you, and I know Charlie will be too. I would love to have your reunion party at my house, however, I have decided to rent it out. It really is such a big place, and I could live somewhere much smaller.

I'd love to have you over, though, and we could have a lovely dinner at my new place (I could possibly seat up to 8). The only difference being they wouldn't be able to sleep anywhere. But you and Dad could have my bed, and I've got a pullout sofa bed. What d'you think?

xxxx Holly

Subject: Charlie

From: Holly
To: Charlie Denham

I had an inspiration about the house thing. I told Mum and Dad I was renting it out.

xxx

tuesday

Subject: What a night I had

From: Holly
To: Jason GrangerRM; Aisha

I woke up in the middle of the night, and guess who was lying next to me?

From: Jason GrangerRM
To: Holly; Aisha

Toby Maguire butt-naked except for a small amount of webbing over his privates, which shimmered invitingly in the moonlight?

From: Holly
To: Jason GrangerRM; Aisha

Oh, we are in a funny mood today, aren't we Jason.

No, anyway, you've ruined it now. I was going to say I woke up to see that PA who hates me so much—Shella—lying next to me. I said, what are you doing in my bed? And she said—'Well Holly (she said the H like she always does... like she's coughing something up), you forgot to book my meeting room, so I'm going to lie here until you do.'

It was most disconcerting, I couldn't get her out.

From: Aisha
To: Holly; Jason GrangerRM

Do you think this is some kind of fantasy you have about her?

Aish

From: Holly
To: Jason GrangerRM; Aisha

No Aish, it wasn't sexual, it's just because she makes me so nervous.

From: Aisha
To: Holly; Jason GrangerRM

Where was James all this time?

From: Holly
To: Aisha; Jason GrangerRM

Not there, we don't sleep with each other every night.

From: Aisha
To: Holly; Jason GrangerRM

Maybe you should. I'd be banging his brains out every night if I were you.

From: Jason GrangerRM
To: Holly; Aisha

Good point Aish, also, if James was in your bed, there wouldn't be any room left for PAs. You should tell him.

From: Holly
To: Aisha; Jason GrangerRM

I'm going now, thanks for your advice you two.
PS—Just remembered, me and Trisha owe you a windup—keep your eyes peeled!

Subject: Rent

From: Nick
To: Holly

Holly,

Just thought I'd send you an email to remind you about your rent this month. I know your landlord will be expecting it on time, and I thought a reminder would help you. All the best.

Yours sincerely,

Nick Harkson

Subject: Bitch from hell

From: Patricia Gillot
To: Holly

That was fun last night.

From: Holly
To: Patricia Gillot

Shella really hates me for some reason, and I don't think she's about to make it easier for me here.

x

From: Patricia Gillot
To: Holly

Init, just watch your back.

Subject: Toby

From: James Lawrence
To: Holly

Toby seems like a stand-up kind of guy. If we're good mates, will this make things awkward?

Subject: My lovely, very cool sister

From: Charlie Denham
To: Holly

What do you know about licensing laws?
Charlie

Subject: Toby

From: Holly
To: James Lawrence

What?

Subject: ?????

From: Holly
To: Charlie Denham

I know nothing about licensing laws, and now your cool sister is very suspicious.

From: Charlie Denham
To: Holly

Don't worry. You don't need to know anything, just need to sign a few forms.

From: Holly
To: Charlie Denham

What forms?

Subject: Toby

From: James Lawrence
To: Holly

Yes, I invited him to Spain with us, hope that's OK?

From: Holly
To: James Lawrence

Of course that's fine. I was thinking, why don't you invite your parents too, my mum is desperate to meet them, and, well, I just think it's time, don't you?

Subject: Your weekend

From: Patricia Gillot
To: Holly

Forgot to ask about your weekend, did you have fun with that pregnant friend of yours. You saw her this weekend, didn't you? She still moaning?

From: Holly
To: Patricia Gillot

She's finding it very difficult. She's always got a headache, always feels sick, and she's single-handedly put me off having children. Her emails are like letter bombs. I'm scared to open them any more, in case she attaches a picture of something nasty she feels like sharing with me. Being pregnant isn't that bad, is it?

From: Patricia Gillot
To: Holly

Why? Has that James been talking about having kids?

From: Holly
To: Patricia Gillot

No, I was just thinking.

Subject: Your registration has been processed

From: Totaljobs.co.uk
To: Holly

Congratulations,

Your job requirements have been entered onto our database. You will now receive job updates which match the criteria you have stipulated.

Good luck in your employment search.

Registration Centre

Subject: My belt

From: Aisha
To: Holly

Lover girl—did you remember my belt?

Aish

From: Holly
To: Aisha

It's under my desk. See you at 5 p.m.

Subject: What forms?

From: Holly
To: Charlie Denham

Now I'm back from lunch—what do you want me to do?

From: Charlie Denham
To: Holly

I'll come clean with you. We're having a few problems finding anyone without a criminal record to hold the licence, seems everyone's got one these days. In fact, the only people I KNOW who don't have one are you and Granny. And I can't see Granny in rubber, luckily.

xxxx

From: Holly
To: Charlie Denham

I'm hoping you can't see me in rubber either you pervert. But anyway:

1: I am not going to be held responsible for a club I don't even work in.

2: Rubber? You said it was just a normal club with lots of strange artwork?

Holly

Subject: SPAIN

From: James Lawrence
To: Holly

OK, let's not take my parents or Toby, OK? You're not getting wound up today. What's wrong with you?

But I am very much looking forward to seeing the Denham clan— what did you say your sister does again?

From: Holly
To: James Lawrence

Landscape gardening, with her husband.

From: James Lawrence
To: Holly

Great, what does your brother do?

From: Holly
To: James Lawrence

Runs a bookshop.

From: James Lawrence
To: Holly

Fab, where?

From: Holly
To: James Lawrence

Israel.

From: James Lawrence
To: Holly

Really?

From: Holly
To: James Lawrence

Yes.

From: James Lawrence
To: Holly

You're such a f*cking liar, Denham.

Subject: Re: normal club with strange artwork

From: Charlie Denham
To: Holly

'Unusual artwork' is what I said, and it is. Mainly naked bodies involved in kinky sex acts, but this doesn't detract from the fact that I need you to front the club and act as the licencee.
Charlie

From: Holly
To: Charlie Denham

What type of club is it then?

From: Charlie Denham
To: Holly

A fetish club.

From: Holly
To: Charlie Denham

You are kidding me—definitely not!

From: Charlie Denham
To: Holly

Oh, come on, it's just like a normal club, only there's more to see, and you make friends a lot quicker.

From: Holly
To: Charlie Denham

Go away.

Subject: My thoughts

From: Jason GrangerRM
To: Holly

Holly,

I've given it a lot of thought today, and I don't think you should let James meet your family. Not yet.

xxxx

Also, have you had your legs waxed??

Have you booked a tan?

Have you booked your nails in? (if I remember, they look awful).

Finally, what underwear have you packed? I'm worried.

From: Holly
To: Jason GrangerRM

Family—we're singing from the same hymn sheet. But the rest of it—you're making me nervous. I'm not worrying about all that. He's seen me naked, with the lights off. We've been together a while now, it's all fine.

xx

From: Jason GrangerRM
To: Holly

It is not all fine. You're about to set foot in a foreign land full of beautiful, stylish women who know how to dress, walk, talk, and eat lunch without spilling gravy down their fronts and will be doing everything possible to get their manicured paws on your perfect marriage material. And you don't even have a battle plan? But if you think it's all fine, then don't worry.

Got to go.

xxx

Subject: Wax Lyrical

From: Holly
To: Jason GrangerRM

OK, I'm definitely having my bikini line done. Right—I'm busy, places to go, people to see.

xx

From: Jason GrangerRM
To: Holly

… and somewhere in London there's a bunch of very scared wax strips making their way to the front of the queue.

xxx

wednesday

Subject: Your house

From: Mum and Dad
To: Holly

Holly,

Morning, dear. It's such a shame you've decided to rent out your house before our reunion, but I've come up with a solution. Just rent it out initially on a short let for about a month. Your father can fly over next week and help you with interviewing potential renters. Then we can still hold our get-together at your place in June. Knowing how little time there is to get going, I've put an advertisement on a couple of websites about it and given them your phone number. I'll book your dad's flight now.

Love, Mum

x

From: Holly
To: Mum and Dad

Mum,

Just read your email. Thank you for being so concerned—and helpful. I've already begun to get a stream of calls to my mobile. But don't book Dad a flight! I can interview people myself and also, having a 1 month let will mean the house is empty for a couple of weeks before you come, which is a waste of money.

Regards, Holly

Subject: REF: Acct 20000389384374 Holly Rivers

From: Southern Debt Management Services
To: Holly

REF: Acct 20000389384374 Holly Denham

Dear Holly Denham:

Thank you for your recent email. Our records have now been updated with your new surname: Denham.

You will also be receiving confirmation via post.

Yours sincerely,

Douglass Granger, Senior Collections Officer

Subject: Butt

From: Aisha
To: Holly

Nice backside.

From: Holly
To: Aisha

Why thank you, Aish, and you have a nice backside yourself.

From: Aisha
To: Holly

Not yours—James'.

From: Holly
To: Aisha

—?

From: Aisha
To: Holly

Nice strong hands, too. I like hands.

From: Holly
To: Aisha

So glad.

From: Aisha
To: Holly

Like the uniform too. Soldier boys, hmmmmmm.

From: Holly
To: Aisha

That was Ralph in the uniform. James was the guy I was talking to (although I am kind of grateful you haven't fantasized about him).

From: Aisha
To: Holly

I know which one he was—I was joking about the uniform. James was the sexy one in the suit, very nice, very public school, confident rugby type, good suit.

Subject: Small favour

From: Charlie Denham
To: Holly

So come on, I'm really stuck here, and you know I wouldn't ask you if there was anyone else I could turn to? This is your brother asking you for a small favour.
Charlie

From: Holly
To: Charlie Denham

Small favour? You've got a club, which is going to be full of rubber-dressed sex addicts (all probably on crack), doing goodness knows what, nasty, yuk, and you want my name on the front door????

From: Charlie Denham
To: Holly

—yes.

From: Holly
To: Charlie Denham

NO!!!!

Subject: Hi

From: Pregnant Pam
To: Holly

I just puked on my foot.
Pam x

Subject: It's not a problem

From: Mum and Dad
To: Holly

Hi,
You don't need to sign off with 'Regards,' darling, just 'Love, Holly'
will do. Also, it's a bit late. I'll email your father's details.
Mum

From: Holly
To: Mum and Dad

I know Mum—I was busy and wasn't looking what I was writing.
What details?

From: Mum and Dad
To: Holly

Holly,
His flight details, of course. And I do hope you make more of an effort
to watch what you're typing when you are writing to other banks.
Mum

From: Holly
To: Mum and Dad

I don't write to other banks, Mum—I'm not sure what you think I do here?? Also, why have you got Dad coming here? This is utter madness. Can you ask me first before organising things???

From: Mum and Dad
To: Holly

He's coming to help you, dear, to meet these people who wish to live in your house for the next month. It's very important you get the right type of people. I've read you can make yourself some good money if you choose wisely for short lets. Anyway, you clearly can't organise things yourself, otherwise you wouldn't have moved into a flat before renting out your house. Would you?
Mum

Subject: Service

From: Ralph Tooms
To: Holly

Holly, can I get something from the shops for you, please?
Ralph

From: Holly
To: Ralph Tooms

No, but thank you.
Holly

From: Ralph Tooms
To: Holly

Do you want me to report at your desk at 4 p.m. sharp?

From: Holly
To: Ralph Tooms

NOT now Ralph, I'm busy.

Subject: Organising

From: Holly
To: Mum and Dad

Mum, you really are unbelievable!!!!!!

From: Mum and Dad
To: Holly

Thank you, darling, so are you.

xxx Mum

PS Do make sure you have clean sheets on his bed, and it would be nice of you to pick him up from the airport.

Subject: Service

From: Holly
To: Ralph Tooms

Ralph, you're a good boy, sorry if I sounded mean. Just having a nightmare day.

Holly

Subject: Your news

From: Holly
To: Pregnant Pam

Hi Pam,

Sorry to hear about the sick. Do get better soon.

Holly

xx

Subject: Club

From: Charlie Denham
To: Holly

So ?

Subject: Heeeeeeeeeelp

From: Holly
To: Jason GrangerRM

Jason, tell me your day is going as badly as mine. I feel I'm being attacked by mad people from every direction???

Subject: JASON!!

From: Holly
To: Jason GrangerRM

WHERE ARE YOU???!!!!!!

Subject: Any jobs going?

From: Charlie Denham
To: Holly

Any jobs going? I mean, I'll be out of work soon, without a nightclub to build. Not forgetting the huge debt I'll be in.

Charlie x

I've done you lots of favours.

From: Holly
To: Charlie Denham

Name one!

From: Charlie Denham
To: Holly

Toby.

Subject: You alright?

From: Patricia Gillot
To: Holly

You don't look good?

From: Holly
To: Patricia Gillot

Just seen a ghost.

xxx

Subject: ? ? ?

From: Jason GrangerRM
To: Holly; Aisha

To be honest, Holly-I'd-prefer-to-let-a-sex-mad-nympho-meet-my-boyfriend-than-Jason, my afternoon hasn't been that good, either.

From: Holly
To: Aisha; Jason GrangerRM

Sorry Jason, but Aisha, if you're there, please explain to Jason you were just meant to be picking up your belt last night, that's all.

From: Aisha
To: Holly; Jason GrangerRM

Grrrrrrrrrr

From: Jason GrangerRM
To: Holly; Aisha

Is it a gay thing, Holly? Is that it?

From: Holly
To: Jason GrangerRM; Aisha

Of course, yes, that's exactly it.
Stop being nasty, I've had a rotten day.

From: Aisha
To: Holly; Jason GrangerRM

Grrrrrrr

From: Jason GrangerRM
To: Holly; Aisha

Not being nasty, only teasing.

Sorry, got to break off this banter for a moment… Aisha, do you want to join the conversation, or are you going to continue to type grrrrrrrrrrrr—hmm?

From: Aisha
To: Holly; Jason GrangerRM

Grrrrrrrrrr

From: Holly
To: Jason GrangerRM; Aisha

What's wrong with her?

From: Jason GrangerRM
To: Holly; Aisha

She's been in heat all day, it's been like having a ravenous wolf sitting next to you. I'm considering sending her home before she attacks someone.

What was James like then?

From: Aisha
To: Jason GrangerRM; Holly

Nice, good butt. Yeah, I'd do him. Can I go home now, Jason? If you don't let me, I'll show you my tits?

From: Jason GrangerRM
To: Holly; Aisha

Go!

thursday

Subject: Monday's meeting

From: Judy Perkins
To: Holly; Patricia Gillot

Dear Patricia & Holly,

I thought our meeting on Monday night was very productive, and I've been liaising with the HR department, Shella, and management to finalise the best course of action.

I've taken on board your views in this matter and will be able to give you a clearer idea of who will be in charge of the conference within the next few days. Do understand, it won't ultimately be my decision.

Judy

Subject: Job Application

From: Holly
To: ChezGerardCoventGarden

Dear Sir or Madam,

Although having no recent waiting experience, as you can see from my CV, I had a regular job as a waitress during the holidays whilst at university.

I am keen, presentable, enthusiastic, willing, and feel this is an area where I could really excel.

Kindest regards,

Holly Denham

Subject: Miss you

From: Holly
To: Jennie Pithwait

Miss you.

x

Subject: Your club

From: Holly
To: Charlie Denham

OK, fine, you can put my name on the licence. But not because of any favour I owe you, just because you're my brother, and I love you, even though you're a selfish git most of the time.

x

What do I need to do then?

From: Charlie Denham
To: Holly

Holly, you're the best, you've saved my bacon. OK, all you need to do is answer a few questions on licensing laws.

From: Holly
To: Charlie Denham

—OK.

From: Charlie Denham
To: Holly

In court.

From: Holly
To: Charlie Denham

Fine.

From: Charlie Denham
To: Holly

Tomorrow.

From: Holly
To: Charlie Denham

Oh please Charlie, no!!

From: Charlie Denham
To: Holly

Go on, you said you would help me.

From: Holly
To: Charlie Denham

Yes, Charlie, next week—help you, next month—help you. I'm going to Spain tomorrow night??

From: Charlie Denham
To: Holly

There's no point helping next month. The court date is tomorrow, go on please? If you don't, there'll be a lot of very sad perverts with nowhere to go.

Subject: What about that then

From: Patricia Gillot
To: Holly

You read Judy's email? 'Not my decision'—she says. Don't like the sound of that. I reckon we'll have Shella sitting down here next week?

From: Holly
To: Patricia Gillot

I think I can feel an illness coming on.

From: Patricia Gillot
To: Holly

No you don't. If she's here, you're here. I'm not sitting with her alone!

From: Holly
To: Patricia Gillot

I think it's glandular.

From: Patricia Gillot
To: Holly

You're not sick.

From: Holly
To: Patricia Gillot

Feel my forehead, it's very hot.

From: Patricia Gillot
To: Holly

You'll feel my hand slapping your cheek in a second.

Subject: Not that cheek

From: Patricia Gillot
To: Holly

I bet the clients would like it though. Where've you been on your holidays this morning, then. Anywhere nice?

From: Holly
To: Patricia Gillot

Tanning shop, Kilburn High Rd.

From: Patricia Gillot
To: Holly

So what about Shella then?

From: Holly
To: Patricia Gillot

I don't know. We'll have to watch our emails for a start. We need some kind of code.

From: Patricia Gillot
To: Holly

Yeah, if you see me raise my arm and bring it down on the back of her head—it means she's p*ssing me off.

From: Holly
To: Patricia Gillot

Like it.

x

Anyway, I don't think there's enough room, not with my big feet. And is it just me, or are all the shops full of baby clothes? NOTHING FITS. EVER.

Subject: Shoes

From: Holly
To: Jason GrangerRM

Got no shoes.

From: Jason GrangerRM
To: Holly

—So?

From: Holly
To: Jason GrangerRM

Got no shoes.

From: Jason GrangerRM
To: Holly

Forget it.

From: Holly
To: Jason GrangerRM

I hate it! None of them ever fit and I end up crying.

From: Jason GrangerRM
To: Holly

I don't like the looks I get when I'm searching for size nines. They think they're for me.

From: Holly
To: Jason GrangerRM

I AM NOT A SIZE 9!

From: Jason GrangerRM
To: Holly

OK, eight and a half, I'm still not doing it. I'll wait outside for you.

From: Holly
To: Jason GrangerRM

From: Jason GrangerRM
To: Holly

OUTSIDE ONLY!

From: Holly
To: Jason GrangerRM

From: Jason GrangerRM
To: Holly

Got to go, there's a pigeon on table five. The daft thing flew in and went straight for the restaurant, and of course, pigeon catching is under my job description.

Subject: Drinks

From: James Lawrence
To: Holly

Everyone from my floor is going for drinks later. You coming?

From: Holly
To: James Lawrence

Would love to, but I can't.

| **From:** James Lawrence |
| **To:** Holly |

Why not?

| **From:** Holly |
| **To:** James Lawrence |

Studying. I'll tell you about it another time.

| **From:** James Lawrence |
| **To:** Holly |

Sounds good. OK, I'll catch you tomorrow.

J

Hey, also, I think your friend Toby is a sexist dork, a complete knob.

| **From:** Holly |
| **To:** James Lawrence |

Why? What's he done?

| **From:** James Lawrence |
| **To:** Holly |

Just saying things about you lot on reception. Don't worry, I had a word with him.

Subject: Gala Dinner

| **From:** Judy Perkins |
| **To:** Holly; Patricia Gillot; Dave Otto; Ralph Tooms; Samantha Graham; Kristan |

Dear all,

The Gala dinner at the Dorchester to commemorate our UK office's 25 years in operation will soon be upon us, and I still haven't had your replies as to who will be bringing a partner with them. I have put all your names down as attending because, as you know, it is an essential night in this year's calendar, and I expect a full attendance from my department.

So names please, people. I need to know by Monday latest to ensure they're booked in.

Yours,

Judy

friday

Subject: Spain

From: Holly
To: James Lawrence

Hi Babe,

Hope you had a good night last night and you're not feeling too rough.

I'm packed and looking forward to Spain (although next time, let's go somewhere cooler, where I can wear more clothes!!).

Holly

Subject: Candles

From: Alice and Matt
To: Holly

Hi Holly,

Know anywhere I can buy candles from?

From: Holly
To: Alice and Matt

Spain (I don't think they're illegal, Alice).

Subject: Battle plan

From: Jason GrangerRM
To: Holly

How are you looking?

From: Holly
To: Jason GrangerRM

In clothes—as good as I get. Bikinis are another matter—the very thought is giving me goose bumps.

From: Jason GrangerRM
To: Holly

Get rid of the goose bumps, they're not helpful. Right let's go through our checklist:
Legs ...

From: Holly
To: Jason GrangerRM

Waxed!

From: Jason GrangerRM
To: Holly

Eyebrows ...

From: Holly
To: Jason GrangerRM

Waxed!

From: Jason GrangerRM
To: Holly

Pits ...

From: Holly
To: Jason GrangerRM

Waxed!

From: Jason GrangerRM
To: Holly

Front bottom?

From: Holly
To: Jason GrangerRM

Waxed.

From: Jason GrangerRM
To: Holly

Good. Brazilian?

From: Holly
To: Jason GrangerRM

No—Hollywood. I thought—in for a penny, in for a pound.

Subject: Witches

From: Alice and Matt
To: Holly

I know you can buy candles here, but I need a lot of them—for my wicker witch nights. I'm getting really into it, it's so enlightening, Holly, really. I think you'd make a great witch. What d'you think?

xxx

From: Holly
To: Alice and Matt

I think I have too many problems already—without being called a witch.

But I love you.

(not to be rude)

xxx

Look on the web for cheap candles.

Subject: Battle plan

From: Holly
To: Jason GrangerRM

Where've we got to? Is that it?

From: Jason GrangerRM
To: Holly

Only just started: Feet ...

From: Holly
To: Jason GrangerRM

Pedicured.

From: Jason GrangerRM
To: Holly

Hands?

From: Holly
To: Jason GrangerRM

Manicured.

From: Jason GrangerRM
To: Holly

Back garden ...

From: Holly
To: Jason GrangerRM

Cut the lawn and pruned the bushes.

From: Jason GrangerRM
To: Holly

Good girl. (Although I have no idea what you mean.)
Sunbed?

From: Holly
To: Jason GrangerRM

Full body—spray tan. Also massage, facial, and cellulite buster.

From: Jason GrangerRM
To: Holly

Like it.

Subject: Witches

From: Alice and Matt
To: Holly

Found a website just for witches, and they sell everything I need. Also, you get points every time you buy!

xxx

Thanks for that.

Alice

From: Holly
To: Alice and Matt

That's great.

Just a thought, when you say points—is it like air miles? Because I can see that will be very useful. Instead of casting a spell from far away, you can go by broom. Make sure it includes—broom tax?

Holly

From: Alice and Matt
To: Holly

You're not funny.

Subject: Battle plan

From: Jason GrangerRM
To: Holly

What about phase two?

From: Holly
To: Jason GrangerRM

Yes, clothing. I kind of ran out of money after phase one, so I'm mixing and matching …

Holly

By the way, do you think my family is a little strange?

From: Jason GrangerRM
To: Holly

Strange isn't the word. Phase three?

Subject: How's work

From: Holly
To: James Lawrence

Didn't see you come through. Are you in yet?

Subject: Phase three

From: Holly
To: Jason GrangerRM

Phase three???? Phase three??
WHAT THE HELL IS PHASE THREE???
Don't tell me I forgot one?

From: Jason GrangerRM
To: Holly

It's where you pretend that you completely forgot about the trip all together!!!!

From: Holly
To: Jason GrangerRM

Jason,

Over the last couple of days I've been pushed, punched, plucked, and preened. I've been sprayed, dyed, sponged, and scented. More behind the scenes work has been carried out on this body than even my Mini, and that, I've discovered, used to be two different cars.

I'm ready to go, and I look good. I know this because Ralph keeps asking for orders… so don't tell me I have to pretend I'd forgotten about it all, because I don't want to! I want to look forward to it. (Besides which, it will never wash; I'll be lucky if he recognises me.)

Agggh, sorry, it's all just a bit much. On top of all this, I'm now the head dom at a fetish club, and I've still not heard from James.

Holly

PS I've emailed him already, twice, and mentioned wanting to wear more clothes.

PPS Don't bother saying anything. I know it wasn't a good move.

PPPS I hate playing games anyway, you know that.

Subject: Jennie

From: Holly
To: Jennie Pithwait

Are we still friends? I miss you???

From: Jennie Pithwait
To: Holly

Sorry?

Holly, I don't know what you mean, We've always been friends, there's no problem with me.

Jennie

From: Holly
To: Jennie Pithwait

Oh good! Have a great weekend then.

Holly

xxx

Subject: Spain

From: Granny
To: Holly

Holly,

Would you like me to register your name with some more flight companies? I'm looking through them now and will get some more over to you in a jiffy.

xxxx
Love, Granny

From: Holly
To: Granny

Granny,
Please don't, I really have so many now. Thank you so much. Are you still on meagre rations since you entertained the troops?
Holly

From: Granny
To: Holly

Holly,
I wasn't 'entertaining the troops,' dear, I was stripping for the troops. It was so much fun. I danced and I danced. It was the first time I've really enjoyed myself here.
They haven't put me on meagre rations, they've cut me off totally. I'm not a child, I don't like being treated like one.
From your Granny
x

Subject: Spain

From: Jennie Pithwait
To: Holly

I hear you're off to Spain—enjoy it, won't you.
Jennie

Subject: Afternoon

From: Jason GrangerRM
To: Holly

Any news from him yet?

From: Holly
To: Jason GrangerRM

Not a thing, I want some attention. There's no point looking this good if you don't have any.

From: Jason GrangerRM
To: Holly

I could tell you something funny to cheer you up?

From: Holly
To: Jason GrangerRM

Yes, please do. I'm so bored. Even bossing Ralph around is becoming tedious. Trish had him standing facing the wall for a while, until Judy came by and told him off (he's meant to be checking passes).

From: Jason GrangerRM
To: Holly

Knock knock?

Subject: Sorry I'm late

From: James Lawrence
To: Holly

Terrible hangover, feel like crap. You look fantastic.

From: Holly
To: James Lawrence

Thanks.

From: James Lawrence
To: Holly

I got some gifts for your family. Got your old man some whisky.

From: Holly
To: James Lawrence

That's nice. I thought we'd agreed we weren't seeing them.

Subject: Hey

From: Jason GrangerRM
To: Holly

I said knock knock!

Subject: No, got that wrong …

From: James Lawrence
To: Holly

Got him some vintage champagne?

From: Holly
To: James Lawrence

What?

From: James Lawrence
To: Holly

You sound moody, so I thought that might swing it??

From: Holly
To: James Lawrence

Sorry, not moody at all. I was just thinking about the whole you meeting the parents thing. Very excited about Spain, and it's very sweet of you to think about taking them presents. I'm just not sure.

xxxx

PS You still look good hungover.

From: James Lawrence
To: Holly

Yeah, how good?

From: Holly
To: James Lawrence

—Hot.

Subject: Hello??? IS ANYONE THERE???

From: Jason GrangerRM
To: Holly

KNOCK KNOCK???

From: Holly
To: Jason GrangerRM

James just arrived.

What gets me is I spend two days making myself look perfect, and he strolls in at ten to four with a hangover, not even bothering to shave, and looks better now than he's ever done before.

MEN HAVE IT EASY.

Sorry, had to get that off my chest… Who's there?

PS Sorry if I sound self-obsessed, I really do definitely want to know who's there.

xxx

Sorry …

Who's there?

AND he wants to see my family????

SORRY, that's enough.

Who is there?

From: Jason GrangerRM
To: Holly

Who cares who's there?? (I was going to make it up as I went along anyway.)

I think you should think long and hard about letting him meet ANY of your family. EVER.

xxx

And that's meant in the nicest possible way.

Subject: Am I hot enough to eat?

From: James Lawrence
To: Holly

Well?

From: Holly
To: James Lawrence

Don't push it Mr, you're late.

From: James Lawrence
To: Holly

I am, and I'm sorry, really really sorry.

James

PS Get your arse in that lift. I need an urgent meeting, Denham.

From: Holly
To: James Lawrence

Forget it.

You'll have to wait.

x

Subject: The problem is

From: Holly
To: Jason GrangerRM

He's just so rude, but …

Anyway, back to what the choices are. I've listed the pluses and minuses about surprising the family in Spain:

The Pluses

Great to surprise the family. Also, Mum would love James and would get off my back about meeting men.

The Minuses

Matt and Alice could be in the middle of some weird snake hunt.

Mum is very difficult to handle.

Alice and Matt could be in the middle of some weird snake hunt, dressed as witches.

The Guardia could be in the middle of taking Dad away for mass producing babies.

Granny could be in the middle of stripping again.

I still haven't told James what I used to do for a living, he thinks I've always worked in reception.

Oh, and he doesn't know I was once married.

What d'you think?

From: Jason GrangerRM
To: Holly

Do you think you love him?

From: Holly
To: Jason GrangerRM

—Yes.

From: Jason GrangerRM
To: Holly

Then I would stay at home for the weekend, don't answer the phone, preferably with a sheet over your head (he can go to Spain on his own JUST IN CASE you bump into your family out there).

xxx

PS I think you've got to tell him the truth soon x

PPS Does your dad really mass produce babies?

From: Holly
To: Jason GrangerRM

In picture form only.

From: Jason GrangerRM
To: Holly

That's a relief, I thought your family had issues, but that takes the biscuit even for you.

From: Holly
To: Jason GrangerRM

Thanks. Why the sheet?

From: Jason GrangerRM
To: Holly

Don't know, added to the image.

x

sunday

Subject: STOP

From: Jason GrangerRM
To: Holly

I just got what I think was a drunken voice mail from you saying you were going to take him to surprise the family… BAD BAD BAD idea, stop NOW. I have left four messages on your phone to stop you. Having said that, if you don't check your emails till Monday, and you're now reading it on Monday—Hey sweetie, don't panic, it's not bad, it's all good, and I'm sure he still loves you. Nothing we can't sort out. Don't worry, xxx Call me.

week 4
monday

Subject: HOLLY ARE YOU THERE?

From: Jason GrangerRM
To: Holly

Did you get my email from the weekend????

Subject: My weekend

From: Aisha
To: Holly; Jason GrangerRM

I've always loved Mondays, but usually because I'm still partying from Saturday. This work thing really sucks.

Subject: Who we'll be working under

From: Patricia Gillot
To: Holly

I spoke to Judy this morning.
They'll be letting us know who's going to be in charge of organising the annual results later today.

Subject: Romantic weekend

From: Jason GrangerRM
To: Holly; Aisha

Holly, if you're there, can you email me? The suspense is killing me. (that and Aisha's perfume)

Subject: Romantic weekend

From: Aisha
To: Holly; Jason RM

Yes Holly, please talk to us. Jason's sense of humour is killing me. He's so bloody funny.

Aish

From: Jason GrangerRM
To: Holly; Aisha

She's stunk the hotel out, Holly. We've even had food returned in the restaurant, because guests can taste cheap perfume on their eggs.

From: Aisha
To: Holly; Jason GrangerRM

Oh, he's such a poof. I'm wearing no more than normal, and it's bloody expensive too.

Aish

Subject: Children, Children

From: Holly
To: Jason GrangerRM; Aisha

Just stop that now! Or you'll be split up and put on separate desks for the rest of the term.

From: Jason GrangerRM
To: Holly; Aisha

We'll behave if you tell us about your weekend.

Jason

From: Holly
To: Jason GrangerRM; Aisha

So:

Saturday night I'd decided it was a fantastic idea, let's surprise the family, drive up there Sunday morning with James, introduce him to Mum. The next day I barely knew where we were heading until we were halfway to theirs—less than an hour away. So when James got out to fill up the car with petrol, I got on the phone to Mum—told her not to mention anything work related or husband related and that's about all I could get out before he got back in.

From: Jason GrangerRM
To: Holly; Aisha

Hold on, what happened on Saturday?

From: Holly
To: Jason GrangerRM; Aisha

The trip up to that point had gone well. Stayed in a great hotel Friday and Saturday, and I'd discovered his legs. Did I tell you his legs are lovely and hairy and tanned, and he looks so good in shorts?

Subject: Your lot

From: Patricia Gillot
To: Holly

Don't be skiving now, darlin. You can do this lot.

Subject: Things in shorts

From: Jason GrangerRM
To: Holly; Aisha

No, you didn't tell us. I think you should.

From: Holly
To: Jason GrangerRM; Aisha

Did I tell you when he came out of the shower in one of those soft white hotel towels—I threw myself back on the bed and had to cover my head with my book, because I was giggling like a schoolgirl? Did I tell you he uses one of those old shaving brushes when he

shaves? He smells of Dunhill shaving soap and hair wax, and it's
intoxicating. Did I tell you this?

From: Aisha
To: Holly; Jason GrangerRM

Am I reading a Mills and Boon?

From: Holly
To: Aisha; Jason GrangerRM

Also that he crawled forward on the bed, took away my book, and
held my hands to the covers while kissing my neck?

From: Aisha
To: Holly; Jason GrangerRM

I am, I'm reading Mills and Boon. Can you spice it up a bit Holly,
tell me how big his stiff cock was.

From: Jason GrangerRM
To: Holly; Aisha

Ignore her, Holly, this is quite enough for my pure mind.

From: Holly
To: Jason GrangerRM; Aisha

Thank you, Jason!!

From: Jason GrangerRM
To: Holly; Aisha

So his balls, small and tight, or big and dangly?

Subject: Laughing

From: Patricia Gillot
To: Holly

Something funny?

From: Holly
To: Patricia Gillot

Just booking this room and forgot to add the food.

From: Patricia Gillot
To: Holly

I can imagine how funny that must be.
Liar.
x

Subject: More

From: Holly
To: Jason GrangerRM; Aisha

I'm trying to write, but we're quite busy here.
x

Subject: Getting the sack

From: Jason GrangerRM
To: Holly; Aisha

You were talking about his balls, come on.

From: Holly
To: Jason GrangerRM; Aisha

Did I call anyone over the weekend?

From: Jason GrangerRM
To: Holly; Aisha

You did, and sent a text saying 'remind me about this on Monday.'

From: Aisha
To: Holly; Jason GrangerRM

OH, I just got Jason's joke about getting the sack. Good, funny.

From: Jason GrangerRM
To: Holly; Aisha

She's that slow with customers too.

From: Aisha
To: Holly; Jason GrangerRM

I don't know if you called me, Holly, although I got a call from someone on my answer-phone that sounded like a mobile had gone off in their pocket while they were walking. Either that, or they were having really slow, dull, repetitive sex—that wasn't you, was it?

From: Holly
To: Aisha; Jason GrangerRM

No, that wasn't me. On the way out there, we'd sat in Business class, had champagne, had fab food. He was joking around a lot, which took my mind off the journey—including a bit where we went through cloud and I thought the plane was on fire—until he pointed out it was the flashing red light under the wing colouring the white cloud and so everything was fine. I had a lovely day by the hotel pool reading a book on the Saturday—while he was out at meetings, but by the time we were flying back, I just felt weird. Mum and Dad were OK, Alice and Matt couldn't make it, they were off up in Madrid buying tadpoles or lizards or something, and we popped by after to surprise Granny, who was so happy to see me, amazingly tactful, and wearing clothes. So really, I should be happy.

From: Jason GrangerRM
To: Holly; Aisha

So nothing drastically went wrong then????

From: Holly
To: Aisha; Jason GrangerRM

You said I should come clean with him, Jason. So I told him SOME things when I realised nothing was fitting. After the meal with my parents, I took him to one side and told him that… I used to be married (but that I don't like talking about it) and that my parents still thought I owned a big house. I expected him to be shocked, but he didn't seem to mind. He was his usual self, joking, but maybe a bit distant. Could have been his work, maybe he just had a lot on his mind with deals going on or something. Maybe he was tired.

From: Jason GrangerRM
To: Holly; Aisha

Jekyll and Hyde. It's nothing, that's a typical Gemini trait. Don't panic, just give him some space. You haven't emailed him yet, have you?

From: Holly
To: Jason GrangerRM; Aisha

—No.

From: Jason GrangerRM
To: Holly; Aisha

Or called him?

From: Holly
To: Jason GrangerRM; Aisha

Yes, didn't answer.

Subject: Lunch

From: Holly
To: Jason GrangerRM; Aisha

Went to lunch, back. So what d'you think?

From: Aisha
To: Holly; Jason GrangerRM

Honey, stuff him. I thought he was a jerk anyway, and who lives with their mum at that age?

From: Holly

To: Aisha; Jason GrangerRM

Not sure that's what I want to hear, but thanks. (He doesn't anyway—his house is being renovated.)

From: Jason GrangerRM

To: Holly; Aisha

Don't worry, it's been half a day!!! He's probably still asleep!

Subject: Help

From: Patricia Gillot

To: Holly

Can I get a hand here. Are you going to help me or just type??? (Don't mean to be bossy, but it's getting busy.)

From: Holly

To: Patricia Gillot

Sorry, I'll keep up.

xx

Subject: A wonderful day

From: Jennie Pithwait

To: Holly

How was your weekend? I do hope it all went well.

x

Subject: Jennie

From: Holly

To: Jason GrangerRM; Aisha

I feel sick. I think Jennie knows something. She knows something's up with him. He must have said something upstairs. She just wrote 'how was your weekend? I do hope it all went well.'

From: Jason GrangerRM
To: Holly; Aisha

What an evil bitch! How could she say these horrible, disgusting things to you, wishing you well. That's just heartless!

You're overanalysing everything. Get on and do some work, and it'll all be fine.

x

Subject: Surprise

From: Mum and Dad
To: Holly

Holly,

What a wonderful surprise! It was so nice to see you and James yesterday. You looked so happy together; he's a great catch, very charming. I look forward to being invited to meet his parents. Just give me a date, and I'll pop it into my calendar.

We love you so much, Holly!

Mum

Subject: You're right

From: Holly
To: Jason GrangerRM

You're totally right. I think I was just being paranoid. It's amazing how you can look at things that were said—and read them a hundred different ways.

Holly

tuesday

Subject: Your Spanish surprise

From: Granny
To: Holly

Holly,

Lovely to see you and your new man. Will you pass on my thanks for making an old woman very happy by bringing you out here. What a lovely treat for me. Keep bringing me these young men.

All my love, Granny

Subject: Annual results

From: Roger Lipton
To: Judy Perkins; Holly; Patricia Gillot; Ralph Tooms; Dave Otto; Samantha Smith
To: Facilities Department

Thank you for attending all the meetings concerning the organisation of the Annual Results. We are very excited to be hosting this event in our UK office, and it is essential that we chose someone to organise it who is committed, experienced, passionate, and driven.

It is, therefore, our pleasure to confirm that Shella Hamilton-Jones is taking charge of the conference, with full support from the facilities department. Please ensure you offer her all the help and assistance she requires from you.

Yours sincerely,

Roger

Subject: Leaving

From: Patricia Gillot
To: Holly

That's it, I'm packing me bags.

From: Holly
To: Patricia Gillot

Shella won't be that bad, surely. When we begin working with her, we'll probably all end up as friends.

Subject: My team

From: Shella Hamilton-Jones
To: Holly; Patricia Gillot; Ralph Tooms; Samantha Smith; Dave Otto

Dear Team,

I am looking forward to getting my teeth stuck into this conference, as I am sure you all are, however, I will be very busy over the coming weeks. If you have any suggestions or would like to ask me questions then please don't call. I have set up a new email account: ShellasAnnualResults@Huerstwright.com.

Commitment is important, teamwork essential; it's for the good of the company, and at the end of it you can feel you've contributed to a wonderful event. When I ask for assistance, I will not be pleased if I hear 'it's not my job' or 'that's outside my normal working hours.' It's going to be very busy, so if you're one of those employees who is constantly taking time off, all I can say is just one thing: Shella will be watching!

Thanks again, and I look forward to working with my new energetic and helpful team.

Shella

Subject: Nice

From: Patricia Gillot
To: Holly

I think that answers your question.

From: Holly
To: Patricia Gillot

We're part of Shella's team. I'm thrilled. 'Shella will be watching'? I wonder where the Big Brother cameras are hidden. You know, she's probably already bugged us?

From: Patricia Gillot
To: Holly

Well, that's pointless, because we're not allowed to talk.
SHELLA STINKS, SHELLA STINKS, SHELLA STINKS.

From: Holly
To: Patricia Gillot

Unless she means they've given her access to our emails???

From: Patricia Gillot
To: Holly

Probably.

From: Holly
To: Patricia Gillot

Oh God, I'd die if anyone could read my emails!

Subject: James

From: Jason GrangerRM
To: Holly

Has he called yet?

From: Holly
To: Jason GrangerRM

NO.

Subject: Toby

From: Patricia Gillot
To: Holly

Come on then??

From: Holly
To: Patricia Gillot

What?

From: Patricia Gillot
To: Holly

You went to the same school?

From: Holly
To: Patricia Gillot

Yes.

Subject: Fetish Queen

From: Charlie Denham
To: Holly

Thanks for Friday, I owe you. So we're all pushing ahead, the big opening. Also, Rubber Ron thinks you should have a stage name.
Charlie

From: Holly
To: Charlie Denham

Charlie,

Please don't put stupid things in the subject boxes like 'fetish queen'?? If someone was going through my emails looking for anything suspicious, this would stand out. Also—stage name?? What?

Subject: James

From: Jason GrangerRM
To: Holly

Has he come in yet?

From: Holly
To: Jason GrangerRM

No—got my eyes glued to the door.

Subject: Company restructuring and necessary redundancies

From: Charlie Denham
To: Holly

Good Golly—it's Rubber Holly?
OR
I'll be Frank—it's Holly Spank?
What d'you think?

From: Holly
To: Charlie Denham

I think you should stop trying to wind me up and do something constructive.

From: Charlie Denham
To: Holly

Waiting for deliveries to show up. Also, I've posted you some forms. Just sign them and post them back.
Cheers,
Charlie

Subject: Toby

From: Patricia Gillot
To: Holly

So, you were Toby's girlfriend at school, and now he's working here.

From: Holly
To: Patricia Gillot

Yes. What's all that noise?

From: Patricia Gillot
To: Holly

May Day protesters.
So how long hadn't you seen him for?

From: Holly
To: Patricia Gillot

12 years.

From: Patricia Gillot
To: Holly

So what did you say when you first laid eyes on him here?

Subject: V exciting!

From: Jason GrangerRM
To: Holly

BL**DY HELL!!! You should see this!

From: Holly
To: Jason GrangerRM

WHAT???

From: Jason GrangerRM
To: Holly

Naked male protesters—and he got it to spin.

From: Holly
To: Jason GrangerRM

That's nice.

From: Jason GrangerRM
To: Holly

Like a helicopter!

Subject: James

From: Holly
To: Jason GrangerRM

Getting all stressed and confused. All that shouting outside isn't helping. Grrrrrr. Waiting for him to arrive. Why isn't he here yet?

Subject: Toby

From: Patricia Gillot
To: Holly

Come on, darlin, you've left me hanging here. What did you say to him when you saw him after all that time?

From: Holly
To: Patricia Gillot

I just told him to get lost. I don't want to think about Toby now. Sorry Trish, will tell you one day.

xx

Subject: I hate this

From: Holly
To: Jason GrangerRM

Spent the night checking my phone every five minutes to make sure I hadn't missed any calls. Then when the phone did ring, it was Alice from Spain. Don't think I was very friendly.

From: Jason GrangerRM
To: Holly

xx

From: Holly
To: Jason GrangerRM

This is it!! Taxi, outside, he's paying for it.

From: Jason GrangerRM
To: Holly

Don't bother looking up!!

From: Holly
To: Jason GrangerRM

He's coming.

From: Jason GrangerRM
To: Holly

Change of plan. LOOK, SMILE, AND FLICK HAIR BACK.

Subject: What's happening?

From: Jason GrangerRM
To: Holly

Tell me?? Is he still there?

From: Holly
To: Jason GrangerRM

I saw a taxi pull up outside, and I thought I could see him through the window, but we've got shaded glass, so it's not always easy to tell.

But it was him.

He got out.

I tried to get myself looking good. I was going to shout over to Trish, but she was dealing with clients who'd just arrived. He opened the door at the end, and I saw his face, but couldn't tell what his expression was, kind of just busy. I looked down as he began walking towards us. My heart was going so fast. I wanted to look nonchalant or even sexy, but I could feel the colour draining from my face, and if he had talked to me, my voice would have been all squeaky because one of the clients decided she wanted to have her pass done by me, and I hit some kind of top C when I spoke. I looked down to tear off the paper and fit it into the plastic wallet. He'd passed.!!!!

Hugely frustrating. I hate this, I hate feeling like this.

Why didn't he stop??

From: Jason GrangerRM
To: Holly

He's really late, what with the May Day thing, probably in trouble with his boss, got stuck in traffic. Also, he might have thought your relationship is so secure now that he doesn't have to try so hard? There could be plenty of reasons. I thought you two were still trying to keep it a bit of a secret anyway?

From: Holly
To: Jason GrangerRM

I don't care about secrets any more. I just want him to come over and hug me, take me to one side, and show some love and tenderness, even a kiss on the cheek would do. Tell me that he's sorry he hasn't been able to call, but he's been thinking about me constantly. Something like that.

From: Jason GrangerRM
To: Holly

I wish I could tell you something to cheer you up. Aisha's been working well today, handling lots on her own. I told her there wasn't any news from your man, and she said to tell you—'he's a d*ck anyway, she'd seen someone much better… who looked like a cross between Clinton and Tyson.' Thought you might like that.

From: Holly
To: Jason GrangerRM

How—how is that possible?

Subject: Our time together in Spain

From: Holly
To: James Lawrence

Hi James,

Great holiday, lots of fun, thanks. It's good knowing someone who you can have a laugh with, as well as other stuff... (talking of which... I had a sexy delivery... from that shop you talked about...)

Just spoke to Judy, who asked me which table I wanted to sit on for the Gala Dinner, etc. I heard you've got a table for the boys and are excluding wives and girlfriends, etc., so I understand if that's the case, but I've got to let her know today.

Holly xx

Subject: I emailed him

From: Holly
To: Jason GrangerRM

I sent him an email, tried to sound sexy and cool. Regretting it now, could try recalling it. Won't bother. I want to go home.

Now.

Wish you were here, wish we were sitting out in the sun, somewhere abroad, on a beach. Please don't email me back and say I shouldn't have written to him. In fact, please don't email me back. I'm going to sit on the Internet now and look at holiday sites.

xxx

Wish you were here.

wednesday

Subject: Morning

From: Jason GrangerRM
To: Holly

Morning,

How are you feeling?

From: Holly

To: Jason GrangerRM

I was glaring at the phone last night for hours and hours before it finally rang. I didn't see him pass for the rest of the day yesterday, so there was also a chance he was under a lot of pressure at work, working hard up in the office till very late. It's amazing how you begin analysing every minute detail. So I had it stuck in my head that he was going to call me in the evening, but got stuck with loads of work that night in the office and horror upon horrors, his mobile had run out of charge, or fallen out of the window, etc. I was going to call it from an anonymous number just to see if it rang.

I then started thinking, he probably isn't calling me because he thinks I mentioned being married in the past for the sole reason of bringing up the subject of marriage and now he's run a mile. I didn't hide my number, I just called his phone, and it rang—it rang, and I hung up before he even answered, because otherwise he'd know it was me.

My phone then rang, and I knew it was him calling me back. But it wasn't him, it was you. Hope I wasn't too short. This morning I've tried thinking where I went wrong—maybe he didn't think I looked very attractive when we were in Spain. I knocked my coffee off the seat on the plane back, and on to my lap and then later made a joke to security (because I was a bit drunk, and also noticing I wasn't getting any attention from James and thought saying anything could be better than getting no reaction from him at all). So I told the girl who patted my leg down that it wasn't pee, then laughed, and she just looked at James and then back at me, like, you've got a classy girl there, haven't you?

But surely that's not right. I mean, we've had lots of fun before, and he laughs with me at these kind of things and usually joins in. He probably didn't like me sitting by the pool in a jumper and thinks I'm insecure about my body (which I am), and he wants some ultraconfident girl. I do remember him noticing other women in the hotel who turned his eye. It wasn't a jumper, anyway, it was like a baggy top. Maybe I shouldn't have giggled on the bed when he

looked so hot in his towel, because then he knew how I wanted him
so much, and it probably ruined it. But surely you don't spend your
whole life playing these games. Surely you can one day say 'yes! I do
fancy you, I do love you, and I think you are fantastic, and I want to
give you my heart and soul, because I trust you, love you and I want
to spend the rest of my life with you and just stop playing these
games!!!!!!!!' I don't want to play these games any more, Jason, I
really don't, I've had enough, I don't want to, I'd prefer to be alone.
Alone is fine, it's OK with me. I'll be alone.

Help

Subject: Just called him

From: Holly
To: Jason GrangerRM

Rang his mobile. It went to voice mail, so I didn't leave a message.
Then after a few minutes thought I should actually leave a message,
so I rang again, and this time left one—'just called to say Hi, but
you're not there, so hope nothing's wrong and you're OK'—said
something like that.

Nothing too clingy.

It's over, isn't it?

From: Jason GrangerRM
To: Holly

That's fine, you checked whether he was OK. He could have been
injured or something. You don't know, do you?

Not clingy at all.

Jason

PS I wouldn't email him again, though, unless it's abuse. I could do
it for you????

Subject: I'm here to help too

From: Aisha
To: Holly

Sorry, not usually very good at this kind of thing, sweetie. How are you feeling?
Aish

From: Holly
To: Aisha

OK.
What d'you think I should do?

From: Aisha
To: Holly

I think you should forward on the below message to him:
You arrogant stuck-up shit bag, crap weazel, sleaze monkey, knob-jockey …

From: Holly
To: Aisha

Thanks.

From: Aisha
To: Holly

Also …
The only orgasms I had when we were going out, were ones when you weren't there.

From: Holly
To: Aisha

xxxxx

Subject: Holly

From: Patricia Gillot
To: Holly

You should check the mirror, darlin.

x

From: Holly
To: Patricia Gillot

Got it, thanks for that.

Subject: Then

From: Aisha
To: Holly

Big-arsed, small-dicked, hairy-backed, jam-rag-muncher.

From: Holly
To: Aisha

Thanks Aish.

From: Aisha
To: Holly

Then I'd make sure I had sex with all his friends. And told them how bad he was in bed. Then I'd stalk him for a while, and finally, send him lots of pizzas he never ordered.

From: Holly
To: Aisha

Does this ever work?

From: Aisha
To: Holly

When you're drunk. But when you sober up, it's kind of worse. Sorry.

Subject: Come on

From: Patricia Gillot
To: Holly

Come on there, Holls, don't think about him, and we'll get through this bunch of idiots a lot quicker. Being busy will take your mind off him, and at the weekend I'll take you down the Island, and you can come out with me and Les. We'd love to have you over.

From: Holly
To: Patricia Gillot

Thanks Trish, that sounds brilliant. I'll get myself together, I promise. I'll pull that smile out in a moment, you'll see.

xx

From: Patricia Gillot
To: Holly

Course you will, darlin. In a moment we'll have a word with Ralph, get him on his knees barking at people when they come in.

From: Holly
To: Patricia Gillot

He'd like that.

From: Patricia Gillot
To: Holly

Course he would, I'll sit on his back and ride him around the coffee table, you whip his arse with that ruler …

From: Holly
To: Patricia Gillot

I can picture it. What would we say to Shella if she decided then to do a spot check on us?

412 holly's inbox—week 4

> **From:** Patricia Gillot
> **To:** Holly

We'd tell her it's what she asked for: team building. Ralph would agree with us (IF we let him take the horse's bit out of his mouth).

Subject: Nonce

> **From:** Patricia Gillot
> **To:** Holly

Can't believe he did that. Gutless, that's what that was.

Subject: News

> **From:** Holly
> **To:** Jason GrangerRM; Aisha

Just saw him.

> **From:** Jason GrangerRM
> **To:** Holly

What happened?

> **From:** Holly
> **To:** Jason GrangerRM

He walked out. Then a few mins later he came back in. Kept my eyes glued to him to make sure I didn't miss it. He didn't look though. It's over.

Subject: NO, I'm not having it like that

> **From:** Holly
> **To:** Jason GrangerRM

I'm not having that. I need to know.

> **From:** Jason GrangerRM
> **To:** Holly

No, wait what are you doing?

From: Holly
To: Jason GrangerRM

I'm going up there. Back in a moment.

Subject: Important

From: Holly
To: Patricia Gillot

Got to go somewhere, can you cover?

x

From: Patricia Gillot
To: Holly

—go!

thursday

Subject: Any more news?

From: Jason GrangerRM
To: Holly

Have you seen him this morning??

From: Holly
To: Jason GrangerRM

No, oh, hold on.

Subject: WONDERFUL WONDERFUL NEWS!!!

From: Pregnant Pam
To: Holly

The most amazing news in the world!!!
IT'S A BOY!!!!

xxxxxxx

From: Holly
To: Pregnant Pam

That's great. I'm so pleased for you, you must be very happy.
Holly

From: Pregnant Pam
To: Holly

Really really happy, although I've already had his room done pink (I was sure I was having a girl). Still, you don't think it'll be too bad if I dress her up in lots of pink, do you (just for the first few years)?

From: Holly
To: Pregnant Pam

You said her—you mean him.

From: Pregnant Pam
To: Holly

What?

From: Holly
To: Pregnant Pam

Don't worry. But you'll have to paint it all blue now, won't you?

From: Pregnant Pam
To: Holly

No, there's no point. With any luck, he could turn out gay???
xxx
I'm emailing everyone else now, talk later.

Subject: Him

From: Holly
To: Jason GrangerRM

That was him, came through. I was busy with some clients though.
Holly

From: Jason GrangerRM
To: Holly

Don't be going up there again, promise me …

From: Holly
To: Jason GrangerRM

Promise. I just stood there like a lemon last time, not going through that again.

From: Jason GrangerRM
To: Holly

People go up in lifts all the time without stepping out. No problem there, you could have forgotten something.

xx

Subject: Time for baby clothes

From: Pregnant Pam
To: Holly

You are totally right, Holly. I need to dress him in blue, at least to start with. So can you meet me later? And we can go shopping together for baby clothes!!!!???

From: Holly
To: Pregnant Pam

I can't, sorry.

From: Pregnant Pam
To: Holly

Tomorrow then!

From: Holly
To: Pregnant Pam

I can't, really sorry, Pam.

x

From: Pregnant Pam
To: Holly

Why?

From: Holly
To: Pregnant Pam

I just can't. Next week sometime.

From: Pregnant Pam
To: Holly

Look, if you don't come shopping at the weekend, I'll come find you, I'll kick you out of his bed, and if need be, I'll drag you both with me!!!

From: Holly
To: Pregnant Pam

Sorry, it's very busy here. I can't chat.

x

Subject: The Clients

From: Patricia Gillot
To: Holly

Are you going to look after those clients, darlin?

From: Holly
To: Patricia Gillot

Sorry Trisha, forgot about them. I'll go and talk to them now.

trisha's
Inbox

week 4

thursday

Subject: Does Trisha need service?

From: Ralph
To: Trisha

Any new requests?

From: Trisha
To: Ralph

Me and Holly were having a laugh yesterday about you, Ralphy. We should get you crawling around this reception area!

From: Ralph
To: Trisha

I wouldn't crawl for no woman. Really, I was just winding you both up.

From: Trisha
To: Ralph

Funny, that's not what you said when you were drunk.

From: Ralph
To: Trisha

Don't remember.

From: Trisha
To: Ralph

So if we told you to kneel down in front of us and be our little doggy, you wouldn't want to do that for us? Wouldn't you want to, Ralphy???

From: Ralph
To: Trisha

OK, but not in front of everyone.

From: Trisha
To: Ralph

RALPH!!! That's great!

Subject: Screwdriver!

From: Les
To: Trisha

Where did you leave the screwdriver?

From: Trisha
To: Les

On the side, by the telly.

Subject: The Clients

From: Trisha
To: Holly

Are you going to look after those clients, darlin?

From: Holly
To: Trisha

Sorry Trish, forgot about them. I'll go and talk to them now.

Subject: The screwdriver …

From: Les
To: Trisha

It's not here.

From: Trisha
To: Les

On the side, by the telly.

From: Les
To: Trisha

There's no point just repeating yourself. I'm telling you, it's not here!

From: Trisha
To: Les

Tell me where you're standing.

From: Les
To: Trisha

What do you mean, where am I standing? I'm on the computer, aren't I? What they feeding you there, Trish, stupid pills?

From: Trisha
To: Les

No, but you must have a prescription. When you aren't on the computer, when you're next to the telly—where are you?

From: Les
To: Trisha

In the lounge, oh, you mean the one in the bedroom.

From: Trisha
To: Les

GIVE THE MAN A PRIZE!

From: Les
To: Trisha

I'll give you more than a prize when you get home, you cheeky cow.

From: Trisha
To: Les

Saucy thing. All right, make sure you come home early then.

Subject: Our friend Holly ...

From: Trisha
To: Jason GrangerRM

Jason,

Do you mind if I email you? It's about Holly. Sorry, but I'm worried for her.

Trisha

From: Jason GrangerRM
To: Trisha

Of course not. Is everything OK? Is she there?

Jason

From: Trisha
To: Jason GrangerRM

She's sitting next to me, can't see my screen though. She's not right, she looks like she's losing it. I know you're her friend, so hoped you could help. It's to do with James not calling, but surely, that can't get to her this much? She looks dreadful. She's my Holls. Don't like to see her this way.

Trisha

From: Jason GrangerRM
To: Trisha

Hi Trisha,

I spent a hour on the phone to her last night. It's never nice being dumped, especially when you think it's your fault and don't know what you've done wrong. We both know it's nothing she's done wrong herself (short of being TOO nice), but she's got that confidence thing. It's been knocked again.

Look after my little friend there please.

xxxx

From: Trisha
To: Jason GrangerRM

I'm doing my best. I've told her to go home sick, because if some of the management see her, she'll get in trouble. She's barely talking to clients when they come in, her head's down, she doesn't look up, and she mumbles to them. Just want to know whether I should be that worried or whether she'll be fine soon?

From: Jason GrangerRM
To: Trisha

If I tell you something, you promise not to tell Holly I told you—if she sees my emails, she'll kill me. I don't think it's a good idea for her to go home. I'd try to keep her there.

From: Trisha
To: Jason GrangerRM

I think she should go home, take a couple of days off, and she'll be fine.

From: Jason GrangerRM
To: Trisha

I don't think that's a good idea.

From: Trisha
To: Jason GrangerRM

Why?

From: Jason GrangerRM
To: Trisha

I just don't.

From: Trisha
To: Jason GrangerRM

If it's going to help, then tell me why. If it's gossip, I don't want to know.

From: Jason GrangerRM
To: Trisha

I DO NOT GOSSIP!

From: Trisha
To: Jason GrangerRM

GOOD.

From: Jason GrangerRM
To: Trisha

OK, sometimes I do, but not about friends!

OK, sometimes about them too, but not about this sort of thing!

From: Trisha
To: Jason GrangerRM

GET ON WITH IT! No wonder she's miserable, when it takes you both this long to get anything out. You're as bad as each other! Come on, darlin, as Les would say—sh*t or get off the pot.

From: Jason GrangerRM
To: Trisha

Who's Les? Doesn't matter. Did Holly tell you she was married?

From: Trisha
To: Jason GrangerRM

YES. But I don't know a thing about it.

From: Jason GrangerRM
To: Trisha

OK, he was one of those men who had an opinion about everything, and his opinion was always right. He (Sebastian) never admitted being wrong, and whenever Holly did anything, it was always like 'I would have done it differently,' which of course meant better. She started being so scared about doing anything off her own back— because she didn't want to look like she'd got it wrong again—she started asking him first. It got worse and worse, until she couldn't decide about anything herself. She gave up making any decisions at all. It got really bad.

From: Trisha
To: Jason GrangerRM

Like?

From: Jason GrangerRM
To: Trisha

I caught her once asking him whether HE thought it was time she was hungry???? Seb-the-pleb, I used to call him. The reason I'm telling you this isn't to gossip (and this sounds like I am). I just want you to know that she's such a sensitive girl underneath everything. After they split up, she went into a huge depression. She didn't go out for weeks. I used to take her food around. She didn't open post, didn't do anything, so yes, I'd be very worried about her, as I am.

From: Trisha
To: Jason GrangerRM

Bloody hell.

From: Jason GrangerRM
To: Trisha

I don't want her going back to that.

From: Trisha
To: Jason GrangerRM

Great! Hold on, darlin, she's just emailed me. Back to you in a minute.

Subject: I forgot

From: Holly
To: Trisha

Sorry Trish, I think I forgot to tell Maxi's clients she was starting the meeting.

From: Trisha
To: Holly

No, you didn't, you spoke to them. They've gone up already.

From: Holly
To: Trisha

Have they?

From: Trisha
To: Holly

Yes, darlin, you're fine.

x

Subject: Re: Our friend Holly ...

From: Jason GrangerRM
To: Trisha

Also, I want to pass some of the pressure over. Sorry to heap this on you, please don't tell her I told you anything. She could be fine with it all, as you said, but it's best that you know this. I don't think it would be good to get her to go home. Once she's out of the routine, there's a small chance she won't go back there.

xxx

Hey, isn't it time we all met???

From: Trisha
To: Jason GrangerRM

I've asked her to come out over our way—you fancy coming?

From: Jason GrangerRM
To: Trisha

Love to, thanks Trish.

Jason

holly's
inbox

week 4
thursday

Subject: Friends

From: Pregnant Pam
To: Holly

Holly!!
It's not fair. Your friends should come first, especially when they're pregnant!!!

From: Holly
To: Pregnant Pam

You do.

From: Pregnant Pam
To: Holly

Seems like it's all James this and James that these days. If you were pregnant, I wouldn't forget you.

From: Holly
To: Pregnant Pam

James dumped me.

From: Pregnant Pam
To: Holly

What??

From: Holly
To: Pregnant Pam

xxxxx

From: Pregnant Pam
To: Holly

Oh sweetie.

Subject: I forgot

From: Holly
To: Patricia Gillot

Sorry Trish, I think I forgot to tell Maxi's clients she was starting the meeting.

From: Patricia Gillot
To: Holly

No, you didn't, you spoke to them. They've gone up already.

From: Holly
To: Patricia Gillot

Have they?

From: Patricia Gillot
To: Holly

Yes, darlin, you're fine.

x

Subject:–?

From: Holly
To: James Lawrence

Is there a reason you're not talking to me? Is it just because we're over, or because you are angry with me about something? If you don't talk to me, I won't know, and I'd at least just like to know?

friday

Subject: Back pain

From: Holly
To: Alice and Matt

Got your message last night. Sorry to hear about Matt's back, hope he's feeling better today.

From: Alice and Matt
To: Holly

It's awful, he can't move at all, not a finger. I managed to get him on to the bed last night, and this morning he's absolutely stuck, the poor love. I'm going off to the chemist now.
Alice

Subject: Flowers

From: Patricia Gillot
To: Holly

Tell us, tell us, are they from who I think they're from???

From: Holly
To: Patricia Gillot

Not sure. I don't think so.
Holly

Subject: Flowers

From: Holly
To: Jason GrangerRM; Aisha

Did either of you two just send me some flowers?
Holly

From: Jason GrangerRM
To: Holly; Aisha

No, I didn't. Did you, Aisha?

From: Aisha
To: Holly; Jason GrangerRM

No.

Subject: Flowers

From: Aisha
To: Holly; Jason GrangerRM

Wait, do they look a little bit odd?

Aish

From: Holly
To: Aisha; Jason GrangerRM

What d'you mean, odd?

From: Aisha
To: Holly; Jason GrangerRM

Like not alive?

From: Holly
To: Aisha; Jason GrangerRM

You want to know if someone sent me dead flowers?

From: Aisha
To: Holly; Jason GrangerRM

Yes.

From: Holly
To: Aisha; Jason GrangerRM

No, Aisha, they're alive. I might not be looking great these days, but hopefully, I haven't reached the stage when people start sending me dead flowers.

From: Aisha
To: Holly; Jason GrangerRM

Oh dear, because I was hoping they were the ones I sent you when I didn't turn up to your party a few weeks ago. I've been hoping they'd arrive. Must be still lost.

Aisha

From: Holly
To: Aisha; Jason GrangerRM

They aren't lost. They didn't arrive, Aisha, because you never really sent them.

Love you though.

SO who d'you think they're from then?

From: Jason GrangerRM
To: Holly; Aisha

Very exciting. Isn't there a message with them at all?

From: Holly
To: Jason GrangerRM; Aisha

They're 'from an admirer.'

Subject: Our Brother Charlie

From: Alice and Matt
To: Holly

I've never been so humiliated in my life. That brother of yours is in big trouble.

Alice

From: Holly
To: Alice and Matt

What's he done?

From: Alice and Matt
To: Holly

He made me promise not to tell anyone.

From: Holly
To: Alice and Matt

He hasn't got you involved in this stupid fetish club, has he?

From: Alice and Matt
To: Holly

What fetish club?

Subject: Him

From: Holly
To: Jason GrangerRM; Aisha

So do you think they're from HIM then?

From: Jason GrangerRM
To: Holly; Aisha

No, can't be. It said from an admirer… so who d'you know who's hung like a horse in that place???

From: Holly
To: Jason GrangerRM; Aisha

They could be from him? Maybe it's an apology?

Subject: Charlie

From: Alice and Matt
To: Holly

Anyway, a month or so ago, he asked me to start buying him Viagra, because you can't buy it in England…!

From: Holly
To: Alice and Matt

You are kidding me? You didn't say yes, did you?

From: Alice and Matt
To: Holly

YES.

From: Holly
To: Alice and Matt

Oh come on Alice???

From: Alice and Matt
To: Holly

You know what he's like, it's difficult saying no. Anyway, that's not the worst bit. When I got him his Viagra last month, I got it from the village's ONLY pharmacist. Stupid thing to do, I know. I go there again today, and my Spanish isn't great, and the shop is quite busy, and I've begun explaining about Matt and his back problem... ?

From: Holly
To: Alice and Matt

And?

From: Alice and Matt
To: Holly

I'm trying to explain to them in bad Spanish about Matt's back, the fact he's lying flat out, he's stuck there, stiff, and it's painful, and he can't get up. The lovely little black-shawled Spanish women in the shop have shaken their heads in disgust, and I've been given a bottle of pills I've only just realised are Viagra again! I can't go back there. I'll have to find a new chemist.

Subject: It's over

From: Jason GrangerRM
To: Holly; Aisha

Come on, Holly, they won't be from him. Men are bastards, and that's that.

Apart from me.

Jason

From: Holly
To: Jason GrangerRM; Aisha

I think they could be???

From: Jason GrangerRM
To: Holly; Aisha

Isn't there anyone else there you fancy???? Come on, think?

From: Holly
To: Jason GrangerRM; Aisha

No there isn't.

From: Jason GrangerRM
To: Holly; Aisha

There must be someone else you want there, it's a big place??

xx

From: Holly
To: Jason GrangerRM; Aisha

I don't want anyone else, I just want him.

From: Jason GrangerRM
To: Holly; Aisha

But honey, you can't have him.

From: Holly
To: Jason GrangerRM; Aisha

You sent those flowers, didn't you.

From: Jason GrangerRM
To: Holly; Aisha

Yes sweetie. Didn't think you'd imagine they were from him.
Sorry.

From: Holly
To: Jason GrangerRM; Aisha

Oh.

From: Jason GrangerRM
To: Holly; Aisha

It seemed like a good idea to cheer you up. All went a bit wrong.

From: Holly
To: Jason GrangerRM; Aisha

OK.

From: Jason GrangerRM
To: Holly; Aisha

So just move on baby.

From: Holly
To: Jason GrangerRM; Aisha

Just wanted him back. So much.

From: Jason GrangerRM
To: Holly; Aisha

I know.

From: Holly
To: Jason GrangerRM; Aisha

I don't want it to be over. Jason, I need to cry now. Got to go. Love you both so much.

x

Subject: Hi Holly

From: James Lawrence
To: Holly

How are you?

From: Holly
To: James Lawrence

OK, where've you been?

From: James Lawrence
To: Holly

I've just been working hard. How have you been?

From: Holly
To: James Lawrence

OK, a bit confused, to be honest.

From: James Lawrence
To: Holly

I know, I've been a bit off recently. I didn't mean to upset you.

From: Holly
To: James Lawrence

So, what are we doing?

From: James Lawrence
To: Holly

How d'you mean?

From: Holly
To: James Lawrence

Are we still together?

From: James Lawrence
To: Holly

I care about you very much, but you know how hard it is having any kind of relationship.

From: Holly
To: James Lawrence

What?

From: James Lawrence
To: Holly

Any relationship is difficult, especially one with people at work.

From: Holly
To: James Lawrence

No it's not. If it's secrecy you're worried about, we can keep it secret. It can be our secret. Barely anyone knows?

From: James Lawrence
To: Holly

Holly, it's not just a secrecy thing. It's just not good, having a relationship with people at work.

From: Holly
To: James Lawrence

We can get through it.

From: James Lawrence
To: Holly

Holly, we can't.

From: Holly

To: James Lawrence

Please James, please don't do this. Call me now, let's go outside and talk about it for a few minutes.

From: James Lawrence

To: Holly

No Holly, sorry.

From: Holly

To: James Lawrence

I'm dialling you now, just pick up the phone please. For me, I need to talk about this.

Subject: PLEASE ANSWER YOUR PHONE

From: Holly

To: James Lawrence

Please answer your phone, please James, I just need to talk to you. Come on, please, I just want to talk to you. I know you're saying it's over, but please.

Subject: HOLLY GO HOME

From: Patricia Gillot

To: Holly

Go home, darlin, please go home. You can't sit there blubbering. Come over here and give me a hug, then go.

xxxx

From: Holly

To: Patricia Gillot

NO I'm NOT GOING ANYWHERE! NO.

From: Patricia Gillot
To: Holly

Please darlin, you'll get yourself sacked, just go.

xx

I don't want to lose you.

xx

month 4

week 1
bank holiday monday

Subject: Call me

From: Alice and Matt
To: Holly

Give me a call when you get my email Tuesday. I've been trying to reach you all weekend.
Alice

tuesday

Subject: News Update

From: Jason GrangerRM
To: Holly

Did you hear about my poor love?

Subject: Morning

From: Patricia Gillot
To: Holly

Nice to see you, fancy a coffee?

From: Holly
To: Patricia Gillot

Hi,
Had some. How was your weekend?
Holly

From: Patricia Gillot
To: Holly

Good. Interesting outfit you've got on. Where's your jacket?

From: Holly
To: Patricia Gillot

Hi,
I forgot my jacket, sorry Trish.

From: Patricia Gillot
To: Holly

That's alright. Get yourself the one from the cupboard the temp wore. It's just been cleaned.

Subject: Booking

From: Jennie Pithwait
To: Holly

Morning Holly,
Is there a problem with my meeting tomorrow?
Jennie

From: Holly
To: Jennie Pithwait

Hi Jenny,
Everything is fine with your booking. It's in the schedule, all confirmed.
Holly

From: Jennie Pithwait
To: Holly

Sorry Holly,
But if you've already put it in the schedule, then why haven't you told me about it? How am I meant to know it's been organised?

| From: Holly |
| To: Jennie Pithwait |

I never usually send you confirmation. You just know I'll do it?

Subject: News!!!

| From: Jason GrangerRM |
| To: Holly |

Important French History was made this weekend. It's the first time the words: 'Paris is going down' didn't refer to either a football team or a sexual act.

? ?

| From: Holly |
| To: Jason GrangerRM |

? ? ? ?

| From: Jason GrangerRM |
| To: Holly |

Paris. Hilton—you know, she's going to prison—didn't you know? ? ? ?

| From: Holly |
| To: Jason GrangerRM |

Sorry Jason, things here aren't going great.
Holly

Subject: Phone

| From: Holly |
| To: Alice and Matt |

Got your email. I turned my phone off at the weekend. Did you need me?

From: Alice and Matt
To: Holly

Is everything OK?

From: Holly
To: Alice and Matt

We've broken up.

From: Alice and Matt
To: Holly

Oh honey,

This is just totally unfair, you can't tell me something like that. How can I give my sister a hug when she's so far away?

xxx

What happened?

From: Holly
To: Alice and Matt

It ended.

From: Alice and Matt
To: Holly

I gathered that. Don't worry, you are beautiful and lovely and you've got a huge heart, and men are just crazy if they can't see that. Do you want to know my advice?

Subject: Bookings

From: Jennie Pithwait
To: Holly

Holly,

I have client meetings all week, and I simply need to know there won't be any hiccups.

From: Holly

To: Jennie Pithwait

No, don't worry, there won't be any hiccups.

Regards,

Holly

Subject: Advice

From: Holly

To: Alice and Matt

What's your advice then?

From: Alice and Matt

To: Holly

Well, did I tell you that Matt now has bad diarrhoea? And he still can't move from his bed?

From: Holly

To: Alice and Matt

No you didn't.

From: Alice and Matt

To: Holly

Well, my advice is this:

When you look for a new man, don't go for a arrogant b*stard banker, who's obsessed with money.

But equally, IF YOU DO go for a sweet, kind, gentle man, make sure he doesn't fill your house full of snakes, then cages full of rats so he can feed the snakes, then, now this is important to imagine, Holly, it'll make you feel a lot better about your situation. Make sure he then DOESN'T DO HIS BACK IN and ask you to cover for him???! So you spend your weekends cleaning up his shit and feeding his rats.

AAAAAAAAAAAAAAAAAAAAAAAAAAAAAAGH

I think it's lucky I love him so much.

From: Holly
To: Alice and Matt

I'll remember your advice. Thanks Alice. xx
Holly

Subject: Outside

From: Jennie Pithwait
To: Holly

Have you been out to lunch yet?

From: Holly
To: Jennie Pithwait

Why—you fancy meeting up?

From: Jennie Pithwait
To: Holly

No, can't, I'm too busy. I'm just going out for a sandwich and
wondered if it was cold—you'd wear a jumper whatever the
weather was though.
x

Subject: Tomorrow

From: Patricia Gillot
To: Holly

You going to be in tomorrow?

From: Holly
To: Patricia Gillot

Of course I will be.

From: Patricia Gillot
To: Holly

Good. I'm proud of you.

From: Holly
To: Patricia Gillot

I did the wrong thing on Friday, didn't I, made a fool of myself.

From: Patricia Gillot
To: Holly

Listen, if you ever want to talk about anything, I'm here.

From: Holly
To: Patricia Gillot

I just really wanted it to work.

From: Patricia Gillot
To: Holly

I know.

From: Holly
To: Patricia Gillot

I thought we went well together, it's been so much fun. I thought it was fun for him too.

From: Patricia Gillot
To: Holly

It would have been darlin, don't worry about him.

From: Holly
To: Patricia Gillot

Have a great evening.

xxxxxx

I'm not usually this wet, promise.

wednesday

Subject: My daughter

From: Mum and Dad
To: Holly

Holly,

We haven't heard from you for a while. What's the news? You don't keep us very informed, do you?

Love, Mum

Subject: Meeting

From: Jennie Pithwait
To: Holly

My meeting this morning was missing a continental breakfast. We had to reorder. If this is the amount of care you put into your relationships, it's no wonder they have a limited shelf life.

Jennie

Subject: JASON AND AISHA! GET YOUR ARSES HERE

From: Holly
To: Jason GrangerRM; Aisha

You two WILL NOT BELIEVE THE CHEEK OF THIS BITCH. HATE HER HATE HER

I'm going up there now.

Subject: Your email??

From: Aisha
To: Holly; Jason GrangerRM

Darling, who are you talking about? And are you sure you want to do this?

Aish

From: Holly
To: Aisha; Jason GrangerRM

Jenny or Jennie, stupid spelling anyway, bitch. She just emailed me and said 'if this is the amount of care you put into relationships no wonder they have a limited shelf life'!!!!!!!!!

From: Aisha
To: Holly

GO UP NOW AND KILL HER.
I'll take the blame. Do it Holly.

From: Holly
To: Aisha; Jason GrangerRM

I'm going to.

Subject: Morning

From: Patricia Gillot
To: Holly

Where are you off to?

From: Holly
To: Patricia Gillot

Upstairs, got to go, back soon.

From: Patricia Gillot
To: Holly

SIT DOWN.

From: Holly
To: Patricia Gillot

You don't understand, Trish, I'll tell you later.

Subject: Jennie

From: Aisha
To: Holly

She's laughing about your breakup, the slut, isn't she?

Subject: SIT DOWN!

From: Patricia Gillot
To: Holly

Subject: READ YOUR SCREEN!!! MRS TYSON SIT DOWN NOW!!!

From: Patricia Gillot
To: Holly

From: Holly
To: Patricia Gillot

It's Jennie, she's so, you won't believe—Trish, I just need some fresh air now.

From: Patricia Gillot
To: Holly

I know, that's it. Now go and get some air and then do your makeup. Give us a hug first.

Subject: All sorted babe

From: Aisha
To: Holly

I've been speaking to an ex-shag of mine, and he knows one of the Adams family, so don't you worry.

From: Patricia Gillot
To: Aisha

This is Trisha—Holly's nosy friend sitting at her desk. Don't start with all that, Aisha. Let her decide if she wants to do it. There's other ways of dealing with this.

Trisha.

Please delete this email.

Subject: Flight back to England

From: Mum and Dad
To: Holly

Holly,

Will you reply to my emails when I write to you! Your father is getting better, better enough to travel again, so I think we should go about booking his flight back to England. It's very difficult to arrange anything with you these days. What day is best for you, so you can pick him up from the airport?

Mum

Subject: Booking

From: Holly
To: Jennie Pithwait

Dear Jennie,

If you know anything about what we do down here, then you'd realise how much care we do take to book a room's facilities. However, if the catering staff don't follow our instructions to the letter, then mistakes can happen; as in this case, I booked the room accurately, the catering staff didn't deliver. So maybe you should take your head out of your arse and check these things before pointing the blame?? I would have thought they'd have at least taught you that up there?

Also, for your information, my relationships only have a short shelf life with those people I decide to push off the shelf.

Holly

Subject: Just Heard

From: Jason GrangerRM
To: Holly; Aisha

You OK?

From: Holly
To: Jason GrangerRM

I am now. Tell me something happy.

From: Jason GrangerRM
To: Holly

I'm going to GAY Saturday, and you can come???

From: Holly
To: Jason GrangerRM

Sorry, I can't this weekend. Just found out I got a job I went for, and I'm working that night. (I'm starting to do some evening waitressing in a restaurant in Covent Garden.)

From: Jason GrangerRM
To: Holly; Aisha

Which one? We'll come and see you!

From: Holly
To: Jason GrangerRM; Aisha

Like that's happening. No telling nothing.

From: Jason GrangerRM
To: Holly; Aisha

Does your work know?

From: Holly
To: Jason GrangerRM; Aisha

No, we can't have two jobs.
dan dan dahhhh. I'm a rule breaker, sue me.

From: Jason GrangerRM
To: Holly

You're going to be shattered.

From: Holly
To: Jason GrangerRM

I know, but bills need paying. Things aren't great in that area.

Subject: The news you've been waiting for!

From: Charlie Denham
To: Holly

Spread the word …

Holly Denham is now …

The official licensee for one dirty and depraved club of filthy perverts!!!

You lucky lucky thing, spread the news!! We passed everything, ready for business.

Charlie

Subject: Money

From: Jason GrangerRM
To: Holly

I didn't know you had any money problems. You always look like such a princess!

From: Holly
To: Jason GrangerRM

You're the best. But a bad liar—like when you suggested that 'suits were the new dresses' when you realised I didn't have the money for shopping so I didn't feel crap about it all.

That was nice.

x

From: Jason GrangerRM
To: Holly

Oh, you're making me all emotional. I'm going to go and hug a stranger.

Subject: Your club

From: Holly
To: Charlie Denham

I'm not going to be spreading the news around, because it's not anything I'm proud of. (So please, don't you tell anyone. That's the last thing I need at the moment!)
(Sorry Charlie, I'm pleased for you though.)

From: Charlie Denham
To: Holly

Ooops, your name is on our headed paper. But don't panic, no one you know will know. Unless you know anyone who's likely to go to these kind of things.
Charlie
PS Opening Night not far away!

From: Holly
To: Charlie Denham

HEADED PAPER!!! I can't talk about this now, but no, Charlie, this is not good. I won't be going to your Opening Night, either. SORRY.

Subject: Apologies from Jennie

From: Jennie Pithwait
To: Holly

Sorry for the misunderstanding. I've checked into it, and I was wrong about the booking.
Jennie.

PS I was right about the shelf life, though. James wasn't exactly pushed. Was he now?

Subject: Jennie

From: Holly
To: Patricia Gillot

Did you see Jennie just then???

From: Patricia Gillot
To: Holly

Yeah, she's just doing it to wind you up.

Subject: Friends you don't need

From: Holly
To: Jennie Pithwait

Maybe he wasn't pushed.

But you certainly were,

pushed,

dumped,

and thankfully, now in the bin.

Enjoy it there, won't you.

Holly

From: Jennie Pithwait
To: Holly

Such a pity.

Going out clubbing with you was really like going out with a younger sister: one who never wore the right thing, never said anything grown up, and never had any money.

Oh well.

xxxx

From: Holly
To: Jennie Pithwait

Isn't there a bone to chew somewhere?

Subject: CV BANK

From: ReceptionWorld.com
To: Holly

Dear Job Seeker,

Thank you for registering your CV with ReceptionWorld.com

Your CV will now be available to many employers across the world looking for experienced receptionists.

ADMIN

Subject: Re: your last message

From: Jennie Pithwait
To: Holly

No bone to chew, but there's your ex-boyfriend to screw. Ooh yes, I think I'll go do that.

xxx

Subject: Embarrassing

From: Jennie Pithwait
To: Holly

If you didn't get that… he wasn't pushed, he was stolen.

Oh, and please don't get your mother writing to my parents again. It was so embarrassing to hear they were begging to have my help. To be honest, receptionists don't make it in the banking world. Oh, except meeting and greeting. Go Holly.

Subject: Need to go

From: Holly
To: Patricia Gillot

Can I go home please trisha, just can't be here any more. sorry.

From: Patricia Gillot
To: Holly

What's wrong, darlin???

From: Holly
To: Patricia Gillot

Can't be here, sorry.

From: Patricia Gillot
To: Holly

What's she done to you now?

From: Holly
To: Patricia Gillot

Don't worry,

Bye.

xxxx

Subject: MORE NEWS!

From: Jason GrangerRM
To: Holly

Got some more news about Paris and Britney, might cheer you up... ??!!!

From: Holly
To: Jason GrangerRM

Hi Jason,

This is Trisha. Holly's just gone home. Can you look after her.

From: Jason GrangerRM
To: Holly

Why? What's happened???

From: Holly
To: Jason GrangerRM

She read something, her face went, shoulders went. Emailed me, told me she had to go. Then got up and walked out into the rain. Didn't take her coat or nothing.

Trisha

Look after her, Jason. You know what it's about—Jennie.

From: Jason GrangerRM
To: Holly

OK, thanks.

thursday

Subject: Can I have an answer please?

From: Mum and Dad
To: Holly

Holly,

I'm getting a little bit annoyed with you, Holly. It's become very frustrating, especially when I need to organize so many important things.

Firstly, your house. We've already begun sending out invitations for our reunion party in England, they have your address on them, so I really do need your father to meet with whoever will be staying there over the next month; now he's well enough to travel.

Secondly, I'd like to invite the Lawrences. I think it would be a great way to meet them, and I'm dropping them an email now. Can you ask lovely James whether they're likely to be staying over?

Mum

Subject: Attention Trisha—from Jason, Holls' friend from the hotel

From: Jason GrangerRM
To: Holly

Trisha,

I don't think Holly will be back there again, so I'm hoping you're still reading Holly's emails. If so, can you delete her inbox, etc.? I've sent this to what I think will be your email address too.

Thanks for this.

Regards,

Jason

Subject: From Trisha—to JASON

From: Holly
To: Jason GrangerRM

OK, darlin, didn't think she would be really. I'll tell everyone. Pass on my kisses to her, poor love. I'll tell Judy, and I'll delete all her messages now. Can you get her pass back off her and her uniform?

Trish

Subject: This might be a nice thing for us to do?

From: Pregnant Pam
To: Holly

I was thinking of something nice we could do together. What about going to feed the ducks? There's some in St. James' Park, and they're so sweet?

Pam

Subject: Service

From: Ralph Tooms
To: Holly; Patricia Gillot

Haven't heard much from you two. If you want, I'm around to get drinks or like if you want food. I'm here to be used, I mean, not

used, I mean, here to be helpful, but you know, if I'm not too busy
and everything. Then I could. If you needed anything. If not, then
that's cool.

Ralph

Subject: Jennie

From: James Lawrence
To: Holly

I heard Jennie's been having a go. Hope you can take it all on the
chin. You know her cutting dry wit, it's just the way she is. Makes
for an entertaining day, though. She drives everyone nuts up here.
You should see her.

Hope we can be friends soon and all go out together. Sorry about the
way things turned out. I'm sure the bank's full of nice guys though,
better than me.

James

Subject: Fabulous sunny day!

From: Holly
To: Patricia Gillot

Hello

xxx

From: Patricia Gillot
To: Holly

Where've you been??????
Trish

From: Holly
To: Patricia Gillot

You told me today to come at 12 p.m.?? The late client meeting??

From: Patricia Gillot
To: Holly

I did, darlin, I did, I forgot. You look great. Really gorgeous, glad you're in, I wasn't sure you'd turn up.

From: Holly
To: Patricia Gillot

Yes, I'm back and happy. Sorry about yesterday. Things will be different today though, I promise you. I'm going to have some fun. Let's see, who's first? I see I have an email from my mum, that should be enlightening.

From: Patricia Gillot
To: Holly

Jason sent you an email, I answered it for you. I think he was worrying about you.
Trisha
Are you sure you're OK. You're not on drugs, are ya? It's not sunny out there, you know?

From: Holly
To: Patricia Gillot

Isn't it? Oh, I'm sure it was when I left home. Maybe it's just my mood.

From: Patricia Gillot
To: Holly

Yeah, or the Prozac.
xx

Subject: Getting it up

From: BEAUTY MAKEUP **From:** TRACEY
To: Holly

Sorry to be sending this you but;s
(*%$Sex life getting you down?

(*&)

Then maybe you need Viagra

$10 x 2 pks

$20 x 4 pks

$40 x 10 pks

Chemist online

From: Holly

To: BEAUTY MAKE-UP From: TRACEY

Thank you ever so much for your kind offer of Viagra. However, I am a single lady, so I can choose to make myself happy with something which doesn't have the option of being limp or small. I do know a couple of people who may be interested, however:

One is CharlesDenham@Artnightclub.com

And the other is JLawrence@huerstwright.com

Oh, and I think the latter would probably be interested in any diverse sexual toys you might stock, plastic sheep, adult baby kits (if they exist), you know the type of thing. Also, I believe JLawrence is also keen to find a bride, if you have any suggestions. Possibly a kennel too.

And I know this is a long shot, but if you have any information on cheap flights or real estate, then he's your man.

Yours,

Holly

Subject: House and renting etc

From: Holly

To: Mum and Dad

MUM

DO NOT WRITE TO ANYONE UNTIL YOU'VE SPOKEN TO ME.

HOLLY

Subject: MUM WHERE ARE YOU?

From: Holly
To: Mum and Dad

?????????????????????????????????

From: Mum and Dad
To: Holly

I don't know, we hear nothing from you for ages, then you're on the phone leaving urgent messages and emailing, demanding attention. I suppose now you need US, we have to be here.

Yes, Holly, what is it?

Mum

From: Holly
To: Mum and Dad

Mum,

Just don't email anyone for the moment. You haven't, have you?

From: Mum and Dad
To: Holly

Why?

From: Holly
To: Mum and Dad

Mum,

Picture this: I'm typing by stabbing the keyboard, and I'm gritting my teeth because you're not answering my question. Please, oh lovely mother of mine, have you or have you not emailed JAMES' PARENTS YET?

From: Mum and Dad
To: Holly

No!

From: Holly
To: Mum and Dad

Good!

Now just stay by the computer, we need to talk. But first I have to deal with a friend of mine who seems to have a duck fixation.

Love, Holly

Subject: Ducks?

From: Pregnant Pam
To: Holly

There may be some ducks closer to you, if you're interested?

Pam

From: Holly
To: Pregnant Pam

Ducks??? Pam, are you OK?

Holly

From: Pregnant Pam
To: Holly

Hi Holly,

Doesn't have to be ducks. We could just sit and eat some sandwiches? Just thought it might be nice?

Pam

Subject: Service

From: Holly
To: Ralph Tooms

Ralph,

Thank you for your kind email.

xx

Yes, you can run off and get me some lunch, if you'd like. You can report to my desk at 1500 hours.

From, your boss.

Just joking!

From: Ralph Tooms
To: Holly

Sorted, I'll be there, cheers.

Oh, with or without the cap?

Ralph

From: Holly
To: Ralph Tooms

With, definitely with!!

Subject: Lunch—sorry

From: Holly
To: Pregnant Pam

I'm sorry, can't do the duck thing.

Holly

From: Pregnant Pam
To: Holly

That's OK.

Pam

From: Holly
To: Pregnant Pam

Don't like ducks. But please please please, can we meet up and do some baby shopping?? Isn't it time you got some clothes that weren't pink? Seen some lovely pooh bear jammies???

From: Pregnant Pam
To: Holly

Yay.

Great, yes yes, this is going to be so much fun. I promise, it won't be dull. Oh, great, I'll start planning where we can go.

Pam

From: Holly
To: Pregnant Pam

Great, and you can fill me in with everything I've missed. xxxx

From: Pregnant Pam
To: Holly

Everything??

From: Holly
To: Pregnant Pam

Yes, even the yukky bits.

Holly

Subject: MUM

From: Holly
To: Mum and Dad

I really really really really didn't appreciate you sending a letter to Jennie's mum and dad, to ask them if she could get me into banking. You will never know how utterly humiliating that was. I told you not to—and you still did. It was really hurtful. I am very happy on reception and don't know a thing about finance, as you'll no doubt find out soon. I wouldn't ever, ever want anything from Jennie. I can make my own way.

Love you.

Holly

From: Mum and Dad
To: Holly

Dear Holly,

I'm sorry if what I did upset you. Jennie's lovely, I'm sure she would have understood all I was doing was looking out for you, so don't worry (I must add, I think you're being a little overdramatic about it all). It sounds to me like someone's fallen out with their best friend from school. What have you done to upset Jennie? You didn't get drunk and sing again, did you? I've told you about the dangers of social drinking. It's best to stay at home on your own if you're going to get drunk.

Love, Mum

From: Holly
To: Mum and Dad

Mum,

No, I didn't get drunk!!! And sitting at home drinking on your own is an awful thing to be encouraging people to do. Sorry, but I'm very busy now, lots of people coming in.

x

From: Mum and Dad
To: Holly

OK, so let's forget about all that, but when are we going to meet with lovely James's parents?

From: Holly
To: Mum and Dad

You won't be meeting with lovely James, lovely Jennie, or either of their lovely lovely parents, because James dumped me. That's right, he dumped me, because he thought I was too keen, or too fat, or maybe it was meeting the weird parents, who knows. But the fact is, he's decided he'd prefer to be shagging lovely Jennie, and Jennie's decided she'd like to make me feel well and truly sh*t about it all. So no, I can't think I'll be entertaining the happy couple, Mum.

Oh, PS, and also, I lost my house.

xxx

Subject: You OK?

From: Patricia Gillot
To: Holly

You OK there?

From: Holly
To: Patricia Gillot

Couldn't be better, thanks.
Holly

friday

Subject: Parents

From: Holly
To: Jason GrangerRM

A bright and crispy morning to you, Jason. I want to know—have you ever told your mum exactly how you feel? I did that yesterday, and it felt great. Probably won't ever speak to me again, but it was at least very relieving.

From: Jason GrangerRM
To: Holly

Yes, I told my mum how I felt when I was sixteen—(that I was gay), she took it pretty hard at first. I think she convinced herself it was all just in my head, then she blamed society for making me gay. We had a huge row, where things were said which neither of us meant, then it was all over. I didn't talk to her again for a few years, which was sad, because she's actually all right.

From: Holly
To: Jason GrangerRM

I like your mum. She is great.

Subject: Her upstairs

From: Patricia Gillot
To: Holly

Morning,

Didn't tell you yesterday, petrol and flames came to mind, but she came down looking for you yesterday.

From: Holly
To: Patricia Gillot

Jennie?

From: Patricia Gillot
To: Holly

No, darlin, the bleedin' queen.

She came down before you got here, looking all pleased with herself. She must have thought you weren't coming back.

Subject: Men

From: Aisha
To: Holly

I haven't been in touch for a bit, because I guessed you were feeling a bit bad. You better now, sweetie?

Aish

From: Holly
To: Aisha

Yes. I know you're not good at the whole consoling thing. But I'm fine. How are you?

From: Aisha
To: Holly

I thought you'd never ask.

I've been lying to Jason for a while now, about a few different things, and I'm still seeing his boss… Also, do you think it's too early to ask for holiday???

From: Holly
To: Aisha

Aisha??? Please tell me you're joking?

From: Aisha
To: Holly

No, and I'm seeing his boss above his boss. I know, I know. But there's no good giving me a lecture now.
Also, I'm kind of pregnant.

From: Holly
To: Aisha

Pregnant??????

Subject: Problems with our Front of House

From: Jennie Pithwait
To: Holly

Holly,
RE: Delivery of accurate messages
Can we revert to the standard company rules when it comes to passing on important client information? I object to being called over in the reception area and having a Post-it note rudely jammed into my hand.
Jennie

Subject: Throwing the towel in

From: Mum and Dad
To: Holly

Dear Holly,

I've given a lot of thought to your last email. It's not our fault you split up with James, but of course, we both feel for you greatly and you must be going through a difficult time. But I want to know if you feel this isn't just another 'Sebastian-type situation,' all over again?

Mum

From: Holly
To: Mum and Dad

What exactly is a 'Sebastian-type situation,' Mum????

From: Mum and Dad
To: Holly

You know, giving up at the first hurdle, letting a good one slip away. Don't have a go at me when I suggest this, but have you thought it could be something to do with you?

Mum

Subject: Pregnant

From: Aisha
To: Holly

I just don't want a lecture, I need a shoulder to cry on and to talk about it all. Are you around tonight, for an Aisha chat?

xxxxxx

From: Holly
To: Aisha

Of course I'm not going to give you a lecture. I'll be around to chat tonight, come over.

Love you,

Holly

From: Aisha
To: Holly

Oh good.

OK, then, I'm not really pregnant, I just didn't want to get the lecture about shagging the bosses. But I honestly do really want to ask Jason for time off to go on holiday… to Ibiza for a week!!! How lucky am I??? All paid for …

xxxxx

Subject: Fridays

From: Patricia Gillot
To: Holly

Busy init?

From: Holly
To: Patricia Gillot

Do you have the sort of friends who would lie about being pregnant?

From: Patricia Gillot
To: Holly

Oh God, yeah, sometimes you got to, to get your man. I've never done it, though.

Trish

Subject: Ex-husbands

From: Holly
To: Mum and Dad

Mum,

I can't believe you've just written that?! I don't think you realize how bad he actually was. Dad knows. Why don't you ask Dad about Sebastian before you write this stuff?

Holly

From: Mum and Dad
To: Holly

Listen, I'm not trying to point the blame, only get you to look at it from our side, darling.
Mum

From: Holly
To: Mum and Dad

Great time to talk to me like this. While you're in the mood, Mum, why don't you go out and kick a kitten or burst a child's balloon? I'm really trying to hold it together here, Mum. Can you get off my back today.

From: Mum and Dad
To: Holly

I don't think me getting off your back will help you at all. Now, on top of all this, you tell us you've lost that lovely house? What happened?

From: Holly
To: Mum and Dad

I'm not talking about this now. I've just split up with a someone I really liked, and I thought my mum would be the last person I'd need to hide from. Can you go away, Mum, please.
Holly

From: Mum and Dad
To: Holly

OK, Holly, I will.
But tell me first, just what exactly did YOU think was so wrong with Sebastian anyway?

From: Holly
To: Mum and Dad

I was frightened of him, Mum, and I don't think you're meant to be frightened of your husband, OK? No, I don't think you should be. Now please, Mum, get lost!

Subject: Hello

From: Jason GrangerRM
To: Holly

Hey,
What's the news?
Jason

From: Holly
To: Jason GrangerRM

Wish I was working there with you.

From: Jason GrangerRM
To: Holly

Come on, it's amazing how you're doing. Love this new napalm-spitting, revenge-battling you!!

From: Holly
To: Jason GrangerRM

It's not really a new me, to be honest. It's the same me, but really battered, really nearly very beaten, the me which wants to hide and hide and hide and never come out to play again.

Each day I get up and I really do fight, Jason, I do. I fight to get him out of my head, because I always wake up thinking of him, and my mornings are spent just staring into space, remembering things, trying to work out what I said wrong, what I did wrong to f*ck it all up.

I come to work, hoping Trish can get me out of it, but it takes a while. She's really wonderful, and I fight, I fight to put it all at arm's length, like try to imagine I'm someone else, like it never happened, like he doesn't work on the floors above me, and that bitch isn't there, too. I push it away, and sometimes I win, I do, and I share a joke with Trish, and by the time I go home at night, I'm feeling better, I've covered it all over, I've bluffed myself and I go to bed, I fall asleep, and the fighting is over. I wake up the next day, and guess what? I dreamt about being back with him. Of course, I was back with him, and it was all so perfect and brilliant and wonderful, then slowly the hammer comes down, and I remember, IT'S OVER !!—and it's all fresh again!! And why did it happen, what did I do to mess it up?? I repeat this cycle of absolute sh*t each day, and I HATE IT! I hate it so much, Jason.

From: Jason GrangerRM
To: Holly

Call me as soon as you can. I'll come and meet you outside your office for lunch, my treat?? I'll bring you ice cream and Smarties and all things fun and bad. I'll just wear a thong—nothing else??? Singing the Macarena? Juggling bananas?

xx

From: Holly
To: Jason GrangerRM

Would the thong be in leopard print?

From: Jason GrangerRM
To: Holly

Of course.

From: Holly
To: Jason GrangerRM

I don't want the red Smarties.

From: Jason GrangerRM
To: Holly

I'll remove them all.

From: Holly
To: Jason GrangerRM

OK. See you at lunchtime.

xxx love you

Subject: Our fun night together!!

From: Aisha
To: Holly

What time do you want me there tonight?
Aish

From: Holly
To: Aisha

I don't.
xxx

Subject: Cruella

From: Patricia Gillot
To: Holly

She's on her way down.

From: Holly
To: Patricia Gillot

Now?

From: Patricia Gillot
To: Holly

Yes, now. She just called.

From: Holly
To: Patricia Gillot

Sh*t. I'm going for a fag.

From: Patricia Gillot
To: Holly

You don't smoke!

From: Holly
To: Patricia Gillot

Then I'm going for an herbal joss stick praying session.

From: Patricia Gillot
To: Holly

Before she gets here, you'll want to delete any messages calling her Cruella.

From: Holly
To: Patricia Gillot

Why, because she'll see what you call her Trisha? THAT YOU CALL HER SHELLA OLD BAT FROM HELL CRUELLA?

From: Patricia Gillot
To: Holly

OK, stop that now. When she finishes talking to him, she'll be able to see my screen!

From: Holly
To: Patricia Gillot

OK, I won't call Cruella anything else, she's lovely. Lovely lovely Cruella. Who doesn't smell bad at all.

From: Patricia Gillot
To: Holly

You are so wrong. You stop giggling.

Subject: STINKS, CRUELLA STINKS, IT'S TRUE

From: Holly
To: Patricia Gillot

This is like Russian Roulette, it's so much fun!!

From: Patricia Gillot
To: Holly

You wait till after school, I'm going to pull your hair.

From: Holly
To: Patricia Gillot

ha ha ha ha

Subject: I'm dying

From: Aisha
To: Holly

I'm dying.

It's true, I didn't want to tell you that before, but there it is. I have two more weeks to live. Poor me.

xxxx boo hoo.

From: Holly
To: Aisha

That's awful.

Oh well.

Holly

Subject: OK OK OK

From: Aisha
To: Holly

I'm not really dying, I admit it.

Aisha

From: Holly
To: Aisha

Good.

From: Aisha
To: Holly

But I am being followed!

From: Holly
To: Aisha

I've told you before, you are not being followed. This is just another good reason to stay off the drugs.

x

Subject: Friends

From: Holly
To: Patricia Gillot

Hey,
Do you have any friends that think they're being followed?
Holly

From: Patricia Gillot
To: Holly

What's with all the 'do you have friends' questions? I don't have any friends who think they're being followed, no.

From: Holly
To: Patricia Gillot

OK.

From: Patricia Gillot
To: Holly

I do have a friend called Mystic Sam, though—tells everyone he can look into the future. Hears voices in his head, telling him about stuff.

From: Holly
To: Patricia Gillot

Do you believe him?

From: Patricia Gillot
To: Holly

Yeah, but you'd hear voices too if you smoked as much weed as he does. He's off his nut most of the day. Actually, he thought he was being followed, but he was: got nicked for dealing. I'm off, goodnight.

xxx

week 2

monday

Subject: Gay clubbing in London

From: Holly
To: Jason GrangerRM; Aisha

AISHA AND JASON,

After thinking long and hard about my life, I've decided I might give it a go at being gay. Alright, maybe not gay, but I thought I'd try hanging out in the odd gay club with you, Jason, get my mind off men.

xxxxx

Sorry to just talk about myself, hope you both had wonderful weekends and are bubbling with exciting news.

From: Aisha
To: Holly; Jason GrangerRM

Get your mind off men, yeah, good one. So you're going to start hanging out in places which are packed with hunky, muscular, oiled, beautiful men, who know how to dance? Yes, that'll take your mind off men.

From: Jason GrangerRM
To: Holly; Aisha

I hate to agree with Aisha about anything, actually (and not that I wouldn't welcome you with open arms). But Aisha's right, the guys do look good, and sensitive too… Which is a bummer for you.

Jason

From: Aisha
To: Holly; Jason GrangerRM

Yeah, what's a bummer is how full of crap you are, Jason.

From: Jason GrangerRM
To: Aisha; Holly

Aisha's upset because after I took her to GAY, she got kicked out of an after party. Two men were kissing, she threw herself underneath them and screamed 'take me, I'm yours!' Neither of them did, and we had to leave. It was really embarrassing.

From: Aisha
To: Holly; Jason GrangerRM

They were really rude Holly. Anyway, I think you should seriously consider the lesbian thing.
Aisha

From: Holly
To: Aisha; Jason GrangerRM

The lesbian thing?

From: Aisha
To: Holly; Jason GrangerRM

Yes. It could be a nice change for you? I've tried, and it's lots of fun. I know a lovely Chinese girl actually, I met her last week. She'd sit on your face for you?

From: Holly
To: Aisha; Jason GrangerRM

I'm OK. Very kind of you though Aisha.

From: Jason GrangerRM
To: Holly; Aisha

Now, I've just finished being sick (thank you Aisha), we're agreed that Holly shouldn't worry about guys, immerse herself in quality magazines, *OK!*, *Hello!*, etc., think lovely thoughts, and just enjoy being single for a while?
Jason

Subject: James Lawrence

From: Alistair Moffett
To: Holly

Hi,

I hope this isn't inappropriate, but I recently heard the news that you are no longer dating James Lawrence from IBD. I was hoping this may mean you would now accept a dinner invitation from me, Alistair Moffett.

Regards,

Alistair Moffett

Alistair Moffett, Legal and Compliance, H&W, High Holborn WC2 6NP

Subject: Annual Results

From: Shella Hamilton-Jones
To: Holly; Patricia Gillot; Samantha Smith; Dave Otto; Ralph Tooms

RE: Annual Results

Dear Conference Planning Committee,

We have a mammoth task ahead of us. With over 500 delegates descending upon our shores, we will need to avoid a minefield of potential disasters, all of which I am confident can be avoided, providing we first ensure we have enough planning and preparation. Owing to the late withdrawal of our Brussels office as a venue, we have just two months to get this right.

A budget has been set and, unlike the Jubilee extension, which was £1.2 billion over budget and 2 years late, and the Channel Tunnel, which was £5.2 billion over budget and 5 years late, this conference will be within budget and on time.

A great deal of research will need to go into achieving the best value for all areas of the conference, and I will be emailing you over the next few days with details of which areas will be covered by which team member.

Yours sincerely,

Shella

Subject: Hot stuff

From: Gavin Oliver
To: Holly

Holly

Fancy a beer after work?

Gav

Gavin Oliver, Equity Derivatives, Emerging Markets, H&W, High Holborn WC2 6NP

Subject: News!!!!

From: Holly
To: Jason GrangerRM; Aisha

I've been asked out by two guys, so I think I'm going to go out with both of them?

Holly

From: Jason GrangerRM
To: Holly; Aisha

Yes, that was always the other option—go out with as many men as humanly possible, at the same time.

From: Holly
To: Jason GrangerRM; Aisha

I'm going to be a slut!

From: Jason GrangerRM
To: Holly; Aisha

Good. Well that's settled then.

From: Aisha
To: Holly; Jason GrangerRM

Oh, goodie, we can be sluts together!! How exciting. Oh oh and we could charge for it??

From: Jason GrangerRM
To: Aisha; Holly

Tell Aisha your problems and suddenly the world seems that little bit rosier.

From: Aisha
To: Jason GrangerRM; Holly

Stop being so grumpy Jason.

From: Jason GrangerRM
To: Holly; Aisha

You split up from someone, and Aisha's way of cheering you up is to offer you a life of prostitution. I admire the way she can find a nugget of gold in any bad situation.

tuesday

Subject: Bet you're glad

From: Toby Williams
To: Holly

Hi Holly,
I heard what happened with James. Glad you realised what he's like.
Toby

From: Holly
To: Toby Williams

I also know what you're like too. So do me a favour and stop emailing?
Holly

Subject: Re your email

From: Holly
To: Alistair Moffett

Hi,

Do you know James then?

Holly

From: Alistair Moffett

To: Holly

Dear Holly,

No, I've never met him.

Alistair

Subject: Legal & Compliance

From: Holly

To: Patricia Gillot

Hey, would the Legal and Compliance lot know the IBD lot?

From: Patricia Gillot

To: Holly

Not really.

From: Holly

To: Patricia Gillot

So, if someone chats me up from Legal & Compliance because he's heard I'm now free, there's no reason he'd know, other than …

From: Patricia Gillot

To: Holly

It's gone around the whole bank.

From: Holly

To: Patricia Gillot

Good, that's what I thought. Nice to know.

From: Patricia Gillot

To: Holly

You lucky cow, all that attention! Come on, give me the goss. Who are they then???

From: Holly
To: Patricia Gillot

Someone called Alistair Moffett?

Subject: Clients waiting

From: Jennie Pithwait
To: Holly

Dear Receptionist,
Tomorrow I'll have quite a few clients coming in for meetings. Be a dear and run them up for me. I don't think I'll be able to come down and collect them myself (unfortunately).

Subject: Dinner invitation

From: Alistair Moffett
To: Holly

Holly,
Does this mean you would be accepting my invitation or not?

Subject: I know Alistair

From: Patricia Gillot
To: Holly

Alistair Moffett, no, you don't want to go near him, he's half your height, darlin.

From: Holly
To: Patricia Gillot

That's not so bad?

From: Patricia Gillot
To: Holly

He has a beard.

From: Holly
To: Patricia Gillot

Short and trendy, or big and scary?

From: Patricia Gillot
To: Holly

Big. And he's a groper.

From: Holly
To: Patricia Gillot

Come on, you're making that up?

From: Patricia Gillot
To: Holly

No, honest.

From: Holly
To: Patricia Gillot

I guess that's it for Alistair then.

From: Patricia Gillot
To: Holly

I think he's married too.

From: Holly
To: Patricia Gillot

Enough, Trish, I get the picture.
xxx

From: Patricia Gillot
To: Holly

Yeah, I wouldn't go near him. Some of the secretaries complained about him last year.

Subject: Dinner Invitation

From: Holly
To: Alistair Moffett

I'm going to have to say no to your invitation, but thank you.

From: Alistair Moffett
To: Holly

Any reason?

From: Holly
To: Alistair Moffett

Yes, I don't go out with married gropers.
Holly

Subject: Alistair

From: Patricia Gillot
To: Holly

Thinking about it, I think he got sacked last year.

From: Holly
To: Patricia Gillot

How can he still be here then?

From: Patricia Gillot
To: Holly

Looking at the directory, I got it wrong, different Alistair. Oh, darlin, your one is lovely, get in there quick.

wednesday

Subject: Chat up lines

From: Holly
To: Jason GrangerRM

I was called 'hot stuff' on an email from a trader. What d'you think?

From: Jason GrangerRM
To: Holly

Very cheesy. Depends what he looks like.

From: Holly
To: Jason GrangerRM

Quite nice, but in a cheaky, chappy, laddie kind of way.

From: Jason GrangerRM
To: Holly

Like the opposite of anyone you'd usually like.

From: Holly
To: Jason GrangerRM

We've got this company dinner at the Dorchester next Friday …

Subject: Lying to friends

From: Holly
To: Aisha

So have you told them you can't go out with them any more?

From: Aisha
To: Holly

I've talked to them, yes.

From: Holly
To: Aisha

Not just talked to them.
HAVE YOU TOLD THEM BOTH you won't be able to see them any more (without wearing your uniform).

From: Aisha
To: Holly

YES.

From: Holly
To: Aisha

And that doesn't mean having sex while wearing it, either. (I just want to make this completely clear.)

From: Aisha
To: Holly

You're like my mum! Yes, I've told them I won't, OK?

From: Holly
To: Aisha

Good.

From: Aisha
To: Holly

Stop stressing. Just cool it, hot stuff.

From: Holly
To: Aisha

Very funny. Tell Jason he's dead.

Subject: Attention: Receptionist

From: Jennie Pithwait
To: Holly

Re: Clients

I heard your message about my clients having arrived down there. I believe they allow support staff to use the company lift, so if you could run them up to me, that would be just fab. Meeting room 20. And try not to dilly-dally.

Jenns x

Subject: HER UPSTAIRS—HELP TRISH

From: Holly
To: Patricia Gillot

Don't tell me I have to do this, I'll die, please Trish. See below what she emailed me:

Re: Clients

I heard your message about my clients having arrived down there. I believe they allow support staff to use the company lift, so if you could run them up to me, that would be just fab. Meeting room 20. And try not to dilly-dally.

Jenns x

From: Patricia Gillot
To: Holly

Oh I wanna kill her.

Go back to the manual and do what it says there. And try smiling, you look like you're going to puke.

Trish

Subject: Attention: Jennie

From: Holly
To: Jennie Pithwait

Unfortunately, owing to your recent request to 'revert to the standard company rules,' I have reverted to the reception manual, which states that it is a security risk for us to be taking clients up whenever we feel like it. It is a shame, because I'd love to help, but company policy clearly states the host of the meeting should come down to collect their visitors.

Have a lovely day 'Jenns'??

Holly xx

Subject: Your useful Gran

From: Granny
To: Holly

Holly,

I've been using the World Wide Web once more. I have registered your name with some new companies. It's been quite exciting.

xxx

From: Holly
To: Granny

Thank you Granny, but you haven't registered me on any more cheap flight sites have you?

Subject: I'm a bit lost

From: Jason GrangerRM
To: Holly

Why are we now looking at barrow boys, and what's the Dorchester got to do with it?

From: Holly
To: Jason GrangerRM

Oh, nothing, I've got this cr*ppy company cr*ppy do next Friday. Jennie and James will be there, probably sitting together. I didn't want to go without a partner, but I haven't got long if I'm going to find someone (need to give Judy a name by Friday). Therefore— thinking about the two dating offers I had. No! This is stupid. I'm not letting her get to me. I'll go alone.

Subject: Reception

From: Jennie Pithwait
To: Holly

Hi,

Are you sure you want to play it like this? I'm very worried you could end up with egg on your face?

Jennie

Subject: JASON!!!

From: Holly
To: Jason GrangerRM

Changed my mind!!! Need a date! ASAP!

Subject: Exciting

From: Granny
To: Holly

Holly,

Have you received anything there yet?

Love, Granny

From: Holly
To: Granny

No Granny, maybe it didn't work. Don't worry though, what is it you wanted to send me?

Holly

Subject: SO YOU ARE SINGLE??? THEN HELP IS ON THE WAY!!!

From: UKSingles
To: Holly

Thank you for registering with UK Singles, Dating Online.

Registration Name Hollylookingforlove
Password Denham
Registration Account number 92482374

Subject: DATING ONLINE—IT COULDN'T BE EASIER

From: DatingDirect.com
To: Holly

Dear Holly:
Thank you for registering with Dating Direct.com. You will soon receive an email with more details.
Admin

Subject: Thank you Granny

From: Holly
To: Granny

Hi Granny,
I think they're coming through now. Thank you for putting my name on dating sites. That's very sweet of you.
Holly

From: Granny
To: Holly

You are very welcome.
Granny
xxx
He wasn't good enough for you anyway.

From: Holly
To: Granny

Thank you for saying that.
xxxx

Subject:—Hi

From: SwingersLife
To: Holly

SWINGING SEX RULES!!!! SO MANY COUPLES SO LITTLE TIME!!!!!!SEX AND THE SINGLE SWINGER !!! ENJOY YOUR REGISTRATION

Subject: One thing though Granny ...

From: Holly
To: Granny

Please don't register me on any swinging sites.

xxx

Holly

From: Granny
To: Holly

Ooops, sorry darling. They were something I had been looking at.

Love, Granny

Subject: Conference planning committee

From: Shella Hamilton-Jones
To: Holly

RE: Annual Results

Dear Conference Planning Committee,

After some careful consideration, I have decided it would be fairer to discuss which areas of research would be most suited to which committee member before delegating these responsibilities. Do keep in mind when volunteering that quite a bit of this work will need to be achieved during your free time.

We have use of meeting room 13 at 7 p.m. and I expect everyone to be there. I can only apologise for the short notice, but I too will have to make sacrifices.

Shella

Subject: Working in the restaurant

From: Holly
To: Patricia Gillot

I can't go to Shella's thing. I've got to be in the restaurant by 7 p.m. tonight!

From: Patricia Gillot
To: Holly

Haven't they sacked you yet?

From: Holly
To: Patricia Gillot

No. It may surprise you, Patricia, but I'm actually very good!

From: Patricia Gillot
To: Holly

It does flipping surprise me. ha ha

You can't miss Shella's 'planning committee meeting.' And my Les won't be happy, you know what he's like. He likes his dinner around 8.

From: Holly
To: Patricia Gillot

I've got to work tonight. What can I tell Shella then?

From: Patricia Gillot
To: Holly

I'll tell her you've got the trots?

From: Holly
To: Patricia Gillot

Great, why not start another rumour about me?

From: Patricia Gillot
To: Holly

I'll stand up for you. I'll tell her clients have been complaining, and we had to keep the front door open all day. It's something to do with all that posh food you eat.

From: Holly
To: Patricia Gillot

Don't you dare! I'll get you, Patricia Gillot!

From: Patricia Gillot
To: Holly

You could have some illness which needs dealing with? I'll just say it's too personal to say, so she won't ask?

From: Holly
To: Patricia Gillot

Sounds good.
Thanks,
Holly

thursday

Subject: Wake up!

From: Jason GrangerRM
To: Holly; Aisha

Come on, we've got work to do... You need to find a man, and we have 24 hours to do it. You need to be psyched and pumped!

From: Holly
To: Jason GrangerRM; Aisha

After sleeping on it, I'm not sure I want the added pressure of finding someone. It's all not necessary. Jennie's obviously got it in for me, and I don't want to come to work everyday thinking about arguments and bitchiness, so I've been looking on www. receptionworld.com and think I'll apply to a few positions.

xxxx

From: Jason GrangerRM
To: Holly; Aisha

Necessary ? ? ?

Necessary??? No of course it's not necessary, but you don't always do things because they are necessary.

You can't just give up!

From: Jason GrangerRM
To: Holly; Aisha

Do you think Aisha broke down and cried when she realised everyone in that flat (apart from me) wanted her to leave? No, she stood up with pride, put her dress back on, slurred a few insults, and stormed out.

From: Holly
To: Jason GrangerRM; Aisha

OK, fine. So what d'you want me to do? (Like the pep talk, very inspiring.)

From: Jason GrangerRM
To: Holly; Aisha

I'll be back in two minutes with a plan.

Subject: Meeting last night

From: Holly
To: Patricia Gillot

How did it go last night?

> **From:** Patricia Gillot
> **To:** Holly

I told Shella you couldn't make it cause you had a problem. She wanted to know what it was. So I said it was a really personal problem, you had an appointment with the doctor, but she still wanted to know. That girl has got one cheek on her, I'm telling you. How did it go in the restaurant last night??

> **From:** Holly
> **To:** Patricia Gillot

So what did you tell her?

Subject: List of potential candidates

> **From:** Jason GrangerRM
> **To:** Holly; Aisha

OK, so we need to draw up a short list of potential candidates. Had any luck with Granny's dating sites yet?

> **From:** Holly
> **To:** Jason GrangerRM; Aisha

No. Not too keen on the dating site thing.

> **From:** Jason GrangerRM
> **To:** Holly; Aisha

OK, what about the two who emailed you on Monday?

> **From:** Holly
> **To:** Jason GrangerRM; Aisha

I didn't reply to the 'hot stuff' email, and the other one is probably out of the question now.

> **From:** Jason GrangerRM
> **To:** Holly; Aisha

Yes, I think you need to get back in touch with both of them. A sexy, well-placed email could bring Alistair back on board. What d'you think, Aisha?

> **From:** Aisha
> **To:** Holly; Jason GrangerRM
>
> I think he sounds like a knob.

> **From:** Jason GrangerRM
> **To:** Holly; Aisha
>
> Not particularly helpful, Aish.
> Go on, Holly, email him something. You can get around him.

> **From:** Holly
> **To:** Jason GrangerRM; Aisha
>
> Oh, OK, I'll give it a go. I suppose there's nothing to lose.

Subject: Trisha, you haven't answered my question

> **From:** Holly
> **To:** Patricia Gillot
>
> What did you tell Shella when she wanted to know what my personal problem was?

Subject: Sorry

> **From:** Holly
> **To:** Alistair Moffett
>
> Dear Alistair,
> I have just realised what a huge mistake I've made. I am truly sorry, please forgive my rude email. I sent it to the wrong Alistair.
> I would love to have dinner with you.
> Holly

> **From:** Alistair Moffett
> **To:** Holly
>
> Holly,
> I don't understand, you know another Alistair at Huerst Wright?
> Alistair

From: Holly
To: Alistair Moffett

Yes.

From: Alistair Moffett
To: Holly

One who gropes people?

Subject: Dating update

From: Holly
To: Jason GrangerRM; Aisha

It's going to take some time, I think. This could be harder than I thought.

Holly

From: Jason GrangerRM
To: Holly

You don't have time, are you working tonight?

From: Holly
To: Jason GrangerRM

No, night off.

From: Jason GrangerRM
To: Holly

Then you need to see them both tonight, so you can decide whose name to give Judy tomorrow.

From: Holly
To: Jason GrangerRM; Aisha

You are joking?

Subject: Hot stuff

From: Holly
To: Gavin Oliver

Hi,
Thank you for your email, sorry it's taken me so long to get back to you. A beer might be nice sometime, yes.
Holly

From: Gavin Oliver
To: Holly

Sounds good, let's go out next week some time.

Subject: Trisha answer please!!

From: Holly
To: Patricia Gillot

What did you tell Shella?

From: Patricia Gillot
To: Holly

You've got hemorrhoids, darlin.
Love, Trish

From: Holly
To: Patricia Gillot

TRISH!!!!!

From: Patricia Gillot
To: Holly

That's why you walk funny.

From: Patricia Gillot
To: Holly

??

| **From:** Holly |
| **To:** Patricia Gillot |

Just kidding. She didn't ask—just said you were sick.

Subject: Communication problems

| **From:** Holly |
| **To:** Alistair Moffett |

Hi Alistair,

It really is a long story. Do you fancy just having a quick drink after work, and I can explain everything?

Holly

Subject: Annual Review

| **From:** Shella Hamilton-Jones |
| **To:** Holly |

RE: Annual Results Conference

Dear Holly,

It was a shame you weren't able to make our meeting last night, but I understand you were not feeling well, etc. Although I would be the last person to wish ill of anyone, I do hope it was nothing trivial (in the nicest possible way). We are trying to organise this event in half the usual time scale.

Organisational and research sectors were allotted to committee members last night, and I'm sure Trisha would have told you by now which one will now be your responsibility. As you are one of the newest employees in facilities and also the one who has needed so much help in achieving a relatively average level of success in their position, I personally would have given you far less involvement. The decision, though, was achieved through an unanimous vote of the members and, therefore, until you prove yourself incapable—the result stands.

I will expect the information provided in Excel with formulas calculating the various packages and offers available. As I'm sure

you will appreciate, you have the largest area to cover in terms of research, so please begin as soon as possible. I wish you all the best.
Yours truly,
Shella

Subject: TRISHA

From: Holly
To: Patricia Gillot

Is there anything you forgot to tell me about last night?

From: Patricia Gillot
To: Holly

I'm off, see you tomorrow.
Lots of love,
Trisha
xxxxxxxx

friday

Subject: Fun fun fun Friday!!!!

From: Holly
To: Jason GrangerRM; Aisha

Today is going to be a fantastic day!!!
Hello, London.

From: Jason GrangerRM
To: Holly; Aisha

What happened last night???

From: Holly
To: Jason GrangerRM; Aisha

I went out with both of them!!

From: Jason GrangerRM
To: Holly; Aisha

You didn't!!!!!

From: Holly
To: Jason GrangerRM; Aisha

No, I didn't.

I called them both, apologised for the ridiculous emails sent—under pressure (thank you, Jason). And cancelled it all, thanking them for being nice. AND NOW I'm going to have a fab day, because I'm lucky just to be alive and healthy and yeeeeeeeeeeeeeeeeeeeeeeeeeeeeeees.

xxxxxxxxxxxxxxxxxxxxxxxxxxxxxxx

From: Jason GrangerRM
To: Holly; Aisha

Aisha!!!! Have you given Holly one of those special mints of yours??

From: Aisha
To: Holly; Jason GrangerRM

Do you mind! I'm being a responsible mother these days. Talking of which, are you two still coming over at the weekend? Shona is looking forward to it.

From: Holly
To: Jason GrangerRM; Aisha

Of course, I'm coming. Now I have to find out what my lovely colleague has been up to.

xxxx

Subject: Morning

From: Holly
To: Patricia Gillot

Trish, my good friend and colleague, is there anything you wish to tell me?

From: Patricia Gillot
To: Holly

Yes, I've been doing this for 20 years, and I'll never get used to people saying 'Hi, Trish' as they go past. They never hang around long enough for you to see who they are. I spend all day looking up for no reason.

Subject: About that meeting last night …

From: Holly
To: Patricia Gillot

Is there anything else apart from that, which may have slipped your mind?

From: Patricia Gillot
To: Holly

Love to talk, but I've got to shoot off for a break.
Love ya,
Trisha

From: Holly
To: Patricia Gillot

I'm not going anywhere, I'll be here when you get back!

Subject: Client

From: James Lawrence
To: Holly

Hi honey,
Last minute call. I'm rushing off to see a client in Birmingham, so tonight's out. We can go Saturday?
James

From: Holly
To: James Lawrence

Hi Honey,

I think you emailed the wrong woman. If you wanted Jennie, she's the one dressed like a slut at the far end on the left. I can forward her your blowout though if you want?

Holly

(You're such a knob)

From: James Lawrence
To: Holly

Hi,

Sorry I'm trying to get out of the door quickly and made a mistake. Hope you're OK.

James

Subject: Meeting

From: Holly
To: Patricia Gillot

What did you sign me up for last night???

From: Patricia Gillot
To: Holly

Nothing happened last night.

From: Holly
To: Patricia Gillot

OK, the night before. Stop being evasive.

From: Patricia Gillot
To: Holly

I'm sorry, darlin, I tried to help. Don't think it'll be so bad.

From: Holly
To: Patricia Gillot

It was a unanimous vote!!!!!

From: Patricia Gillot
To: Holly

I know, I was going to vote against them, then I thought it actually might be good for you?

From: Holly
To: Patricia Gillot

WHY????

From: Patricia Gillot
To: Holly

To be honest, keep your mind off things.

From: Holly
To: Patricia Gillot

The second job is doing that fine, I don't have much time left. What am I meant to be doing then?

From: Patricia Gillot
To: Holly

You're doing accommodation.

From: Holly
To: Patricia Gillot

What?

From: Patricia Gillot
To: Holly

Like hotels, etc.

From: Holly
To: Patricia Gillot

You mean, where everyone stays?

From: Patricia Gillot
To: Holly

Yes.

From: Holly
To: Patricia Gillot

Where 400 delegates stay?

Subject: Gifts

From: Alice and Matt
To: Holly

What would you do if you had a queue of people bringing jam jars full of creepy crawlies into your flat every day?

Subject: Annual Results

From: Holly
To: Patricia Gillot

When do I have to do this by??

Subject: Night of the Naughty Nurses vs Rubber Ron's Running Bottoms

From: Charlie Denham
To: Holly

It's an idea for the opening night? I'm not sure myself?

From: Holly
To: Charlie Denham

Go away.

Subject: Annual Results

From: Holly
To: Patricia Gillot

I said, when do they need this by?

> **From:** Patricia Gillot
> **To:** Holly

Not for a couple of weeks.

Subject: Conference planning committee

> **From:** Shella Hamilton-Jones
> **To:** Holly

Hi Holly,

As we need to begin finalising which hotels can offer us the best packages as soon as possible, I'd like your initial offering to be handed in by next Friday. Hope this is OK with you?

Regards,

Shella

Subject: Leather Mistresses from Pangea vs The Naughty Knights from Ikea

> **From:** Charlie Denham
> **To:** Holly

Maybe we could get sponsorship from Ikea??

Charlie

Subject: It's one week

> **From:** Holly
> **To:** Patricia Gillot

I have one week, not two.

> **From:** Patricia Gillot
> **To:** Holly

Sorry babe, I'll help you.

xxx

Subject: Witches

From: Holly
To: Alice and Matt

Sorry Alice,

Are you OK? Why do you have a queue of people outside bringing you creepy crawlies? It's not something to do with that witch thing you've started, is it?

From: Alice and Matt
To: Holly

No, Holly, that's voodoo, and I'm not practicing voodoo. The witch thing is just a hobby, like stamp collecting or chasing buses.

From: Holly
To: Alice and Matt

Who chases buses? I know you live out in the sticks, but you must know those people you see chasing buses in London are trying to get on them—to get to work?

From: Alice and Matt
To: Holly

Ha ha, you know, I mean counting them or whatever those people do—train spotters, etc.

From: Holly
To: Alice and Matt

OK, but train spotters don't turn people into frogs then fly away cackling on broomsticks.

From: Alice and Matt
To: Holly

Neither do I?

From: Holly
To: Alice and Matt

Oh, good. So why all the creepy crawlies in jam jars?

From: Alice and Matt
To: Holly

It's to do with the snakes—because Matt has become such a revered figure out here, for his knowledge of reptiles and insects, people think he'd be interested in whatever they can trap and stuff in a jar. Actually, he just likes snakes, but we haven't got the heart to tell them.

So about every other day we get one excited visitor or another coming to the house, and there they sit on the other side of the table from Matt and between them… there's usually a musty old jam jar with a sad creature looking out from behind the glass. One woman comes at least once a week with something she's spattered inside a jar. There's also this guy who keeps giving Matt lumps of sh*t he thinks are pupai. I mean, how would you like it if people brought you their sh*t all day?

From: Holly
To: Alice and Matt

They do—I'm a receptionist—I get to hear everyone's problems all day long, and because I've got to stay at my desk, I can't escape. (I know I've taken what you've said as a metaphor, but I can't get my head around being brought the real thing.) xxxxx

Good luck with it all. I'll call you over the weekend.

week 3
monday

Subject: Party at the Dorchester

From: Holly
To: Patricia Gillot

Morning Trish,
Are you going with Les to the dinner thing on Friday?
Holly

From: Patricia Gillot
To: Holly

No, darlin, I don't want him there. I thought we'd have fun together.
Trish

From: Holly
To: Patricia Gillot

I love you Trisha and I want your children.
xxxx

From: Patricia Gillot
To: Holly

Take em, darlin. But they're a handful, I'm telling you.

From: Holly
To: Patricia Gillot

Thanks Trish.

From: Patricia Gillot
To: Holly

So are you going to tell me what happened with Toby?

From: Holly
To: Patricia Gillot

When?

From: Patricia Gillot
To: Holly

You know when, at school. There's got to be a good reason you spit each time you say his name.

Subject: Procedure

From: Jennie Pithwait
To: Holly

Holly,

I've spoken to a senior director here, and she said there's no reason you shouldn't walk our clients up, it's part of your job, so next time get your skates on, eh Hols???

x

From: Holly
To: Jennie Pithwait

Dear Jennie,

Unfortunately, as previously emailed, this is against company policy, so until company policy changes, it is really out of my hands.

Kind regards,

Holly

tuesday

Subject: Story time

From: Patricia Gillot
To: Holly

So you're at school and?

From: Holly
To: Patricia Gillot

I didn't really fit in.

From: Patricia Gillot
To: Holly

Was it your hair or your singing?

From: Holly
To: Patricia Gillot

Thank you Trish.

I think because the school started at 13, and I came from a comprehensive when the others came from prep schools. That could have been one reason, the other reason was my skirt.

From: Patricia Gillot
To: Holly

Below the knee?

From: Holly
To: Patricia Gillot

Ankle length.

From: Patricia Gillot
To: Holly

Your mum cracks me up.

From: Holly
To: Patricia Gillot

She's hysterical. I was also very unconfident.

From: Patricia Gillot
To: Holly

What about sport?

From: Holly
To: Patricia Gillot

I used to hide. Sometimes I hid behind the chapel during matches and smoked cigarettes.

From: Patricia Gillot
To: Holly

You dirty smoker! I'd never have guessed, so where was Jennie?

From: Holly
To: Patricia Gillot

What—while I was smoking? Probably winning tennis matches, surrounded by boys. She invited me to a party at her house. I was so excited (she was popular), but it turned out she invited most of our year. They had this amazing place, a pool, they even had waiters serving us drinks—alcoholic drinks.

From: Patricia Gillot
To: Holly

Nice, responsible parents.

From: Holly
To: Patricia Gillot

It was amazing. They had a dance floor and bar in a marquee! So I had a party at mine, I thought it might help me make friends.

From: Patricia Gillot
To: Holly

Dance floor?

From: Holly
To: Patricia Gillot

My dad in a chef's hat, cooking burgers on the barby in the garden. We had Top-deck Shandy—you know, the nonalcoholic stuff for kids (unless you drink about 100 of them). And when Jennie arrived with some other girls, they went straight up to the off-licence and brought alcohol back. Of course, my dad confiscated it. Everyone seemed to leave after that.

From: Patricia Gillot
To: Holly

So where was Toby?

From: Holly
To: Patricia Gillot

He was this recluse. I actually met him smoking behind the chapel. I wasn't inhaling, just doing it to make myself feel better about things. Mostly I think I did it because it was something my Mum hated, and she'd have killed me if she'd found out. He was there, smoking. He was very cool, very bad.

From: Patricia Gillot
To: Holly

Bad boy Toby, like the sound of him... so come on.

Subject: Important reminder

From: Holly
To: Holly

3 DAYS LEFT TO GET FUNERAL DRESS!!!!

Subject: You lucky boy

From: Holly
To: Jason GrangerRM

I got all your messages!!! So pleased you're back together.
xxxxx

From: Jason GrangerRM
To: Holly

It's great. You still worrying about Friday?

From: Holly
To: Jason GrangerRM

It's going to be one huge, massive, unbelievably huge chance for Jennie to rub my face in it all. Can you think of how I can avoid utter embarrassment and the desire to plunge a steak knife into her back?

From: Jason GrangerRM
To: Holly

Don't go?

From: Holly
To: Jason GrangerRM

Can't not go, no way, can't do it. I was thinking about asking Aisha to go in my place. What d'you think? Obviously in a mask?

From: Jason GrangerRM
To: Holly

I think they'd notice. Apart from the fact it's NOT a fancy dress party (so she might stand out a little), she's also got black hair, oh and in case you'd forgotten, black skin too (you haven't).

From: Holly
To: Jason GrangerRM

So I guess that idea is out???

From: Jason GrangerRM
To: Holly

Yes it is, so stop mulling over it—Oh, and don't imagine for one instance that she could wear a full costume, either, not even if you get permission to wear one.

From: Holly
To: Jason GrangerRM

How do you always know what I'm thinking??

From: Jason GrangerRM
To: Holly

I know you. Also, from what I've heard, Aisha only goes to fancy dress parties dressed as a bunny girl, and that's not a full costume, that's a thong and a bit of fluff taped to her backside. The other obstacle is she'll be on a plane to Ibiza.

From: Holly
To: Jason GrangerRM

You've let her go???

From: Jason GrangerRM
To: Holly

Yes, don't ask.

xx

Subject: Birth

From: Aisha
To: Holly

Did you tell Pam not to worry about the birth?
Aish

From: Holly
To: Aisha

I did. Thank you for that. She sounded much less scared after I spoke to her.

From: Aisha
To: Holly

People just like to wind everyone up about it. If giving birth was that bad, the tubes wouldn't be so packed, would they?
Aish

Subject: Story time

From: Holly
To: Patricia Gillot

He was kind of the opposite to me. People wanted to be his friend, but he didn't want it. The first time I saw him, he didn't say anything to me. I was sitting up on a water barrel, and he just kind of nodded, that was all. It was just the two of us, smoking quietly. I could faintly hear the shouts of the girls from my house, playing hockey. I always knew when I had to run back, when I heard the final whistle.

From: Patricia Gillot
To: Holly

What did he look like then?

From: Holly
To: Patricia Gillot

Not much different, same build, slim. At first the other boys didn't think much of him. He came from a comprehensive too, that's how we first started talking.

From: Patricia Gillot
To: Holly

Go on, I'll do this lot, you just write!

From: Holly
To: Patricia Gillot

Aren't you going to lunch?

From: Patricia Gillot
To: Holly

I'm going nowhere, neither are you. We'll get Ralph to get us something, he's been desperate for orders. So, what happened next?

From: Holly
To: Patricia Gillot

I was always the substitute. It was so rare that they ever needed me for games. I think they used me once in about a month. So when I heard this voice shout my name, I nearly jumped out of my skin.

Subject: Judy

From: Holly
To: Patricia Gillot

Sorry, I'm so late back. I got collared by one of the directors who wanted to know why it was such a problem taking clients up to meeting rooms.

From: Patricia Gillot
To: Holly

We do it as a favour to the host IF we can't get hold of them, but it's THEIR responsibility to come down and collect THEIR guest. We're not skivvies for that bitch Jennie. She's just doing this for power play. She'll get her comeuppance one day.

From: Holly
To: Patricia Gillot

Judy told me to ignore him anyway. So, where'd we got to?

From: Patricia Gillot
To: Holly

You were behind the chapel ...

From: Holly
To: Patricia Gillot

I used to sit under this tree where I had my cigarettes buried in a plastic bag, watching the game, well, not really watching the game. I'd begun watching the path to the chapel. I got the timing right on a couple of occasions. I used to pick up my hockey stick and run like the wind, stand for a couple of minutes catching my breath behind the building, doing my hair, then saunter nonchalantly around the side.

From: Patricia Gillot
To: Holly

Oh, you're such a tart!!!

From: Holly
To: Patricia Gillot

I was not a tart, Patricia, I was just very keen. So after I'd put some lipstick on, lip liner, mascara, eye shadow, etc… I walked around the side.

From: Patricia Gillot
To: Holly

TART!!!!

From: Holly
To: Patricia Gillot

I'm joking, we weren't allowed any of that there (OK, I smuggled lipstick in, but that's all). SO the path to the chapel split in two, one path took you to the chapel and the other off to one of the other houses. I couldn't see him there, so guessed he'd gone to the house. I swore, and then I remember seeing his legs on the ground next to me. He was sitting with his back against the chapel, looking right at me.

From: Patricia Gillot
To: Holly

Sh*t, what did you say? You could have been swearing about anything.

From: Holly
To: Patricia Gillot

Exactly, so I didn't say anything. This was the third time I'd been there with him without saying a word. Then this girl appeared from our house, someone had been injured, and they'd been searching for me. She made some bitchy comment about being from a comprehensive and smoking then ran off to get me in as much trouble as she could.

From: Patricia Gillot
To: Holly

Was this girl Jennie?????

From: Holly
To: Patricia Gillot

No, one of her friends, but she had lots (and I can't blame her for that). After she ran off to tell them, I remember getting my things together to go back, and Toby said something like 'From a comprehensive too?' And I nodded and then—he smiled. But that smile, to me, meant a lot, it meant, it's all sh*t and don't worry about it, and you'll get through it, and I respect you because I'm also from a 'comp,' and lots of lovely things like that.

From: Patricia Gillot
To: Holly

He just smiled! He was probably thinking, I can't wait to get her clothes off.

ha ha ha

Look out!!!!

From: Holly
To: Patricia Gillot

What?

Subject: Nasty

From: Holly
To: Patricia Gillot

I can't believe Shella!!!!

From: Patricia Gillot
To: Holly

What did she do??

From: Holly
To: Patricia Gillot

She ripped off my cutsie bunny picture and threw it in the bin!!!
And worse... my picture of Mr Big!! Told me to grow up! Clients
can't see it from their side!!!!!

grrrrrrrrrrrrrrrrrrrrrrrrrrrrrrrrrrrrrrrrrrrr

From: Patricia Gillot
To: Holly

Shella's a class act. Don't worry, I'll plaster rabbits and Mr Big all
over the desk tomorrow.

From: Holly
To: Patricia Gillot

Are you OK?

From: Patricia Gillot
To: Holly

Cramps, had them years, they just come on. Sometimes are worse
than others.

From: Holly
To: Patricia Gillot

You should have that looked at??

From: Patricia Gillot
To: Holly

I will.

So where did you and Toby do it then? I want all the details, want
the colour of the moon, where the snooty girls were playing hockey,
where the naughty boys were filming it from. I want the full story.

wednesday

Subject: Trisha is off today

From: Judy Perkins
To: Holly

Holly,

Unfortunately Patricia called in sick this morning, but instead of arranging a temp, Shella will be covering for her during the busy period—from 11 a.m. to 3 p.m. I've looked at the meeting-room schedule, and it does look like a fairly busy day, so it will be good to have someone working alongside you who understands our systems here, etc.

Any problems, give me a call.

Regards,

Judy

From: Holly
To: Judy Perkins

Hi,

OK Judy. I was thinking, couldn't Ralph cover? I'd look after him.
Holly

From: Judy Perkins
To: Holly

It's not his shift today, and Neil is too new to know what's going on.
Judy

Subject: TRISHY!!!

From: Holly
To: Patricia Gillot

Trishy,

Just heard you're sick today, so this is a Get Well Soon email. Of course, hopefully you'll read this when you're back to work, and I'm praying it will be Thursday, because I've got to work with Cruella today, and that's just not fair! I can picture you'll be laughing yourself silly when you read this. Yes, that's right, you've made me have to work next to that viper all day!

Oh, and I'm worried about you too (not just thinking of myself). Please be better.

Xxxxxxxxxxxxxx Xx

Subject: Passwords

From: Judy Perkins
To: Holly

Holly,

Do you know Trisha's password?

Because Shella will need to check her emails to make sure there aren't any about bookings. I know they should go to the main booking email address, but sometimes Trisha emails PAs who are friends of hers directly.

Judy

Subject: EMERGENCY HELP HELP HELP

From: Holly
To: Jason GrangerRM

Sh*t! I need you urgently, where are you? Why don't you keep your mobile on?? How d'you recall email, I need to know—if you don't know yourself, then can you let me know someone who does know? This is really really really urgent.

Subject: URGENT HEEEEEEEEEELP

From: Holly
To: Charlie Denham

URGENT

How do you recall emails? I'm in deeeeeeeeeeeeeep shit.

Subject: Reception Assistance

From: Shella Hamilton-Jones
To: Holly

Holly,

I'll be working with you on the desk today. Some of my tasks here needed completing, but I'm on my way down now, so don't panic. I'm probably not as easygoing as Patricia normally is, so be prepared for that.

Essentially, today our front of house will perform like a well-oiled machine.

Yours,

Shella

Subject: nok nok

From: Joseph
To: Holly

Hellow Arnty Holly,

nok nok

Subject: Your son

From: Holly
To: Alice and Matt

I guess you've given your son my email address, because Aunty Holly just got an email from him.

Subject: Passwords

From: Judy Perkins
To: Holly

Holly,

I can't get through to Trisha's mobile, so I've contacted IT, and they're cancelling her password and reissuing a new one, so don't worry. If Trisha calls, just let her know it's nothing important now, and I wish her a rapid recovery.

Regards,

Judy

Subject: nok nok

From: Joseph
To: Holly

arnty nok nok

Subject: YOUR EMERGENCY

From: Jason GrangerRM
To: Holly

I don't have my mobile on for the same reason you don't, because you can't have them ringing on reception. Now calm down, what's the problem?

From: Holly
To: Jason GrangerRM

It's OK now. Trisha's off sick, and so they've got Shella (Cruella) to cover. So I sent Trisha a jokey email for when she gets back which wasn't exactly complimentary towards Shella, then I find out Shella's using Trisha's login name to keep track of any stray bookings. I don't know what Trisha's passcode is to delete my message, so I called her, but she's not answering. Then I got through to Pam, who told me how to recall the email, so I've done that, so it should be OK now.

xxxx

PS She's sitting here now, grrrrrrrr, what a day I'm going to have.

Subject: nok nok

From: Joseph
To: Holly

nok nok

From: Holly
To: Joseph

Sorry Joseph,
I was busy, but it's nice to hear from you—how is school?
Oh, and 'Who is there?'
Love, Holly

From: Joseph
To: Holly

Im App

From: Holly
To: Joseph

I'm App Who?

Subject: WAIT NO NO NO

From: Jason GrangerRM
To: Holly

Sorry sweetie, just found out, that recall thing doesn't work. It just sends them another email after the first message, showing you're desperate to recall it. It's pointless. If she opens the RECALL message first and agrees, then you're OK… chances are, though, she'll open the other one first, THEN see you're trying to get it back …
Sorry.
Xxxx

Subject: ha ha ha ha ha ha

From: Joseph
To: Holly

You just sed Im a poo
ha ha ha arnty holly is a poo
arnty holly is a poo

Subject: Help!

From: Holly
To: Jason GrangerRM

OH, GOD.

She's opened up the system now and is reading through things. How will I know if she clicks on the RECALL first or the other one first?????

From: Jason GrangerRM
To: Holly

From what I gather, you either get a message saying Recall Success or
Recall Failure …
Good luck.

Subject: Recall failure

From: Patricia Gillot
To: Holly

Your message
Subject: TRISHY!!
Could not be recalled

Subject: Holly

From: Joseph
To: Holly

arnty holly is a poo
arnty holly is a poo
arnty holly is a poo
arnty holly is a poo
HA HA HA
Love, Joseph

xxxxxxxx

From: Holly
To: Joseph

I get it, Joseph, that's very funny.
Thank you.
Love,
Holly

Subject: Oh No!

From: Holly
To: Jason GrangerRM

Crapola.
It got opened.
?

Subject: Holly

From: Patricia Gillot
To: Holly

Holly,
I'll be working from both my email and Patricia's today, therefore, I may email you from either, just in case you get confused.
Also, there seem to be an awful lot of people that aren't down in the schedule arriving for meetings. Is this because Patricia hasn't bothered updating the system?
Regards,
Shella

From: Holly
To: Patricia Gillot

Nothing to do with Trisha. Sometimes it's because the secretaries or PAs don't give us all the names, but mainly it's just because there are new additions to the original meetings.

And no one's bothered letting us know (so the first we know about it is when they are standing in front of us, demanding a badge).
Holly

From: Patricia Gillot
To: Holly

Holly,
But how do you fill in their details on the badges program whilst making the appropriate changes in the scheduler?
Shella

From: Holly
To: Patricia Gillot

You have to flip between screens, by using CTRL and the tab button. (It's easier if you keep all five screens open at once.)

Subject: an email sent

From: Aisha
To: Holly

I hear you're about to be sacked again—what's naughty Holly been up to now?
Aish

From: Holly
To: Aisha

I'm not about to be sacked!

From: Aisha
To: Holly

If you are, though, fancy coming to Ibiza on Friday?

From: Holly
To: Aisha

I'm not going to be sacked!!!

535

Subject: Clients

From: Holly

To: Shella Hamilton-Jones; Patricia Gillot

That couple on the second couch, I think they've been there a while. Is it all sorted?

From: Shella Hamilton-Jones

To: Holly

Holly,

Of course it is, you don't have to watch over me. I've informed the host, so it's their responsibility now.

Shella

Subject: Justin Tanworth

From: Shella Hamilton-Jones

To: Holly

Justin Tanworth just blew his top at me, because I had left his guests sitting around down here. But I informed his secretary, so surely it's her fault?

From: Holly

To: Shella Hamilton-Jones

It should be, but we get the blame, because ultimately, his secretary has a better relationship with him than we do, and the PAs and secretaries are used to relying on us to continually remind them to inform the host.

They might call the host and say their guests are waiting for them down here, but if the Director forgets this and the PA thinks they've done their job, if the guests are still down here, it's our fault for not telling them again.

From: Shella Hamilton-Jones

To: Holly

But the director was already in the meeting?

From: Holly
To: Shella Hamilton-Jones

Then we can text him, or call the phone in the meeting, or if we can't leave the desk and his secretary is not around, then we have to get someone else to go into the meeting, etc.

From: Shella Hamilton-Jones
To: Holly

Well, this has got to change, it's just not right.

Subject: REMINDER

From: Holly
To: Holly

ONLY 2 DAYS LEFT TO GET FUNERAL DRESS!!!

Subject: what'sziz name

From: Holly
To: Jason GrangerRM

I've just thought, what kind of idiot signs his name off as 'J' anyway??

From: Jason GrangerRM
To: Holly

Hiya,

Only complete tits do that.

xx

PS We are talking about James, aren't we? I don't think I've ever done it.

From: Holly
To: Jason GrangerRM

No, you haven't. xx

No feedback yet from my email. She can't have read it.

From: Jason GrangerRM
To: Holly

Something else on your mind?

From: Holly
To: Jason GrangerRM

Yes, I still haven't got a dress for Friday, because there is nothing in the shops that fits me. The shops are just full of TINY CLOTHES FOR TINY PEOPLE, and I don't think any of those people exist. The clothes are just put in shops to upset me!!!!!

From: Jason GrangerRM
To: Holly

Do you want me to come with you?

From: Holly
To: Jason GrangerRM

I bet SHE will be going to the Gala in something which makes her nasty, vindictive, evil, heart-stabbing, boyfriend-robbing body look great, and it's not fair! I bet she goes windsurfing too.

From: Jason GrangerRM
To: Holly

Windsurfing?

From: Holly
To: Jason GrangerRM

That's what HE likes doing, because HE wanted a sporty girlfriend, and SHE's always in the gym. I bet she does sky hopping, wind surfing, river bashing, crappy pooh fart yuk.

From: Jason GrangerRM
To: Holly

Are we being childish?

From: Holly
To: Jason GrangerRM

Yes.

From: Jason GrangerRM
To: Holly

Do you want to meet me tomorrow to find something?

From: Holly
To: Jason GrangerRM

Yes. Please, Jason.

xxx

Sorry for being childish.

Subject: Assistance please

From: Holly
To: Alice and Matt

Can you put a spell on someone for me?

From: Alice and Matt
To: Holly

I can give it a go? Are they sick?

From: Holly
To: Alice and Matt

No, not yet. I was hoping you could make them sick??

From: Alice and Matt
To: Holly

I'm studying to be a white witch. That means we help people get better, not the other way around. Sorry, xxx

(I can pray for her?)

thursday

Subject: Catering

From: Shella Hamilton-Jones
To: Holly

Holly,

I think it would be quicker and make a lot more sense if we simply called up the catering team to let them know if there are extra meals needed.

Shella

From: Holly
To: Shella Hamilton-Jones

No, you have to update the scheduler, too, otherwise the wrong costs are allocated to the host, etc.

From: Shella Hamilton-Jones
To: Holly

What happens if you fail to update the scheduler?

From: Holly
To: Shella Hamilton-Jones

There's a chance you'll get shouted at, the host or the catering team will be on your case. Best to do it right first. Also, it keeps a record that you've done it, so there can be no arguments.

Holly

From: Shella Hamilton-Jones
To: Holly

They can't really shout?

From: Holly
To: Shella Hamilton-Jones

Not in front of clients, but they do.

Subject: RE your email

From: Charlie Denham
To: Holly

Just picked up your message from yesterday. No, I wouldn't bother recalling it, it'll look worse.

Charlie

From: Holly
To: Charlie Denham

Thanks, Charlie, for your rapid response. I know this NOW.

Regards,

Holly

Subject: She's still here

From: Holly
To: Aisha; Jason GrangerRM

I've got to work with Shella again! Trish is still poorly.

Poor Trish.

Subject: Sick

From: Les Gillot
To: Holly

Hey there, darlin. You doing OK without me?

From: Holly
To: Les Gillot

Why Leslie, I never thought you'd ask… Does Patricia know you're emailing me?

Holly

From: Les Gillot
To: Holly

You think you're so funny! Leslie! I'll tell him. I hear we've got a new girl on reception.

From: Holly
To: Les Gillot

Yup,

Sitting next to me right now.

Dan dan daaaaah

How are you feeling?

From: Les Gillot
To: Holly

Bit better, sitting up in bed now. So how bad is she? Tell us?

From: Holly
To: Les Gillot

She's actually quite good. She's introduced a lot of new procedures, which seem to be working out well, etc. It's been a breeze.

From: Les Gillot
To: Holly

What new procedures???? Don't like the sound of this one. What's she after?

From: Holly
To: Les Gillot

Sorry. Really bad thing to wind up a sick person. heee heee

It's so so so bad here, you won't believe it. Really missing you!!

From: Les Gillot
To: Holly

Oh thank God for that. I was hoping you would miss me… and I was sitting here thinking the bitch was after me job!!! You're a cruel girl, Holly. You wait till I get back.

From: Holly
To: Les Gillot

Are you back in tomorrow?

From: Les Gillot
To: Holly

Yes, then I want to know about Toby, and you better make it good.
I've been looking forward to story time with Holly.

xxxxx

Trisha (keep smiling)

From: Holly
To: Les Gillot

Promise I'll tell you everything. I hope you really are in tomorrow,
I can't go to that thing on my own …

xx

Subject: Ibiza

From: Aisha
To: Holly

How's your day going? Did I tell you I'm going to Ibiza with a
millionaire?

From: Holly
To: Aisha

Yes you did. I can't email much today, Shella keeps watching my
screen. Have a lovely time in Ibiza, you lucky thing.

xxxx

friday

Subject: She's back!!

From: Holly
To: Patricia Gillot

Nice to have you back. What did the doctor say?

From: Patricia Gillot
To: Holly

They don't know what's wrong with me. What was she like then, the new girl? Don't tell me she did well?

From: Holly
To: Patricia Gillot

She started off the day with a quick meeting. She sat me down and told me she wanted to improve the company's 'front of house' with some new procedures. She said I had to keep my wits about me, because SHE wouldn't be as 'easygoing' as you are.

From: Patricia Gillot
To: Holly

What were these new procedures??????

From: Holly
To: Patricia Gillot

When people come in and the phone rings, instead of answering it and smiling at the clients to let them know you've seen them… She wanted to let the phone ring continually while tutting at the clients and saying 'hold on, hold on, can't you see I'm trying to do two things at once!!'

From: Patricia Gillot
To: Holly

Ha ha ha, oh, that's cheered me up. Did she lose it?

From: Holly
To: Patricia Gillot

It was her first time.

From: Patricia Gillot
To: Holly

Flipping marvellous!!! I've wanted this for years… for her to see what it's like. Don't ruin it for me by saying you got on with her—remember, this is the woman who screwed up your little rabbit picture! Did she lose her rag with anyone?

From: Holly
To: Patricia Gillot

She did, it was actually quite satisfying. You would have loved it… at one point, she was shouting at a PA, and I had to remind her where we were.

From: Patricia Gillot
To: Holly

OH OH OH YES YES YES

From: Holly
To: Patricia Gillot

OK, anyway, I need a toilet break. Are you OK for a moment?

From: Patricia Gillot
To: Holly

I think Shella's right about one thing, though, I'm too easy on you… this place is going to be run more professional from now on, so sit your arse down, I'm off for a f**king fag.
Trisha ha ha ha ha
Oh, then after your break, it's story time!

Subject: Holly Denham, star of the show …

From: Jason GrangerRM
To: Holly

Good luck tonight—and remember, go easy on the booze and try and keep this in mind for when you're staring out drunkenly across the room. The sea of faces glaring back at you, their expressions are not of 'wonder' but are in fact of 'fear,' they are scared, so sit down. This is NOT, I repeat, NOT the Albert Hall/Stars in their Eyes/Opportunity Knocks/The Royal Variety Show/X Factor, and although your singing is quite good, you are a receptionist called Holly Denham, NOT one called Leona Lewis.

xxx love you xxxx

Jason

From: Holly
To: Jason GrangerRM

Please have some faith in me. I will be a picture of grace and decorum.

xxxx

Subject: Ibiza

From: Holly
To: Aisha

Have fun in Ibiza. Don't do anything you don't want to, just because it's a nice boat or villa or whatever and you feel grateful… call me if you need me.

Love you

xx

From: Aisha
To: Holly

Yes Mum, I promise Mum.

Re: your night tonight, I know you don't often listen to my advice, but sometimes I can help—?

From: Holly
To: Aisha

Tell me???

From: Aisha
To: Holly

OK, well this is how I got a bit of revenge once. Are any men making speeches there tonight?

From: Holly
To: Aisha

Yes.

From: Aisha
To: Holly

Good, when you get there, find out who's going to be making a speech, choose the best looking of the bunch. And simply do a little flirting.

From: Holly
To: Aisha

That's it?

From: Aisha
To: Holly

Yes... when I did it, and he was called to make a speech, he was under my table giving me head!!! You should have seen it, there was a spotlight looking for him and everything!!
Xxxxxx enjoy.

From: Holly
To: Aisha

Thanks Aish, I'll take your advice onboard.

Subject: Story time!

From: Patricia Gillot
To: Holly

Why was Toby bad then?

From: Holly
To: Patricia Gillot

OK, when I first began talking to him, we were both 15, but I'd known OF him since we'd both started there. There's kind of an unwritten law which says the new boys joining the school are the lowest of the low—it's easier for the girls, but that first year is really tough for the boys. They do all the cleaning chores, sweeping and keeping the house and dorm spotless, etc., and the older boys talk down to them. A year later, and it's their turn to pick on the new boys—it's kind of a tradition in private schools.

From: Patricia Gillot
To: Holly

What nice traditions you lot have. So Toby went for one of them did he?

From: Holly
To: Patricia Gillot

I heard he had about three fights with the older kids when he started, he just wouldn't accept it. In the end they all left him alone, and he kept this bad boy reputation. He wasn't a troublemaker, though, he just didn't like the school much.

From: Patricia Gillot
To: Holly

Good for him.

From: Holly
To: Patricia Gillot

I got in lots of trouble after I was caught smoking and then the teachers knew where everyone had been going to smoke, so then that was then out. It was a couple of weeks before I saw him again. I was just sitting on a bench in the sun outside the school library, and he sat down next to me. He started chatting about the school and the cliques and everything, and he told me they had a new secret place for smoking. I had decided smoking wasn't really for me by this time, but I wanted to go there anyway.

From: Patricia Gillot
To: Holly

I bet you did, you naughty tart.

From: Holly
To: Patricia Gillot

We went to the chapel, but this time inside it. I remember thinking, it must be some kind of awful joke and there's going to be my classmates there laughing, and it would be a setup or something. We worked our way along a pew and sat down. Then he reached down and pulled up this wooden hatch in the floor. It was dark, and he jumped down and disappeared. I waited for a moment and then, asking God to watch me, I went in after him.

From: Patricia Gillot
To: Holly

Holly Denham, you surprise me.

From: Holly
To: Patricia Gillot

I surprised myself. Down in the dark, I sat until he lit a light. It was this whole passage network of kind of tunnels, in the foundations. You couldn't stand up, but he'd set the place up with cushions and bean bags, drinks, and there was a Walkman, I couldn't believe it.

He said he went there to get away from everyone. It was so good. I began meeting him there regularly, and we'd read, chat, or listen to music. I kissed him on my second time under the chapel. I didn't do any more smoking, but I'd found something much better.

From: Patricia Gillot
To: Holly

What? What had you found… and I bet your mum would have been just as annoyed.

From: Holly
To: Patricia Gillot

More, when she found out. More later, got to go.
Xxx

From: Patricia Gillot
To: Holly

Oh Holly!!!

week 4
bank holiday monday

Subject: Toby

From: Alice and Matt
To: Holly

About Toby.

I've been thinking about it over the weekend, and you need to speak to him, find out why he never wrote to you. There might be a reason, it can't have been easy for him, either. You were both very young.

xxx

Alice

tuesday

Subject: The reason he never wrote

From: Holly
To: Alice and Matt

He never wrote to me, Alice, because he's a bastard. I'm sorry, but he broke my heart, and it's taken a long, long time to get over him, and now I've done it. If he'd have cared at all, even a little bit, he'd have got in touch and I don't think being young is an excuse.

xxxx

From: Alice and Matt
To: Holly

OK. I didn't mean to sound pushy.

Also I think Joseph is playing up more and more. Today I couldn't find my favourite shoes, I asked Joseph if he knows anything about them, because I saw him holding them yesterday. He gave me an innocent explanation, filled with so much detail (a real epic) that I know he was lying, but he won't admit it. Happy days.

Alice

Subject: Toby

From: Patricia Gillot
To: Holly

Can't believe what happened at the party. You've got to talk to him now?

From: Holly
To: Patricia Gillot

No thanks.

From: Patricia Gillot
To: Holly

You told me the good bits about when you two were young, so I can't see what the problem is, until you tell me what went wrong?

From: Holly
To: Patricia Gillot

I missed my period, and for him, that was that.

From: Patricia Gillot
To: Holly

You were pregnant?

From: Holly
To: Patricia Gillot

I didn't get my period for weeks. It was a boarding school, so these things aren't easy to keep quiet and our school was in the country, so no way of getting to any shops, so no pregnancy tests either. In the end, I was so scared, I told Toby. We had an argument. The next thing I knew was he'd done a runner and never came back to school.

Finally, I discovered I wasn't pregnant, but with typical school gossip, everyone thought I'd had an abortion. I was really in love with him, head over heels. You know what it's like with first love.

I never heard from Toby again though.

From: Patricia Gillot
To: Holly

Oh.

Subject: Conference

From: Shella Hamilton-Jones
To: Holly

Dear Holly,

Organising a conference is not an easy feat; I need to have everything prepared as soon as possible. Have you managed to get some of the research started for the hotels? If not, can you get yourself in gear and get it done ASAP?

Regards,

Shella

From: Holly
To: Shella Hamilton-Jones

Shella,

Yes, I've finished it, let me know when you want it?

Regards,

Holly

From: Shella Hamilton-Jones
To: Holly

Holly,

If you honestly think you are ready to show me a professional project-managed production of the information requested, then I need to see it ASAP. Therefore, I have requested you work upstairs with me tomorrow afternoon to go through your presentation;

we've organised a receptionworld temp to help cover the desk with Trisha.

Regards,

Shella

Subject: It's so exciting …

From: Jason GrangerRM
To: Holly

Let me know the gossip (like if he says anything else).

From: Holly
To: Jason GrangerRM

I'll never forgive him for dumping me at my hour of need—so drop it!

From: Jason GrangerRM
To: Holly

SORRY.

From: Holly
To: Jason GrangerRM

Didn't mean to sound grumpy, just had everyone ask me this morning. He's always been a strange boy, it doesn't change a thing.

Subject: Dorchester

From: Patricia Gillot
To: Holly

Sounds like you're right, then. He's not worth thinking about, darlin. You fancy going for a drink some time this week?

From: Holly
To: Patricia Gillot

That sounds good.

Re: Shella—I can't believe she's still such a bitch. What is wrong with that woman??

From: Patricia Gillot
To: Holly

Maybe she did read your email slagging her off?

From: Holly
To: Patricia Gillot

No, she couldn't have done. She would have crucified me happily if she had.

From: Patricia Gillot
To: Holly

Looks like she is anyway—presentation?? Project managed?? I'd take the day off sick, sounds like a ritual killing to me.

From: Holly
To: Patricia Gillot

Thanks.

From: Patricia Gillot
To: Holly

Also, you haven't heard from Jennie or James yet???

From: Holly
To: Patricia Gillot

Not yet, d'you think I'm going to be in trouble?

From: Patricia Gillot
To: Holly

For doing what? They were acting like idiots.

From: Holly
To: Patricia Gillot

I'm sure I'll hear something from Jen soon, though. She reminds me of a shark who's gone back down below to lick her wounds—before she comes back up for an even worse attack.

From: Patricia Gillot
To: Holly

Can I at least say I like Toby's style?

From: Holly
To: Patricia Gillot

He's got a way with words, always had.
But that's about it.
xx

wednesday

Subject: Your brother

From: Alice and Matt
To: Holly

I'm not happy with Charlie. When you next talk to him, you may want to tell him how unamusing he is.

From: Holly
To: Alice and Matt

No, I'm not being blamed for anything he does, he's OUR brother. (What's he been up to now?)

Subject: It's all about me!!

From: Aisha
To: Holly

Guess where I am?

From: Holly
To: Aisha

Ibiza?

From: Aisha
To: Holly

OK, yes, but where exactly??

From: Holly
To: Aisha

Having sex with someone??

From: Aisha
To: Holly

No, actually, Miss Holly-pants, although I think I might later. I am on a lovely boat!!

From: Holly
To: Aisha

You're not on a boat. How can you be emailing me from a boat?

From: Aisha
To: Holly

It's a big one, and the guy who owns it has let me shower in his place and use his stuff. I think he said I could use his stuff, cause I am. Holly my bestist bestist friend, this is going to surprise you, but I was thinking about you, and the party seems to have got a bit dull anyway and I wanted to know what happened, at that party.

From: Holly
To: Aisha

You want to know what happened to me???

From: Aisha
To: Holly

No. Not really, I'm going back upstairs.

bye

x

Subject: Office party thing last Friday

From: Aisha
To: Holly

I do really want to know.

Tell me please, Holly-pants, before I get kicked off his computer (I might look at some dirty pictures in between your emails if you don't mind) (men on this ship aren't much to look at) (all old and fat) (and some with beards). But tell me, because i really want to know!!!!!

xxxxx

From: Holly
To: Aisha

Are you OK?

From: Aisha
To: Holly

Why wouldn't I be? I'm on holiday, having just the best time, it's all fab.

xx Tell me

From: Holly
To: Aisha

It was really strange, and I don't know what to make of it yet. The Gala all began as expected. I was nervous the whole day, I only managed to eat breakfast and a bag of crisps for lunch. I wore that dress I wore to your party, the black-and-white one, and I added some long white gloves and my new shoes. Not looking too bad. It was raining, so I purposely made sure I'd ordered a cab with plenty

of time to spare. Kept my hair out of the rain between cab and
Dorchester and followed the signs down to the function room—
massive place, people were arriving as I went in. I was one of the
first few, and the others were in small groups of their own (people I
didn't recognise), so I thought about heading back out and going to
a bar until everyone else arrived, but then Trish and the boys from
the post room turned up.

From: Aisha
To: Holly

Had you seen her yet?

From: Holly
To: Aisha

No.
The place began filling up, and I began to hope that maybe she
wasn't going to come at all, that she'd be too scared of confrontation,
and they'd both decided to boycott it out of a sense of proportion or
kindness or something. I got a couple of drinks down me and then
of course, Jennie did turn up.

From: Aisha
To: Holly

What was she wearing?

From: Holly
To: Aisha

A tight red slinky dress, of course—it was as if the nightmares I'd
had were premonitions. Everyone was looking at her while she
pranced around like some kind of princess, both of them together,
him in a black tux.

From: Aisha
To: Holly

She's a dirty whore.

From: Holly
To: Aisha

Thanks, Aish.

After watching this for a while I realised I had to leave, I couldn't be there. I thought they'd at least have kept their relationship a little secret. I mean, when I was with him it was oh so important no one knew, bastard, but they walked around the place arm in arm, her like the cat that got the cream. That's when I first began feeling sick.

From: Aisha
To: Holly

You didn't puke, did you??? No, Holly, not in front of everyone?

From: Holly
To: Aisha

… I remember thinking, this is it, I'm going to throw up over myself, all over my dress, and everyone's going to laugh. The more I thought about it, the worse I got. I felt myself turn cold. I got to the bathroom and locked myself in a cubicle, shaking like a leaf and fighting the urge to throw up. I wanted to go home. I couldn't picture even being able to make it to the exit door of the building. I remember thinking I'd happily spend the rest of my life locked in there, with food and water passed under the door—as long as I didn't have to go out and face everyone.

From: Aisha
To: Holly

Poor baby, I would have saved you, if I hadn't been on a plane drinking champagne.

From: Holly
To: Aisha

Trish found me in the end and insisted I come out (or she was going to 'kick the f***ing door in'). She's so lovely, I owe her. I hope one day I can be there for her. She made me down four drinks she'd got waiting for me and put more makeup on. Luckily, Jennie didn't come in while I was wiping mascara off my cheeks.

I avoided her until we were all seated—and that's when it all began to go wrong.

I could still see them through a gap in peoples' heads—their table was on the other side of the room, and although there were about a hundred people in between us, I could see them kissing, laughing, and all over each other.

I tried not to think about them and at first managed to get involved in conversation—and alcohol. Problem was—I couldn't eat anything, because I was so worked up, so food came and went and I kept drinking, and by the time the dessert had been served, I was well on the way.

From: Aisha
To: Holly

I've a feeling someone wants to use this room (I've locked the door). Who cares? So you're sitting there drunk?

From: Holly
To: Aisha

I remember thinking as I approached them that they needed to be told—so they both could know what heartless bastards they were. I was going to appeal to their better instincts, and I thought I had something worked out, which would make them feel really small about their behaviour. But as I began getting closer to them, squeezing through past people's chairs, etc., I bumped into someone who knocked a drink (luckily) down themselves. After I'd apologised and began heading off again towards Jennie and James, I'd forgotten everything I'd planned to say.

James had now noticed me, so I couldn't exactly turn back. I carried on till I got to their table. He nudged Jennie, and then she looked up, and whatever I had left to say, went. She looked me in the eyes and immediately, that smirk began building on her lips. I began saying something, and from recollection it went—'I think—you

two—well people think—I think you are,' and that's as far as I got
before Jennie said: 'Sorry—Holly, is it? I think you're at the wrong
table. You're over there with support staff.'

At which point, I felt myself go red, and things seemed to wobble.
I heard her laugh, I must have garbled something, and just then I
heard a voice say:

'I think what Holly's trying to say is "James, if you want a bed, rent
a room, this is an office party, not a brothel, so scrape that whore
off your arm and go find one!!!"' It was Toby, and he was standing
next to me and then him and James seemed to launch themselves at
each other. At that point, I was being led away by Trisha, and it all
seemed to fizzle out. I went home soon after. No one's said anything
yet from upstairs, but I'm waiting …

What d'you think?

From: Aisha
To: Holly

Go Toby!!
I think I would have punched the bitch, or poured a drink over her,
or thrown food in her lap
So you getting back with Toby?

From: Holly
To: Aisha

No, definitely not.

From: Aisha
To: Holly

He needs bagging quickly. Got any pictures of him?

From: Holly
To: Aisha

No, go back to your party. Wait, scratch that, GO TO BED!
zzzzzzz
(for sleep)

From: Aisha
To: Holly

Might need to talk to you later.

From: Holly
To: Aisha

Bed bed bed, Aisha needs to sleep.

Say night-night to everyone, Aishy.

(I'll be here if you need me)

thursday

Subject: Envelopes

From: Shella Hamilton-Jones
To: Holly; Judy Perkins; Patricia Gillot

Dear Judy,

Having now spent some time on the reception desk myself, I know that both Holly and Patricia are very busy for most of their time. However, during the quieter times e.g., at the beginning and end of each day, I was hoping to utilise their able dextrosity in communicating an urgent message to employees and delegates. If this is OK, I'll have the envelopes which need stuffing delivered to them now.

Yours,

Shella

Subject: Shella

From: Holly
To: Patricia Gillot

Able dextrosity???

From: Patricia Gillot
To: Holly

Hand me my boots. I need to pay her a visit.

From: Holly
To: Patricia Gillot

If she's always this rude to everyone in the company, how come she hasn't been sacked years ago??

From: Patricia Gillot
To: Holly

They're too scared.

From: Holly
To: Patricia Gillot

But she's a PA. It's not like she's bringing money into the company or anything?

From: Patricia Gillot
To: Holly

That's not why they're scared. It's not a money thing.

Subject: Mum

From: Alice and Matt
To: Holly

Don't you think it's time you called her? She really is feeling bad about everything.
Alice

From: Holly
To: Alice and Matt

I'm not calling her yet. Maybe I will soon.
So tell me, what did Charlie do?

From: Alice and Matt
To: Holly

Our delightful brother called up on Monday night around 7 p.m., drunk, and I know he feels awkward when my children answer the phone, because he doesn't know what to say to them, but I really do think he should work on something—anything except telling little Joseph how to make a magic sweet tree… ???? Do you know how to make one?

From: Holly
To: Alice and Matt

No, but I'm guessing it's fun?

From: Alice and Matt
To: Holly

Apparently you need to empty a bag of sugar and a slab of butter into one of mummy's shoes and bury it in the garden (or so Uncle Charlie told him).

You know how my son looks up to Bad Uncle Charlie. He'll do anything Charlie tells him.

Can you have a word with Charlie for me? He just laughs when I tell him, and then gets upset when I don't find it funny.

From: Holly
To: Alice and Matt

Sorry, I tried not to laugh, I did maybe a teeny bit. But I guess not funny when it's your shoes full of butter. I'll have a word with him I promise.

xxx

Haven't actually heard from him in a while.

Subject: And as if by magic …

From: Holly
To: Patricia Gillot

The desk was swamped in envelopes!

Grrrr

From: Patricia Gillot
To: Holly

We should get Ralph to help, he'd love doing this for us.

From: Holly
To: Patricia Gillot

No he wouldn't.

From: Patricia Gillot
To: Holly

He would if we made him do it kneeling in the middle of the reception??

From: Holly
To: Patricia Gillot

Funny, and when Judy catches him, I can picture her face now, utter confusion??? (Followed by rage.) Best not.

So tell me why people are frightened of Shella (apart from her charming persona)?

Subject: Where are you these days?

From: Holly
To: Jason GrangerRM

Not heard a squeak from you?

xxx

Subject: Envelopes

From: Patricia Gillot
To: Holly

Pass me some more.

And answering your question, when I joined, Shella had already been here a while. There were a lot less of us back then, and she was the PA for Mr Wright before he died …

From: Holly
To: Patricia Gillot

So?
So what are you saying??????

From: Patricia Gillot
To: Holly

That she knows that Mr Huerst killed Mr Wright!

From: Holly
To: Patricia Gillot

?

From: Patricia Gillot
To: Holly

And Shella and Randy Randolph Huerst have been having an affair for 20 years!!!

From: Holly
To: Patricia Gillot

??

From: Patricia Gillot
To: Holly

Stop sending over those flippin question marks, it's true!

From: Holly
To: Patricia Gillot

Sorry Trish, but I feel this may be just your imagination?

From: Patricia Gillot
To: Holly

It's true. Randolph Huerst and Shella Hamilton-Jones have been sharing the same bed for years, and they killed Mr Wright.

From: Holly
To: Patricia Gillot

They did, did they?

From: Patricia Gillot
To: Holly

They did, and they had a kid, and this is the best bit. It's my job to tell you, darlin, it's you.

From: Holly
To: Patricia Gillot

I am the love child of Shella and Mr Huerst?

From: Patricia Gillot
To: Holly

Yes.

Subject: WORK WORK WORK

From: Jason GrangerRM
To: Holly

Haven't had much chance to gossip, been busy since Aisha's away. Also got two more off sick.

xxx

Subject: The truth is

From: Patricia Gillot
To: Holly

OK, I'm lying.

From: Holly
To: Patricia Gillot

That's a shame, I was going to ask Daddy for some cash.

From: Patricia Gillot
To: Holly

Anyway, Shella must know something big, some dark secret they don't want coming out.

Also, I thought you said James lives in Richmond?

From: Holly
To: Patricia Gillot

He does (please refer to him as scumbag—makes me happier).

From: Patricia Gillot
To: Holly

But then who lives in Islington—his parents?

From: Holly
To: Patricia Gillot

No, his parents live in Chelsea—I went there once—nice house, scumbag parents (didn't meet them). (But probably are.)

Why, who lives in Islington?????

From: Patricia Gillot
To: Holly

I've got his letter here, Mr James Lawrence—140 Elgin Drive, Islington.

From: Holly
To: Patricia Gillot

Are you sure?????

From: Patricia Gillot
To: Holly

Yes. I think he's been telling you porkies?

Subject: When you come back

From: Patricia Gillot
To: Holly

Hope you and Shella had fun together. I've been thinking about this address thing, and there must be a reason he's been a lying little toe rag.

friday

Subject: Bite Marks

From: Patricia Gillot
To: Holly

How did yesterday with Shella go? You look happy, why aren't you missing some teeth? Can't see no bite marks on your arms either?

From: Holly
To: Patricia Gillot

We talked about everything I'd put together. Shella looked at it. Didn't pass any comment at all, said she'd review it and get back to me this morning. So... aaaaaaaaaagh viper email at any moment.

Subject: A bright sunny Friday to you Miss Hilton

From: Jason GrangerRM
To: Holly

Looking forward to meeting Trisha tonight. Where are we going then?

From: Holly
To: Jason GrangerRM

Don't know. I was thinking about Henry's bar in Covent Garden?

Subject: Nightclub

From: Holly
To: Charlie Denham

I haven't heard from you for a while, is everything going OK with the club?
Holly

Subject: I'll pray for you darlin

From: Patricia Gillot
To: Holly

Tell me when Shella sends that hate email, and I'll go pick us up some chocolate cake from catering.

Now more important things:

Mr James Lawrence

140 Elgin Drive

Islington

That's Islington, NOT Richmond. What's that about then?

From: Holly
To: Patricia Gillot

He definitely lives in Richmond, with half the house covered in tarpaulin, massive extension on the back. Maybe this is a friend's place?

From: Patricia Gillot
To: Holly

How d'you know he lives in Richmond?

From: Holly
To: Patricia Gillot

He told me.

From: Patricia Gillot
To: Holly

Yeah, but he could be lying.

From: Holly
To: Patricia Gillot

OK, but why would he lie?

From: Patricia Gillot
To: Holly

That's what we need to find out. So, you never saw this huge house in Richmond or any pictures of it with this amazing extension?

From: Holly
To: Patricia Gillot

No, I wanted to go one night, but James said something about it being too far out of town to bother—in Richmond? So do you think he lives in a tiny flat in Islington, and he made the other one up?

From: Patricia Gillot
To: Holly

I hate to bring her up, but where does Jennie live?

From: Holly
To: Patricia Gillot

No, she doesn't live in Islington.

From: Patricia Gillot
To: Holly

Richmond's too far, but if he said it was in Islington, you could have been over there in a shot. I think he's lying. He tells girls he lives in some swanky palace in Richmond, while really he's slumming it in some rat hole in Islington?

From: Holly
To: Patricia Gillot

Islington's still quite expensive though?

From: Patricia Gillot
To: Holly

Still might be a hole. He might even be putting on a fake accent. My guess is he speaks more like me. When he's with you, he's all 'just a gin and ha ha yar'? and back home he's 'gizza pint an some scratchins, you muppet!'

From: Holly
To: Patricia Gillot

Stop making me laugh, I need to pee!

From: Patricia Gillot
To: Holly

It's probably not even his real name. He's probably called Jimbo. He's probably got a Mark 2 Escort hidden somewhere.

From: Holly
To: Patricia Gillot

What's that?

From: Patricia Gillot
To: Holly

Ask him. When he walks past say: 'Oi Jimbo! Next time I'm in yer mannor give us a butches at yer Mark 2 you can't.'

From: Holly
To: Patricia Gillot

That's it—you've done it—I've got the giggles—I'm off, before I have an accident.

xx

Subject: Wanted to talk

From: Toby Williams
To: Holly

Hi.

Subject: Why I've been quiet

From: Charlie Denham
To: Holly

I lost the club.

Charlie

From: Holly
To: Charlie Denham

What? Why didn't you tell me—are you alright?

Subject: Annual Review: Your research

From: Shella Hamilton-Jones
To: Holly

Holly,

I'm keen to get together for another meeting some afternoon next week. Let me know when would be suitable for you.

Having had time to study your submission for longer, I found myself considerably impressed, and you've left me rather intrigued, because I can't see anywhere on your CV the mention of any training at all in events or project management?

Regards,

Shella

Subject: Talk

From: Holly
To: Toby Williams

Why are you emailing me?

From: Toby Williams
To: Holly

I want to talk to you.

From: Holly
To: Toby Williams

No, Toby, please.

From: Toby Williams
To: Holly

I know you were married.

From: Holly
To: Toby Williams

What?

From: Toby Williams
To: Holly

I know he was a bastard, and you've no reason to trust men, but please, Holly. I just need to get everything straight. Can I see you tonight?

From: Holly
To: Toby Williams

Toby, don't do this. Please. I don't want to go back. Please Toby, just leave it all alone.

From: Toby Williams
To: Holly

Come out tonight and let me explain. Please.

Subject: Pain

From: Patricia Gillot
To: Holly

My arse is killing me on this seat. I'm going for a fag, you alright?

From: Holly
To: Patricia Gillot

Fine.

x

From: Patricia Gillot
To: Holly

Looking forward to seeing your Jason tonight—back in a mo.

Subject: Annual Review: Your research

From: Holly
To: Shella Hamilton-Jones

Shella,

I'm fine any day next week—it's just Judy and Trisha who I would need to check with, etc.

Re:—events & project management training—I just looked on the Internet, etc.

Kindest regards,

Holly

From: Shella Hamilton-Jones
To: Holly

Holly

Let me get this straight; you went on to the Internet, and you learnt all that in a week?

Shella

From: Holly
To: Shella Hamilton-Jones

Yes.

Subject: Shella

From: Holly
To: Patricia Gillot

Is it likely that Shella could have a copy of my CV?

From: Patricia Gillot
To: Holly

Of course. Why? Also, you decided what we're going to do about James's dodgy address thing?

From: Holly
To: Patricia Gillot

I'm not going to do anything about his address thing—what's there to do?

Subject: Tonight

From: Toby Williams
To: Holly

You haven't answered me. I'm not going to push this forever. I'd really like you to come out so I can talk to you. If not, then that's fine, and I promise this will be the last time you will hear from me.
Toby

Subject: Internet

From: Shella Hamilton-Jones
To: Holly

Holly,
I find this very difficult to believe, but the work is very good, which is the most important thing.
I will email you a time for us to meet up again next week.
Shella

Subject: Hello

From: Holly
To: Toby Williams

Are you there?

From: Toby Williams
To: Holly

Yes.

From: Holly
To: Toby Williams

I just didn't want to write something which could be read by everyone up there, while you were at lunch or something.

From: Toby Williams
To: Holly

No, I'm here, no one's around. I think most of them are in the bar still.

From: Holly
To: Toby Williams

Thank you for last Friday night.

From: Toby Williams
To: Holly

You're welcome.

From: Holly
To: Toby Williams

I wasn't doing so well.

From: Toby Williams
To: Holly

You were doing fine.

From: Holly
To: Toby Williams

No, I wasn't.

I thought that kind of thing would get easier, but it's got harder the older I've got. I've lost a lot of what I used to have.

From: Toby Williams
To: Holly

I don't think you have.

From: Holly
To: Toby Williams

I have. You remember when we'd take on all the cliques and gangs, and give them as good as we got?

From: Toby Williams
To: Holly

Of course.

From: Holly
To: Toby Williams

When I was standing there last Friday, I suddenly felt like I was back in that cafeteria, and you were there with me, and we were giving as good as we gave. It was weird. Very strange.

From: Toby Williams
To: Holly

For me too. I just want you back Holly, give me a chance.

From: Holly
To: Toby Williams

I can't.

From: Toby Williams
To: Holly

Holly,

I've never stopped loving you, ever. Just give me a chance.

Please.

From: Holly
To: Toby Williams

I loved you too, so so much.

I can't go back though, please understand this. When you left, it was so difficult. Too difficult. I want to get myself stronger now, and I don't want to lean on your shoulder, or anyone else's ever again. Too many ups and downs. I can't cope with it all. Sorry Toby.

xx

From: Toby Williams
To: Holly

I'm coming down, Holly. I'm not giving up.

Subject: Going out

From: Holly
To: Patricia Gillot

I'm going out. If you see Toby, tell him no.

Sorry.

x

From: Patricia Gillot
To: Holly

No, what? What's going on? Do you need me, babe?

Subject: Me

From: Aisha
To: Holly; Jason GrangerRM

Got very drunk, got married.

Picture attached

month 5

Subject: Wedding??

From: Holly
To: Jason GrangerRM

Hiya,
Tell me when our lunatic friend gets in!!!
xxx

From: Jason GrangerRM
To: Holly

She's not coming in.

From: Holly
To: Jason GrangerRM

So you've spoken to her???

From: Jason GrangerRM
To: Holly

She called in sick, of course.

From: Holly
To: Jason GrangerRM

So? What was our naughty sparrow doing in a wedding dress?

From: Jason GrangerRM
To: Holly

The question is, was it a wedding dress?

From: Holly
To: Jason GrangerRM

Stop teasing me. Do you know or not?

From: Jason GrangerRM
To: Holly

No.

Didn't speak to her myself, now she's not answering the phone. I'll keep you updated on Mrs—whoever. At least this is the kind of thing I can imagine her wearing to her wedding.

From: Holly
To: Jason GrangerRM

Yes, totally inappropriate, looking a complete trollop and the kind of thing I could only dream of being able to get away with (at a fancy dress party).

Love her.

Subject: Rent

From: Charlie Denham
To: Holly

Unless we come up with the back rent, they're not going to let us back in the club.

Charlie

From: Holly
To: Charlie Denham

I heard. How long have you got?

From: Charlie Denham
To: Holly

Maybe a few weeks. I hope.

From: Holly
To: Charlie Denham

If I could help you, I probably would (as much as I'd fight against doing it). Sorry, Charlie.

xx

Subject: Friday night

From: Holly
To: Patricia Gillot

Morning you drunkard. Had a great time Friday night. Thanks.
xxxxx

From: Patricia Gillot
To: Holly

I was in a right old 2n8 when you left. Good, wasn't it, and we love gorgeous Jason. He's so funny. He had me and Les in stitches the whole night. Me Vikki was after him, and she wishes she could change him!

Subject: Your ex

From: Patricia Gillot
To: Holly

So, what are we going to do about James' address thing?

From: Holly
To: Patricia Gillot

Nothing?

From: Patricia Gillot
To: Holly

Don't you want to know why he lied?

From: Holly
To: Patricia Gillot

I'm happier not thinking about either him or Jennie at all.

From: Patricia Gillot
To: Holly

Well I'm not leaving it, I'm a right nosy so-and-so and I want to know.

Subject: Reference for you

From: Jason GrangerRM
To: Holly

A Hillary just called from 'the HR dept at Huerst & Wright' wanting a reference for you. When I tried to give them one, they didn't sound too impressed, like they wanted to check it with our personnel dept etc. I gave them all this months ago?

From: Holly
To: Jason GrangerRM

I bet that's something Shella's stirred up. She sounded very suspicious last week.

From: Jason GrangerRM
To: Holly

That's your own fault then. I told you not to be such a smarty-pants.

From: Holly
To: Jason GrangerRM

I wasn't being a smarty-pants, just doing my best. Anyway, that's not helpful. What will your HR say if they go directly there for a ref?

From: Jason GrangerRM
To: Holly

They'll probably confirm the dates, that you were here two weeks and not two years ...

From: Holly
To: Jason GrangerRM

Oh joy. Fab, that's just great.

From: Jason GrangerRM
To: Holly

You should probably come clean now.

From: Holly
To: Jason GrangerRM

I can't do that, they'll definitely sack me then.

From: Jason GrangerRM
To: Holly

If you'd told Trisha the truth, you could ask her. (Holly! Stop glaring at me.)

From: Holly
To: Jason GrangerRM

It's a bit late now, but I know, I know.

Got to go, conference stuff with Shella again.

x

tuesday

Subject: I've been thinking

From: Jason GrangerRM
To: Holly

I want a baby.

From: Holly
To: Jason GrangerRM

I'm not ready for them Jason, besides which, I'm not your type (I have nasty breasties).

From: Jason GrangerRM
To: Holly

I know, quite repulsive.

I'm feeling blue.

| From: Holly |
| To: Jason GrangerRM |

Are you getting paternal again?

| From: Jason GrangerRM |
| To: Holly |

Yes.

| From: Holly |
| To: Jason GrangerRM |

OK, I found this in our receptionists' magazine. You could sponsor a child. You get a letter from them and school reports and everything. Check it out. http://www.frontofhousemagazine. co.uk/loveachild.asp

If that doesn't work, I could get pregnant Pam to give you a call, that should put you off?

xxxxx

| From: Jason GrangerRM |
| To: Holly |

Thanks.

x

Subject: Holly

| From: Shella Hamilton-Jones |
| To: Holly; Judy Perkins |

Dear Judy,

Is it possible to borrow Holly for another couple of afternoons this week? I'd like to get her involved in other areas of the planning of this conference. (I've copied Holly into this email.)

Regards,

Shella

Subject: Granny

From: Alice and Matt
To: Holly

Hi Holly,

I spoke to Mum today. She was telling me how Granny has been going to church more and more these days. Mum says it's because Granny's thinking about the next life, and what it might have in store for her.

Subject: Dad's army

From: Holly
To: Granny

Hi Granny,

How are you? Everything here much the same. Also, did you get those tapes I sent you of Dad's Army?

Love, Holly xxx

From: Granny
To: Holly

Holly,

Thank you so much for the tapes. I haven't received them yet, but you know what the post is like. Have you spoken to your mother? I know she has a tendency to put her foot in her mouth whenever she opens it, but she usually means well. It's best not to let these things dwell, or one day you'll find it's just too late to make things up. It's your decision of course, and you can tell your nosy grandmother to bog off if you want.

Love, Granny

xxx

From: Holly
To: Granny

Thanks Granny, I'll get in touch today. Of course I love her lots, just wanted to punish her a bit first. Also, that comment you emailed—

about needing to get things straight before it's too late. You're not having any morbid thoughts, are you—Alice mentioned you've been going to church a lot?

Holly

From: Granny
To: Holly

Holly,

I'm not having any morbid thoughts, dear, I just don't think arguments should go stale.

Yes, I am going to church a lot. Not so I can get closer to God, as your mother thinks, but to get closer to the communion wine, as I can get quite sozzled on the port if I'm left to hold the chalice long enough. Unfortunately the parish priest, at some stage, snatches it back and offers it to the next poor sinner. Still, I guess he has a job to do. If I was treated as an adult instead of a child, I wouldn't have to go to church.

Your Gran, as always,

Elizabeth

xxx

From: Holly
To: Granny

Granny,

You have an amazing way of always making me smile!

xxxx

trisha's
inbox

tuesday

Subject: I'm waiting

From: Les
To: Trisha

So what's the news?

From: Trisha
To: Les

I'm still waiting, Les, he hasn't emailed yet.

From: Les
To: Trisha

Tell me when he does, won't you?

From: Trisha
To: Les

I said I would, didn't I?

Subject: Hello

From: Les
To: Trisha

Any news?

From: Trisha
To: Les

No, Les.

Subject: So?

From: Les
To: Trisha

Any news?

From: Trisha
To: Les

Les, can't you p*ss off and leave me alone? Find something else to do?

From: Les
To: Trisha

Alright, I'm only asking. Do you think I should go with him?

From: Trisha
To: Les

I don't know. I'll find out when he emails, OK!

Subject: Tests

From: Dr. Goth
To: Trisha

Dear Patricia,

We still need to organise a time for you to come in again for further tests. Please can you contact the surgery when you have a spare moment.

Kelly C

Admin

Subject: Psssssssssssssst are you there?

From: Jason GrangerRM
To: Trisha

All set, I'm going there from 6 p.m... waiting... How exciting!

From: Trisha
To: Jason GrangerRM

At last, I thought you were going to bottle out on me. Did you sort yourself out with everything you need?

From: JasonGrangerRM
To: Trisha

The essentials required for any modern agent or gay spy (we like to be known as WAGS).

From: Trisha
To: Jason GrangerRM

Darlin, that spells MAGS.

From: Jason GrangerRM
To: Trisha

I know, just realised, but who cares, I just want to be a WAG. Anyway, I got our chef to rustle us up a great selection of food and drink, which I've packed into a cooler. There's enough there for when Les swaps over.

From: Trisha
To: Jason GrangerRM

Oh he will be happy. Does he need to take anything with him?

From: Jason GrangerRM
To: Trisha

I'm hoping I'll have seen it all by the time he does a handover (although I saw diddly-squat for 2 hrs last night, so who knows). I have: a camera, digital with zoom, of course, and lastly, I'm not only a supercool agent, I'm also the master of disguises!!! I've found the perfect outfit. It's a kind of Lily Savage meets Inspector Clueso… (basically a moustache, a raincoat, and a red wig I borrowed from a tranny friend of mine). I'm so excited, I can't breathe.

From: Trisha
To: Jason GrangerRM

James doesn't know what you look like, does he?

From: Jason GrangerRM
To: Trisha

No?

From: Trisha
To: Jason GrangerRM

So what you doing?

From: Jason GrangerRM
To: Trisha

You've got to do it right, Trisha. You can't sit in a car, watching someone's house, dressed as you are. It's no fun at all.

From: Trisha
To: Jason GrangerRM

Babes, if you go dressed like a clown, you'll get arrested.

From: Jason GrangerRM
To: Trisha

You're right, damn. OK, I'll go as I am.

From: Trisha
To: Jason GrangerRM

You spoken to Holly?

From: Jason GrangerRM
To: Trisha

Yes, to throw her off the scent, I've been pretending to be moody all morning, said I wanted a baby. Five minutes later, she's sent me something for sponsoring a child, bless her—might do it too. This has been so much fun!! Shame Aisha's going to miss it.

From: Trisha
To: Jason GrangerRM

Holly wouldn't let us do it if we mentioned it to her.

From: Jason GrangerRM
To: Trisha

Don't tell her, whatever you do.

From: Trisha
To: Jason GrangerRM

What time are you heading off?

From: Jason GrangerRM
To: Trisha

In about 3 hours… My heart's already going.

From: Trisha
To: Jason GrangerRM

Don't get caught. You want my Les to meet you there? You might be better off with some muscle behind you.

From: Jason GrangerRM
To: Trisha

Oh Trisha, if you'd said that in a gay club… I AM fighting the urge to make any number of innuendos. If nothing's seen by the morning, then he can take over. I've got your number.

From: Trisha
To: Jason GrangerRM

OK, darlin, call me as soon as you see anything, whatever time it is. xxxx

From: Jason GrangerRM
To: Trisha

I will, mon pretty Island conspirator.

Subject: Why so happy?

From: Holly
To: Trisha

Why are you looking so pleased with yourself?

From: Trisha
To: Holly

No reason.

From: Holly
To: Trisha

Come on now Trisha, tell me. Why do you keep giggling?

From: Trisha
To: Holly

Can't a girl giggle to herself sometimes? Isn't it allowed now?

From: Holly
To: Trisha

Smiling's OK, but being genuinely happy probably isn't allowed.
I'll check the manual.

From: Trisha
To: Holly

Fffrrrrrrrrt

From: Holly
To: Trisha

Patricia Gillot, did you just blow a raspberry at me????

From: Trisha
To: Holly

YES Ha ha.
Oh, and I'm not happy you keep getting stolen off my reception
desk by Shella. It's not fair. I don't want to work with a temp.

From: Holly
To: Trisha

Sorry.

Subject: News

From: Trisha
To: Les

He's got everything sorted. He even had a moustache and wig.

From: Les
To: Trisha

What's he want that for?

From: Trisha
To: Les

He's just getting excited about it. He got you some food an' all, but he doesn't need you there tonight. You go along in the morning, if he's seen nothing.

From: Les
To: Trisha

OK, OK. What we having for dinner?

From: Trisha
To: Les

Lobster with orange sauce, followed by coconut truffles. Happy?

holly's
inbox

tuesday

Subject: Why so happy?

From: Holly
To: Patricia Gillot

Why are you looking so pleased with yourself?

From: Patricia Gillot
To: Holly

No reason.

From: Holly
To: Patricia Gillot

Come on now Trish, tell me. Why do you keep giggling?

From: Patricia Gillot
To: Holly

Can't a girl giggle to herself sometimes? Isn't it allowed now?

From: Holly
To: Patricia Gillot

Smiling's OK, but being genuinely happy probably isn't allowed.
I'll check the manual.

From: Patricia Gillot
To: Holly

Fffrrrrrrrrt

From: Holly
To: Patricia Gillot

Patricia Gillot, did you just blow a raspberry at me????

From: Patricia Gillot
To: Holly

YES Ha ha.

And I'm not happy you keep getting stolen off my reception desk by Shella. It's not fair. I don't want to work with a temp.

From: Holly
To: Patricia Gillot

Sorry.

Subject: Truce?

From: Holly
To: Mum and Dad

Do you want to be friends again?

Holly

From: Mum and Dad
To: Holly

Yes, Holly, I'd like that very much.

From: Holly
To: Mum and Dad

I don't like falling out with you, Mum, I really don't.

From: Mum and Dad
To: Holly

I don't like it, either. These last few weeks have been truly horrid.

From: Holly
To: Mum and Dad

Then you must stop meddling. Please, Mum. I know it's all done with the best intentions, but it doesn't usually work out well for anyone.

From: Mum and Dad
To: Holly

Will you call me please? I just want to talk to my daughter again. Please, can you call me now?

Mum

From: Holly
To: Mum and Dad

I'll just ask Trisha and call you from a meeting room.

Love you

xx

wednesday

Subject: The Post Room??

From: Jennie Pithwait
To: Holly

Holly,

I couldn't help but noticing you down there madly folding envelopes on Friday as I passed. Your mother must be so proud of you! I bet you can fold twenty a minute if you really try hard!! I hear these are for the Annual Review, which I will be attending, so please make sure you get my letter out on time, dear.

xJ

Subject: Oi Part Timer!

From: Patricia Gillot
To: Holly

Do I get you for the rest of the day? Or are you off gallivanting upstairs again?

From: Holly
To: Patricia Gillot

Sorry Trish. How was your morning?

From: Patricia Gillot
To: Holly

Cr*p, to be honest, darlin. I've got used to your face, as sad as it sounds.

From: Holly
To: Patricia Gillot

I got an email-nasty from Jennie, she is the most despicable bitch ever! I thought she'd changed since school, but ...
Holly
I couldn't help but noticing you down there madly folding envelopes on Friday as I passed. Your mother must be so proud of you! I bet you can fold twenty a minute if you really try hard!! I hear these are for the Annual Review, which I will be attending, so please make sure you get my letter out on time, dear.
xJ

From: Patricia Gillot
To: Holly

For less than the price of a new Merc, I could have her disappear?

From: Holly
To: Patricia Gillot

I haven't got that much. What about the price of a secondhand Mini with engine trouble?

From: Patricia Gillot
To: Holly

I'll have one of her nails broken?

From: Holly
To: Patricia Gillot

Real or false?

From: Patricia Gillot
To: Holly

For real, I'll give you a number. He hangs out down at The Gun. (Joke—I know what you meant.)

So, you writing back to the cow upstairs?

From: Holly
To: Patricia Gillot

I think I might send her one back. I really want all this to end—I'm really tired of it and to be honest, I can't carry on much longer. It makes me so on edge and my heart races and I get worked up and angry. I don't want to feel like this at work. I don't want her getting to me, but she's so good at being awful. It's hard keeping up with her. She's a nasty piece of work.

From: Patricia Gillot
To: Holly

What goes around comes around, I just wish it would hurry up.

PS—Don't you dare leave me!

xxx

Go on, write something back, she deserves it. I dare you ...

From: Holly
To: Patricia Gillot

She's even started signing off with J—like he does... grrrrrrrrr

Subject: Important

From: Holly
To: Jennie Pithwait

Jennie,

My parents are very proud of me, because I've turned out to be a well-balanced human being, with moral values; not a psychotic tart with delusions of grandeur.

Love,

H

xx

Subject: Aisha

From: Holly
To: Jason GrangerRM

Any news from our miscreant friend yet?
Her phone's still off.

From: Jason GrangerRM
To: Holly

Zilch.

From: Holly
To: Jason GrangerRM

Are you OK?

From: Jason GrangerRM
To: Holly

Yes, just tired.

From: Holly
To: Jason GrangerRM

I was thinking of telling Trisha the truth?

From: Jason GrangerRM
To: Holly

Good luck sweetie.

xxxx

Subject: I'm sorry ...

From: Holly
To: Patricia Gillot

I'z been lying to you.

From: Patricia Gillot
To: Holly

About what, darlin?

From: Holly
To: Patricia Gillot

Quite a lot, but it's not my fault.

From: Patricia Gillot
To: Holly

Don't tell me you're gay? If you're about to come out to me, darlin, I'm happy for ya and all, but you're not my type. I like girls with more meat.

From: Holly
To: Patricia Gillot

I'm serious Trisha.
Anyway, how much meat do you want?

From: Patricia Gillot
To: Holly

A lot more than you've got. So what's up?

Subject: Little white lies

From: Holly
To: Patricia Gillot

When I first met you, I didn't know you well enough to tell you the truth. Then I did start knowing you better, but by then, it was too late to tell you the truth. So I didn't. You see, it's really not my fault, Trishy.

From: Patricia Gillot
To: Holly

You posh people really don't know how to spit things out, do you. Come on you dirty lying whore-bag, tell your Aunty Trisha!!!

From: Holly
To: Patricia Gillot

I only spent 2 weeks as a receptionist in a hotel.

From: Patricia Gillot
To: Holly

I could have told you that. I've met some bad receptionists in my time, but you took the biscuit. I guessed you were lying about doing the job for years, either that, or you were as thick as f*ck. So come on, what you been up to? You weren't working as a Mile End slapper, were you??

From: Holly
To: Patricia Gillot

No Trisha, I wasn't. I ran a small events company with my husband.

From: Patricia Gillot
To: Holly

I know you did. He was a right b*stard from what I heard, used to beat you up and everything. I had a man like that before Les. Talking of which, that was him on the phone, got to go meet him. It's dead anyway. I'll see you tomorrow.

xxx

Ha ha, love you, you lying cow.

Subject: PS ...

From: Patricia Gillot
To: Holly

You should have a word with your friends, they haven't half got mouths on them. That Jason for instance, can't keep secrets. ha ha

From: Holly
To: Patricia Gillot

I'll kill him!!! Have a good night.

Subject: Bad bad girls!!!!

From: Jason GrangerRM
To: Holly

I just called Aish, and I'm sure it rang with a foreign ring tone before going dead. I think she's still in Ibiza, or Russia or Egypt. Actually, I don't have a clue where she is, but she's not in this country and not in this hotel.

I'm going to give that young lady a steeeeeern talking to when she resurfaces.

thursday

Subject: Hold the front page!!!

From: Jason GrangerRM
To: Holly

Aisha's coming in!!!! Today gets more exciting by the second.

From: Holly
To: Jason GrangerRM

At last!! What else is exciting??

From: Jason GrangerRM
To: Holly

Oh Holly, so many many things, it's a funny old world really, isn't it?

From: Holly
To: Jason GrangerRM

What's a funny world? Have I missed out on some celebrity gossip?

From: Jason GrangerRM
To: Holly

No. Promise.

Subject: What a great day it is

From: Patricia Gillot
To: Holly

Morning Holly.

From: Holly
To: Patricia Gillot

Morning. Why are you beaming at me?

From: Patricia Gillot
To: Holly

Didn't know I was beaming.

From: Holly
To: Patricia Gillot

You are, and it's scaring me. Please stop. What's wrong? Have you put something sticky on my seat again?

From: Patricia Gillot
To: Holly

No.

From: Holly
To: Patricia Gillot

My skirt wasn't tucked into my knickers, was it?

From: Patricia Gillot
To: Holly

I'm just happy. Life is just one big surprise, init?

Subject: Ibiza chick

From: Holly
To: Jason GrangerRM

Is she there yet? I still couldn't get hold of her last night either. Where is the little misfit?

From: Jason GrangerRM
To: Holly

She's sitting about four metres away, sniffing and snuffling and hoping someone notices she's got a cold, trying to look very sorry for herself.

From: Holly
To: Jason GrangerRM

Are you buying it?

From: Jason GrangerRM
To: Holly

Am I, hell.

From: Holly
To: Jason GrangerRM

Can I email her, or has she been sent to Coventry? And what's the news? Is she, or isn't she?

From: Jason GrangerRM
To: Holly

Well that's where the confusion lies. I've no idea. She said it's a long story, and she's not well enough to tell it yet. She knows we're both dying to know, so she has every intention of dragging it out until I'm nice to her. She's trying to check people out without opening her mouth to speak to them.

From: Holly
To: Jason GrangerRM

Oh poor love. She might be ill??

From: Jason GrangerRM
To: Holly

She's not sick, unless the doctor has started prescribing whisky for colds—she smells like an old drunk from the park. She's just hungover. I'm watching her now, and she knows I'm watching her, and she's trying to look as feeble as she can. Oops, there she goes, head up, and at last she's seen me.

Subject: To the sick one

From: Jason GrangerRM
To: Aisha; Holly

To the sick one:
Hello sweetie, not feeling well, are we? A long week in bed recovering from life-threatening illnesses? Say hello to your friend, Holly. She's been worried about you too!

From: Aisha
To: Holly; Jason GrangerRM

Holly,
Hi baby, how are you? Have you heard how horrid Jason is being to me? I'm trying to recover from the flu, and he's made me do all the checkouts. He doesn't love me any more.

From: Holly
To: Aisha; Jason GrangerRM

I think he's being very patient, young Aisha. Now, I would call you Aisha Peters, but I've no idea if that's your name—is it or not?

From: Aisha
To: Holly; Jason GrangerRM

I'll always be Aisha Peters to you, Holly, although Jason just calls me 'the sick one.' Poor me.

From: Holly
To: Aisha; Jason GrangerRM

Stop doing those faces—as Jason always tells me, it's not cute or clever. Now, are you married to your boss?

From: Aisha
To: Holly; Jason GrangerRM

No.

From: Jason GrangerRM
To: Aisha; Holly

Are you a lethargic waste of space?

From: Jason GrangerRM
To: Holly; Aisha

Holly,

I can see that mischievous smile creeping on to her face. She's trying to hide it under her hand, but I can see it there.

From: Aisha
To: Jason GrangerRM; Holly

Oh, you are really on my case, Mr Jason. Poor Aisha, and on her honeymoon too.

From: Jason GrangerRM
To: Aisha; Holly

TELL US!!!!!

From: Aisha
To: Holly; Jason GrangerRM

OK, are you sitting comfortably?

From: Holly
To: Aisha; Jason GrangerRM

YES!

From: Jason GrangerRM
To: Aisha; Holly

YES!

From: Aisha
To: Jason GrangerRM; Holly

Then I shall begin.

Firstly, Jason, can I have a lickle break? I'm ever so hot and tirsty, and my poor lickle head is so hot, I tink I shall surely die.

From: Jason GrangerRM
To: Aisha; Holly

OK, OK, whatever you want. You can go home after this. Just tell us!

From: Aisha
To: Jason GrangerRM; Holly

OK, it was just a fancy dress party.

Thanks Jasey, love ya. I'll call you tomorrow, Holly. Jason, I'll tell Maria to take over on this desk. See you tomorrow.

Love and kisses,

Aishy

614   holly's inbox—week 1

From: Jason GrangerRM
To: Holly; Aisha

I need a drink.

Subject: Story time

From: Patricia Gillot
To: Holly

Tell us about this company then?

From: Holly
To: Patricia Gillot

We used to do events, weddings, parties, lots of fun at the beginning.

From: Patricia Gillot
To: Holly

What happened? Why did it go bust?

From: Holly
To: Patricia Gillot

Who said it went bust?

From: Patricia Gillot
To: Holly

Then where is it? What happened to your house?

From: Holly
To: Patricia Gillot

I'm a little ashamed to admit it, but I was a bit of a mess when he left. He was frightening. He got me to sign over the company and took all the equity out of the house we had. I messed up, really, couldn't pay the bills, and just left it all to rot, just couldn't get everything together to sort things out. Jason was great, he was such a sweetie, looked out for me, got me back on my feet, etc. He's just the best friend anyone could have.

From: Patricia Gillot
To: Holly

Don't you dare be ashamed. Where's Sebastian now?

From: Holly
To: Patricia Gillot

Don't know where he lives. I know the company is doing well. It's in Canary Wharf.

From: Patricia Gillot
To: Holly

How well?

From: Holly
To: Patricia Gillot

Very well.

From: Patricia Gillot
To: Holly

Like?

From: Holly
To: Patricia Gillot

Like they recently did the music awards. They do all the biggest shows. Jason's really annoyed, he wants to meet all the celebrities. Anyway, it's gone, it's over. I'm very happy now.

From: Patricia Gillot
To: Holly

I wouldn't be. I feel as sick as a parrot. Can't you get it back?

Subject: Aisha

From: Jason GrangerRM
To: Holly

She's lying.

I know she's married and I promise I didn't mean to, Holly, but I clicked into her phone line earlier, and she was telling her daughter about it. Just don't know who to.

From: Holly
To: Jason GrangerRM

???

But why would she lie to us?

Subject: Toby

From: Holly
To: Mum and Dad

Mum,

I've been thinking about Toby more and more recently. What did you really think of him?

From: Mum and Dad
To: Holly

Holly,

Darling, it's good to hear from you. But why are you asking me about Toby?

Love, Mum

From: Holly
To: Mum and Dad

I'm asking you, because you might be able to add something. You met him a few times. I don't know anyone else that knows him.

From: Mum and Dad
To: Holly

He was nice enough, bad manners. I remember he had bad hair, terrible hair, Holly. But I don't see why you want to know. You're not thinking about getting back together with him, are you darling? I didn't think you were talking to him?
Mum

From: Holly
To: Mum and Dad

He has better hair now, Mum, you'll be pleased to know. How did he leave when he came around that day? What did he say to you?

From: Mum and Dad
To: Holly

I told him you were very upset and probably that you were both too young to be having such an obviously sexual relationship. We argued, he left. Holly, have you been speaking to him again?

From: Holly
To: Mum and Dad

He has blue eyes. I didn't think about them much at the time, but they are blue. James has brown eyes.
No, Mum, I'm not. Don't worry.
Just thinking.

friday

Subject: Wedding

From: Jason GrangerRM
To: Aisha; Holly

So where was this fancy dress party then, Aish?

From: Aisha
To: Holly; Jason GrangerRM

Dhurrrrr—Ibiza?

From: Holly
To: Aisha; Jason GrangerRM

And it had a wedding theme?

From: Aisha
To: Holly; Jason GrangerRM

That's what I said, yes.

From: Jason GrangerRM
To: Aisha; Holly

I presume someone went as a priest or vicar, Aisha?

From: Aisha
To: Jason GrangerRM; Holly

Yes?

From: Jason GrangerRM
To: Aisha; Holly

Aisha—did this vicar or priest get you to repeat some vows during the evening?

From: Aisha
To: Holly; Jason GrangerRM

Maybe.

From: Holly
To: Aisha; Jason GrangerRM

Baby, at some point did you exchange rings?

From: Aisha
To: Holly; Jason GrangerRM

Maybe.

From: Jason GrangerRM
To: Holly; Aisha

That wasn't a party. That thing you were attending was what we call a 'wedding,' Aisha, and it sounds suspiciously like you were the 'bride.'

Subject: Urgent

From: Judy Perkins
To: Holly; Patricia Gillot

Dear Trisha and Holly,

I've just had a very angry call from Adam Yastovich regarding our new policy of NOT escorting clients up in the lift when we can't get through to the relevant host. I was unaware of this new policy—can someone explain to me what all this is about?

Regards,

Judy

Subject: MY WEDDING

From: Aisha
To: Jason GrangerRM; Holly

OK you two. I've had enough of this spotlight, grilling thing. I got married to a millionaire, he's handsome and rich, and it was a fabulous wedding. I just didn't want you being jealous, OK?!

From: Holly
To: Aisha; Jason GrangerRM

Sweetheart, that's wonderful. Why would you not want to tell us? I'm really happy for you. Tell us about him. Where did you meet him? Have you got any more photos?

From: Aisha
To: Holly; Jason GrangerRM

No, I'm so upset, the camera was stolen. It was fantastic though. I didn't invite you, because I thought you'd think bad of me. Because we hadn't known each other for long. So I wanted to keep it a secret. His name is Julian, and he's so kind and sweet and caring.

It was amazing. I was in that dress in the picture I sent you, and it was in this huge, beautiful old church. There was this big reception afterwards. I arrived there by horse and carriage. Guests drinking champagne in the sunshine, flowers everywhere, it was so pretty.

From: Jason GrangerRM
To: Aisha; Holly

Are you OK Aisha?

From: Aisha
To: Holly; Jason GrangerRM

I'm happy, so happy, OK.

From: Jason GrangerRM
To: Aisha; Holly

Aisha, take a break, go on.

From: Aisha
To: Jason GrangerRM; Holly

I wanted that wedding, I wanted it just like that, I did. It's just lies. Do you want to know why I got married?????

Subject: Jason, what's happening there?

From: Holly
To: Jason GrangerRM

Is Aisha OK?

> **From:** Jason GrangerRM
> **To:** Holly

I tried to put my arm around her, and she ran off. She's crying her eyes out. I've sent one of the other girls to go after her. She's gone to the toilets.

> **From:** Holly
> **To:** Jason GrangerRM

What's up with her? I'll see if I can take my lunch early and come over?

> **From:** Jason GrangerRM
> **To:** Holly

OK, just wait, she's coming back. I'll keep you informed.

> **From:** Holly
> **To:** Jason GrangerRM

If you get to give her a hug, give her one from me!!!

xxxx

and loads of kisses

Subject: Sorry

> **From:** Aisha
> **To:** Holly; Jason GrangerRM

Sorry, I lied.

I got married in Spain—to Shona's dad.

> **From:** Holly
> **To:** Aisha; Jason GrangerRM

What, that man who ran off and left you both? Don't tell me you're back with him, Aisha????

From: Aisha
To: Holly; Jason GrangerRM

I'm not back with him. I had to pay him to go, OK?

From: Jason GrangerRM
To: Aisha; Holly

I don't understand?

From: Aisha
To: Holly; Jason GrangerRM

There was no huge wedding, no carriage, no flowers. He turned up drunk. I paid for him to have a holiday in Ibiza, otherwise he wouldn't do it, that was the condition. I paid for my fucking husband to marry me, OK? There was no lovely church, I signed some bits and pieces, he f*cked off. I've spent my life dreaming about the perfect wedding, Holly, remember you and me always wanted it just perfect? It wasn't f*cking perfect. I'm relay really relayl slukupset OKUPSET and now Jason, can I go home?

From: Jason GrangerRM
To: Aisha; Holly

Only if I can give you a hug. Why did you marry him, Aisha?

From: Aisha
To: Holly; Jason GrangerRM

For Shona. she's at scholl, and I wanted her to say she had a dad. Stupid, I know, but taht's it.

From: Jason GrangerRM
To: Aisha; Holly

Go home, sweetie.
xxx Holly, I'll give her kisses for you.

From: Holly

To: Aisha

We all love you, Aish.

Don't worry.

Subject: Clients

From: Patricia Gillot

To: Holly

When you come back on Monday, don't worry about Judy's email, she's just trying to cover her own a*se. If they're Jennie's clients, I'll take them up so you don't have to see her nasty face.

Trish

trisha's
inbox

week 2
monday

Subject: Pssssssssssssssst

From: Jason GrangerRM
To: Les; Trisha

I hear the Russian Ballet is good at this time of year, but why are you wearing a tutu?

From: Les
To: Jason GrangerRM; Trisha

What?

From: Jason GrangerRM
To: Les; Trisha

I said 'I hear the Russian Ballet is good at this time of year, but why are you wearing a tutu?'

From: Les
To: Jason GrangerRM; Trisha

Because it's cold and me nuts are freezing. Look Jason, I don't want to be 'The Fish' any more, it's sounds sh*t, I want to be 'The Jackal' or 'Wolf?'

From: Trisha
To: Les; Jason GrangerRM

Les, grow up. So what we doing next?

From: Les
To: Jason GrangerRM; Trisha

Why don't we meet up?

From: Jason GrangerRM
To: Trisha; Les

What's the name of that pub we went to last time?

From: Les
To: Jason GrangerRM; Trisha

The Prince Arthur in Eversholt Street?

From: Jason GrangerRM
To: Trisha; Les

I can be there by 6 p.m.?

From: Trisha
To: Les; Jason GrangerRM

Sounds good. See you both there and let's get a plan together.

From: Jason GrangerRM
To: Trisha; Les

OK, I'm bringing Aisha along. I thought she could be useful. From working with her for a while, I can vouch for her deviousness and ability to lie.

From: Trisha
To: Jason GrangerRM; Les

That's agreed, and remember Les, it's your round.

Subject: Holly

From: Toby
To: Trisha

Hi Trisha,
Has she mentioned me at all?
Toby

From: Trisha
To: Toby

Not for a while, sweetheart. If I thought I could change her mind, I'd say something again. I did try for you a couple of times.

From: Toby
To: Trisha

I know you did, Trisha. Thanks.

From: Trisha
To: Toby

So when you off?

From: Toby
To: Trisha

Last day here tomorrow. I start work in France on Monday.

From: Trisha
To: Toby

Good luck, darlin.
Trisha

Subject: A letter for me?

From: Holly
To: Trisha

Here's a letter addressed to Holly Denham, Staples and Paperclips Division.

From: Trisha
To: Holly

Sorry babes, I told you I was bored. You shouldn't spend so much time up there.

toby's
inbox

week 2
monday

Subject: Holly

From: Trisha
To: Toby

So when you off?

From: Toby
To: Trisha

Tomorrow night. I start work in France on Monday.

From: Trisha
To: Toby

Good luck, darlin.
Trisha

Subject: Coming home

From: Toby
To: Steve

I'll be expecting a beer waiting for me at 11 p.m. on an outside table, opposite the square in Deauville tomorrow.

From: Steve
To: Toby

I'll line them up, mate. I thought we'd just have a few drinks, have a big night out on Friday. I've got a girl I want you to meet.

From: Toby
To: Steve

Who, Elise? I've met her.

From: Steve
To: Toby

Not for me, for you. She's a friend of Elise's. She's got that independence you wanted from a woman. I'm sure she's just like Holly, no difference.

From: Toby
To: Steve

You haven't met Holly. Anyway, independence as in—she doesn't want to hang around you two all night?

From: Steve
To: Toby

Yeah, yeah, whatever. I try and do you a favour. So this girl I've found you is one of your lot (unless you've had enough of nice girls and want to go back to bad ones????).

From: Toby
To: Steve

I just want to lie on the beach and forget it all.

From: Steve
To: Toby

The beach is a good place to start. Once you've seen these French women, you'll forget your own name. I said you were wasting your time in London. I did say you were, mate.

From: Toby
To: Steve

Everyone thinks about their first girlfriend. You've mentioned yours before.

From: Steve
To: Toby

But I didn't take a job just to be with her, did I????? Did you tell her in the end?

From: Toby
To: Steve

What?

From: Steve
To: Toby

That you only joined the company to be with her?

From: Toby
To: Steve

No, she still thinks it was a coincidence. I couldn't see the point.

From: Steve
To: Toby

Good, you would have looked like an even bigger idiot (if you'll pardon the honesty). At least you've kept some of your pride intact, kind of. I'd take the piss a bit more, but I'm guessing you might be a bit cut-up about it all, so I'll let you off the hook for a couple of days.

From: Toby
To: Steve

I didn't think she'd still be mad at me.

From: Steve
To: Toby

Mad is the right word. Just as well you didn't get back with her. You did everything you could to get her back at the time. You were in France, for God's sake, in a boarding school. You wrote to her, you said you were sorry. It wasn't your fault anyway. Your parents put you there and she never wrote back to you, not once. How many letters was it?

From: Toby
To: Steve

Don't remember.

From: Steve
To: Toby

A lot, a lot of f*cking letters you wrote her.

From: Toby
To: Steve

A few.

From: Steve
To: Toby

Right, so forget her.

From: Toby
To: Steve

I'll see you tomorrow.

Toby

holly's
inbox

week 2
monday

Subject: A letter for me?

From: Holly
To: Patricia Gillot

Here's a letter addressed to Holly Denham, Staples and Paperclips Division.

From: Patricia Gillot
To: Holly

Sorry babes, I told you I was bored. You shouldn't spend so much time up there.

tuesday

Subject: Clients

From: Jennie Pithwait
To: Holly

Receptionist,

I heard I'll soon be seeing you scurrying past me with my clients. There's a good girl, behaving at last. It's just a shame it had to come to this… I really didn't want to make you feel so small, but I guess you know your place now?

From: Holly
To: Jennie Pithwait

Sadly, you won't see me taking your clients past, because Trisha is very kindly doing yours (on the odd occasion you can't be contacted).

love,
Holly

> **From:** Jennie Pithwait
> **To:** Holly

By the way, if you hadn't already guessed it… I was shagging James the night before you both went to Spain. He was late to work… because he wanted to do it again. Maybe I gave him something you weren't very good at??

PS I was there in Spain, too, took a flight out after you. He came and met my family before yours in Marbella.

PPS We're so so in love now, and at last, he's told me he's ready to settle down. That's right, Holly, we're thinking of getting married. Kiss kiss.

Have a fab day.

Subject: You OK?

> **From:** Patricia Gillot
> **To:** Holly

You don't look so good. Anything I can do?

> **From:** Holly
> **To:** Patricia Gillot

I'm OK.

> **From:** Patricia Gillot
> **To:** Holly

Is it more hate mail from Jennie?

> **From:** Holly
> **To:** Patricia Gillot

A bit.

From: Patricia Gillot
To: Holly

Forward it on?

From: Holly
To: Patricia Gillot

Can't, I feel sick.

From: Patricia Gillot
To: Holly

Hold on to it, darlin.

xxxx

Subject: Your References

From: Roger Lipton
To: Holly

Dear Holly,

We have been unable to obtain an accurate reference to cover the period of time you said you were working for the LHS Hotels Group. Can you explain why this is the case?

Yours sincerely, Roger

From: Holly
To: Roger Lipton

Dear Roger,

Yes, sorry, I was self-employed.

My husband and I ran an events company during the time I should have been working in the hotel. I did work at the hotel, but for just two weeks. I have no explanation other than I really wanted to work here and prove myself. My CV wouldn't have been noticed without having previous reception experience. In the last few months I hope I have managed to show you the dedication, loyalty, and vigilance you require from a member of your reception team.

Kindest regards,

Holly

Subject: Got rumbled

From: Holly

To: Jason GrangerRM

Think Shella got me in trouble... I've been rumbled by HR, and they don't sound happy. I told the truth. Think it's the best thing to do.

Subject: Your references

From: Roger Lipton

To: Holly

Holly,

So you admit you were lying on your CV, and you have no previous receptionist experience?

From: Holly

To: Roger Lipton

Yes, apart from the two weeks in the hotel.

Holly

From: Roger Lipton

To: Holly

Holly,

Since your employment here, we have come to believe you are a dedicated worker and have fitted in well, carrying out your responsibilities to the standard we require from employees. Huerst & Wright is a financial institution, and our clients empower us with a huge amount of responsibility in dealing with their financial operations.

Security is therefore at the forefront of all our minds, and employees who have fabricated their previous work history, exam credentials, address, or any other such details, are dealt with according to company rules. This is an area we take very seriously.

This position as 'Receptionist' had always been offered subject to references, and you are still within your six-month probationary period. Therefore, it is with deep regret that I inform you of the termination of your contract with Huerst & Wright as of today.

Please hand your pass back and any other Huerst & Wright property to Judy Perkins at 5 p.m.

Yours sincerely,

Roger Lipton

Subject: Gone

From: Holly
To: Patricia Gillot

That's it, I'm out. They're getting rid of me, Trisha.

From: Patricia Gillot
To: Holly

What????

From: Holly
To: Patricia Gillot

Something about security and me lying on my CV.

From: Patricia Gillot
To: Holly

Yeah yeah, very funny.

From: Holly
To: Patricia Gillot

Trish, look at me.

From: Patricia Gillot
To: Holly

They're F*CKING having a f*cking laugh!!!!

From: Holly
To: Patricia Gillot

It's my own silly fault.

From: Patricia Gillot
To: Holly

OH, darlin, what you going to do ???

Subject: Missing?

From: Shella Hamilton-Jones
To: Holly

Holly,

At 12 p.m. you were meant to be waiting for me in meeting room 5, which is where I am. Have you forgotten??? Are you still on reception or have you been sacked?

From: Holly
To: Shella Hamilton-Jones

Yes, I've been sacked.

I imagine someone's had a word with HR about me, and they're getting rid of me (well done, Shella??). So no, I can't be bothered coming up for your meeting, because I don't have to take any more crap off you.

Holly

Subject: What happened???

From: Jason GrangerRM
To: Holly

Have they come back to you yet ??

From: Holly
To: Jason GrangerRM

Yes, I'm out the door, gone.

From: Jason GrangerRM
To: Holly

You're joking?

Subject: Oh dear dear dear …

From: Jennie Pithwait
To: Holly

Ex-Receptionist

It looks like I WIN, after all.

After finding out you had lied to us all, it only took a couple of calls to set the ball in motion …

So it's good-bye from me and good-bye from James.

Taraaar

Subject: Missing?

From: Shella Hamilton-Jones
To: Holly

What a ridiculous thing to say, why would I be happy? I'll have to find someone else who's good at this now. Why on earth are they sacking you?

Shella

From: Holly
To: Shella Hamilton-Jones

Jennie told them I lied on my CV (I've never been a receptionist before.).

From: Shella Hamilton-Jones
To: Holly

So what has Holly been up to?

From: Holly
To: Shella Hamilton-Jones

I managed an events company with my husband.

Subject: Holly Denham

From: Shella Hamilton-Jones
To: Holly; Roger Lipton

Roger,

I must say, I find the way you have reformed company policy within the whole of HR rather refreshing. Your ability to remove the 'bad eggs' within our company is always achieved with so little fuss, and your decisions in this area are always spot on.

In the case of Holly Denham I cannot believe, however, what a total pig's ear you've made of it. For what reason are you sacking her?

Shella

PS Please keep Holly involved in your reply, as I may need to verify some facts with her.

From: Roger Lipton
To: Holly; Shella Hamilton-Jones

Shella,

I am sorry you feel this way, however, Holly has lied on her CV, and our company policy is clear and unambiguous in this area.

From: Shella Hamilton-Jones
To: Holly; Roger Lipton

What was she doing instead of reception, Roger?

From: Roger Lipton
To: Holly; Shella Hamilton-Jones

Shella,

I think it would be better if we had a chat in my office tomorrow regarding this matter, however, I believe Holly was self-employed.

Roger

> **From:** Shella Hamilton-Jones
> **To:** Holly; Roger Lipton

She ran an events company with her husband, Roger, and what project are we currently working on together?

> **From:** Roger Lipton
> **To:** Holly; Shella Hamilton-Jones

The Annual Results.

> **From:** Shella Hamilton-Jones
> **To:** Holly; Roger Lipton

The Annual Results, very good. It is, if you've failed to notice, the biggest event of our calendar. Holly Denham ran an events company, which is exactly the kind of experience I need to help me put together this conference in such a short space of time.

Will you cancel the termination immediately, and let's not hear another word about it. I know you meant well, Roger, but now I am thoroughly busy with the conference, and time is running out.

Please do not email me again unless it's about a different matter.

Regards,

Shella

PS You may like to look into why Jennie Pithwait sounds like she's taken it upon herself to do her own referencing?

Subject: Working

> **From:** Shella Hamilton-Jones
> **To:** Holly

So you will have to take more cr*p off this 'Viper' then, won't you?

Oh, and if you get any more trouble from that woman—the one who I can see today has come in wearing a skirt, which would shame a prostitute, then let me know. I'm the only one who can be mean to people in this company.

Shella 'Cruella'

PS I really think you should chase after Toby. He's much better looking.

From: Holly
To: Shella Hamilton-Jones

Not sure what to say!!!!
Thank you so so much, Shella, you've just made me so happy!
Holly
xxx !!!
(Sorry about the Viper thing.)

Subject: Sad news

From: Holly
To: Patricia Gillot

Only joking! I'm BACK!!!
YIPEEEEEEEEEEEE ha ah aha aha ha ha
Trisha, I love ya, 'Darlin" !!! hee hee hee!! I want to give you a big kiss, but first, I've got an important message to send someone.

From: Patricia Gillot
To: Holly

What???
How?
Tell me now!!!!!!

From: Holly
To: Patricia Gillot

She knew!! She read that email I sent about her!!! And she is still nice??? ?? What? I think the world is turning upside down today. Oh, got an email to send, taraaaar.

From: Patricia Gillot
To: Holly

???

From: Holly
To: Patricia Gillot

Don't be starting with the question marks, trishywishy. Hee heee

Subject: Wake Up

From: Holly
To: Aisha; Jason GrangerRM

Stinky and stinky?? I've got something to tell you!

Subject: Going

From: Holly
To: Jennie Pithwait

OH, I guess I'm off.

From: Jennie Pithwait
To: Holly

You still here?

Would you like to hand ME your pass before you go? If you want, I can send you down an empty box of cornflakes to put your pens and pencils into?

boo hoo

It's the end of an error.

From: Holly
To: Jennie Pithwait

Don't be dumb; I mean, I was just popping over the road to get a coffee …

They haven't sacked me, it was just a terrible error (you were right). Got a call from Roger Lipton apologising. Such a shame for poor little vindictive you… BOOO HOOO

HA HA H A HA

This feels good der na ner na ner na ner—like I knew it would

Love and kisses,

mwah mwah

Holly

PS...... Shella says to watch your back. ooops naughty naughty Jennie

From: Jennie Pithwait
To: Holly

Is that so???

WELL I'LL SHOW YOU SOMETHING THAT WILL BREAK POOR LITTLE HOLLY'S HEART ANY MOMENT!!

From: Holly
To: Jennie Pithwait

What is it?

OH MY GOD!!!

You're not... about to show me you've had your breasts enlarged again???

You're right, that would be SO sad.

Or maybe you're about to reveal you're dating Mr Big, that WOULD break my heart.

Oh no, forgot you can't, you're still dating my castoffs.

Shame.

Subject: Here

From: Holly
To: Jason GrangerRM; Aisha

You two just won't believe what's been happening here!!!!! Are you around????

Holly

x

Subject: Jennie

From: Holly
To: Patricia Gillot

What d'you think she's up to? She just said she was coming down to quote 'break my heart'—psycho???
Having said that, I've had some great fun emailing her.

From: Patricia Gillot
To: Holly

I hope it's not what I think she's going to do, she wouldn't.

From: Holly
To: Patricia Gillot

What????

Subject: TELL US!!!

From: Jason GrangerRM
To: Holly; Aisha; Patricia Gillot

What's happening then, Holly??????

From: Holly
To: Aisha; Jason GrangerRM; Patricia Gillot

Well:

I heard from Jennie that she had been with James all the time I was on holiday with him. Don't have to say anything, trying to forget that bit. Then I got sacked (wasn't the best start to a day). Then reinstated. Yipppeee (because Shella told them they had to. Incidentally, she had read that email calling her a Viper) (and she's got a sense of humour, very disturbing?!) Then I sent a few ha ha emails to Jennie. Now she's coming down to break my heart (she says). Oh, and here she is now. With James? Oh, I hope they're not going to.

From: Jason GrangerRM

To: Holly; Aisha; Patricia Gillot

WHAT????

Subject: WHAT ARE THEY NOT GOING TO DO?

From: Jason GrangerRM

To: Holly; Aisha; Patricia Gillot

WHAT is happening??????

From: Holly

To: Jason GrangerRM; Patricia Gillot; Aisha

She's kissing James in the middle of the reception.

From: Patricia Gillot

To: Holly; Jason GrangerRM; Aisha

Silly girl, she's about to get a huge shock.

From: Holly

To: Aisha; Jason GrangerRM; Patricia Gillot

What?

From: Patricia Gillot

To: Holly; Aisha; Jason GrangerRM

See that client there putting down the newspaper?

Subject: That's …

From: Patricia Gillot

To: Holly; Aisha; Jason GrangerRM

That's his wife.

From: Jason GrangerRM

To: Holly; Patricia Gillot; Aisha

Sh*t.

From: Holly
To: Patricia Gillot; Jason GrangerRM; Aisha

What? How did you know? What wife????

From: Patricia Gillot
To: Holly; Jason GrangerRM; Aisha

Oh, now that would be telling.

xxxx

Subject: URGENT

From: Judy Perkins
To: Holly; Patricia Gillot

What is going on down there? I've just had reports of a security risk and shouting coming from reception? Whoever they are, get security to remove them from the premises, if necessary, by force. NOW!!!

Subject: Do you want to or shall I?

From: Patricia Gillot
To: Holly

Shall I tell them, or do you want to?

From: Holly
To: Patricia Gillot

Ooo, I think I can handle this one. Might get Ralph to stamp on some feet as he goes.

Subject: Please forgive me

From: Mum and Dad
To: Holly

Holly,

I have had a long, hard look at myself since our last chat. As much as this may drive you to hate me, I need to let you know this.

Toby did write to you. He actually wrote to you many times. I didn't let anyone else in the family know, not even your father. I was so angry with him, I tore up most of the letters. I kept one. This is the final one, which, with the help of your sister, I've scanned and am about to send to you now.

Love, Mum

Subject: Happy???

From: Patricia Gillot
To: Holly

I thought you'd be jumping up and down, laughing your head off. What's wrong?

From: Holly
To: Patricia Gillot

I don't know, I'll tell you in a minute. When did you say Toby was leaving?

From: Patricia Gillot
To: Holly

Today. He'll be here till 5. Why?

From: Holly
To: Patricia Gillot

I'll tell you in a second.

Subject: Letter

From: Holly
To: Mum and Dad

Where's the letter??????

Also, how could he have written? I didn't get anything at school. Why would he write to you???

From: Mum and Dad
To: Holly

He didn't write to me. I'm sorry, I had the housemaster intercept anything from France. Sorry Holly. His letter is attached.

Mum xxxx

Holly Denham

Rosemont School

Guildford

England

22nd Oct 1994

Holly,

It's 6 a.m. I'm sitting on my bed in my dormitory. I've been lying awake all night again, picturing the same thing, the thing I always picture these days. It was different when I first came here. I spent so much of my time thinking of all the funny, crazy things we did together. Even when I was down and you wouldn't leave me alone. You're so damn sexy, Holly. Even when I wanted to be mad at you, I couldn't be.

When I wrote to you, I had so much confidence. I had no doubt we'd stay together through this. I knew how I felt about you, and I blindly assumed you felt the same way about me. I thought I'd spend a year here, and we'd be back together, even if it was two, we'd see each other in the summer, when we broke up. I think of how sure I was then, and it was only 2 months ago. I imagine how you looked at me when you said you loved me. I try to remember that look because, as beautiful as you are, I just need to think of your face, your eyes, how they looked, whether you meant it as much as I did. When the post was handed out yesterday, I was there again, hoping there would be one from you. When I see a postmark from England, I realise the writing isn't yours, but then, and how stupid is this, I start hoping they'll mention you in their letter instead.

Anything which tells me you miss me as much as I miss you. If I knew you did, I'd run away now, I'd get on a train, I'd walk if I had to. I'd get to you though, Holly, if you'd just let me know how you feel.

I'm not going to write again. I know if you'd have turned out to be pregnant, I'd have been the happiest man alive, but that wasn't to be. I know just getting a letter from you saying you're thinking of me would now make me the happiest man alive.

I love you, Holly, and I just hope one day, you'll love me back. I'm going to go down to the field now at the back of the school. I do this most mornings before everyone else gets up. It's as far away as I can get from people. I listen to the quiet, I enjoy the silence, and then I scream as loud as I can, Holly. I shout my head off. I don't know why, I just need to do it.

I love you, Holly.

Toby

From: Holly
To: Patricia Gillot

Oh my God, I've got to go.

From: Patricia Gillot
To: Holly

Where? Why?

From: Holly
To: Patricia Gillot

Because I've just realised something. I'm going upstairs.
xxxx Wish me luck.

From: Patricia Gillot
To: Holly

Go get him now!!!!! go go!!!!

trisha's inbox

week 2

tuesday

Subject: So??

From: Les
To: Trisha

What's happening now?

From: Trisha
To: Les

Holly's gone upstairs to tell him.

From: Les
To: Trisha

Tell him what, he knows, doesn't he? The whole bank must know now?

From: Trisha
To: Les

Don't be so dense, Les. Not James, Toby.

From: Les
To: Trisha

She's gone to tell Toby what?

From: Trisha
To: Les

That the photocopier ran out of paper halfway through a print job.

From: Les
To: Trisha

So?

From: Trisha
To: Les

And we got Leslie Grantham waiting for him in Reception.

From: Les
To: Trisha

Leslie who?

From: Trisha
To: Les

She's gone to tell him she loves him, you doughnut!

From: Les
To: Trisha

How am I supposed to know that then? If you don't tell me, how am I meant to know that's what you're talking about? So, what's he said then?

From: Trisha
To: Les

I don't know, she hasn't come back yet.

From: Les
To: Trisha

You got a letter from the doctors here, shall I open it?

From: Trisha
To: Les

You can if you want. It's probably just giving me the all clear. Hold on, here she comes. This can't be good.

holly's
inbox

week 2

tuesday

Subject: He's gone

From: Holly
To: Patricia Gillot

He's not there. They said he left 10 mins ago, must have gone out the fire escape.

From: Patricia Gillot
To: Holly

Well, you wouldn't want to walk past us again, would you? Poor lad. So, what you doing about it?

From: Holly
To: Patricia Gillot

I can't do anything, can I? I suppose I'll have to get his number or an address for him.

From: Patricia Gillot
To: Holly

Yeah, just send him a letter, or email, or text, or something.

From: Holly
To: Patricia Gillot

You think?

From: Patricia Gillot
To: Holly

No, I don't think!!!! I'm not sitting next to you with that wet, soppy love-hurt look on your face. Get off your arse and go chase after your man! You love him, don't ya??

From: Holly
To: Patricia Gillot

Yes, a lot.

From: Patricia Gillot
To: Holly

Then go after him. He's on the Eurostar. It's not exactly hard to find, is it? He's going from Waterloo!

From: Holly
To: Patricia Gillot

Will you be OK here on your own?

From: Patricia Gillot
To: Holly

Oh, p*ss off! Go before I fling you out!

Subject: That's it

From: Patricia Gillot
To: Holly

I'm coming over there!

From: Holly
To: Patricia Gillot

I'm going, I'm going. If he calls, give him my mobile number.
xxx

From: Patricia Gillot
To: Holly

He won't call, darlin, so run!!!!!!!!!!!!!!!!!!

trisha's
inbox

week 2

wednesday

From: Trisha
To: Jason GrangerRM

Anyone heard anything?

From: Jason GrangerRM
To: Trisha

No, and I'm worried about her.

From: Trisha
To: Jason GrangerRM

She can't be sitting up there sulking. We'll have to get her out of her house.

From: Jason GrangerRM
To: Trisha

If I've heard nothing from her by lunchtime, I'm going to her flat.

Subject: Sick

From: Holly
To: Trisha

Sorry Trisha,

I know I can't lie to you, I never could. I was going to say I was sick today, some kind of flu or bug. But I know you wouldn't believe me. The only bug I've got is being in love, so in love it's painful. So I won't be in until I get over it, and I'm really really going to try to get him out of my head, Trisha. Problem is, it's so so difficult when he's lying next to me!!! Heee hee. xxxxx

I caught up with him in the station, I literally saw him by the ticket barrier as I came in. I shouted, he turned around. I didn't know what I was going to say. I actually said 'Why the HELL didn't you tell me you'd written to me!!!!!' He didn't answer, he didn't need to. I ran over, and I saw that he was still in love with me, and I'm not sorry to say I threw myself on him. We kissed and kissed and at some stage, we were lying on the floor in the middle of Waterloo station kissing, with people passing us by. We actually lay there until we got told to move. Covered in dust, not at all classy. I had a McDonald's wrapper stuck to my bottom when I got up. I now wish I had kept it, as a souvenir.

I'm writing to you right now from the beach in France. We're lying together, and yes, I'm writing to let you know I'm in love, and so I won't be in today. I'm sick. Heee hee hee. No idea what to do next, but got to go, there's a chest that needs my head on it.

xxxxxxx

Love you, Trishy,

Holly

PS I'm just about to call Jason (or Dad) to stop him worrying too. Bad Holly.

PPS There's a picture of me and Toby together in the next email I'm sending you. (I think my holiday snaps could be better this year!)

xxx

Dear Reader,

So that's the end of my story... for now! I really hope you enjoyed it.

Lots of love,

Holly xxx

PS I'll be back soon!